JORDAN'S BEND

CAROLYN WILLIFORD

THOMAS NELSON PUBLISHERS
Nashville • Atlanta • London • Vancouver

Copyright © 1995 by Carolyn Williford

Published in Nashville, Tennessee, by Jan Dennis Books, an imprint of Thomas Nelson, Inc., Publishers, and distributed in Canada by Word Communications, Ltd., Richmond, British Columbia.

Scripture quotations are from the KING JAMES VERSION of the Bible.

The stanzas of the poem by Madeleine L'Engle which appear as epigraphs for each chapter of this work are from her book *The Irrational Season*, © 1977 by Crosswicks, Ltd., reprinted by HarperCollins, Publishers, Inc., New York, New York. International rights held by Raines & Raines, Inc., New York, New York. Used by permission.

Library of Congress Cataloging-in-Publication Data

Williford, Carolyn.
    Jordan's Bend / Carolyn Williford.
        p.   cm.
    ISBN 0-7852-7707-2
    1. Tennessee Valley Authority—History—Fiction. I. Title.
PS3573.I45633J67   1995
813'.54—dc20   95-45627
                                                                          CIP

Printed in the United States of America

1 2 3 4 5 6 — 00 99 98 97 96 95

To Diana
who showed me that a Southerner loves
with depth and truth

and to Jo and June
who proved that Northerners do also

Prologue

Although over twenty-five years have passed since I last saw McKenney Way, the longing to stroll the slopes of those gentle hills and push that rich, fertile soil through my fingers can still press at my heart in an urgent wanting. Some would say I'm merely tormenting myself to put down onto paper those impossible longings. But I feel compelled to—not even knowing myself all the reasons and whys of it.

I suppose more than anything it's a pulling at the back of my mind on something that Granny Mandy often said. After Daddy harvested our rye with a cradle, bundled it, and let it cure for a while, the old thrasher'd come round to separate out that rye. But Granny Mandy's daddy didn't have any thrashing machine, so they had to beat the rye over a hole in the ground, collecting the rye that had fallen in.

Problem was, there was a good bit of chaff in there to separate out. So on a windy day they'd get a handful of that rye and pour it from one sack into another. That way the wind just blew away the chaff. So, often when I was stewing over something in my mind, trying to put right what so-and-so had said, Granny Mandy would tell me to "grab a handful an' see what the wind blows away, Rachael." 'Course, then she was there to help me see what needed to be blown away—and what was worth hanging onto. How I could still use her help! So I guess that's why I'm putting this all down—to see it, feel it, know it as if it's all just happening—and then maybe that chaff'll blow away in the wind.

Seems like I might have trouble bringing to mind all those memories, but they do come, carrying with them the sight of the dogwood looking like Mama's crocheting scattered among them hills along Spring Tide Creek, the feeling of putting my feet in the clear, cool water in Granny Mandy's springhouse and always, always, the sound of the dinner bells ringing. Ringing for a hungry family when we'd lay by the corn, ringing for the birth of another young'un, ringing to warn that the law was somewheres nearby, and ringing for the final time for one of our own—my own. Granny Mandy, is it the chaff that brings the hurting and must be blown away? Or is it the rye itself carrying the pain, bringing joy in the end after it's been purified by the good Lord? The telling will take some time, and the healing—what about the healing? Will it come too? But now I'm getting ahead of myself, for right now the wind's blowing and it's time to get about the work of remembering, sorting, separating, harvesting, and storing the memories before the healing can even begin to come about. Yes, Granny Mandy, I'm fixing to grab a handful.

1

Who shoved me out into the night?
What wind blew out the quavering light?
Is it my breath, undone with fright?
This is the Kingdom of the Beast.
For which will I provide the feast?

Andy! Don't you dare be shootin' that there starlin'! Put your slingshot down and leave the poor thing alone!" I glared down at him with all the commanding a big sister can gather up, knowing that the bird's very life was depending on me being able to convince Andy—or "O.A." for Ornery Andy, as I often called him—that I meant to win this scuffle. He was an excellent shot with his flip-jack, and I couldn't count on him missing.

"Oh, what's it gonna hurt, Rachael? 'Sides, Daddy don't like starlin's nohow. That'd be one less to bother with." He continued to take aim, slowly pulling back the slingshot and narrowing his McKenney eyes at his intended prey. Those eyes were known round this county—bright green with the unusual dark lashes. 'Course, the sandy-red hair and freckles were part and parcel of the McKenney look too. No way any of us McKenneys could get away with anything around here. He slowly picked up one bare foot and used a big toe to rub the back of his leg. "Durn bugs is gonna make me miss!"

"My daddy don't like 'em neither," chimed in little Earl Purser, shifting his eyes from Andy's flip to the bird and back again. He and his sister Daisy, who lived with their parents just above our farm, were on their way to school with us. The Pursers didn't own any land, being only tenant farmers, but Daddy said they sure worked the land hard. Most times Daddy thought tenants were lazy and shiftless, but the Pursers were different. We hoped that some day they might be able to get a homestead of their very own, but times were sure hard right now, with the Depression and all.

"Don't hurt 'em, Andy, please." Daisy looked up at him with such innocent pleading in her big, blue eyes that I hoped he couldn't resist her. She twisted one of her short, blond curls nervously round a small finger. "'Sides, I'll tell Miz Travis that you got a flip-jack at school!"

That did it. Andy quickly jammed the slingshot back into his pocket, picked up the lunch bucket he'd set down to get the best aim, and give Daisy a "you'd best not" kind of stare. Telling was next to breaking your word around these parts, so I didn't think Daisy'd really squeal. But she sure saved that bird.

"I ain't takin' it to school, anyways," Andy said, looking around at all of us. "I'll be hidin' it before we even get there, so you can just keep quiet about it. There!" Slingshots were absolutely not allowed on the school grounds by Miz Travis, but all the boys had them. They just kept them in their secret places and then picked them up after school. Me and my best friend Merry Jo'd often tried to find those slingshots and throw them in the Tennessee River, but we hadn't found them yet. Not that we'd give up.

"When you gonna hep me make my flip-jack, Andy?" Little Earl came up to take Andy's hand, looking up at him with near adoration. Earl often clung to Andy's hand since he was most generally tripping over his rolled-up britches. The Pursers always made their young'uns' clothes with plenty of growing room.

"Well, I s'pose we can be lookin' for the right kinda forked stick right now. On the way to school's prob'ly the best time to find a good 'un. While we're a-walkin' along here, just keep your eyes peeled for one like mine." Andy pulled his out of his pants pocket again and held it up to be admired. I had to admit to myself, grudgingly, that he could nearly hit a blackberry clean across the cornfield.

As I glanced over to Andy's slingshot, I caught a glimpse of some buds on a dogwood tree just past the edge of the road. Now I noticed that all around me things were greening up and tiny buds were coming up everywhere. While Andy and Earl searched for a stick to make a slingshot, I caught sight of some of my most favorite wildflowers—spring beauties—peeking through the piles of leaves and underbrush. Later I'd be sure to pick Mama and Granny Mandy a bouquet.

Spring was coming early, and I peered through the trees to see if any redbuds were out. Sure enough, there were some just over the ridge. We'd had an easy winter, since we'd seen only one slight covering of snow and only one kindly cold spell. Come February, we'd already put in the Irish potatoes (how I was looking forward to them fresh taters baked in Granny Mandy's fireplace), and tomorrow, since it was a full moon, we'd be putting in Mama's and Granny's gardens.

I swatted a bunch of gnats away that were bothering about my face. Sure didn't take them bugs long to find out it's spring. Daddy says that's another sign of an early summer a-coming; makes him anxious to try and get two good crops in this year. The bugs only make me anxious to watch I don't get stung, bit, or bothered. Them chiggers! Already I could be tasting the sweetness of fresh-picked blackberries, but how I hated them bites.

"Rachael, what be ya thinkin' on so sincere like?" Daisy touched me lightly with her hand. "Could you be thinkin' 'bout Tommy Lee? Ere you two sparkin' yet?"

"Daisy!" I looked around quickly to see if Andy had heard. I certainly didn't want him to hear this conversation. "Now you just be quiet about me and Tommy Lee. We're a mite young to be thinkin' on courtin'. Besides, we're only friends. Just like me and yer brother Earl."

"That ain't what everbody says. I heared he's sweet on you an' . . ."

"Hey, Andy! Got yer flip?" I nearly jumped a foot as Tommy Lee come rushing up to us, panting and out of breath. Behind him come Lester and Anna Ruth Dickerson, Lester all rumpled and tousled, as usual, and Anna Ruth looking as neat as ever. Why, she could run and keep up with the big boys and still not pull the hair out of her pigtails. I quickly smoothed out my skirt and pushed some stray hair back from my face; my hair was always escaping from wherever I attempted to put it. Glancing over at Daisy, I seen she hadn't missed a thing. That little one was just too quick.

"Look at this new 'un I made just last night. Daddy's shoes plumb wore out so's he give me the tongues. Ain't it a fine one too?" Andy took it from Tommy Lee to test the pull, aiming it at some far-off target. "I tested her out this mornin' an' couldn't wait to show her off! That's why Lil' Lester an' me caught up with you earlier than usual. We run clean like . . ." He turned around, noticing Anna Ruth was there too. "Anna Ruth, how'd you get here so quick?" He looked at her with disbelief and was it—no, couldn't be, could it?—admiration? That Anna Ruth!

"Guess it ain't only boys can run these hills." She gave him a smug smile and then glanced over at me.

"Good mornin', Rachael and Miss Daisy." Tommy Lee bent over in an exaggerated bow for Daisy, causing her to break into a fit of giggles. I swear that Tommy Lee could charm a hog into prancing to the smokehouse.

"Mornin', Mister Tommy Lee!" Coyly looking up at him, Daisy was certainly pleased with Tommy Lee's attention too. Couldn't rightly say I blamed her or Anna Ruth. Just turning fourteen, he was already tall for his age and built sturdy from farming. His thick, dark brown hair had waves that he constantly pushed back from his forehead and ears. Sure, his shirttail was always coming out and his hands were generally rough and dirty from choring, but no other boy in this county had eyes like Tommy Lee's. Doe's eyes, they were. And just as soft and gentle. I never seen the like of them in someone so strong and hardworking.

"Come on. We'd best be hurryin' to school or we'll be late," I urged. I'd heard enough of this chatter, so I turned and hurriedly walked on, though I could still hear snatches about finding ammunition and hunting little round stones. Since we girls always walked together and the boys kept off to themselves, the two groups drifted apart. When we come to Small Creek, I concentrated on getting across without slipping off the few dry stones. Normally the creek wasn't nothing but a trail of stones, but since it was spring, it had a fair amount of water heading on to the Tennessee. Up ahead we'd cross Possum Trot Creek. It was a good bit bigger and had a bridge. If we followed it to the river, we'd come to Blackberry Bluff, one of my most favorite spots. Oh, if I was only on my way there instead of to school and . . .

Anna Ruth broke into my dreaming. "Rachael, where is yer mind off to now? Seems like yer always—"

"That's what I just told her!" Daisy exclaimed. "An' I asked if she was a-thinkin' 'bout—"

"Daisy, you hush!" I certainly didn't want her bringing up Tommy Lee now. "Yonder is Miz Harris scrubbin' out her wash. Now let's wave and holler *hey* loud enough so's she hears us. You know she's breakin' fast. Gettin' mighty hard of hearin'. Hey, Miz Harris! How you be doin' today?"

"Hey, young'uns!" Miz Harris looked up from her black iron pot and waved the stirring paddle at us. Her and Mister Harris were getting up in years, although the look about her lined, aged face and the arm she waved at us still contained much strength. Their homestead was kindly worn down though. The rail fence round the front was failing, though the "worm"—the first row—had been laid skillfully and would probably last a good bit longer.

My eyes followed what was left of the stake and rider fence to the house and barn, both in bad need of repair. The cabin's foursquare foundation, like the fence, was solid and strong. But them old logs were beginning to rot away and parts of their puncheon floor showed through. The old barn was leaning so bad, it looked to be falling over any minute.

The land—mostly the cornfield—looked even worse. Daddy said the Harrises never give their land a rest, and that like in the Bible, even good soil deserved a spell to leave off. One time we were riding by on the mail wagon, and Daddy looked over their fields, shaking his head, saying that the soil reminded him of a child feeling poorly. He said there ain't nothing you can do that'll make that child put on some flesh and look healthy and good. It's ailing, deep down inside.

I had to agree with him. As we walked on, Anna Ruth and Daisy chattered on about school and whatever, but I couldn't keep from studying that field and remembering what Daddy had said. The soil wasn't a deep red color anymore like ours was. Instead, it looked dull and bleached out, tired like in its grayness. I remembered Daddy telling about walking across grass that was so thin you could fairly see the copperheads right along the bare ground. That didn't seem like such a bad thing to me at the time, but now I thought about our upper pasture and the thick, evergrowing grass that thrived there. You surely wouldn't be seeing any copperheads in that grass before they were on you.

"That ain't right, is it, Rachael?" Daisy was tugging on my arm again.

"Ain't what right?"

"Your brother James Junior ain't goin' on relief, is he?"

"He certainly is not, Daisy Purser! An' I'll tell everbody it ain't so! He's goin' to work with the CCC—the Civilian Conservation Corps. Now don't that sound important?" My but Daisy was hitting every sore spot I had lately. I didn't even want to think about James Junior leaving, it hurt so much, but here she'd brought it up and added a shiftless meaning to it too. Going on relief might be something them Northerners would do, but not anybody in *my* family, and including most folks in this whole county too.

"Well, then what does this CCC do then?" Anna Ruth asked, throwing out her words in a challenge.

"I'm not right sure, but it has somethin' to do with plantin' trees and workin' with the soil. Like the Harrises' we just passed. Did you notice how poorly it looked? Well, James Junior's goin' to learn us how to heal land like that. I'm not rightly sure all he'll be doin', but James Junior don't take no handouts. What money he gets he's gonna earn by workin' hard, just like he always has. And we're gonna miss him kindly awful, and I just don't want to talk about it anymore, you hear?" Looking towards town, I attempted to seem very interested in who was passing through, quickly blinking back the tears that were pushing at my eyes. I wasn't about to let Anna Ruth see me cry about James Junior or anything else. Besides, Granny Mandy doesn't cry. Neither does Mama. Taking a deep breath, I decided this McKenney wouldn't neither.

I turned to see if Andy was up ahead of us—suddenly realizing that I'd plumb forgot again to watch for where he hid his slingshot—and saw that Jessie, Eugene, and Billy Ray Dickerson had joined the boys' group. I'd been so busy studying on the Harris property that I hadn't even seen or heard them come along. I told myself I'd just better quit the daydreaming before I got to school or Miz Travis'd be put out for sure. She expected a lot from me, being older and setting an example for the little'uns. I was most anxious to be pleasing her.

We took our usual shortcut through the southern part of town and walked across the main north-south highway that went right through the middle of Jordan's Bend. It wasn't a kindly big town, but it wasn't so small either. I guess you'd call it middling size for a southern town. If you was to take the main east-west road right out east about two miles, following along the bend of the Tennessee River, you'd come to our homestead. We walked this road every day to school and sometimes, if we were lucky, we got to ride home with Daddy when he drove the mail wagon.

Seemed like the normal everyday activities were going on; I could see a few wagons outside the general store and a few people toting in eggs 'n such. James Junior used to bring our eggs in, but real soon now that'd be my chore. Then I'd have to be mighty careful crossing Small Creek while toting them eggs.

We took a shortcut through the yards of the homes here on the edge of town, and then we could spy the schoolhouse—our church on Sundays. That's why the sign out front of the one-room building said "Jordan's Bend Baptist Church." There were other churches outside of town, but most people around here attended this one, and because of its central location, we used it for school and all sorts of town meetings too.

Seeing the schoolhouse brought a rush of excitement. Every part of the learning—the feel of a book in my hands, knowing I had the correct answer to the arithmetic problem, or making my penmanship fine and neat—was a part I enjoyed and wanted to someday teach. Next year I'd be old enough to attend the high school over to Chattanooga, and I was hoping like anything that I'd be able to go. I was most anxious to be a teacher like Miz Travis. 'Course that meant boarding at the school, and I didn't know yet if Daddy and Mama would let me. Every time I wanted to ask them about it, seems another problem for Daddy would come up. Now we had to say good-bye to James Junior. I was sure Mama and Daddy wouldn't want to be thinking about me leaving right now too.

I caught sight of Verna Mae, Merry Jo, and Nellie and give them a quick wave. Verna Mae Hickman lived in town with her parents; they owned the biggest general store in Jordan's Bend. Merry Jo was

Preacher Morgan's daughter and they lived in the parsonage right next door to the church. Nellie Smith's folks were farmers, and since she usually walked the last part of the way to school with us, I figured she must've got a ride to town that morning with her daddy. Us three girls, along with Tommy Lee and Clyde Travis, were the oldest pupils Miz Travis had. All of us together numbered twenty-eight, and that was plenty for Miz Travis to handle.

"Hey, everbody!" I said, and then turning to Nellie, asked, "How'd you get here so quick?"

"Daddy brung me in the wagon with him since he had some tradin' to do at the store." Suddenly her eyes got real big, and she looked around to see if anyone else was near. Whispering with a sound of importance in her voice, she asked us, "You know what we seen on the way?"

Now Nellie loved tales and being listened to, so I wasn't much concerned. Knowing Nellie, she could be talking about anything from a copperhead sunning itself on a rock to a new sign for the remedy "666" (which supposedly cures ailing from the malaria) on somebody's fence. But Merry Jo, sweet person that she was, looked at her with interest. "What, Nellie?"

"Me an' Daddy saw one of them outsider's automobiles settin' by the road!" She was plainly puffed up with her news, since now we were all interested. Few people round here had a car, but even more rare was seeing a stranger in Jordan's Bend. We even knew everybody's kin clear into the next county, so they weren't considered outsiders, of course. "Daddy was right put out! He went on an' on 'bout this bein' a government automobile—somethin' 'bout the license plate spellin' TVA. Any of you ever hear tell of that?"

To our puzzled no's, Nellie continued on. "Well, Daddy said he's gonna keep an eye on this intruder an' everbody else in Jordan's Bend had better too!"

Miz Travis started in to ringing the school bell then, hollering, "Come on, young'uns! Come on now!"

Giving each other a "we'll finish this discussion later" kind of look, we headed towards the steps into school. I know I was certainly thinking on why this government car would be in our county and just what he wanted. Could it have something to do with the CCC and my brother? I was going to be anxious to see Daddy come afternoon.

We always began the day by raising the flag and saying the Pledge of Allegiance. Usually I enjoyed watching the flag rise slowly up the pole, but today I had trouble fixing my attention on it. Just too many things were happening, breaking into the normal way of things. I couldn't help but worry what this news meant, and somehow I knew most surely that it wouldn't be good.

As we all filed into the schoolhouse—little'uns first—I heard muffled giggles ahead of me. Several looked back at me and then pointed to Tommy Lee. *Oh no!* I groaned inwardly. *What now?*

Giving the room a quick scan, my eyes soon lit on the big blackboard we had mounted on the back wall. "Rachael loves Tommy Lee!" was written in a bold scrawl. Instantly, I felt the rush of what I knew to be bright red cover my face, highlighting the sprinkling of freckles across my cheeks and nose. And when you've already got sandy-red hair and green eyes, adding more red to that face makes it light up like a pine knot catching in the fireplace. I wished I could disappear.

"Come now, children! What's everyone dawdlin' about?" Miz Travis come from behind the last one in and looked quickly around the room. As soon as she spied the message she headed right for the blackboard. Taking a rag in hand, she wiped out the words with one good swipe. "Now, who had the mean spell come over 'em, hmm?" She let her narrowed eyes trail round the whole room, but mostly she stared at O.A. (boy, was he going to get it if he done it), Clyde Travis, and Willie Snodderly. That Willie was a mean spell. All of them Snodderlys were. One of those young'uns was always in for it at school.

Everyone found their places on the benches, setting there fidgeting or trying terrible hard to look innocent. I was still wishing I could head right back out the door, stroll out to Blackberry Bluff, and pretend this'd never happened. I was dying inside to know how Tommy Lee was taking this, but I daren't look at him just now. He was probably suffering more than I was. So instead I just stared down at my feet, twitching my toes and praying mightily that Miz Travis would just forget about it all and go on with our lessons.

"Seems we won't be havin' a recess this mornin' 'til someone decides to have 'im a little talk with me!" Several let out loud groans. And Willie looked over at me like it was my fault! "Just let me know when you's ready. Now, you little'uns get up to the blackboard for your 'rithmetic. Lester, Jessie, Lena, and Willie, I want to see some fine penmanship. You're to begin copyin' the number ten exercise in your books. You older ones are continuin' to read Shakespeare from wherever you left off yesterday. Rachael, I want you to read for a spell and then help the younger girls with their readin'. Everyone get busy!"

The morning seemed to last about as long as trying to churn blinky milk. That's what Granny Mandy calls milk that hasn't yet clabbered.

And believe me, that's a long time churning. Since no one 'fessed up to writing the blackboard message, it wasn't until dinnertime that we were allowed out the door, and then we come fairly bursting out. Me, Merry Jo, Nellie, and Verna Mae fetched our lunch pails from the creek and then headed for our favorite spot. We'd claimed the biggest crab apple tree as ours, for it give a good bit of shade and privacy for our "grown-up" talk. The little'uns didn't pester us when we were there—unless one needed help—and so our tree became a special place to tell secrets and whisper to our hearts' delight. Today, though, I was not of a mind for whispering and giggling.

I pretended to be very busy setting out my piece of salt-cured ham, cornbread, sweet tater, and milk. We most always had cornbread, and the sweet taters could still taste right pleasing even after being stored all winter in the smokehouse. Yet I was sure ready for some fresh garden vegetables. We'd had just a piddling of "blackberry winter," but that would be enough to bring on the blackberry blossoms. And that was the best sign to be putting in the garden too. Along with the moon being just right. Even though I didn't enjoy looking like a McKenney, I sure had the McKenney blood in me, for I loved feeling the soil in my hands, seeing the dark, rich color of it as I hoed up the fresh and turned under the old, planting the tiny seeds, and watching them begin to sprout. Oh, there was work to be done in gardening, but there was reward too.

"Ere you be ready to talk about it now, Rachael?" Merry Jo glanced up at me and then quickly looked back down at her dinner. I could tell she was embarrassed to mention it, but too caring and concerned for my hurt feelings not to. "We don't have to talk about it if you don't care to. But I thought you might want to say what's pullin' at yer mind."

I could feel tears forming for her caring as a friend. What would I do without Merry Jo? "Thank you, Merry Jo, but there's nothin' to bother about. I surely was embarrassed, and I'm feelin' low for Tommy Lee too. But mostly I aim to find out who was so rotten mean! Andy can be awful ornery sometimes, but still he's got a tender place down in him somewheres. I don't kindly think he'd do that. I'm guessin' it's Willie Snodderly, since he don't take to me or Tommy Lee. What are you all thinkin'?"

"My daddy says all them Snodderlys got a mean streak long as the Tennessee River," Nellie agreed. "'Sides, they's been whisperin' 'bout Willie, too, but I'm not s'posed to tell."

"Oh, Nellie, you can't just go hintin' like this an' then not tell! Come on, what's goin' round that we ain't heard yet?" Verna Mae probed. If Mama was there right then she would've said that Verna Mae was growing up to be the spitting image of her mama. Since Miz Hickman helped out at the general store, she knowed most every bit of news—and gossip—in probably the whole county. Granny Mandy said that gal knows more about people round there than the good Lord, almost.

"Well, you got to cross your hearts and promise not to tell!" Nellie put her own hand on her heart to emphasize the solemn duty we were about to do.

"I'm thinkin' you best not say anythin', Nellie," Merry Jo quickly put in. "I know the Snodderlys is mean folk, but Daddy says we must love 'em like the Bible says."

"Bible also says to speak the truth 'bout people, and them Snodderlys is all shiftless! 'Member that TVA automobile I was tellin' you all about? Well, Daddy said more 'bout that too than I told you before. He was wonderin' if the Snodderlys had somethin' to do with them outsiders bein' here, and that's when he told me that you couldn't trust any of 'em—'cause most of their young'uns is wool colts!"

"Nellie!" Merry Jo wasn't merely shushing her; she was mad. Fixing a determined glare to her eyes and setting her chin firmly, Merry Jo announced, "I'm goin' to eat the last of my dinner and see 'bout playin' a game of Steal the Pines. If you all want to join in, you'd best hurry and finish up." I thought to myself that maybe Merry Jo should become the teacher instead of me. She was knowing how to put on the "Miz Travis look" just fine. Finishing up her last bit of milk, Merry Jo grabbed up her lunch pail and headed towards the group of boys over by the woodshed.

Me, Nellie, and Verna Mae tagged along behind since we were still feeling a bit chastened. I know I was feeling kind of—just what was it—put out? Resentful? Who was Merry Jo to be preaching at us so? Just because she was the preacher's daughter didn't give her the right to be preaching at us.

"Hey, boys! How 'bout a game of Steal the Pines? I see you all are settin' round the woodshed again. I guess you just naturally head that way 'cause you spend so much time gettin' switched here anyways!" Merry Jo reached down to pick up a pine twig about six inches long. Twirling it between her fingers she teased, "This one seems to be 'bout right. Bet all of us girls can find a dozen faster'n you boys can!"

With that challenge, everyone went running everywhere. Each team—boys against girls—needed to find a dozen twigs to put into the "pot," an area we would circle to look like a big old soup pot. Then we'd put the twigs, the same number for each team, into the pot. The object of the game was to sneak each others' pines without being tagged.

If you were tagged, you had to join the other team. At the end of recess the team with the most pine twigs won. Since there weren't any boundaries, sometimes one of us would be so far away, it'd take a while to get back to school when we heard the bell ringing. One time Clyde didn't come back 'til we were well into geography. And when he come in prancing like a yearling colt, Miz Travis wasn't one bit impressed that he still had his pine twig clenched proudly between his teeth.

There were several scrub pines all over the area, so it didn't take us no time to collect our twigs. When we put them on the ground, Merry Jo and Tommy Lee drew big circles in the dirt around them with a rock. And as soon as Tommy Lee finished, he looked up at her with a twinkle in those eyes of his. His hair was falling over his forehead again and there was a bit of a smudge of chalk dust on his cheek. But his tousled look didn't take away anything from the determined set of his mouth and chin. Tommy Lee obviously meant to win this game!

"Ready, set, go!" Tommy Lee hollered and instantly grabbed up a twig from our pot. I set off after him, keeping my eyes peeled on the bright red of his shirt flapping behind him as he ran. He was heading for the back of the school and then on across the road towards the creek. I figured he'd probably go up the creek towards the mills, so I took a sharp turn to the right to cut him off. Just about the time I was giggling to myself that I'd catch him for sure, I heard someone behind me. Anna Ruth!

Now why is she taggin' after us, I wondered, *unless she's just nosin' about for more to be teasin' me with?* "Anna Ruth!" I strained to half-whisper, half-holler. If Tommy Lee heard us, my plan wouldn't work atall. "Go on back! You hadn't oughta be leavin' the pot too!"

"You know I can run quicker'n you. Let me catch 'im!"

I stopped for a second, placing my hands on my hips and preparing to give her a good talking to. "I'm older than you and I say go back! And if you don't do as I say, me, Merry Jo, Nellie, and Verna Mae won't be speakin' to you for a week!" Since the younger girls looked up to us, I figured this threat ought to work.

"Rachael, you're just plain mean! Maybe I don't want to be speakin' with any of you all if yer goin' to be so ill!" We stared at each other for a minute or so, each of us huffing and puffing from running so hard. Then suddenly she turned around and walked back towards the school, her head down and shoulders slumped. And with her back turned, I could still see them neat pigtails shifting back and forth as she walked.

I guess that must've been the last egg I could handle in my basket, because I just plopped down right there. I wanted to cry something awful, but I knew if I started in now, there'd be no stopping for a good bit. I stared hard at an old log that was rotting away there on the ground, blinking my eyes so tight and concentrating on the log, the leaves scattered here and there, the honeysuckle vine growing round a limb: anything to keep the tears from coming. I glanced over at a sapling and then immediately thought of James Junior planting trees. That would never do. I had to be thinking on something else!

"Rachael, is somethin' wrong? Did you hurt yerself?" Tommy Lee sat down on the log beside me, his words rushing out in concern. I'd been concentrating so hard on not crying that I hadn't even heard him coming.

I closed my eyes and drew a deep breath. If I thought about the caring in his voice, I'd be crying for sure. "No, I'm fine. I just . . . needed to set a spell and collect my feelin's together. Sort 'em out, I guess."

He ran his hand through his hair, pushing it back behind his ear. "I know just what yer meanin'. Sometimes I like to climb this big ol' shag bark hickory out on the ridge of our upper pasture. An' I just set there, thinkin' on things awhile. It helps."

I had to swallow several times again to keep from blubbering. Certainly that was not what Tommy Lee'd be wanting a gal to do right now. How could I not let him know my heart was nearly full of feeling for him? A gal just didn't do that until the fella'd spoken to her daddy, and we weren't quite ready for that yet. At least, I was surely counting on him speaking for me to Daddy some day.

We could hear Miz Travis ringing the bell off to the school. As I stood and dusted off the leaves clinging to my skirt, Tommy Lee cleared his throat nervously. I looked up at him with worry. *What is he fixin' to say now?*

"Um, I'm mighty sorry 'bout the message somebody put on the blackboard, Rachael. I know it embarrassed you an', well, I mean to find out who done it. He's goin' to catch it from Miz Travis and me!" His eyes sought mine, and I could see the promise in them. He was trying to make it right. For me.

"Tommy Lee, Nellie says she and her daddy saw an outsider this mornin' in a car with plates sayin' TVA. And her daddy says they's mixed up with the Snodderlys. D'you know anythin' 'bout all this?" We were hurrying now to get back to school, jumping over logs and stepping around heavy brush.

"No, don't reckon I've heard tell of anythin' like that. But I do think even them Snodderlys wouldn't likely be tied in with any outsiders. Prob'ly 'specially the Snodderlys."

"Ain't that the truth? My daddy says even their kin don't rightly care to mess with 'em."

By now we were just within sight of the schoolhouse. Tommy Lee stopped and put his hand on my arm. "Wait just a minute, Rachael. So's no one'll tease you again, you'd best go on this way and I'll go round to the other side." Looking intently at the ground, he pushed at a rock with his toe. "I don't like folks to be hurtin' yer feelin's any." And with that he took off running the other direction.

I just stood and looked after him for a minute, again collecting my thoughts. Maybe I wasn't too young to be thinking about sparking. After all, Mama was only thirteen when she and Daddy were married, and I was nearly a year older than that now. But then, Mama didn't go to high school neither. Would Tommy Lee wait for me?

As I come round the corner of the schoolhouse, I saw Tommy Lee heading to the steps. I noticed he gave a quick look in my direction, then bounded on up the steps and through the door. Already he was looking out for me in so many ways. It was comforting to know that.

The rest of the afternoon I studied geography and then taught the little'uns their lessons. Pupils like Daisy and Earl Purser and Eugene and Billy Ray Dickerson were so quick to catch on. It was such fun to see their eyes light up and a big smile come when they answered my questions correctly. Others took a fair amount of patience. All them Snodderlys did for sure. Some of them had the trachoma, and that must've been hard on them trying to read with sore eyes and all. I don't think they ever brought much in their lunch pails either; I could hear their stomachs growling nearly all afternoon. And they all generally looked so tired. I suppose all those reasons could be why they were hard to learn. Could be they never even had a chance before they walked in the door.

When Miz Travis let us out, I said good-bye to Merry Jo and Nellie, warned O.A. to watch the young'uns, and then walked up to town with Verna Mae. If I hurried, I might be able to catch up with Daddy before he set out on the mail wagon. Daddy delivered the mail along the roads that headed out of town, and his last route was out our way so's he could be home to do the chores before supper. Most times I walked on home to keep an eye on the young'uns. But today I needed to talk to Daddy. Alone.

The drizzling rain from the day before yesterday'd left Jordan's Bend a mess. The streets were mostly dried out, but a tolerable amount of mud had been tracked onto the sidewalks, which were made out of uneven boards. Now that mud had dried into clumps—clumps which were then tracked into the town's businesses. "I imagine yer mama's havin' a time keepin' the dirt outta your store," I remarked to Verna Mae as we walked gingerly through the mess. "Best watch that you don't track in any. See you tomorrow!" I waved good-bye to her and thought to myself that she'd be working that broom good most likely.

As I looked at the boarded-up storefronts, I again felt the sick worry that the Depression had brought to all of us. I'd heard Daddy say that the Northerners kept the South so poor, we hardly even noticed the Depression. But we had felt it right here in Jordan's Bend. The Albert Owenses—they're kin to Mama—used to own the store right in the center of town. Wasn't nothing in there now but cobwebs and mice. And the hotel, well, Daddy said he doesn't know how they kept it running. Not many folks coming through Jordan's Bend those days. Even the gristmill and lumberyard didn't do business anywhere near like they use to. Everything seemed to be slowing down.

I caught sight of Old Mean Dean hitched to the mail wagon, tied up just outside the post office. Our mule was named that for a reason, and I was careful to avoid his hind legs. Since I figured Daddy must still be inside the post office, I climbed into the wagon seat to wait for him, setting my lunch pail in my lap. Noticing Miz Hickman across the street, I hollered, "Hey, Miz Hickman!" and waved. I couldn't help chuckling to myself, noticing that she was busy trying to sweep the dried clumps of mud out the door! When she handed the broom over to Verna Mae, Verna Mae looked over at me and rolled her eyes. It was going to be a long evening for Verna Mae!

"So, gal! You'll be expectin' a ride home, I reckon?" Daddy give me one of his ornery grins. No wonder Andy was mean as the dickens! "Needin' to make only two stops. Totin' mail here for the Harrises an' yer Uncle Evert an' Aunt Opal."

"I was figurin' you prob'ly be needin' someone to show you the way," I teased. "Otherwise you just might get lost in these here hills." At least I could hold my own up against him and O.A. Most of the time, anyways.

Daddy unhitched Old Mean Dean, put the mailbag and his pistol behind our seat, and climbed up beside me. It was the law here in Franklin County that the mailman had to carry a pistol for protection from revenuers, Daddy says. Giving the reins a quick slap on Dean's back and calmly saying, "Come on now, Dean," the mule slowly began to lumber on out of town.

"How ever do you get that mule to goin' like that, Daddy? He won't never do that for me!" I always reacted with disbelief to Daddy's way with animals. Most would come to him when called, move on when ordered, and even Ezra and Nehemiah, our mangy hound dogs, would sit when he hollered *Set!* He was a powerfully built man, with broad shoulders and huge forearms from the constant choring he did. 'Course, he also had the McKenney look—green eyes, dark lashes, fair but weathered skin covered with freckles. But while Andy and I had sandy-red hair, Daddy's was bright red.

"Don't rightly know. Jest wish my gals'd be movin' 'bout as easily with the orderin' as my mule does!"

"Oh, Daddy. You're so bad to tease!" And we both broke into laughter. It felt good to laugh after such a long day.

"So how did yer learnin' go today?" Daddy mostly kept his eyes on the road (Mean Dean had a tendency to stray towards anyplace that might be a good resting spot), but he glanced at me with a look of concern. He could always figure when I'd had a bad day.

"I finished readin' William Shakespeare's *King Lear*. It sure put me to thinkin'. And then I helped the little'uns with their readin'. Later I studied on the countries of South America and then taught the young'uns again. Daddy, I do love learnin' them. Bein' a teacher like Miz Travis must be wonderful!"

"I reckon it must be a good deal of work an' carryin' a load too. Most any chorin' is. Anythin' special happen to school?"

"How do you always know when somethin's botherin' at me?" I looked at him in amazement. Daddy was uneducated by any standard, but he was the smartest man I knew.

"Guess the freckles do the tellin'. Some of 'em must've been so riled, they done moved round." Pointing to my cheek he said, "See, this one was on yer nose this mornin', I'm sure!" I looked up at him and giggled, knowing this was his way to help me work out all the cares of the day. I felt a rush of feeling for this caring daddy of mine.

"Oh, they was somethin' . . ." I was back to studying on my feet again. How come I always looked at them when I was most anxious about something? I rubbed my fingers back and forth along the handle of my lunch pail. Telling Daddy the scribbling on the blackboard might bring on a pile of questions I wasn't sure I wanted to answer. Or worse yet, would he tease me about this too?

"Sometimes somethin' that hurts right bad feels better in the tellin'. Kinda like lettin' steam outta the boilin' pot o' beans. Other times it's best to keep the lid on a stew what's simmerin'. You're old enough to know the diff'rence."

I took a deep breath, but decided I just couldn't talk to Daddy about the blackboard. Granny Mandy would be more to my liking for this kind of talk. Instead, I thought about Nellie and her news about the strange car. "Nellie said somethin' that's just not settin' well with me. Told us her and her daddy spied an outsider this mornin' in an automobile with license plates that had the letters TVA on them big as you please. You didn't see the likes of them, did you? And what could he be wantin' here, Daddy?"

"Don't rightly know anythin' 'bout it, Rachael. I heared the news in town though. Folks is all talkin' 'bout it, but they ain't got many answers to why. I reckon the law is just spyin' round again. 'Bout that time a year for moonshinin', you know."

"But the revenuers ain't never had them kind of license plates, has they?"

"Don't b'lieve so."

"Nellie says they's mixed up with the Snodderlys."

"Seems to me Nellie says plenty!" Again he grinned at me. "Come on now, Old Dean! Don't you be slowin' down on me." He give the reins another slap and let out a low sigh. "Good Lord says a man should do him a day's honest labor and be mindin' his own business 'stead o' everbody else's. The Snodderlys got a heap o' troubles of their own, gal. They don't be needin' anybody addin' to 'em, I'm thinkin'."

"Do you think the outsider has anythin' to do with the CCC?"

"Reckon not." His features suddenly looked older, and he got that deep line between his brows like he gets whenever he's thinking hard on something. I could see the muscle twitching in his jaw. James Junior's leaving was hurting him too.

"Daddy, Anna Ruth says James Junior's goin' with the CCC's like goin' on relief. I told her that ain't so!" I could feel my heart fairly thumping under my flour sack blouse, and I clutched my lunch pail even tighter. Looking up at Daddy for reassurance, I asked, "She ain't right, is she, Daddy?"

"James Junior's a God-fearin' man too, Rachael. He ain't never asked for what he ain't earned. Seems like plenty o' gals was talkin' to hear their heads rattle today." He turned to wink at me and then nodded towards the Harrises' farm. "Washin' day for Miz Harris, I see. Well, she'll be happy to set a spell and read her letter, I reckon. Over this way, Dean. We ain't headin' on home just yet!"

He drove the wagon up the Harrises' worn and rutted pathway. Miz Harris was checking the clothes hanging out to dry all around her fence. She hardly needed to bend over to move them this way 'n that, she was so bent over herself. When she reached down to check some overalls, I saw her put a hand to her back. But when she straightened up to welcome us, she looked as sturdy as the standing tall white oak next to our spring.

"Hey, Miz Harris! How you be doin' today?" I noticed Daddy hollered so that Miz Harris wouldn't have no trouble hearing him. He climbed down from the wagon and reached back for his mailbag.

"Thankee, I be doin' fine, Mister McKenney. Hey, Rachael." She looked up at me and smiled.

"Hey, Miz Harris. Good to see you again."

"Eh? Speak up, Rachael!" She squinted up at me and cupped her hand round her ear.

"I said 'Hey! Good to see you again!'" Seemed I was near to straining to be heard.

"Is Mister Harris somewheres about?" Daddy asked.

"My ol' man be a-totin' wood. I reckon he be comin' anytime now. You all be welcome to stay fer supper."

"Thank you, Miz Harris, but before I left for town, Miz McKenney were cookin' up a storm. I'm thinkin' she's expectin' us to be comin' on home right hungry. My missus would want to pass on a friendly *hey* though."

"Well, be sure'n tell her I said *hey* too."

I knew Miz Harris must be mighty anxious to see that letter she'd received, but the code of the hills always called for these pleasantries, and no one violated them here. It wasn't that we thought on doing them; it was just part of daily living and being civil to people.

"Hey, Mister McKenney! Hey to you too, Rachael." Mister Harris come round from the back of the house and extended a handshake to Daddy. He was short and heavyset, probably from eating so much of Miz Harris' good cooking. Everybody loved her blackberry pies. Hooking his thumbs to the suspenders of his worn and dirty overalls, he leaned back against the fence to jaw with Daddy awhile. "Hear a gov'ment automobile was round here this mornin'. You hear tell 'bout it?"

"Eh? What's that?" Miz Harris asked, leaning towards Mister Harris.

"Automobile! I's askin' Mister McKenney 'bout that automobile!"

"You best be askin' Mister McKenney 'bout that there automobile we done heared 'bout!" Miz Harris said, nodding her head with importance.

"That's what I'm sayin'!"

I covered my mouth quickly to hide a big grin, but Daddy just acted like nothing unusual had happened. The Harrises had hollered back 'n forth like this for years now, but it still most always made me giggle when Mister Harris repeated—every time, too—"That's what I'm sayin'!"

Daddy slung his mailbag to the ground and leaned against the wagon. Crossing his arms on his chest he said, "Yep, I heared. Don't make much of it, though. Them government people comes through now 'n then."

Miz Harris moved closer to Daddy, one hand pressed to her back and the other still cupped round her ear. It was obvious that she didn't want to miss out on nothing being said.

"They best not be nosin' round too much!" Mister Harris pointed one thumb towards his cabin, adding, "Got me a rifle mounted over the fireplace I'm itchin' to try out on some stiff Yankee britches!" His eyes were twinkling with mischief as he continued, "'Course, that be if they's on Arnold's land," nodding eastward now with his head. Suddenly his face turned more serious as he narrowed his eyes, and a faint red coloring come to his cheeks. I could feel my cheeks redden slightly too at the mention of Tommy Lee's name. "Anybody sets foot on my land sets hisself fer a heap o' troubles."

"Now, Mister Harris," Miz Harris anxiously cut in. "Ain't goin' to be no outsiders on our land. You's workin' yerself up 'bout nothin'. Ain't that right, Mister McKenney?" Miz Harris looked to Daddy for help. I knew Mister Harris was prone to getting riled pretty easy, and he'd had several "spells" over the last few years when he got a bit too excited about something.

"Reckon yer right, Miz Harris. I don't s'pose we'll see anymore of them cars for some time. Hey, I most forgot 'bout yer mail here. I best be gettin' about my route. Got me more to deliver and Miz McKenney'll be waitin' supper." Daddy reached down into his mailbag and pulled out one envelope, handing it to Miz Harris.

"Hit's from Donnie Junior! Thankee, Mister McKenney! Be sure to say *hey* to Miz McKenney. Come an' set a spell, Mister Harris. Let's us see what Donnie Junior's got to say!" She headed toward their run-down breezeway with its comfortable old rocking chairs. I knew they'd be setting there for awhile now, enjoying the news from their only son. Donnie Junior had a job over to Spring County in a mine, and they were right proud of him. They had six daughters spread over the whole county with a passel of grandkids, but Donnie's being the onliest boy made him special. A letter from him was like gold to the Harrises.

Daddy climbed back up into his seat and waved good-bye to them.

Don't suppose that they noticed, though. Miz Harris was already busy reading the letter to Mister Harris. He didn't know how to read, so Daddy always give the mail to Miz Harris. Don't know if that helped Mister Harris not to be embarrassed, but it was like Daddy to be that way. Hill people were proud folk, and Daddy knew their dignity was important to them. It was important to all of us. Granny Mandy always said we don't have much else to hang on to.

"Now, come on, Old Dean," Daddy coaxed. "You know that ain't goin' to get you home soon 'nough." He give Dean another nudge, and we headed to kin of Mama's—the Dickersons' place—just down a bit on the other side of the road. Didn't seem to be anybody about just now. Daddy must've been thinking on the same thing because he said, "Everbody must be a-chorin'. Can't see a body anywheres. Hey! Anybody to home?"

Suddenly young'uns come running from every which direction. Billy Ray, the second littlest, scampered down the steps of the house and Jessie and Eugene raced from the barn. Couldn't hardly tell what any of them were saying, they were all shouting and carrying on so.

"My land, young'uns! Hush up so's yer Uncle McKenney can talk!" Aunt Opal strode out the door with baby John Evert straddled on one hip. She was a pretty little thing, Mama's brother Evert's wife, but you could tell that keeping track of all them boys was telling on her. She pushed some stray hair back from her face into the bun at the back of her head and mopped her forehead with her sleeve. "Hey, Jamie! Hey, Rachael! Won't you all come in an' sit to supper with us?" She switched her plump toddler to the other hip. I couldn't fancy how she toted him all day.

"Thank you, Opal, but me and Rachael need to get to home. You all are welcome to come join us though. Miz McKenney would love to be visitin' with you a spell." He reached down into his mailbag and pulled out a letter. "Hey, Jessie, hand this to yer mama, please."

"I would right love to visit with Mae a good while. But Evert's out workin' the back field. 'Spect him home any minute now, an' he'll be plenty hungry!" She looked up at the sky a minute and then back at Daddy. "Fine weather, and the moon be as full as she's goin' to get. You all puttin' yer gardens in tomorra?"

"Yes, ma'am," Daddy answered, nodding his head. "Granny Mandy's been fairly itchin' to for some time now. Have to hold her back ever year to let me or James Junior get her truck patch plowed up. One o' these years she's goin' to beat us to it, I reckon!"

"Yer mama don't never slow down none, does she?" Aunt Opal said, chuckling.

"No, ma'am, an' don't figure she be dawdlin' any soon, neither! Still threatens to whup me now an' then when I don't move quick enough to please her!" I noticed the boys were all listening with their mouths hanging open. Guess they were picturing Granny Mandy chasing after Daddy with a switch! "Well, we best be movin' on. Nice visitin' with you, Opal. Tell Evert *hey*!"

"Be sure to tell Mae hello, and I'll be lookin' forward to seein' her come Sunday. Thank you for the mail!" She took the letter from Jessie, holding it up to examine it. The boys immediately took off running every which direction again, and I seen Aunt Opal shake her head. "Jessie, tote in some more wood for my stove! Eugene and Billy Ray, hunt for yer Daddy an' see if he needs help with anythin'! Come on now! Stop yer scufflin' an' do as yer mama says!"

I grinned at Daddy and shook my head. "Reckon if they have any more boys Aunt Opal'll get the rheumatism from runnin' after them?"

"Seems to me she does just fine a-hollerin' from the porch! Now, Old Mean Dean, let's us head on home." We pulled out onto the road, crossing Small Creek and its fair bit of water trickling on down to the Tennessee. We both settled back to enjoy the ride home, still keeping watch, though, for a neighbor to be hollering at. We passed Uncle Les and Aunt Samantha Dickerson's (Les is Mama's older brother) and then Tommy Lee's house. Both looked quiet except for the smoke coming from their chimneys. Most everybody would be getting supper ready this time of day.

"Look how that smoke's a-risin', Rachael." He pointed out the Pursers' chimney. "Headin' straight up to the good Lord's heaven, it is. Goin' to be one fine day tomorra for puttin' in yer mama's and Granny Mandy's gardens."

We crossed the gap-board rickety bridge over Clear Springs Creek, and then we could look over the McKenney homestead. It covered both sides of the road, with our home on one side and Granny Mandy's cabin on the other next to the Tennessee River. Dogwood Springs joined Spring Tide Creek to form a big Y up the hills a ways and then flowed down across the rest of our land to the Tennessee. With all them creeks—and flooding about every year too—the soil gets a good many drinks to keep it good and fertile.

Granny Mandy told me that her great-grandaddy took one look at this land and said it certainly belonged to the Lord, so rich and green and pretty nestled up to the Tennessee the way it is. Said too that he was right sure that the good Lord would want him to care for and tend it along with his sons to come. McKenneys have been on this piece of land ever since, and probably every one of us has thought the same thing: this *is* God's land. Looking over it this way, I always swell up with pride and loving for the dark, rich soil, the strong, wind-whipped oaks and sturdy hickory trees, and the gentle slope down to the river. Didn't rightly know nothing about the homesteads up or down the Tennessee, but us McKenneys were sure we had the best viewing of the river anywhere.

I looked over to Granny Mandy's, trying to catch a glimpse of her somewheres in the yard, but she must've been inside cooking too. Her cabin wasn't our kin's first, many having already burned to the ground over the years. But it was a good many years old, with the original foundation probably the same. I smiled to myself as we passed by, noting the plain, foursquare cabin, built solidly on a somewhat level spot in this hilly area. I say somewhat because nothing's rightly level here; folks say even the cows are born with two legs shorter for standing on the hillsides. Daddy says that his grandaddy used to tell him a story about how he had to tie his old mule to an oak tree. Kept him from falling out of the field when he laid off plowing!

Granny Mandy had a barn, several outbuildings, and a springhouse built by my Great-Grandaddy McKenney (the best in the whole county, most said). But since my Grandaddy McKenney had died several years ago, she didn't have no need to keep up all those buildings. Daddy and James Junior did all the farming now, with Daisy and Earl Purser's daddy doing some tenant farming too. I didn't care to think about how Daddy'd be doing it all with James Junior leaving, so I concentrated on spying out Lookin' Point best I could. There's a fair-sized clump of trees near Spring Tide Creek where it dumps into the Tennessee, and Lookin' Point is a big old rock setting right there by the river. Granny Mandy says sure as anything that rock's watching the river go by, so's anybody there ought to join in. Soon the leaves would be on and I wouldn't be able to see past the trees, but today I could just glimpse the river. It still looked fairly muddy from the rain we'd had.

On the northern side of the road was our home, and right out front was the "truck patch," the garden, all plowed up and ready for tomorrow's work to be done. We had a larger home than Granny Mandy, although it hadn't always been that way. It was built by Daddy and about everybody else round here for him and Mama's house-raising when they were married. They built just a small, square house with one fireplace, but when the young'uns started coming (and Daddy was bringing in extra for swapping with the good crops he was raising even those early years), Daddy put on another room with a breezeway in between. Like the Harrises, we kept rocking chairs setting out there too. They were the best place to be on a muggy summer's night.

We had pasture on the northwest and west sides of the farm, cornfields on the northeast and east (this was the most fertile land from flooding and therefore the best for growing corn), and a wheat field on the west side of Granny Mandy's land. The corn grown in the middle of the Y made by two creeks was always the best in the county. It grew so thick and tall over Daddy's head that you couldn't hardly see him atall when he was only one row in. Folks all over the county envied our corn so much they even give it its own name—McKenney Way Corn. That's because whenever a buyer from out of the county come in and saw Daddy's corn for the first time, he'd most likely ask, "Where'd that come from?" Folks got so use to answering, "Oh, it's from out McKenney's way," that pretty soon it just come to be called McKenney Way Corn. Saved time for the asking, most said.

We had every sort of outbuilding scattered about the place. The barn was a good many years old, and showing its age too, Daddy'd say. We had toolsheds and woodsheds, a chicken house, smokehouse, a shed for the pigs, and a corncrib for storing corn. We also had our own springhouse, although it wasn't near as fine as Granny Mandy's, and of course we had an outhouse next to the creek. There were all sorts of farm tools, wagons, sleds (upside down when they weren't being used so the runners wouldn't rot), and some sort of animal everywhere. We had a stake and rider fence around most of the place too. The most important fence, though, was around the corn and the truck patch to keep the animals out rather than to keep something in. We let our hogs roam all over the hills (Daddy said they always got fatter that way rather than eating slop all year), and the cows moved freely in the pastures. If that fence ever come down and the hogs or cows got in—'specially if they got into Mama's garden—somebody were going to catch it for sure!

As we turned into our path up to the house, Ezra and Nehemiah come running from the house, yelping and wagging their tails. When they got near to Old Mean Dean they knew to slow a bit and stay back from that mule though. Didn't take but one kick each and them dogs learned quick. Daddy pulled the wagon up to the barn and said, "Hol' up there, Dean. I'll be settin' you out now. You must've smelled Miz McKenney's cookin' to be a-hurryin' like this. Rachael, you best get yer milkin' done right off and then go on in an' see to helpin' with supper. Soon's I see Andy I'll send him on to help you."

"Yes, sir," I said and climbed down from the wagon. I put my lunch pail by the back door and walked over to the pasture to find our three cows—Eenie, Miney, and Moe, Daddy'd named them. (He always prided himself on "o-riginal" names, as he said it. Too bad we'd had to sell Meanie last year; kind of ruined the sound of saying them names all together. But Meanie had lived up to her name: she was a kicker!) I figured they'd be moseying on into the barn like they always did this time of day. Never did need no clocks with animals around; they knew when it was eating time.

Didn't see them outside the barn, though, so I peered inside and there was Andy milking them already. "O.A.! How'd you get home so quick? An' how come yer helpin' me with chores without even bein' asked to?" I looked at him suspiciously.

"Me an' the boys raced near the whole way home. Tommy Lee won, though, like always." He moved the milking stool a little to get a better hold on Miney. "Thought you might want a bit of help today. Figured it were a pretty long day for you."

My first thought was that Andy was feeling guilty about that blackboard writing because he was responsible, and I was mighty tempted to blurt that out. But then I figured I'd best ask my questions carefully or I'd never pull the story from him. Cautiously, I asked, "Why you figurin' it were a long day?" Andy cleared his throat. *That don't seem to be a good sign,* I thought to myself.

"Um, 'cause o' the blackboard an' all."

"What about the blackboard?"

"You know, Rachael! That teasin' writin' that some rascal wrote. Tommy Lee was a mite upset too, you know!"

So Andy had been talking to Tommy Lee about it. Well, I reckoned I could trust Tommy Lee not to say too much. I suppose the milking was Andy's way of making it up to me and Tommy Lee. I wondered if he knew who'd done it. "You know who wrote it?"

"Nah, but I wouldn't tell if I did know. Us boys gotta stick together, even if it was a mean thing to do." He cleared his throat again. "I just mentioned kind of easy like, though, that whoever done it best not be pickin' on my sister for any more mean spells. Seein' as when James Junior's gone, I'll be the man of the house next to Daddy . . ." His voice trailed off and I could hear the hurting in it, but I knew I daren't let Andy know that I'd noticed.

"I'll be takin' this milk on to the springhouse then." I made an effort to keep my voice flat and even. "You can bring that on in the house for supper when yer done. An' thanks, Andy." I grabbed up the pail of milk and walked back out to the welcome sunlight. There was too much gloom sitting in that shadowed barn.

The springhouse was just next to Spring Tide Creek, which flowed by our barn and house. A pile of rocks at a bend in the creek produced the sweetest, coolest water from way down in the ground. Daddy had built our springhouse there from mostly rocks and some wood. It looked like a small building, and inside he'd built shelves for storing our milk and the cheese and butter me and Mama made. The water from the spring come up through the rocks at the back of the spring-house and Daddy had constructed it so the water flowed all the way through, cooling the whole building. It stayed about the same tempera-ture all year round so that milk stored in there didn't even freeze in the winter. I poured the milk into a large jar and put it back into the springhouse. Picking out some butter for supper, I noted that me and Mama'd be needing to churn again soon.

I walked on down to the house, wondering what Mama was fixing for supper. Cooking wasn't my most favorite thing to do—I'd much rather be reading down at Lookin' Point or gardening—but I did enjoy helping to cook up a supper that Daddy and James Junior'd like after a hard day choring. When he'd finished eating, Daddy'd most always push back in his chair and say, "That there was one fine meal, Miz McKenney!" Though he'd say that whether we'd had beans and cornbread or fried chicken and sweet taters, I could tell that Daddy meant it true. Seeing the replying twinkle in Mama's eyes and the slightest turn upwards at the corners of her mouth brought a big grin to my face too. Knowing I was a part of that made cooking fine.

I patted Ezra and Nehemiah, who were tagging at my heels, snatched up my lunch pail, and headed on up the steps into the cabin. Soon's I opened the door I knew why they were following so close like. Mama was cooking something special again. The smell of her candied sweet taters brought me a feeling of pleasure and pain at nearly the same time. Candied sweet taters were one of Mama's specialties, and we were in for a treat whenever she made them. But I knew she was making them special for James Junior, and so none of us would likely be enjoying them taters quite the same as usual. They were too much a reminder of James Junior's going away.

"Hey, Mama. Smells mighty fine in here!" I set the butter on the table, plopped both pails by the sink, and then washed up with some water from the pump. Last year Daddy'd put in our latest "con-ven-ience" (Daddy always drawed it out that way) when he piped in water from our spring into the cabin. That pump meant me and O.A. didn't have to tote water as much as we use to. We'd still have to fetch some for bathing, cleaning, and washing clothes, but the pump had sure saved us many a trip to the creek.

Mama was stooped over the big old oak meat box we kept next to the stove. In there we'd layered shoulders, middlings, and ham, with salt in between to cure the ham for keeping. It was my job to empty the pan underneath the meat box whenever it was full of the dripping salt. "Hey, Rachael." Mama's voice sounded weary. "You best be emptyin' the pan soon. Looks to be 'bout full again." Usually Mama'd ask me about school, but I could tell she wouldn't be offering much extra talk tonight. "You come keep a eye on the ham a-fryin' whiles I check the taters. Then you can set the table."

"Yes, Mama." I moved over to the stove and pushed the ham around a bit in the large cast iron frying pan, making it sizzle and spatter grease. Mama'd put on a kettle of beans too, with a bit of saltback to flavor them; they were simmering on the back of the stove. Up above we had a warming closet, and a quick peek in there showed that Mama had made biscuits for supper too. I noted with another quick jab in my heart that everybody else's favorite was cornbread. James Junior's was biscuits.

As Mama opened the oven to check the candied sweet taters, I noticed the same weariness of movement I'd seen in Miz Harris. With one hand to her back, she leaned over to pull out the pan and check for any signs of burning. Mama'd never offer one word of complaining or even sigh so's I could hear her, but something in her movements about the kitchen seemed to speak of being tired—tired from the heart.

Studying on Mama always made me wish I'd known what she was like as a young gal. Sometimes a sparkle'd come in her eyes and a easy laugh'd escape that showed she must've been different years ago. Her dark brown hair must've been the prettiest in Jordan's Bend and was still her best feature. It was so thick and full of waves that she always had trouble keeping it tucked into a married gal's proper bun. Pretty waves were always pulling out round her face. I don't think Daddy helped none either though. He'd generally be pulling at it, like he just enjoys the feeling of touching them curls. Looking at it now, I spied plenty of gray showing here and there.

Her face was still pretty with its sharply defined cheekbones and high forehead, but it was lined about her mouth and eyes. Lines from fretting about providing for us young'uns, lines from working her garden on a hot summer day when the sun was beating down, lines from pain—body pain and the heart-hurting pain of life. What had she looked like before the wearing down of daily living?

She put the taters back into the oven and closed the door, turning off the oven's heat control. "They oughta be just fine by the time everthin' else is ready. Ham comin' along?"

"Everthin' looks wonderful, Mama. James Junior's sure to be pleased." I moved away from the stove to fetch the plates, forks, and knives. We'd always coveted the crated boxes that the fruit come in to the general store in town. Several of those crates were nailed to our walls for storing any number of things, and from one of these I pulled out our plates. The table was set pretty much in the middle of the room, with the rough stone fireplace covering most of the east wall. Mama rarely cooked over the fireplace, since she had such a fine, big wood stove, but Granny Mandy used hers for cooking right often. She insisted that fireplace cooking tasted ever so much better than in any newfangled stove.

The room had just two windows—front and back—and two doors. One was the back door that I'd come in and the other opened up to the breezeway or "dog trot," as we often called it. Don't rightly know who named it that, but I was sure Ezra and Nehemiah would be doing just that time we set down to eat.

I suppose you'd call this room pretty rough, seeing how it had a puncheon floor made of poplar that was worn right smooth in most places but could still give a nasty splinter to our feet now and then, and the crude table and chairs, walls, and nailed-up crates certainly didn't give it a neat look. But Mama'd added touches here and there that give it a softer, homey kind of feeling. Frilly gingham curtains hung at the windows, a rag rug set by the back door, a colorful quilt hung over the back of a ladder-back rocker next to the fireplace and a safe (as we called it) that stored better serving dishes and knives, forks, and spoons leaned against one wall. The front of the safe had tin on the doors that had holes poked in it, holes that made pictures of flowers and interesting shapes. It wasn't exactly pretty, but like all them other things in the kitchen, it also added to that homey feeling. Mama'd told me once that she made our clothes and linens for the needing of them; she added crocheting to the pillowcases and frills to the curtains for the needing of her heart.

The door suddenly banged open and James Junior come fairly bounding in. "Mama, do I smell yer candied sweet taters a-bakin'? If I'm mistaken, my stomach's goin' to be plain sorry!" He gave Mama a quick kiss on the cheek and opened the oven door. "I knew it! I can nearly smell yer sweet taters a mile away. Even upwind!"

"James Junior, you best be gettin' outta there! You'll ruin 'em for sure!" She looked stern about her mouth, with her lips tight in a firm line. But there was a twinkle in her eyes, and James Junior and me both knew she wasn't really put out. He looked over at me and gave an exaggerated wink. He sure took that winking after Daddy. One of them two was most always winking and teasing at me about something. Was I going to miss that too?

He went over to the pump to wash his hands, saying, "Got Granny Mandy's garden all plowed up and ready for plantin' too. Daddy an' Andy'll be in any time now. They're just finishin' up in the barn. Did you know that scrawny tabby cat looks to be havin' kittens again soon, Rachael? As if we don't have 'nough already." Wiping his hands on the old piece of quilt we used for a dishrag, James Junior turned to again inspect all that was cooking on the stove.

I pulled forks and knives out of the safe. "Daddy told me she can't have any more kittens. He says we've plumb run outta names to give 'em!" I finished setting the table, moving plates just so to make it look special nice for James Junior.

"Daddy'd best have a good talk with the tabby, then! Doubt that'll do him much good though. Seems a mite late to me . . ." He put a bite of green beans in his mouth, mumbling, "Mmm, them beans are tastin' fine too, Mama."

I could hear O.A. scuffling with the dogs out in the yard, and then him and Daddy come in the door. "Didn't need to be ringin' no bell for supper tonight, Miz McKenney! James Junior could smell them taters clean across the cornfield. Everbody round the county's goin' to be envyin' us them sweet taters!" Daddy bent down to give Mama a kiss on the cheek and then joined Andy washing up at the sink. James Junior reached over to tousle O.A.'s hair. When he wasn't winking at me, he was most likely ruffling Andy's hair.

Me and Mama set the beans, ham, and biscuits out on the table, and then we set the candied sweet taters right in the middle since they were special. Soon as I poured the milk for me and Andy and coffee for Mama, Daddy, and James Junior, we were ready to hold hands round the table. Mama said we held hands to pray because it was nice to pray that way as a family. I always thought it was to keep O.A.'s hands out of trouble while Mama and Daddy had their eyes closed.

"Lord, we be most thankful for what Thee has provided for us. Thank Ye for this food, our home, our family. Mostly we be thankful today for James Junior and this new job Thee has given." Daddy's voice seem to catch just a bit, and I peeked up at him. He cleared his throat and went on. "Bless our remainin' time before he goes away. Amen."

We all echoed, "Amen," and Mama started in to dishing out our food. When she served up the taters, I noticed James Junior's helping covered nigh to half his plate.

"Daddy, did you tell James Junior 'bout the government car?" I asked.

"What's this?" James Junior looked up from his plate with interest. He'd already put a good dent in that helping of taters.

"Heared in town that a automobile with the license plates spellin' out TVA was parked just outside of town. Everbody's jarrin' an' jawin' 'bout what the feller was up to," Daddy said in between bites.

"Reckon he's recruitin' more for the CCC?" James Junior asked.

"Nah, don't rightly think so. Prob'ly nosin' round for moonshinin' again. Best be watchin' where he's puttin' his nose though. Them taters taste even better'n they smell, Miz McKenney."

She looked up at him with one of those special grins again. *Wonder if I'll ever smile at Tommy Lee just like that*? I thought to myself.

O.A. turned to Daddy with a puzzled look. "But what's the letters TVA stand for? I ain't never heared tell of that before."

"Maybe they's short for . . ." I could tell Daddy was thinking on another of his tales. "Trappin' Varmint Andy!"

We all laughed at that one—even Andy, though he give Daddy a scowl at the same time.

"Heaven help them Yankees if they catch him!" James Junior added, causing us to laugh again.

I took a big drink of milk, concentrating on swallowing down the cool-tasting drink and my anxiousness. I could tell Daddy and James Junior were doing their best to make these last few meals when all of us could be together just like all the other suppers we'd spent round this old table. Mama may be fixing special dishes of James Junior's favorites, but Daddy was fixing to make us forget about the empty seat we'd see here come Monday.

"Anybody want another helpin' o' taters?" Mama asked. "Don't be backwards none. They's plenty here for everbody to have more." She reached over from the table to grab the coffee pot off the stove. "Bet yer coffee needs hittin' up, Mister McKenney. Yers cold too, James Junior?"

Mama moved round the table, filling their coffee cups. I noticed how she let her hand rest a moment on James Junior's back.

"Spoke with Mister an' Miz Purser 'bout goin' in with the CCC. They ain't never heared of the Civilian Conservation Corps. Had to explain it all to 'em. Mister Purser seemed right interested." James Junior took a drink of coffee and then set down his cup. "Said he'd sure like to get paid just for plantin' pines."

Daddy had been just about to put another forkful of ham in his mouth when he suddenly put the fork back on his plate. "Hope you set 'im straight 'bout that." Mama was still eating, but I could tell she wasn't missing a word.

"Yes, sir, I did at that. Told him 'bout the educatin' of farmers we'd be doin'. Givin' 'em phosphates for fertilizin' an' 'bout puttin' to pasture some of their cornfields that's wearin' down. That's when he perked up an' listened. He knowed you been restin' yer land off an' on for years. An' he knowed you be raisin' fine crops too."

Andy wiped his mouth with his sleeve and asked, "But James Junior, why you plantin' trees? Seems we got plenty of them." He shook his head in bewilderment.

"Some places don't got 'nough trees, Andy." James Junior pushed back from the table so he could spread out his arms better. "See, trees got roots, right?" He held both hands up, fingers pointing down. "Well, say the spring tide comes in this year an' she's a big 'un. Them roots is deep in the soil an' they hold onto it when them floods come. Keep that soil from washin' away." He held his fingers down firmly. Then lifting his fingers, he said, "If they ain't no roots, that good soil washes right into the Tennessee. Makes big gullies too. If you got trees growin', them roots holds tight an' keeps that good topsoil from washin' away."

Andy watched James Junior in fascination, nodding his head. *Bet he ain't never listened to Miz Travis like that,* I thought to myself.

Daddy pointed his now empty fork at Andy. "That's why my Daddy called the Tennessee a Yankee river."

"Why's that, Daddy?" Andy looked mighty puzzled again.

"'Cause she starts up north, curves down to us, an' then goes back up Yankee way again. In the meantime, she's snitched us of our good topsoil, takin' it back up to them thievin' Yankees!"

James Junior grinned and added, "Well, we mean to stop her with them pines. Government's plannin' to control the tides by buildin' dams too. Somethin' called the . . ." He paused a moment, concentrating on it. "Tennessee Valley, . . . don't rightly 'member for sure." He shook his head. "Can't bring it to mind. Anyways, I'm needin' some more of them taters. Won't be none of these left for the slop bucket, I reckon!" He dished the last bit onto his plate, giving Mama another smile.

"Been workin' on gettin' yer clothes all mended before you leave," Mama said, keeping her eyes on her plate. I noticed she hadn't eat much. Seemed like she'd just kind of pushed it round like O.A. did tomaters. "You reckon yer shoes'll hold out for awhile?"

"They's got to. Least 'til my first paycheck. Most all the rest I'll be sendin' home to you all."

Mama suddenly got up from the table and started clearing away the dishes. Daddy put a hand on her arm to stop her a minute. "Now, James Junior, we ain't havin' you to go off an' support us none. We's doin' jest fine, you hear?" Daddy's look was stern. And proud.

James Junior looked to Mama, then Daddy, and back to Mama again. "Yes, sir, I know that. But I'm wantin' to help out too, an' I know they's needs comin' up. Like Rachael's schoolin'."

The sudden mention of my schooling made me nearly drop my cup of milk. I put it down quick and stared at my plate. If I hadn't been at the table I probably would've stared at my feet again. I could hear Mama take in a big breath of air and then I could tell she was busy again, carrying dishes to the sink for washing. "Rachael, get some water outta the reservoir from the stove. Time we done up the dishes. You need to head over to Granny Mandy's before dark. Said she's a-needin' to talk to you 'bout plantin'."

Daddy and James Junior stared at each other a moment before Daddy sighed and got up from the table. James Junior put his head in his hands for a minute and then fairly jumped out of his chair. As he opened the back door, not looking our way but gazing towards the upper pasture, he said, "I'll be workin' on one of the sleds. Looks as though the runners might need replacin'." He went out, easing the door closed behind him.

"Andy," Daddy said, "you best be cuttin' more wood for the firebox. Get started tonight an' you can finish up tomorra."

Andy nodded, saying, "Yes, sir." They both headed out, but Daddy stopped a minute, holding open the door and looking back at Mama.

"Mae." Daddy rarely called Mama by her given name. He most always called her Miz McKenney. She didn't turn to look at him but stopped washing, holding her head up straight and staring at the wall. "Everthin'll be fine."

I wondered if he said it to convince Mama . . . or himself.

We done up all the dishes and then Mama give me the slop bucket, telling me to give it to Ezra and Nehemiah. There wasn't much left tonight though. Them dogs was going to be mighty disappointed.

Going out the back door was like getting out of church when Preacher Morgan was long-winded on a hot summer's day. I was most anxious to escape the kitchen; thinking on all that had happened and was going to happen made me feel impatient to run to Granny Mandy. She'd help me sort it all out. I spilled the slop bucket's contents out onto the ground (Ezra and Nehemiah had been waiting on me all right), watched them gobble it down (did they even chew atall?), and took off running for Granny Mandy's.

I run down our pathway past the garden and across the road. Granny Mandy's garden was plowed up nicely too. "Granny Mandy! Hey, Granny Mandy! You to home?" I started in to hollering soon's I stepped foot on the other side of the road. We rarely bothered with knocking. Wasn't no need after we'd hollered so loud.

By the time I got to her rickety door (it always looked as though it would fall off its hinges any minute), she was there, opening it wide for me. "Well, come on in, Rachael! I's jest 'bout to make my cornbread fer supper. They be plenty fer sharin'." Granny Mandy and me rarely hugged, but the welcoming look she always give me meant just as much.

Her face was deeply lined all over, and when she smiled—as she did just then—the lines went deeper and farther, pointing out the spark in her deep-set gray eyes. Her hair was snow-white and thinning out a bit. She always braided it and wrapped the long braid round and round at the back of her head. Granny Mandy wasn't a big woman, but she was strong. Once I seen her lift a huge rock out of her truck patch, saying only that it was "takin' up room fer my cabbage." After seeing that, I always figured Granny Mandy could do about whatever she set her mind to. She wore one of her faded, frayed dresses (I'm thinking she only owned three to her name—two for every day and one for church) and a starched, clean apron.

As I went in through the door, I felt like I was entering the safest, warmest place ever. Granny Mandy's cabin was my city of refuge like I'd learned about in Sunday school in the Old Testament. I wasn't no refugee, of course, but I sure needed a place to run to now and then for comfort. Her cabin was very small, with only one room and a fireplace that was years and years old. Although several cabins had burned down, our kin had always rebuilt whatever was left of the chimney. The one bed was close to the fire where Granny Mandy kept it most of the winter to keep warm. In fact, most everything was pulled close to the fireplace since she did a good bit of her cooking there.

As always, the first thing I looked at when I come in the door was her walls, since they were covered with pasted up pictures from magazines. She put them up because they were pretty and on account of her and Grandaddy didn't have no money for wallpapering. But mostly she put them up to teach Daddy and Aunt Hettie their ABC's. Pointing out letters on them pretty pictures made it a fun game for them, and Granny Mandy said they'd caught on right quick.

One of my favorite stories that Granny told was one time when she was making the paste to put up more pictures. She made it with flour, water, and a little bit of hot pepper to keep the mice from nibbling at it. Well, she had it simmering on the back of the wood stove when Grandaddy come in from working. First thing he did was reach for a spoon to taste what was cooking in the kettle—the paste! Granny Mandy said he learned mighty quick why the mice don't bother her pictures none.

The cabin contained a few chairs, a small table, the assortment of crated boxes, of course, and a chest or two for clothes and such. She wasn't needing or wanting much, I'd often heard her say, and she also would share more than half of everything she had. A string of leather britches (green beans which we strung on thread) hung by the fireplace, and Granny'd set the table for one—which she remedied quick by adding a setting for me.

"You'll be eatin' with me now, won't ye, Rachael?"

"Thank you, Granny Mandy, but we already ate. I might could put down some of your cornbread, though, if I was to try real hard!"

"Just need to get her in the fire. Won't be long a-bakin'. Now what went with that spoon I had? Things be hidin' from me these days." She looked about her working space and table, searching for her stirring spoon.

"Here it is, Granny Mandy. It was under your dishrag." I picked up the rag to use as a hot pad, planning to use it to pull the preheating pan from the hot coals. Granny Mandy called it an "old-timey oven." It looked like a large frying pan with a rounded bottom, but it also had four little legs and a tight-fitting lid. All I know is, that pan made the best cornbread I ever had. "Is the old-timey oven ready now? Want me to take it outta the fire so's you can pour in the batter?"

"She should be hot 'nough. Go ahead an' pull her out, Rachael." Granny Mandy walked over to the fireplace, stirring her batter.

As I carefully pulled the hot oven from the coals, I stood back a bit so Granny Mandy could pour in the cornbread batter. It sizzled up soon's it hit the pan, meaning she'd heated it just right. Reaching for the lid with a pothook, I placed it on top and then pushed the pan back onto the coals on the hearth. After putting more coals directly on the lid (the lid had a lip round it to keep the coals from falling off), we stood back to wait a spell. I was known for getting anxious at this point.

Granny Mandy generally said I expected it to bake as quick as we poured it in.

"Might as well set a spell." Granny Mandy pulled one of her rockers closer to the fire and sat down. "Set yerself down too, Rachael." Nodding towards the fireplace, she added, "I'll take a peek soon to see how she's a-comin'." She pushed the rocker back and forth, making that familiar creaking sound against the puncheon floor that was so comforting to hear. We'd had us many a talk in these old rocking chairs by the fire.

"Granny Mandy, did anyone ever tease you about Grandaddy when you two was sparkin'?" I blurted it out quick lest I lose my courage. Staring at the fire made it easier to talk too. Watching the coals was soothing somehow.

"Heavens, yes. That's part'n parcel of bein' that age, I s'pose. Still, I recollect that I didn't much care fer it then iffin the trick was fer hurtin'. Some was fun—like findin' the red ear o' corn." She rocked faster, and I could tell she was going to tell me a favorite story. Granny Mandy always rocked faster in the telling.

"You mean you done the kissin' game at a corn shuckin' too? If a boy found a red ear while shuckin', then he got to kiss a gal? Or a gal who done the findin' got to be kissed?" I looked at her in amazement. I'd thought only us young folks did them things!

"'Course we did! You young'uns didn't think up that one!" She shook her head at me, giggling, all them lines round her mouth deeping again. Her eyes were really sparkling now. "One time, though, ol' Albert Stooksbury—he's passed on now many a year ago—he had a mean spell come over him. Well, he knowed my James Henry an' me was intended. But when he found a red ear he come waltzin' right over to me an' put a big ol' smack right on my cheek."

"No! What did Grandaddy do?" Grandaddy McKenney had died about one year after I was born. So any time Granny Mandy'd tell a story about him, I was most interested.

"Well, right 'bout then yer grandaddy found him 'nother red ear o' corn. So he come prancin' right over to where me an' Albert was standin'. 'Course I was still blushin' to beat the band. An' I was mighty feared James Henry was 'bout to haul off an' knock Albert a good 'un. But you know what he done?" Granny Mandy could tell a story right well. I wasn't rocking any more atall but was setting right still on the edge of that chair.

"What'd he do, Granny?"

Then Granny rocked forward in her chair and stopped so's her knees were touching mine. She gripped the rocker's arms tightly and dropped her voice to a near whisper. "He come so close to Albert that he put his face right up to Albert's face. Why, I'm right sure Albert could feel my James Henry a-breathin' on 'im. An' then," at this point her voice suddenly grew louder, "James Henry kissed 'im! Smacked 'im a good 'un right on the cheek!" I broke out laughing in amazement and Granny Mandy set back in her chair, rocking faster again, laughing all the time in between her words. "My James Henry couldn't o' surprised 'im more iffin he had a-knocked 'im! I'll never forget the look on Albert's face! Hit was somethin', that look was!"

I hadn't even told her about the teasing on the blackboard, but somehow she'd helped to ease the hurting. Just didn't seem quite so important anymore.

"Iffin anybody gets to teasin' on you, jest you think 'bout poor Albert. Somebody'll get 'em one o' these days!" She got up from the rocker and picked up the pothook to check the cornbread. Carefully raising the lid, she said, "Looks to be 'bout done."

The smell of that baking cornbread made me take a deep breath. I could nearly taste it already. "Maybe I am a mite hungrier than I thought," I told her. "Mama made candied sweet taters tonight"—she looked up at me in surprise at that, knowing sweet taters was only for special occasions—"but I didn't eat much. Didn't feel like it."

"Sweet taters? Oh, ain't them James Junior's most favorite? I see." She'd understood right off Mama's needing to do something special for James Junior. "We's all goin' to miss James Junior. Yer Mama takin' it hard?" I helped Granny Mandy lift the old-timey oven out of the fire and place it on the table. Placing a plate on top, we turned over the oven and let the cornbread fall onto the plate for serving.

"You know Mama. She don't say nothin'. But her eyes shows it. Seems she touches James Junior whenever he's near her too, like storin' up the feelin' of him for when he's gone. That it, you think?"

As Granny Mandy cut the cornbread, I watched the steam rise from the lines she made. Putting a big piece on my plate, she said, "I b'lieve so, Rachael. When yer Grandaddy was a-dyin', I kept holdin' on to 'im. Not fer tryin' to keep 'im here; I knew he was a-headin' for glory! But 'cause I wanted to 'member what he felt like, the special feelin' that was yer grandaddy's an' yer grandaddy's alone. I wanted to store 'em up fer when he were gone."

"Do you still 'member what he felt like?" I asked for Granny and I asked for me, thinking on James Junior. And Mama.

Her eyes took on a misty and faraway look for a minute. "Mostly."

I could tell she was studying hard on it. "I 'member the rough feel o' his shirt from the chorin' he'd done. An' his overalls was worn nearly soft from the wearin'. Mostly I 'member the feel o' his hand holdin' mine—strong an' firm an' yet gentle at the same time." She looked down at her hands for a moment, as if picturing Grandaddy's there too. "He could break a good-size board right in two with them hands when he wanted to, yet still hold a newborn kitten right gentle like." She moved over to the stove where she had cooked up some of the leather britches. "Want some beans too?"

"No thank you, Granny. Guess I want to save all my room for yer cornbread."

She spooned a helping onto her plate and sat down. "Thank ye Lord fer this food. It's fixin' to be a might cold out there tonight an' I'm thankful fer my warm fire. An' fer the company of Rachael. Amen." Granny Mandy wasn't one for long praying. Said most of your praying should be shown in the doing.

I put a good hunk of butter on my cornbread, letting it melt down into the warmth of the bread. Most times we ate cornbread with beans and chowchow, but Granny Mandy's sweet butter was a treat on anything. "Anyways," I continued, "things is sure goin' to be different like when James Junior leaves. Seems we's all tryin' to get ready for his goin', and ever one of us is goin' about it in their own way."

"How 'bout you?"

"I s'pose I'm tryin' to be like Mama. Doin' special things for James Junior. She ain't cried none. I'm tryin' not to."

"How do ye know yer mama ain't cried?"

"She ain't that I've knowed." I glanced up at her in surprise, wondering that Granny would even suggest that Mama might cry.

"You ain't knowin' what she does in her own bed of a night." I looked at Granny Mandy intently. She and Mama had never been close like me and Granny. At least, they never talked like we always had. But something in her voice, the certainty in the way she was saying it, made me feel sure she was right. I felt a sudden aching for Mama.

I was still studying on it when Granny Mandy said, "I'm most anxious to be puttin' in my garden tomorra. Yer mama says she'll give ye some time off from workin' hers to hep me." She got up to get another helping of beans. "How 'bout ye come first thing of a mornin' then."

"Yes'm, Granny Mandy." I finished off the last bite of cornbread, licked my fingers, and got up to put my dish in Granny's big bowl for washing dishes.

"You go on now, Rachael. I'll do up these few dishes myself; yer mama'll be wantin' ye to home."

"Thank you, Granny Mandy. That cornbread tasted gooder than . . . gooder'n sweet taters even." I looked down at my feet again.

"Maybe them sweet taters had too much hurtin' 'round 'em to be tastin' like they should."

Again I could feel tears pushing to spill over. I fought to hold them in.

"Rachael, ain't no one knows what you do in bed of a night neither."

I looked up at her, saying thank you with my eyes. The slight nod of her head was answer enough.

She opened the door for me, whispering, "'Night, Rachael," and I quickly run down the steps. As I hugged my arms to me to keep out the night's chill, I heard Granny Mandy close the door behind me. Now the warmth and comforting of her cabin was closed to me too. I could glimpse light from our fireplace shining through the window, but I didn't think it would greet me with warmth and comforting—only reminders of what was coming.

I went in through the breezeway, patting the dogs on their heads and hearing the thump-thump of their tails against the floor in response. I waited just a minute, listening for voices, but the occasional crackling of the fire was the only sound I heard. Slowly opening the door, I first noticed Mama and Daddy in their usual places close to the fire. James Junior was back a ways, just staring at the flames. I assumed Andy must've already gone on to bed in the loft. Mama glanced up from her crocheting and pulled her shawl closer round her shoulders. Opening the door had let in some of the evening's chill.

"Grandy Mandy doin' well this evenin'?" Daddy asked after his mama.

"She's lookin' forward to puttin' in her garden. I reckon she'll be up long 'fore the sun is."

"Reckon so," Daddy said, putting down his work and reaching for the box of pine knots. He was working on a new axe handle and every so often when him and Mama'd need more light, he'd put another pine knot on the fire. We had a kerosene lamp, but the kerosene it used cost more than we had to spend. Using it was a luxury only for when we had guests or it was terrible hot out. Daddy found a middling-sized pine knot and tossed it in. The fire instantly blazed up, sparking and lighting the room in its brightness. I could see Mama's work and was surprised to note that she hadn't done much since last night. She gazed intently at the needles, but her fingers were still.

James Junior stood up and yawned, stretching his long arms up over his head. "I'm still a mite restless yet. Reckon I'll take a walk round the pasture. Moonlight's nice for it." He didn't wait for a response, but reached for the door and ambled out. I could hear Ezra and Nehemiah rouse themselves to tag along.

Mama turned and stared at the already closed door, her look one of concern. She looked like she wanted to go along, but I suppose we all knew James Junior was needing to be alone. Like me.

"I'll be goin' on up to bed now. 'Night, Mama. 'Night, Daddy. Wake me if I sleep too late. I'd like to be up soon's Granny Mandy."

Mama put her crocheting down and rested her hands in her lap. She stared without blinking at the fire. "'Night, Rachael. Don't be forgettin' yer prayers." Her voice sounded as if she was far away and tired. Spent, was it?

"'Night, gal," was all Daddy said, but he turned to give me a slight smile and just the hint of a wink. I smiled back and climbed the stairway to our loft. I was nearly halfway up when I remembered I needed to take a trip to the outhouse. How I wished we had indoor plumbing like Verna Mae.

Climbing back down, I reached for the hot board which we kept warming by the fire, explaining to Mama and Daddy, "Almost forgot to visit the outhouse. Think I'll take the hot board for my feet." Daddy nodded and I went on out the door.

The outhouse wasn't far, unless it was a freezing night. 'Course then it seemed a mile aways. The hot board was a smooth board we used often during the colder months. Putting your feet on it while setting kept your toes from getting too chilled. I hurried into the outhouse and finished quick; I was kindly looking forward to my bed by now.

On my way back to the house I glanced over to the pasture and saw James Junior with Ezra and Nehemiah trailing behind him, now and then chasing after a smell with their tails wagging furiously. I stopped to watch him, storing the picture in my heart. The full moon outlined the downwards slope of James Junior's shoulders and head. He knew that pasture so well—where every stump lay, where every hole's waiting to make you trip, and where every scrub pine growed. But you'd never knowed it watching him now. He walked like it was the first time he'd ever been there, picking his way along like he was. I closed my eyes shut tight, deciding instead to make the picture before me disappear. And then I hurried on inside the house.

"'Night again," I called to Mama and Daddy as I put down the hot board and fairly run up the steps. A rush of cooler air hit me as I climbed the last one. The loft was always middling cold of a wintry evening. When Daddy'd built the loft, he put a hole in the floor so's the heat from the fireplace could rise, and that helped a bit. Now that the days were getting warmer, the loft wasn't nearly so bad, but it was still kindly chilly up here tonight.

My eyes hadn't fully adjusted to the darkened room yet, but I peeked round the quilt we'd hung from the ceiling to see if Andy was asleep. I could just barely make out his form on his bed, and when I moved a bit, making the floor squeak, he didn't move atall. Assured that he was sound asleep, I began to quickly undress and climb into my bed. We both had straw mattresses laid on homemade beds of railings with slats. On top of the mattresses Mama had put a big, heavy quilt and then we had sheets and another quilt on top for covers. Every year we'd clean out our mattresses, burning the old stuffing and replacing it with fresh-smelling new straw. Since my mattress was beginning to poke me now and then, I was getting anxious to be changing the straw again. Tonight, though, my bed felt wonderfully cozy, and after I'd squirmed around awhile, nice and warm too.

From a small window near the foot of my bed, a stream of moonlight poked through and highlighted the room's contents. We'd pretty much divided the room in two, one side for O.A. and the other for me. The old quilt hung from the ceiling gave us a bit of privacy, but not as much as I'd liked. We also stored a good deal of supplies up here. Mama had leather britches hanging from the ceiling, over in the corner was a barrel of apples, and here and there were dried cushaw, punkins, onions, and seed corn. Besides me and Andy's chests for clothes, we also had us a trunk for storing baby clothes—clothes that our baby brother and sister wore before they died. Sometimes Mama'd open that trunk, take them clothes out and hold them awhile. Me and Andy's baby clothes had long ago wore out and was even past being rags. But the clothes in that trunk would last about forever just setting there, I supposed.

I was just beginning to say my prayers when I heard Daddy's voice above the crackling of the fire. I laid real still so's I could make out what he was saying.

"Mae, there ain't nothin' to be doin', that's all." He'd called her Mae again. Twice in one day now.

"I ain't sayin' we can be doin' anythin'. I'm just sayin' they's more a-comin'. I know it. I feel it. Changes is comin'. More changes." Mama's voice still sounded flat and strange somehow, kind of like the old pump organ did when the preacher's wife was ailing and Miz Hickman tried to play on it. She didn't pump on it right so when the notes come out, they just didn't have no roundness to them, no form like, no feeling. That old organ just kind of wheezed along, and we all tried to cover it up best we could with our singing.

"What changes? Gettin' all the chorin' done with James Junior gone? I don't want you a-frettin' over them things. Andy's gettin' bigger'n you think."

"No, nothin' like that. I'm meanin' somethin' much bigger. Bigger'n me an' you can even think on right now. Feels like a storm's a-comin', rushin' down on us from the hills. An' there ain't no stoppin' it, just like they ain't no stoppin' a storm."

Mama and Daddy fell silent then, and though I strained to hear more, Daddy must've put another log on because I couldn't hear anything for the noise of the fire. I was afraid I'd heard too much already. Turning to look out the window, I seen the moon and just a few clouds slowly passing by. Then they all blurred together as the tears that had threatened to pour out ever since this morning suddenly wouldn't be held back no more. I held the quilt up tight over my head, sobbing out the hurt into my old mattress.

The bottom quilt was soaked before the tears stopped. Granny Mandy's words come back to me then—*Rachael, ain't no one knows what you do of a night neither.* But Granny Mandy knew.

As I rolled over to find a dry place on my mattress, the picture of James Junior walking in the pasture pushed into my mind, and then I thought on Mama and Daddy setting by the fire. Rocking. Not saying anything. Just waiting.

Changes, Mama'd said.

Oh, Lord, I whispered in a hushed, frantic prayer, *what's comin'?*

2

Who once was daft, with fear am dafter.
Who went before? Who will come after?
Who in this darkness sends me laughter?
I cannot pray, but I am prayed,
The prey prepared, bedecked, arrayed.

I woke up to the familiar sound of the kitchen door slamming shut. Even the rooster wasn't crowing yet, but I slid out from underneath the warm quilt and into my clothes, hoping I was getting everything on right in the near-darkness. The soft sound of Andy's breathing proved he was still sound asleep; he wouldn't be as anxious as me to get at today's chores.

The aching feeling for James Junior's leaving and the worry at the sound of Mama's voice from last night were still with me, pulling at me to fret on them. But as I buttoned up my blouse and adjusted my skirt, I decided to put it all aside for now. I pictured tucking the worries away like we holed away cabbage for the winter; after we'd used fresh what we wanted, Mama dug a trench where we'd bury the rest. I knew the problems weren't gone—like the cabbage—only just covered up and waiting for the digging up later. But right now the gardening was waiting and no batch of worrying was going to keep me from it.

Before going downstairs, though, I put a match to the candle I kept by my bed and positioned it and my mirror on the windowsill. The light reflected and flickered in the mirror, pointing out the hills and hollows of my face in light and shadow. What I saw there made me frown, like always. Freckles. On my cheeks. On my nose. Sprinkled across my forehead and dotting my upper lip. Even in the poor light of just a small candle, those freckles seemed to glare back at me as I glared at them in the mirror. It was no consolation atall that I had Mama's pretty eyes, although they were McKenney green like Daddy's. And though I didn't have Daddy's bright red hair, it was still too red for me; I'd much rather have had Mama's deep brown. But it was the freckles that made me sneer at the image and shake my head in frustration. I made a promise to myself that I wouldn't forget to wear my wide-brimmed straw hat. It often got in the way when I was bending and standing so much, but it kept the sun out of my eyes, and hopefully it would keep more freckles from sprouting on my face.

I pulled a comb out of my chest and run it through my hair a minute. It didn't have Mama's waves or soft feel to it either, being more coarse and stubborn like Daddy's. But it was healthy and thick, and I could make it shine when I'd washed it and the sun caught the red glistening here and there. I quickly braided it in one long braid, hoping that would keep it out of my way while I was gardening. Then, giving myself one last look in the mirror, I stuck out my tongue at the face staring back at me. I blew out the candle, snatched up my hat, and nearly run down the steps to hear the sounds of Mama putting wood into the firebox of the stove. I was up early if Mama hadn't even got the old stove going yet.

As I walked into the kitchen, I watched her blowing on the fire a bit, easing it into a steady burn for fixing breakfast. She blew evenly, and I noticed the waves of hair framing round her face lift slightly from the air that bounced back onto her. Without even glancing up at me, she said, "Mornin', Rachael. Gather the eggs before you come back in. We'll be needin' 'em for breakfast." Her voice at least sounded better this morning. I knew Mama always looked forward to planting her garden too; maybe that had cheered her up a bit.

"Yes, ma'am." I pushed open the back door and headed for the outhouse. The morning air was chilly and the ground felt slippery wet with dew on my bare feet, but as I glanced back over my shoulder at the stovepipe coming out of our roof, I could see the outline of the smoke against the dark sky. It was heading straight up again—another good sign. It was going to be a perfect day for planting.

When I came from the outhouse, I run right over to the chicken house. Picking up the wire basket we used for gathering eggs, I stepped inside, standing still a minute to try and let my eyes adjust some to having even less light. Even if there wasn't any light atall, though, I'd surely know the chicken house by the rotten, vinegary smell that smacked at my face every time I come through the door. The chickens clucked and cackled a bit, sounding put out at me for disturbing them. But they didn't mind me none, and I knew my way round here fine, even in the dark. In no time atall I had my basket full of eggs.

I was just coming round the corner of the house to go in the back door when I caught sight of James Junior toting the milk pails. He glanced up just then and seeing me said, "Thought since you'd be workin' so hard today helpin' Mama an' Granny Mandy put in their gardens that you could use some help with the milkin'." A bit of milk sloshed over the side as he moved toward the door. "Don't know that I'm quite as graceful as you be a-carryin' these pails though. Seems I've spilt 'bout as much as I milked!"

Knowing he probably hadn't spilt much atall but appreciating his help and the compliment, I smiled at him gratefully and said, "Thank you, James Junior. I will be a might anxious to get at the gardenin' soon's breakfast's done up. Not havin' to milk'll mean I can get to workin' right quick." I held open the door for him and immediately caught the smell of baking biscuits. "Mmm! Smell Mama's biscuits."

"Here's the milk, Mama," James Junior said to her, placing it by the sink. "I'm goin' back out to help Daddy. We'll be listenin' for the bell." Mama turned to give him a quick nod, and then he went on out the door.

"Plenty of eggs today, Mama. Do you need me to parch some coffee beans?" I pumped some water and washed up in the sink, giving my face a quick splash too.

She quickly smoothed her hair back behind her ears and then leaned over to check the oven's temperature. "Yes, we used up all the coffee last night at supper. Have to wait 'til the oven seems cooled off 'nough from bakin' the biscuits. Ain't wantin' to parch them beans too fast an' burn 'em. You know yer Daddy don't like 'em scorched atall. Pour a fair amount in the pan, Rachael."

I got the coffee sack out of one of our crates and poured the beans into the pan we always used just for this purpose. It had long since turned coal-black, like every other pan or kettle we owned. But Mama always said the fixings tasted better out of a well-seasoned pan anyways. I put the pan into the oven and began to set out the breakfast dishes.

"Run an' get some taters, Rachael. I'll keep an eye on the coffee beans for you."

"Yes, ma'am." We kept the Irish taters in a big hole out by the smokehouse. They kept real good there by first putting leaves in the bottom. Then we'd pile in the taters, clean above the level of the ground. We covered them with more leaves and then dirt. Finally, we'd dig a small hole tunneling right down to the taters, and as Granny Mandy'd often said, them taters'd "come walkin' right to you" when you'd dig them out of that small hole. I reached in and pulled out a half dozen good-sized ones, putting them in my skirt which I'd gathered up to use like a satchel.

When I come back inside, Mama had the oven door open to check on the coffee beans. "Look to be 'bout done," she said to me. "I'd give 'em a minute more maybe. You go ahead an' peel them taters."

I put the taters into the sink and began to scrub them off. They felt cold to the touch, as did the water coming from our creek. I rubbed my hands together to warm them up. "Reckon I could go help Granny

Mandy first thing this mornin'? I know she'll be at it right off. Then I could help here after dinner." I moved to the stove to check on the beans again. Seeing that they were done, I took out the pan to let them cool awhile.

"That'd be fine, Rachael. I know yer Granny's grateful for yer comin'. Andy can help me this mornin'. I hope to get most of it done before this afternoon."

At the mention of Andy's name, he came into the kitchen, yawning and rubbing his eyes. "Everbody's up early this mornin'. You all ain't eat breakfast yet, have you?"

"Surely have, an' they ain't nothin' left for you neither," I teased him.

"'Tain't true, Andy," Mama said, opening the warming doors and showing him the waiting biscuits. "But you best get yer chores done so you'll be back in time, or it all might be eat up. Rachael, reckon you can ground them coffee beans now?"

I poked them carefully with a finger. "Still a might warm, but I b'lieve so."

Mama began slicing the taters into the pan, and I poured the beans into the coffee grinder we had mounted on the wall. I wasn't one to favor the taste of coffee—although I did drink a cup now and then—but I sure did love the smell of them roasted beans. Grinding them only made them smell better. I closed my eyes a moment and sniffed in the aroma. "Mama, how come I'm appreciatin' the smell of them beans so, but I ain't one to be drinkin' much coffee? Don't make sense that I'm a-hungerin' for the smell and not the tastin'."

"Yer Granny Dickerson used to say coffee beans be like temptation. Ain't deliverin' what they's a-promisin'."

I giggled. "I reckon she wasn't likin' coffee neither?"

Mama stirred the taters and onions, sending up more delicious smells. "She tolerated it. But my mama was always one to long for tea. Reminded her of her mama—and England's ways, I'm a-thinkin'."

Wasn't long atall before I was outside ringing the bell to call everybody in. I never grew tired of ringing that bell neither. Every home in these parts had a dinner bell, and each one sounded a bit different. We knew what each neighbor's sounded like and could easily recognize who was ringing their bell. Ours had a more mellow sound, one that carried about the farthest of any of them. On a foggy day, you could hear it miles away. I clanged it good this morning, enjoying the sound of it ringing, the smell of taters and ham frying, and thinking on planting those gardens. This was going to be a good day!

Mama rapped her knuckles on the window, and although the window was good and streaked with dirt, I could still plainly see her look was a stern one. "Rachael!" she said distinctly and loudly, for her. Mama rarely hollered. "Don't you think that be 'bout enough ringin'? Come on in here an' pour yer an' Andy's milk."

I sheepishly come back inside, my enthusiasm cowed a bit, but still threatening to swell up and run over. "Sorry, Mama. Guess I got just a bit carried away by the beautiful mornin' and all." I decided I'd better settle down for now; Mama wouldn't be appreciating my excitement popping out much more in her kitchen.

Daddy, James Junior, and Andy soon come in, wiping their feet, pushing up sleeves and washing up at the pump. Although the sun was beginning to come up and the kitchen was fairly light, Daddy poked at the fire to make it brighter. Then he pulled the big family Bible down from a shelf and opened it up. The rest of us all sat down and waited for Daddy to read.

He handled the Book with great reverence, opening it and turning its pages carefully. The outside was so old that the leather had worn smooth; it was discolored too from being rescued from floods and fires and from so much handling through the generations that had passed it down. The binding creaked when Daddy opened it, looking to be falling apart any time, and the pages were yellowing and getting brittle. Us young'uns weren't allowed to page through it by ourselves, but sometimes Mama or Daddy would look through it with us, allowing us to ponder over the family history printed in the front. Our great-great-grandparents' names were recorded there—McKenney was one, of course, but other names sounded so foreign to our ears. Their birthdates and marriages were duly recorded along with baptisms and, of course, deaths. Our Grandaddy James Henry McKenney's death was written in there, and the dates our brother Joseph and sister Leah died. Seemed strange to see their names recorded there along with ours, not knowing them. If it wasn't for that trunk of baby clothes in the attic, it would be even harder to believe they were babies that Mama once held and that should have growed up to be our kin.

I could tell Daddy was turning to the book of Psalms again. When times were troubling, he usually read from there. Clearing his throat and smoothing out the page, almost like he was caressing them words, Daddy began to read, "'God is our refuge an' strength, a very present help in trouble. Therefore will not we fear, though the earth be removed, an' though the mountains be carried into the midst of the sea; though the waters thereof roar an' be troubled, though the mountains shake with the swellin' thereof.'" His voice rose and fell with the words he read. Daddy always seemed to find great meaning in them. "'There is a river, the streams whereof shall make glad the city of God, the holy place of the tabernacles of the most High. God is in the midst of her; she shall not be moved: God shall help her, an' that right early. The heathen raged, the kingdoms were moved: he uttered his voice, the earth melted. The LORD of hosts is with us; the God of Jacob is our refuge.'"

Daddy closed the Book gently, rising to put it back on its honored place on the shelf. When he sat back down, we'd already closed our eyes for prayer, knowing he would now pray like he had every other morning. "Dear Lord, we be thankful for another day to work hard to Yer pleasin'. Thank Ye for this food that Ye hast provided. Thank Ye for this family and that we be healthy an' all together." He stopped for a minute, and the quiet felt terrible uneasy like. I was sure he was thinking on Monday morning and James leaving us. "Help us now as we go 'bout our chores. Amen."

Mama kept her head bowed a bit longer, causing us all to look at her, waiting awkwardly for her to get up from the table. Mama always did the serving of the meals, unless she was at a Granny Frolic—the birthing of a baby. Then I was the one who made and served up the food. When Mama did look up, she looked flustered and irritated, the crease being there between her brows again. She got up quickly and reached for the biscuits in the warming oven and fairly plopped them on the table. "Rachael, pour yer Daddy's an' James Junior's coffee," she said over her shoulder as she served up the gravy, ham, taters, and eggs. Her voice sounded tense and short too.

"I be 'preciative of the fine breakfast, Miz McKenney," Daddy said. "Me an' James Junior aim to cut the field o' hay above the pasture. Need a fillin' meal to do that chore. Reckon Rachael an' Andy'll be workin' hard 'nough to 'preciate them eggs, taters, an' ham a-stickin' to their bones too." We usually just had biscuits and cornmeal mush for breakfast. But like Daddy said, Mama liked to give us a good meal when we had extra choring to do that day. I knew I sure agreed with Daddy. I'd eat it, but mush wasn't my favorite atall.

"Reckon the hay be tall 'nough to cut already?" Mama asked.

"Oh yes, ma'am," James Junior put in. "This fine spring weather has—"

Ding! Ding! Ding!

Uncle Les—our closest neighbor—was ringing their bell and all of us stopped to listen. Three rings followed by a short pause and then three more rings meant trouble: either the law or outsiders were snooping around. We used this system to warn neighbors whenever one of us spied intruders. Seemed we all held our breath listening to see if Uncle Les would ring it three more times.

Ding! Ding! Ding!

Daddy and James Junior immediately jumped up, Daddy's chair falling backwards to the floor in his haste. Andy started to jump up too, but Daddy turned to him and said sternly, "No, Andy. You stay here with yer mama an' Rachael. Me an' James Junior will take a look-see. You all can come out to the breezeway, but I don't want you goin' no farther." O.A. didn't say nothing; there was no arguing with Daddy when he spoke in that tone of voice. Daddy reached for his gun, which was mounted above the fireplace, and sorting through a small box on the mantel, he pulled out ammunition and stuffed some into his overalls pocket. Many kept their guns loaded, but Daddy said that wasn't safe. Instead, he stored his bullets close by in a box.

I could feel my stomach tighten and it seemed hard to catch a breath. Whenever Daddy felt the need to grab up his gun because of the warning bells I felt plenty anxious. I glanced over at Mama to see how she was reacting and saw that she stood behind her chair, grabbing the back of it so tight that her knuckles were fairly white. She followed Daddy's every movement with her eyes and then stiffly walked to the door behind him and James Junior.

We could hear Ezra and Nehemiah carrying on already. Them dogs knew those warning bells as well as us, it seemed. But when we all headed out the front door, we could see what they were barking about. A car was slowly coming up the road and Ezra and Nehemiah went tearing after it, dirt flying up in big clumps behind them. The car stopped just down from our house but the two men inside didn't get out. Reckon the sight of the dogs raising a racket was more than they were wanting to greet soon's they stepped out of their car doors.

Daddy and James Junior took their time ambling down the hill to the road. No way Daddy was about to let any outsider rile him or hurry him none either. Especially when they were on our land. My eyes were drawn immediately to the license plate. It said TVA. So this was the car that Nellie was full of talk about! Now maybe we'd be able to find out what they were about. The dogs were having a fit, running from one side of the car to the other, barking, jumping round, slobbering, and carrying on something awful. I know I was just mighty glad that although Daddy'd said we were to stay put on the porch, Mama, Andy, and me could see everything. This was much too interesting to miss!

Then the man driving the car rolled down his window a few inches. Silly! He was acting like Ezra and Nehemiah—big as they are—could climb on in if he rolled it down any farther! "I don't suppose you'd care to call off your dogs, would you?" he hollered out the window. "We're government people, and we need to survey this land. Can't very well be about that with these dogs trying to eat us."

"Them dogs got better sense than to eat a Yankee!" Daddy grinned, but his look was not a teasing one like he gives us. He was sizing up those men, and he meant to let them know it. Switching his gun from one hip to the other, Daddy subtly let them know what he was toting too, though I'm sure they'd already taken note of that. He said nothing to Ezra and Nehemiah. They were still bothering about them doors. "What you be surveyin', an' why you be on my land?"

"Got government work to do. We're surveying all along this road. Around most of this county, as a matter of fact. Got permission right here on this official piece of paper if you want to see. Don't suppose you can read?" The man peered out at Daddy, holding the piece of paper through the slit of opened window.

I put my hands on my hips and muttered under my breath, "What's he mean thinkin' Daddy can't read?! Them Yankees all s'pose we're ignorant! Bet Daddy can read better'n he can!" Mama shushed me with one quick, harsh look in my direction.

"Take the paper, James Junior," Daddy said. James Junior reached for it and began studying on it.

Daddy was just standing there, still staring at the man at the wheel. *Why doesn't he read the paper?* I thought to myself. *The men will surely think that Daddy can't read now!* I could hardly hide my frustration, but I was afraid to say anything out loud. Mama was already irritated with me.

"Says they's surveyin' for a government project of some sort. Don't say what on here though." James Junior handed the paper back to the man. "Looks official enough, Daddy."

The men waited a minute for Daddy to say something, but Daddy just stood there, leaning back casually with his weight on his left foot. He rested the gun on his hip and slipped his hands into his pockets.

"So, you going to call off these dogs so we can get to work?" The man was plainly getting frustrated with Daddy.

"Reckon so. What you be surveyin' for?" Daddy still didn't move a muscle or speak to Ezra and Nehemiah.

"Can't say yet. There'll be a community meeting this Monday night. Government people will explain everything then. Now can we just get to our job?" The man was getting more impatient every minute. The other feller just kept nervously watching the dogs pace back and forth.

"Ezra! Nehemiah! Git on home!" The dogs instantly backed off at Daddy's command. "Git now!" They scurried up the hill and onto the breezeway with us, but Ezra kept whining and Nehemiah growled softly.

Daddy motioned with his head to James Junior, and they slowly walked up the hill. The men still didn't come out of their car though. The driver rolled his window down a bit farther and yelled out, "Those dogs won't come back down here, will they? Don't you think you should tie them up or something?"

Daddy didn't even bother to turn round but answered as he kept on walking. "Don't never tie them dogs. They'll be fine long as you don't be steppin' foot on up this way."

The men looked at each other, shrugging their shoulders and shaking their heads. It was obvious they weren't too happy with Daddy or too trusting of Ezra and Nehemiah.

Only when Daddy and James Junior reached the porch—and both dogs were setting down—did the men move atall. They climbed out of the car cautiously, keeping their eyes on the dogs every second. Ezra was whining even louder now, and suddenly he stood up, tense, shivering all over in his excitement and ready to sic them trespassers. Glancing down at the men, I seen they was froze like statues, ready to jump back in their car. I smuggled back laughter, enjoying seeing them squirm so! But then Daddy said "Hush!", Ezra laid down, and those cowardly men went about their work.

They walked around to the back of their car, a black station wagon, and started in to pulling out funny-looking equipment. "That's the surveyin' tools," James Junior told us. "They'll be takin' measurements with 'em. Calculatin' the lay of the land an' distances an' all. Maybe they be measurin' to widen the road or somethin'."

Daddy shook his head. "Don't rightly know why they'd be doin' that. Ain't no need." He studied on them a minute and then shook his head again. "Reckon that be 'bout like them government people though. Buildin' an' spendin' money on what ain't needed. Maybe they's tryin' to figure out if the road be there in the first place. Yer Grandaddy used to say once you blowed out the candles of a night, a Yankee couldn't find his own nose with both hands. But I don't aim to be standin' here all day neither, wastin' my time tryin' to figure out what some fool government people is doin'. Take another fool to figure that out, I reckon." He looked over at Mama. "Reckon yer fine meal is ruint by now. Best go eat anyways. Got chorin' to do, Yankees or no." He held the door open for us all and we filed in.

"Daddy, would you've let Ezra an' Nehemiah eat 'em? Would you shoot 'em too?" Andy's eyes were full of excitement. He looked like he was still hoping for a big scuffle.

Daddy chuckled at him. "Reckon there wouldn't be nothin' to shoot if Ezra an' Nehemiah eat 'em, now would there? You know how they go after that slop bucket!" Daddy put his gun back on the fireplace and then picked up his chair and set down, reaching for his coffee. "Middlin' cold now. Would you hit it up, Rachael?"

"Yes, sir." I took the coffee pot and filled his cup with more steaming hot coffee. "You too, James Junior?" He only nodded since he'd already taken a mouthful of taters. Guess he didn't mind if they was cold. "Mama?"

"No, Rachael. Seems my appetite done disappeared." She began scraping her food into the slop bucket.

"Should I be ringin' the bell to warn the neighbors, Daddy?" Andy asked. He already had one hand on the door and was tensed to open it.

"Reckon so. If them Yankees be goin' on up the way, Albert be needin' to know 'bout it."

Andy scurried out the door and we all sat quietly for a minute, listening for the three rings. After Andy'd rung it three more times, he came promenading back into the kitchen with his chin held up like a dog scenting rabbit holds up his nose. Plainly he was right proud that Daddy let him ring the bell.

"Think Mister Owens heared it?" Andy asked Daddy.

"B'lieve so. He ain't been one to miss nothin' before."

Mama began cleaning up the stove, dishing out the rest of the fixings and taking the dirty dishes to the sink. Daddy, Andy, and James Junior ate just like nothing had happened, but I felt the same as Mama. My stomach was churning too much to eat anything, so I just got up to help Mama do up the dishes. I was fairly dying to ask Mama a question but couldn't until Daddy had gone and we were alone.

No one said much of anything more atall until Daddy finished up and announced, "Goin' to check on them men before me an' James Junior head out to the pasture. You all just stay inside."

I had stopped working and was watching Daddy go out the door when Mama said, "Hand me them dishes, Rachael, an' get on with cleanin' them plates. Time's gettin' on. I'm thinkin' yer Granny's already laid a row o' lettuce."

Her words jerked me back into action. Time was passing, and I wanted to get to Granny Mandy's quick.

It wasn't long before Daddy come striding in through the door, saying, "They's spread out. One's down the road a ways an' they's got them tools set up, peerin' through 'em like. Reckon they won't bother us none. Anythin' you be needin' before me an' James Junior go, Miz McKenney?"

"Can't think of anythin'. Andy'll be here if I need help. Rachael's goin' over to Granny Mandy's." She used a luffa gourd to scrub hard on a particularly dirty pot, the one the eggs were cooked in. Leaving them to get cold in there had made 'em stick good.

"Ring the bell if you be needin' to." His meaning was clear: if those men bothered us. "Andy, you go get the gardenin' tools out an' ready for yer mama an' you."

"Yes, sir." Andy run out the door, letting it slam behind him.

"Reckon that boy can ever go out that door without it slammin' shut?" Daddy asked. "You be ready, James Junior?"

James took one last drink of coffee and nodded his head. "See you at dinner, Mama," he said, giving her a quick kiss on the cheek before heading on out the door. James Junior'd never kissed Mama like that before—just to go off for choring of a morning. I looked at her face, expecting some kind of reaction, but she just kept on doing up the dishes. I wondered if she'd even noticed.

I checked to make sure Daddy was out of earshot and then fairly let my question burst out. "Mama, why didn't Daddy read that government paper? Why'd he let them Yankees think he didn't know how to read?" I hurried to wipe the dishes, shoving them away in the box shelves as fast as I could.

Mama turned, jerking her whole body round to face me square. Her eyes flashed when she said, "Yer daddy don't need to prove to no Yankee that he can read. He don't never need to prove nothin' to nobody. You best be knowin' that right now, Rachael! Let anybody think what they be a-wantin' to. It don't matter none to yer daddy. 'Cause he knows what he is an' can do. An' that's all that matters!"

The anger and force in Mama's words took me by surprise. Why, she'd thrown those feelings at me, it seemed. I just stood there, blinking simple like at her, trying to sort through it all. I suppose I understood her words fine, but the meaning still puzzled me. *Why wouldn't it be important to Daddy that others knew he was a learned man?* I just couldn't figure that out atall. I'd have to wait to ask Granny Mandy if I wanted to ask more though; Mama was definitely not the one to be asking right now.

We done up the rest of the dishes in silence. After making sure there weren't more chores to do, I rushed out the door and into the morning sunshine. Only then did I remember my promise to myself to wear a hat. "Almost forgot my hat," I said to Mama, running back in the door to grab it quick and then on out again.

I tied it on hurriedly as I raced on down the hill. I could see both the men up the road a ways; I supposed they moved on farther every time they finished their measuring. I was glad we'd warned the Owens by ringing our bell. Reckon Mister Owens was already toting his gun to have him a look. Then I glanced back up the hill for Ezra and Nehemiah and saw they were still setting on the breezeway like Daddy told them to. But they were also watching the men intently. I smiled to myself. *Reckon those men are still keepin' an eye on Ezra an' Nehemiah too!*

I could see Granny Mandy just inside the rickety paling fence that stretched all the way round her garden. When I got closer I seen that Granny had her gun resting on one hip. I should've known that Granny Mandy wouldn't have missed nothing! "I see you took note of them Yankees too!" I said to her, nodding to her gun. I couldn't help grinning. Seeing Granny Mandy toting that gun always made me smile, although Daddy said she was a crack shot.

"Yep. I seen 'em comin' way up the road even before I heared Les's bell." She was eyeing them still, glaring at them, maybe daring them to come back?

"But it was still barely light then. How'd you knowed they was outsiders?" I looked at her with awe. Granny Mandy's "sight"—as everyone called it—for spying outsiders was known all over the county.

"Jest knowed. 'Tain't many round here with a automobile that'd be ridin' out here this time o' day. 'Sides, them Yankees got they own pecul'ar stink too." She wrinkled up her nose. "I's knowin' they's about quicker'n ye can spit an' holler *hey*, seein' how I could smell 'em a-comin'!" Then she turned towards me and winked, reminding me of Daddy. She climbed up the steps of her porch and rested her gun against the wall of the cabin. "Reckon I'll jest keep this handy like. Feel better iffin it's close by. Now, how 'bout that gardenin'?" She walked over to the garden and then stopped, gazing at the newly plowed ground with what appeared to be great pride.

"Are we all ready to plant? That ground looks fine!" I quickly scrambled over the fence to join her.

"Yep, Rachael. I do b'lieve I'm 'bout ready as this ground. An' it surely looks to be in good heart, don't it?" She looked into my face and smiled. "I fetched the tools a'ready. Let's us be puttin' them seeds in!"

I walked a ways into the garden first though, enjoying the feel of my toes pushing through the rich soil. Then I knelt down to grab a handful, clenching it in my fist. The dirt felt moist and clumped together in my fingers. Opening my hand, I examined the soil a minute, noticing the bits an' pieces of plant that remained from last year and that I knew enriched this year's earth. It was good soil. Good and rich and ready for planting! I started to turn around when I noticed Granny Mandy'd come to stand beside me. She also stared intently at the clump of dirt in my hand.

"Did ye ever hear why the soil round here has so much red in it?" She looked up from the dirt to my face. I caught a sense of sadness in her question.

"No, don't reckon I have." Examining the clump again, I noted that although it was tinged with red, it didn't contain as much bright red clay as some areas in this county. Daddy'd told me that was because ours was bottomland—land that was flooded often and thus enriched by the areas above us. Those yearly "tides" brought a runoff that give us a blacker soil than most had, and therefore better crops too.

"Some say it's from the Indians' blood that was spilt all over this land."

I jerked my head up to look into her eyes. I knew she must not really believe that tale, but the sadness in her voice made me think about the people who must've lived here so many years ago. *Did Indians live right here?* I wondered. *Did some die here too?*

"Plenty of yer kin had blood spilt by Indians too." She reached out a finger and almost tenderly poked at the dirt I still held. "I reckon that's why the good Lord 'spects us to take good care of what He done give us. Blood's been spilt on 'bout ever piece of land I s'pose. Gives it a value we'uns cain't rightly figure. Tendin' this here piece of land—" As she said this she held up her arm, pointing out the whole McKenney homestead, "—workin' it, plantin' it, givin' it what it needs to feed itself fer growin' a good crop next year—that's what the Lord be expectin' of you an' me." She moved a mound of dirt with the toe of her old shoe. "Hit's good land, Rachael. And I'm mighty pleased you be a-seein' that in it too. Yer grandaddy would be right proud."

I looked back down at the dirt in my hand and then let it slowly filter through my fingers back onto the ground. Granny Mandy's compliments were rarely handed out. I knew I would remember and treasure this one forever.

"Now." Her voice had changed instantly back to the strong and lively one that comforted me so often in its familiarity. "Let's us see to them seeds!"

We'd done this for several years now, and so we moved and worked together easy. I knew it was my part to dig the holes and then Granny'd drop in the seeds. We'd work this way for a good stretch, resting in between rows or the changing of seeds.

Mama always varied her garden every year, trying putting onions on the outside one year, or one row in the next. But Granny Mandy's was always the same. She put herbs and spices along the outside, a row of lettuce inside them, and then onions come next. She liked the "multi-plyin' kind" which meant that we'd plant big ones in the spring. Later these would make a passel of little ones, and then these little ones would produce another batch of big onions.

Next we'd plant several rows of early peas; as soon as May we'd be enjoying them. We also put in carrots, cabbage (what we didn't eat fresh or make into chowchow or kraut we'd bury to keep year round), and beets. We'd have to wait 'til sometime in April to finish, putting in corn, sweet taters, okra, and tomaters. Punkins and beans we planted in the cornfields after the first whippoorwill hollers. Punkin seeds we'd just scatter here and yonder; the beans would run up the corn, using them like poles as they grew. 'Course, whatever we put in, Granny Mandy always insisted on planting by the signs, saying anything that grew underground had to be planted by the "dark of the moon." If not, potatoes, okra, and turnips only went to tops, she said. Even though the moon was still full, it would soon be waning, so I was thinking Granny'd be itching to plant much as we could get in today.

One thing Granny Mandy and Mama both did alike. The very richest ground in the middle was reserved for something special: a patch of flowers. We'd put in bachelor's buttons, zinnias, marigolds, and touch-me-nots. I suppose those flowers were always my most favorite to plant in the whole garden.

Granny Mandy always planted a fair amount of spices and herbs too. We'd put in garlic, dill (how I loved it in Granny's dill pickles), ground ivy, sage (this was important for sausage), horseradish, and parsley. Mama planted peppermint, but it grew wild round Granny Mandy's springhouse, so's she didn't have to plant any. We used peppermint for tea.

We'd just finished up the peas when I remembered to ask Granny Mandy about Daddy. If I was going to get any answers about this atall, Granny was the one who might tell me. "Granny Mandy, did you hear Daddy speakin' with them government people this mornin'?" I patted some dirt into a nice mound and moved to dig another hole.

"Yep. Didn't miss hearin' ary a word. Yer daddy handled them Yankees right well!" There was pride in her voice for her only son.

"But Granny Mandy, why didn't Daddy read that piece of paper they had? He let them think he couldn't read!" I dug at the ground with jerking motions, taking out my frustration in the doing.

"So now them Yankees think yer daddy can't read a lick. Be that the truth?"

"No, but that ain't the point." She was questioning me rather than giving me answers, just like always! I knew that she'd get around to helping me figure it all out, but she would make me work at it awhile. I'd end up digging for those answers just about like I was digging in this here dirt.

"So yer worryin' 'bout them thinkin' on somethin' that ain't even so. Seems a waste o' worryin' to me." She scratched her chin, taking her good sweet time about the scratching—and the answering. "Worryin' takes a good bit from a body. Save it fer somethin' that's worth the troublin', Rachael. But who ere ye really frettin' 'bout?"

I stopped working to think on that a minute. "Why, Daddy, of course, Granny Mandy!" I knew my frustration was coming out in my voice now, but I couldn't stop it.

"Yer daddy? Sakes alive, Rachael. It ain't no concern of his what they think!"

"That's just what Mama said. But, Granny Mandy, it should be!" I squinted up at her from underneath my hat. I pulled the brim down as much as I could since the bright sun peeking round her shoulders was shining in my eyes.

"So why you be stewin' on what yer daddy be thinkin' about? Ain't that like the lid on the kettle o' boilin' beans?"

"The lid? What are you meanin'?"

She stooped down to look me square in the eye, and I squirmed a bit under her look. I was wishing now that I could pull that brim down even more. "You been thinkin' on that lid too much! What's in that kettle? Rachael, who ere ye really carin' about?"

The truthful answer came to me suddenly, and I quickly looked down and away from her firm and steady gaze with great shame. "Me!" I fairly choked on the word. "I was feelin' shame for me." Saying it out loud was hard, but spitting it out like that was a release somehow too. "Why, Granny Mandy? Why was I feelin' shame when it should've been *Daddy*?"

"Yer daddy don't be needin' to put on airs fer nobody. An' especially no outsiders, Rachael."

"But why?" I realized it was so important to me to know because I wanted to be that way too.

"Reckon it's 'cause he knows deep down who he is. A good man made by the good Lord. An' that's all he's a-wantin' or needin' to be. He's content, Rachael. That's somethin' not many in this ol' world even know what 'tis, let alone grab ahold of."

"I s'pose that means I don't know yet who I am. Or even what I want to be or do. I know for sure that I ain't content." I set back on my heels and sighed.

Granny Mandy reached over to put her hand on my shoulder "Rachael, don't reckon many yer age is. Time'll change all that soon enough. Let yerself be a young'un jest awhile yet. Tommy Lee an' the rest o' all that's in this world will wait a bit."

I looked up at her in surprise. *How was she always knowin' so much?*

"When yer daddy be needin' to give his say, he'll be a-doin' it." She grinned at me, and them eyes twinkled again. "He's knowin' that when a body has somethin' to say to a mule, he's a-speakin' it to his face. Count o' it pays to be up-front with some critters!" Granny Mandy stood up then, putting a hand to her back and straightening up slowly. "Whew! My back be breakin' fast on me, I do b'lieve! Time was when I could work this garden mornin' 'til night an' scoot right on in the house, grabbin' up yer daddy on one hip, yer Aunt Hettie on the other, an' fixin' supper in no time atall." Granny Mandy stretched her back out a minute and then walked briskly over to the fence. She sure didn't look tired to me. "Wonder how yer mama an' Andy ere comin'?" she asked as she leaned against the fence and peered across the road to our garden.

I stood up and found that I too was stiff. Rubbing my back as I walked over to Granny, I watched her in amazement. *She doesn't look sore atall! How can she be movin' round so easy like?* I thought to myself.

"Hey there, Andy!" Granny Mandy hollered. Our garden was across the road and just a ways up the hill between the house and the road. Andy was stooped over, obviously putting some sort of seed down into a hole. Mama was nowhere in sight; she must've been getting a drink or something. "Where's yer mama?"

"Hey, Granny Mandy." He stood straight up, and I noticed dirt covered most the whole front of his overalls. I knew they would be a chore to scrub come wash day, and I felt a good deal of irritation with him. "Mama went to fetch us a cold drink. How you all be comin'?"

"We be doin' tolerable well. Thinkin' on a cold drink surely sounds fine. Rachael, how 'bout we go get us a sip or two from the spigot?"

I rubbed the dirt off my legs and shook out my skirt the best I could. "Oh yes, ma'am. That would be fine!"

"Tell yer mama we said *hey*, Andy." She put her hand to her forehead, cupping it over her eyes, and peered up the road. "Can't hardly see them Yankees no more, they's so fer up the road a piece." Then she turned and looked at their car still setting there by the road just below our house. "Reckon they got to walk on back to get this automobile though. That is, iffin they's smart 'nough to 'member on its bein' here. Likely to be plumb lost by then too!" Granny Mandy shook her head, chuckling. She'd always enjoyed jawing on any Yankees she could. "Come on, Rachael. Let's see to that cold drink."

I followed her round the back of her cabin to the spigot that Grandaddy had put in not long before he died. The spigot itself was made out of a hollowed out log, as was the underground pipes that ran the water from their spring to the spigot. Grandaddy had built it well, even to having that pipe cross a gully where the ground dipped down below the pipe, exposing it above ground. Here he'd put a hole in the bottom of the pipe so rocks and sand could drain out; a plug could be screwed back in when you were done draining the pipe of the silt. After the water ran on through the spigot, it went on into the springhouse— one of my most favorite places on a hot summer's day. Don't rightly know if it was the smell of the peppermint growing wild along the outside walls, the cool water flowing through my toes, or the smell of the damp rocks inside the springhouse that made me feel so fine on a particularly sticky day. But I know I pined to sit in that springhouse every day come the dog days of summer.

"Us McKenneys surely been blessed to be having this good, bold spring," Granny Mandy said, reaching for the small gourd that had one side hollowed out and a long, narrow top to make a perfect dipper with its own handle. She scooped up a dipperful and handed it to me.

"No, Granny Mandy! You be drinkin' first. I can wait."

She lifted the gourd to her lips and took a long drink. "Yes'm. Yer grandaddy always said 'twas the finest, best-tastin' water round these here parts too. Don't rightly know that I've tasted everbody's spring water, but reckon he jest may o' been speakin' true 'bout that." She lifted up another dipperful and handed it to me. "Don't know why anybody'd want to be moonshinin' when this here water is all a body needs an' more!"

"Had me a drink from Verna Mae's pump a while back. Weren't nowhere near as sweet tastin' as this."

Granny Mandy took another sip and then studied on the gourd a minute. "This here dipper reminds me of a story yer grandaddy once told."

I recognized the beginning of one of Granny's tales and smiled already in anticipation. Granny's stories were always worth listening to.

"Seems him an' his brother, William, was on a swappin' trip to Crawleysville. 'Twas hotter 'n hades an' twice as dry, so's they's scoutin' a good place at the creek to get 'em a drink." Granny Mandy's eyes sparkled with excitement; she was obviously enjoying the tellin' too! "Well, 'bout that time they come upon a woman a-washin' her clothes. Mister McKenney said she was the filthiest thing he ever done seen in his whole life! Would put a wallerin' hog to shame, he'd tol' me. Knowin' some of 'em what lives round here, I couldn't rightly imagine that. But he kept sayin' 'twas true, she were the worst. He said they wasn't one inch on her that wasn't caked with dirt. Thick too!" Granny Mandy wrinkled her nose, evidently recalling too well Grandaddy's description. "An' stink! Whew! Mister McKenney said him an' William walked round to the other side of her; they was a-needin' to get upwind 'twas so bad!"

We both began chuckling at that point. "Then why was she a-washin'? Seems a body what stunk so bad wouldn't be needin' to do that chore!"

"Yer grandaddy was wonderin' the very thing but said he didn't get the notion to ask her before William done opened his mouth an' says, 'Hey there!' right friendly like. 'Does you know a good drinkin' place on this here creek?' An' she speaks right up an' says, 'Tain't no place better'n right here! E'n got my dipper fer you all to use. Go 'head! I be pleased to be a-sharin'.' Well, yer grandaddy took 'nother look at her an' then a good look at that there dipper, an' you know what he was a-thinkin'. He be thinkin' that gourd be 'bout as dirty as she was."

"What'd he do?"

"Well, wouldn't be kindly to say no, so they's stuck. So yer grandaddy kindly steps aside to let William go first, seein's how he got 'em into this fine mess, carryin' on like they was close 'nough to use the same toothpick. Then when it's yer grandaddy's turn and she hands 'im that dipper, he turns it round an' drinks outta the littlest hole at the end o' the handle 'stead o' drinkin' from the hollowed out part. Yer grandaddy thought he was right smart fer thinkin' on doin' it thata way."

"He surely was!"

"Yes'm, he was mighty pleased with hisself 'til he done finished that drink an' looked over at that woman. She was a-grinnin' from ear to ear, yer grandaddy said. An' then she says, so proud like, 'My land! Just cain't b'lieve hit! Didn't know they was 'nother body on this whole earth what drank outta the end o' the gourd jest like I does. Now I done seen all!'"

I wasn't expecting Granny Mandy to end her story nothing like that, and I had just started to take another drink out of the dipper. Of course I burst out laughing right off, causing me to choke, laugh, and cry all at the same time. Besides laughing at her tale, me and Granny Mandy had to laugh at me coughing, sputtering, and slobbering like some fool! I was still coughing in between chuckles when we headed on back to the truck patch to get back to work. And the whole rest of the morning, every time I'd think on that story, I'd start chuckling all over again. Every time I did Granny Mandy'd add something like, "Best be watchin' who you be askin' fer help!" or "Don't be drinkin' outta the end o' no gourd; you don't know what critter was at it first!"

We were just about done—except for the flowers, which Granny Mandy would plant by herself—when my stomach was telling me it was getting on to dinnertime. "Reckon I oughta be headin' home to help Mama with dinner. You be wantin' to come eat with us?" I asked Granny Mandy.

"Thank ye, Rachael, but I b'lieve I'll just cook up a quick batch o' cornmeal mush. Then I'll be a-finishin' up here, puttin' in the flowers I'm a-fancyin'."

"What you be puttin' in this year?"

"Don't rightly know jest yet. Whatever strikes my fancy. Flowers 'bout the onliest thing I change round ever year; got to make sure I enjoy the va-ri-e-ty!" She rolled the word out slowly, obviously enjoying the sound of the word. "Thank ye fer yer hep, Rachael. Always makes the chorin' pleasurable to be workin' with ye. You best be hepin' yer mama after dinner. Since her garden's bigger 'n mine, takes a mite longer to get put in."

I nodded and then added, "Thank you for lettin' me help. An' I mostly thank you for Grandaddy's story. Reckon I'll tell that one at the dinner table!"

Granny Mandy started chuckling again. "Well, you jest be sure not to tell it when someone's takin' a big ol' drink. I don't want to hear tell o' nobody chokin' to death on account of my jawin'!"

I laughed at her and then waved good-bye as I ran out of her yard and across the road. I couldn't see them men anymore, but their car was still setting there in the same place as this morning. I noticed Andy still digging in the garden. "Mama fixin' dinner already?" I asked him.

"Yes'm." He stopped a minute to wipe the sweat off his face with his sleeve. "Gettin' mighty hungry too."

"Won't take us long." I hurried on up the hill and made a trip to the outhouse before going in to help Mama. She was already busy fixing dinner when I come in. "Hey, Mama. How did yer plantin' go? Me an' Granny Mandy did fine." Washing up at the sink, I was surprised at how much dirt was all over me. *Guess O.A. ain't that much worse than me,* I thought to myself.

"Reckon we still got a fair amount to do." She worked at the table trimming meat with swift movements. I always worried that Mama'd cut herself good with that knife. But she was right handy with it; she'd never slashed herself that I knew of. Today I felt especially anxious though as she hacked at the fat so quick like. I kept watching the knife—and Mama's fingers working—as she pulled at it here an' there. She seemed impatient with her progress as she worked on the meat with such hacking, jerking movements. "How Granny Mandy be doin' today?" She strained to slice a piece of fat away, pulling at the meat with one hand and holding the fat down with the knife in the other.

"Just fine. She told me a story 'bout Grandaddy that I'm anxious to tell when we all set down to dinner. Are you goin' to fry them pork chops? You be plannin' to bread 'em first?"

"Uh-huh. Run upstairs an' fetch some apples for fryin'." I hesitated a moment, not rightly knowing why. Guess I had a feeling that something was about to happen, and I just couldn't seem to take my eyes from Mama. Glancing up at her face, I seen that her jaw was set firm, her lips pulled in a tight line. Since she'd rolled up the sleeves of her blouse, I saw the muscles on her firm arms tense and her knuckles turn white from the straining. Mama seemed to be attacking that meat instead of just cutting it up. "We'll have them leftover biscuits, an' I'll stir up some more gravy for—*ouch!*" I had surely knowed it was coming and yet couldn't do nothing to stop it. The knife had cut a good clean slash into her finger, and she held it up to study the cut, grimacing. But seeing her look, I couldn't tell—was it a paining expression? Or was she angry?

"Mama! Is it a bad 'un?" I watched the blood begin to pour out now from the thin, straight wound. One minute it looked clean and whole, just a tiny line showing. And then the blood come squeezing out, dripping faster and faster from the opened slit of skin. She moved to the sink to wash it off and grabbed up a dishrag to wrap round the finger.

"'Tain't bad. Nothin' to be mindin' 'bout atall." She shook her head at me—out of frustration? Was that tears filling her eyes? "Go on, get them apples, Rachael. We'un's need to get dinner on the table if we're goin' to feed everbody, an' I need to get back to chorin' in the garden, an' . . ." She stopped suddenly in mid-sentence. Putting both hands palm down with her fingers spread out on the table, Mama leaned over it heavily, letting her head hang so low that it nearly touched the table too. The wisps of hair framed round her face hid whatever feelings I might have seen etched there.

I just stood still a moment, not knowing what to do. Don't think I even took in a breath while I was standing there. Mama didn't move except for the faint rising and falling of her shoulders as she breathed. Finally I turned and quietly walked out, closing the door softly behind me. I took my time going to get them apples out of the loft, sensing that Mama needed some time alone.

When I come back across the breezeway, I stood and waited a minute before opening the door, listening for the sounds that would tell me what Mama was doing. The soft sizzle coming from the stove told me that she was back to work fixing dinner, frying up them chops. I opened the door and, avoiding her eyes—like I was sure she would mine—I moved straight to the table and began to slice up the apples for frying, taking special care with the knife. It seemed strange working together like that in complete silence. Mama was never one for talking much; she wasn't like Granny Mandy. But this was different. Even the sounds of my knife cutting into the meat of them apples seemed to intrude upon the silence between us.

By the time dinner was ready, I rung the bell again. But I only rung it a few times, and I can't rightly say I enjoyed it. It'd suddenly become just another thing I did to get through the day.

When I heard Daddy, James Junior, and Andy talking outside the back door, I quickly glanced over at Mama to see what I could read in her face. But except for the same tightness about her mouth, she was closed to me. I couldn't help but feel that tightness mirror back in me. *How were we goin' to get through another meal with all that was happenin' weighin' on us so heavy?* The door creaked open, and Daddy come in first followed by James Junior. "We'll sharpen the scythe before we go back out," Daddy was saying to James Junior. "Downright frustratin' to be workin' with a dull blade." James Junior nodded in agreement. Daddy went straight to the sink and washed, as usual. He'd pushed his sleeves up, and I noticed sweat staining the front and back of his shirt. He took a handkerchief out of his overalls pocket and wiped the sweat from his forehead. Just then O.A. come rushing in, letting the door slam once again. Mama jumped. "Andrew, reckon that door just might open an' close without yer slammin' it? You 'bout scared yer mama to death."

"Sorry, Mama," Andy sheepishly apologized.

"How be the gardenin' comin'?" Daddy asked, and then he saw the rag round Mama's finger. "Did ye burn yerself?"

"Gardenin' be comin' along fine. Cut myself with the knife like some fool. A body would think I could trim chops by now." Mama didn't stop working to answer him but just kept finishing up stirring the gravy and putting everything on the table.

I watched her with amazement. *How can she act like it wasn't nothin'? Just minutes ago she was terrible upset!*

"Be it a bad cut?" James Junior asked.

"'Tain't nothin' atall," Mama insisted, setting down in her chair. "Am I fergettin' anythin'? No? Then let's eat. Mister McKenney, we's ready." Her short sentences seemed to cover over her emotions like Miz Hickman wearing them store-bought dresses. When you look close like, you can see the callouses and scars of a gal what's worked the fields. Them fancy clothes weren't doing away with her notions of "ungenteel livin'." They were only covering them up.

Daddy prayed then, but I found myself not hearing him. I squeezed my eyes shut tight like I was praying, but all I could think on was Mama. Things just weren't in their regular ways and patterns, and I felt puzzled and confused. Mama wasn't acting right. James Junior was going away. Strange men were up the road. Even so, we were moving through the same motions, but everything seemed skewed, off. *Was I actin' funny too somehow? Would I even know it if I was?*

"Rachael? Ere you be that tired that you plumb falled asleep?" Daddy was looking at me with surprise.

"Oh no, Daddy. Sorry. Guess I was thinkin' right hard on somethin'." I thought about telling Granny Mandy's story right then to change the subject quick, but I just didn't feel like it no more.

"Pass yer daddy the gravy, Rachael," Mama said. She give me a quick look that said as plain as day, *Don't say nothin'.*

"Granny Mandy's garden 'bout in?" Daddy asked me. He took a big spoonful of gravy and poured it over his biscuits.

I felt jolted trying to move from Mama's warning to concentrating on what Daddy was saying. "Um, yes, sir. All she's got left is the flowers. Figured I'd help Mama this afternoon." Even though I'd been so hungry earlier from the hard work, now my stomach was churning again. I took a small bite of fried apples, hoping they'd taste good and settle that jumping feeling in my stomach.

"Hay cuttin's comin' along slow like. Scythe needs sharpenin' bad." I glanced at Mama's finger. She'd took off the rag and a smudge of dried blood covered the wound.

"Still hope to get it all cut an' raked out today so's it can cure," James Junior added.

He didn't say what the rest of us were surely thinking: that he wanted to get this chore done today since he was leaving Monday morning.

"If the scythe's so dull, mebbe we oughta be usin' Mama's knife instead," James Junior teased. "Seems it's a-cuttin' right well!" James Junior and Daddy chuckled while Andy grinned. But I glanced up quickly at Mama just in time to see her drop her fork. It made a loud clattering sound when it hit the plate, adding another chip too.

"Seems I'm all thumbs today," Mama said. She acted flustered as she rose from the table to fetch another batch of biscuits from the warming oven. "More biscuits?"

"Yes, ma'am, please!" Andy reached for another anxiously. "Didn't see no more o' them Yankees, did you, Daddy?" he asked. "They went up the road a fer piece."

"Me an' James Junior kept an eye on 'em best we could 'til they went outta sight. Reckon they'll be back soon to get their automobile."

"You goin' to that town meetin' they talked about?" Andy was full of excitement still from this morning.

"Reckon so. Best be hearin' what they's up to."

"They's up to no good, that's what they's up to," Mama said, getting up suddenly again and cleaning her plate into the slop bucket. I noticed that she hadn't eat much this meal either.

Daddy followed Mama's every movement with his eyes as he continued to eat. But his thinking on her was about to be interrupted; I could tell O.A. wasn't finished with his endless questions yet from the way he had lowered his brows and skewed one corner of his mouth over into a deep crease. He always got that look when he was about to ask what he considered an important question.

"Can I go?" Andy asked.

"Go to what?" Daddy plainly was pondering still on Mama.

"To the town meetin'!" Andy stuffed another big bite of biscuit into his mouth. He at least was eating enough to make up for me and Mama.

"Don't rightly know. Best be findin' out more 'bout this meetin' at church tomorra." Daddy put down his fork, still staring at Mama. "You sure that finger ain't painin' you any, Miz McKenney? Ere you be wantin' me to put some black pepper on it to take out the soreness?"

"'Tain't worth messin' with! We'uns need to get the dishes done up an' get back to the gardenin'." She moved about the kitchen, clearing off the table and putting things away. I got up to help her, but as James Junior and Daddy started to go out the door, I found myself wishing like anything that I was going with them instead of staying with Mama. As much as I loved putting in our garden, today I would easily choose cutting hay over planting seeds.

"Anythin' you all be needin' before we go?" Mama shook her head, and Daddy went on, "Well, then we'll be sharpenin' up the scythe an' headin' back out to the field. Me an' James Junior'll take a look-see 'bout them Yankees before we go." He paused a moment like he was wanting to say something else, but he only stared at Mama with concern. She must've felt his eyes on her. But she did not look at him.

When he finally let the door close softly behind him, I turned back to finish washing up the dishes. But when I picked up Mama's knife to wash, I stared at it intently, hearing so many questions push into my mind. "Be right back, Mama," I said, rushing out the door like the house was afire. Too late I realized that I'd let the door slam like Andy, but I was intent on catching up with Daddy. "Daddy!" I called, trying hard to keep my fears from sounding in my voice.

He'd just picked up the scythe and was leaning the long curved blade towards him, feeling the curve of it with the palm of his hand. He didn't look at me but kept studying on the scythe. "Feels tolerable sharp up here yet." Dull and used as it was, the blade caught the sun's light and flashed in my eyes. I squinted at the pain from it. "Reckon it be needin' sharpenin' mostly 'bout here at the bottom o' the curve. You be needin' me, Rachael?"

Watching Daddy feel the blade brought the picture of Mama cutting herself sharply back to mind. He moved his fingers over it once more, and I sucked in my breath. Now Daddy looked up at me. "Rachael?"

"Daddy, please be careful like sharpenin' the scythe."

His face eased from concern for me to being amused that I was concerned about him. He grinned his slow, easy smile. "I'll be right careful, Rachael. Now you go on back in an' help yer mama."

I turned to go but then stopped to ask the question that was pushing in my head so hard that it pounded against my temples, crowding all the other questions out. Or did it gather up all the others in one big bunch? I only hesitated a moment, gathering my courage to spit it out. "Will it be all right, Daddy?"

"Oh, I reckon she'll sharpen up jest fine!" He chuckled again, probably wondering at my concern. "Don't you be a-frettin' 'bout yer daddy. Ain't like you! Go on now."

But he hadn't understood my meaning atall. Aching with disappointment, I looked at him a moment longer. *Should I explain to him my meanin'? And did I even know what I was seekin'?* I turned and slowly headed back into the house, staring down at my toes pushing against the dark red soil. Again I longed for Granny Mandy. She would listen to not only my words, but also my heart.

We finished putting in Mama's garden that afternoon, even planted plenty of flowers. But I seemed to just be going here an' there, doing them things without really feeling them. The government men eventually come sauntering back down the road, toting them funny-looking tools. Ezra and Nehemiah raised a ruckus again, but they stayed on the porch like Daddy'd told them. The men didn't pay no mind to us. (Don't Yankees say *hey* to people?) Me, Mama, and Andy were still working in the garden, and I saw Granny Mandy watching their every move with her gun resting on her hip again. They didn't hardly give us no more than a glance, but I noted they did pay mind to our dogs. They kept peering up at them nervous like about every other minute, even after they got in their car and started driving off towards town. Reckon they was still thinking that Ezra and Nehemiah could go right through them windows.

By the end of the day I felt especially low, knowing that I'd somehow missed out on one of my most favorite times of the year. Funny how a body can do something and yet not really feel like he done it after all.

When I crawled under the quilt that night, I listened again for Mama and Daddy's voices. I kept the quilt pulled up close to my ears though, knowing that at the same time, I was afraid to hear what Mama might say. I might want to quickly pull the quilt up over my ears. But all I heard was the crackling of the fire and the creaking of their rocking chairs against the puncheon floor. They didn't say nothing, and I fell asleep listening to the sounds of silence. And my own unspoken fears.

"Rachael! Ere you goin' to stay abed all day?" Andy was pinching my toes, and I come awake with a jolt.

"Stop that! I'm awake already!" I sat up slowly and rubbed my sore toe. It wasn't like me atall to not wake up afore O.A. I kept soothing my pinched toe, trying to figure out why I'd slept so late when I suddenly realized it wasn't getting any earlier with me just setting there.

Easing my feet out from under the quilt and onto the floor, I stood up slowly. I felt so heavy. Like I was pulling a load of wood on the sled. *Why am I draggin' so?* I thought to myself. And then I remembered. This was James Junior's last day to home. Tomorrow morning he'd be saying his good-byes, heading off to the city to get his orders from the CCC. I set back down. I was staring at my toes again when O.A. came bounding round the quilt that separated our sleeping areas.

"You sure ain't movin' 'long very quick like this mornin'." He looked at me with amazement. "Ain't you got chores to do before we go to church?"

Church! I'd completely forgotten that this was Sunday. How could I be forgetting that when I'd always looked forward to going to church for as long as I could remember? At that I stood up again and began doing up my bed. Out of the corner of my eye I could still see O.A. watching me with puzzlement. "Ain't *you* got chorin' to do?" I threw back at him. "Go on and leave me be to get dressed!"

"I'm a-goin'! I'm a-goin'!" He turned, shaking his head, and fairly run down the steps. Faintly I could hear him muttering, "Like Tommy Lee always says, 'Ain't no figurin' out gals! No sir!'"

Tommy Lee! Now why did O.A. have to mention his name this morning? I put on clothes for choring, laying out my good dress and socks an' shoes for changing into later. Sunday was about the only day me and O.A. wore our shoes except for Children's Day. That was when all of us school children recited, sang, and put on a play for our parents. We'd decorate the school right special too, and then after Children's Day, school would be dismissed until the fall. We did this every May, and thinking on it cheered me up a little since I always looked forward to it. And then I remembered it would be my last one. *Why does everythin' I think about this mornin' seem to be the last of somethin'?*

I hurried down the steps, wondering to myself if I'd have time to take a bath after my chores were done. Usually I did bathe on Sunday morning, but usually I was up a mite earlier too. When I come into the kitchen, though, I saw that Mama'd already pulled out the tub (looked like she'd took a bath already herself) and had more water heating on the stove.

"You best be a-hurryin' if you want to take a bath," Mama warned. She looked like she wasn't too happy with me neither for sleeping so late.

"Sorry I be runnin' behind, Mama. Don't reckon I know why I slept so late like." I gave her an apologetic look, knowing me being late wasn't helping her to get everything done this morning. "I'll be hustlin' to get my chores done tolerable quick. If I don't have time to eat, that'll be fine."

I was nearly out the door when I heard Mama say, "No, that won't be fine. You need to eat breakfast."

"Yes, ma'am," I said and sighed, turning to race out the door. At the last moment I remembered to not let the door slam, and I reached out to grab it just in time. I glanced at Mama through the worn screen—it was full of holes and didn't much keep out many bugs atall—giving her a sheepish grin. "Least I remembered 'bout slammin' the door!"

For just a moment she gave me one of her sweet smiles. They come so few an' far between these days. But when she did smile, her whole face changed. The sternness that was most always there give way to a softness, and the waves that framed her face made her look years younger. *Is this a glimpse of what Mama looked like when she was my age?* I was wasting time again, and Mama's face changed back quickly. "Rachael! You know I can't spell no bein' tardy!"

"Sorry, Mama! I'm a-goin'!" I yelled over my shoulder, running for the outhouse first off. Next I milked the cows, unfortunately finding Moe particularly twitchety this morning. I swear she knowed when I was hurrying and purposely made me take longer with her. Then I fed the chickens, collecting the eggs so quick that I dropped one too hard like in the basket. It broke and made a mess all over the other eggs. This day wasn't starting out well atall.

Mama'd rung the bell for breakfast long before I got back inside, but she had some mush waiting for me. Daddy give me a perplexed look. "Ain't like you to be sleepin' late, Rachael. You feelin' poorly?"

"Feelin' fine, Daddy," I said, reaching for a biscuit. "Just didn't wake up as early and . . ." I stopped, remembering something way at the back of my mind. "Seems I was dreamin' somethin' I can't quite recall." I concentrated, chewing slowly on a bite of mush. Uneasy feelings of—despairing, was it?—come rushing over me. "I recollect I had a awful dream. Somethin' 'bout Yankees workin' here on our land, ruinin' our truck patch, Mama. And I recollect flashes of pain in my eyes, pain what . . ." The look on Mama's face made me stop my rambling. She'd just put a bite of mush in her mouth, but she stopped chewing and stared at me.

"Well, t'were only a dream," Daddy said. "You best be eatin' right quick if you's goin' to have 'nough time gettin' ready." Then he glanced over at Mama. She was chewing now, but her eyes were still intent on mine. "Prob'ly dreamin' 'bout Yankees since they was pokin' round here yesterday." Mama looked over to Daddy and nodded. But the crease between her brows was there again.

"I'd like to see the Yankee that tried to hurt Mama's truck patch. Or Granny Mandy's! That'd be a good scuffle!" Andy was excited again about the prospect of shooting a Yankee. "Granny Mandy'd put holes in their britches in no time, an' I'd fetch my flip-jack too an' . . ."

"Andrew, ain't no call to be goin' on like this. No Yankee's ever goin' to be settin' foot on McKenney property," Daddy said, stating and drawing out them words like they was quoted from the Good Book.

As soon as he said them, everything in me wanted to shout, *Take 'em back! Take 'em back, Daddy!* The words hung up above our table like the fog of a morning when it has rained all night. Seemed like if I was to reach out, I could fairly touch them. And oh, how I wanted to—to grab them up and rip them like me and Mama ripped up worn-out sheets to make strips for braiding a rug. But that was just foolishness! They were no more than words, gone with the saying of them. And besides, of course no Yankee would ever set foot here. Daddy wouldn't never abide that!

"Rachael, I swear you be tetched in the head this mornin'. Yer mama be needin' yer help an' you be needin' to get ready for church," Daddy said, again giving me a puzzled look.

How long have I been starin' at the air, thinkin' there was words out there that I could grab ahold of? What's the matter with me? I quickly ate the last bites of mush, deciding to not grab up another biscuit— though I surely wanted to—and helped Mama do up the dishes. Daddy, James Junior, and Andy went off to finish their choring, and Mama helped me get my bath ready. Usually I enjoyed just setting in the tub awhile, but this morning there wouldn't be no time left for just soaking. I had to get washed up and get out right quick. I run up to the loft to fetch my good dress so's I could put it on when I was ready.

Setting in the tub, I scrubbed a particularly dirty knee. Once again I concentrated on the dream I'd had, trying to remember all the details. I was just recalling some more when Mama said, "We be havin' fried chicken for dinner. Want you to pick out a fat 'un an' get it ready soon's we get home from church, Rachael. Think you can remember to do that today?"

I could tell she was tolerable put out with me. "Yes, Mama. I'll remember." Still, I couldn't help feeling frustrated myself, seeing as now I'd lost the part of my dream that I was just about to recall. *I'll work on it some more durin' Preacher Morgan's sermon,* I thought to myself. *Mister Harris an' Mister Owens always fall to sleep. Mister Harris even snores! And Miz Harris can't hear nothin' nohow, so they's no reason I can't just think on somethin' else.* I scrubbed my hair, too, and then Mama rinsed out the suds with clean water from the stove.

After I got out of the tub and dried off, I pulled my Sunday dress over my head. Mama noticed me struggling with the buttons up the back of my dress and come to help. "Gettin' a bit snug on you," Mama said, pulling it tight to button it properly. "You's growin' up. Gettin' to be a full-growed woman." She sighed. "Best be thinkin' on makin' you a new dress. This 'un ain't goin' to button up no more before long. Reckon we ought to be sewin' before Children's Day."

I smiled at the idea of a new dress, but talking about a "full-growed woman" dampened my happiness. Thinking on that made me think on Tommy Lee and marrying, and then I worried about high school. I tried to dry my hair some more, but since it was so thick, it always took a good while. "I'm goin' up to put on my shoes and fetch my comb, Mama. Anythin' else I needs be doin' before we leave for church?"

Mama shook her head no. "Reckon I'll go change now. Yer daddy an' James Junior an' Andy should be in soon." We both went across the breezeway and into the other part of the house. Mama moved behind the quilt hung from the ceiling by her and Daddy's bed that she always dressed behind. I raced up the stairs, wondering how I was ever going to have enough time to get my hair done in time. I generally tried to do it special on Sundays, but doubted that I'd have time today.

Plopping down on my bed, I picked up a sock and began tugging it on. Mama had a pair of lady's stockings that she wore on Sundays. I held up one leg to study, trying to imagine my legs in stockings and wearing shoes like was in the picture books at the general store. Some of them weren't even brown or black. Imagine that!

When I tied up my shoes, my feet felt all pinched and hot. Since I only wore them on Sundays they also generally hurt like fire the whole time I wore them. But that didn't mean I didn't like wearing my shoes. I knew Miz Travis wore hers every day (though they weren't like in the picture books, being only black ones like Mama's), and I wanted to be a schoolteacher just like her. Shoes stood for schooling in my mind. Educated people. And I aimed to wear mine every day too. Someday.

I took just a minute to admire them on my feet, wondering if Tommy Lee noticed how nice they looked on me. They were dark brown and tolerable shiny, although not nearly so as when they were brand-new. When it was raining and muddy, I wouldn't even put them on 'til I was just outside the church door. I spit on both of them and shined them up with a rag I kept just for that purpose. I turned them this way an' that, admiring them once more, and then I snatched up my comb and run down the steps, noticing the "clunking" sound my shoes made against the steps. When I was barefoot, you couldn't hear anything when I went down the steps—especially since I knew where all the creaks were. Whenever I was sneaking somewhere, I stepped around all them places. But wearing shoes was a different thing. Everbody'd hear me in them.

Mama was combing her hair when I raced through the room. Again I thought about how I envied her that beautiful rich brown color. I was so tired of looking in my mirror and seeing the red of mine. I went to the fireplace in the kitchen, and pulling a chair over by the warm fire, I began to comb my tousled hair. It was knotted up good, and every time my comb hit a tangled place I grimaced.

I heard steps coming up the back porch and Daddy, James Junior, and Andy come in. Andy let the door bang closed, like always, but Daddy didn't say anything. He just looked at O.A. and shook his head. Andy didn't even notice; he'd already gone out the door to the breeze-way, but I heard Mama's voice and Andy come sauntering back into the kitchen. "Fergot to wash up," he explained to Daddy's questioning look.

My hair was drying slowly. There was no way it would be dry enough for me to fiddle with it any. I was feeling right disappointed when Mama walked in. I turned to look at her, knowing she'd be wearing a blouse that I thought was just beautiful beyond saying. Most of my blouses were made out of the sacks that our flour come in (though they were getting mighty snug too), but Mama had to make hers out of material bought at the store since them sacks weren't big enough for her. Most of her blouses were simple and plain for every day, but her Sunday one was special. She'd embroidered a lace edge round the collar that looked so lovely. It made me think on the Queen Anne's lace that growed along the road in the summer. On wash day I enjoyed washing that blouse just so I could admire the work and feel the tiny little stitches. Of course

I always handled it with great care. I wouldn't have hurt that collar for anything. That was Mama's work, and it was special.

Daddy, James Junior, and Andy'd all finished washing up and gone to get changed into their Sunday clothes. Mama moved to just behind my chair, and I waited for her to tell me what I'd done wrong now. Seems that's about all I'd done the whole morning—either doing what I wasn't supposed to be doing or not doing what I was supposed to. When I glanced round at Mama though, she was just standing there, staring at my hair. Her head was tipped to one side and her face looked soft again, although she wasn't smiling right then. She reached out and put one hand on my hair.

"Yer hair be gettin' prettier ever year, Rachael."

I stared at her with my mouth open. *How could she think mine pretty when hers was so much more so?*

"Can't hardly b'lieve how you done growed up so quick." She was stroking my hair now, and I stopped combing it. "Won't be long before yer a-goin' off too, makin' yer own home somewheres." Her stroking felt so good that I felt the prickles come on the back of my neck. "I'm right proud ye got yer daddy's hair, Rachael. 'Tis a blessin' havin' hair the color o' the flame."

She took the comb from my hand and began pulling it slowly through my hair. The feel of the warmth of the fire against my skin, the gentle touch of her hands caressing me as she lifted and combed my hair, and the soothing sound of her words made me feel as if I was dreaming again, only this time it was a wonderful dream. I closed my eyes, hoping it would last a long time. "How 'bout we pull the sides up this a way?" Mama asked. "That would look right pretty." She pulled a ribbon out of her pocket. "We'll gather it up with this ribbon, tyin' a nice bow."

I let her continue to comb it, parting and pulling it up the way she suggested. With Mama's help it was nearly dry now, and it felt full and thick. She wrapped the ribbon round the hair pulled up to the top and then carefully tied a bow. When she was done, she went to the window to get the mirror that we always kept there; Daddy used it to shave by of a morning. "See there. Looks nice, don't it?"

I held the mirror up, expecting to only see them hated freckles once again. They were still there, but they weren't all that I noticed. With my hair pulled up at the sides, my face looked thinner. The babyish looking fat was gone. Only my cheekbones stood out, making my eyes look bigger than they'd ever seemed before. The bow on top was a beautiful color of green. And then I realized the ribbon was the same shade as my eyes, making even their color pleasing to look at.

I looked up at Mama, wanting like anything to say thank you, but more so, to say what was in my heart. To say thank you for helping me like this. To say thank you for the sweet words and the caressing touch. To say thank you for making me feel pretty, whether the mirror really said so or not. To say thank you for these few moments of a gentleness and softness from her which I would treasure in my heart forever. *Why was it always so hard for me to talk to Mama? Why couldn't I tell her all that was wellin' up inside of me?* The words were pushing at my heart, but instead all I said was, "You done it right nice, Mama. Thank you." But I looked up at her with all them thank-yous shining in my eyes, hoping that she would know what my eyes were saying.

She touched my cheek for just a moment, and then she abruptly moved away, taking the mirror back to the windowsill. "Bet yer daddy's ready to go. We best be headin' out." She opened the door and called out, "You all 'bout ready?"

I faintly heard James Junior answer that he was going to fetch the wagon, but just for a moment, I wasn't thinking on James Junior and him leaving, church, or nothing else. I could still feel the touch of Mama's hand against my cheek if I thought on it right hard. And I didn't never want to forget that touch.

Daddy come into the kitchen then, dressed in his Sunday clothes. He wore the starched white shirt that Mama took such pains to wash and iron. Them stiff shirts made him and James Junior both get red round the neck—probably from them being so tight and from them both tugging at the collar all day. Daddy was pulling at it already. His pants were worn, like everything we owned, but the crease was still sharp as ever. And Daddy's bulb-toed shoes looked as though he'd spit-polished them like I'd done mine. Even though Daddy did look almost awkward and funny without his overalls on, he stood tall in them Sunday clothes. I felt proud that this broad shouldered, respected man was my daddy.

"Reckon we's ready?" he asked. "Miz McKenney, ere you 'bout to forget yer hat?" He picked it up off the table and handed it to Mama.

"Ain't fergot. Just was fussin' with Rachael's hair." Mama walked over to the mirror again, and placing the straw hat squarely and levelly on the top of her head, she pushed the pin through the back of the small hat. The color was a deep blue, and although it had faded, it was still blue enough to match the blue of her eyes. She moved her head to look at it from both sides and then turned to me and Daddy.

"Still say that's one fine lookin' hat. Best part bein' the pretty head it's a-settin' on though!" He grinned at me and Mama shook her head, motioning with her hand that it was time we were going out the door.

But as Daddy held the door for us to go out, I noticed Mama give him a slight grin back.

James Junior and Andy were waiting for us outside with the wagon and Old Mean Dean. Daddy helped Mama climb into the front, and then he give me a lift up into the back with James Junior and Andy. We generally took the wagon to church, picking up Granny Mandy and anyone else we passed along the way and could fit in. Old Mean Dean wasn't anxious to go nowhere, just like usual, but Daddy persuaded him to get along. We could see Granny Mandy was already down the road a ways; we were a mite late and she must've got tired of waiting. And then I noticed she was toting her gun again. I knew Daddy always carried his under the wagon seat, but Granny Mandy had never took hers to church before that I knew of.

'Bout that time Andy noticed what Granny Mandy had too. "Daddy, Granny Mandy's got her gun! What's she doin' totin' it to church?" he asked. Them eyes of his were lit up again, and he anxiously leaned out over the side of the wagon.

"Reckon ye be needin' to ask yer Granny Mandy 'bout that," Daddy said. "Could be anythin' from huntin' for hairy varmints to scoutin' for Yankee varmints!"

"Whoa up there, Dean!" Daddy hollered. "Help ye up, Granny Mandy?" Daddy climbed down quickly and gave her a lift up.

Andy never could wait worth nothin'. "Why you be totin' yer gun, Granny Mandy? Ere you be lookin' for them Yankees? Is you goin' to shoot 'em?"

She settled herself comfortably on the seat next to Mama and Daddy before answering, smoothing out her Sunday dress. "Never did trust no Yankees. Never will. Best be keepin' an eye on them what's so crooked they needs to be screwin' on their socks." She laid the big gun across her lap, looking left and right of the road. For Yankees, I assumed. Then she adjusted her hat a minute, making sure it was setting straight. "Don't know that I'd need to shoot 'em though. They's skeered 'nough o' them dogs yesterday. Thought they was goin' to get eat up, I guess! Iffin I was to point this barrel at 'em, s'pose they'd just shrivel up in pure terror!"

Andy chuckled and slapped his leg. Wasn't anything that pleased him more, it seemed, than a tussle. I shook my head at him.

The wagon ambled along, bumping us here and there every time it hit a rut, which was most all the time. But it was better than walking (especially in shoes what pinched), and I enjoyed watching the sights go by. I looked for more redbud trees and also for any dogwood that might be in bloom. They weren't quite all the way out yet, but they were getting close. Daddy, Mama, James Junior, and Granny Mandy were talking more about the government men, but I didn't want to listen. I glanced over at O.A. just in time to see him pull his flip-jack out of his pocket.

"Andy!" I whispered at him, though I don't rightly know why. He'd be in for it if Mama knew what he'd brought with him. "You best be puttin' that right back in your pocket. You know you ain't allowed to bring it to church."

"Ain't plannin' on shootin' it none." He give me an indignant look. "Just thought Tommy Lee an' me might stretch 'em out a bit. Need to keep 'em good an' limbered up like."

"Tommy Lee don't take his flip to church no more."

"How do you know?"

"'Cause. I just do." Saying anything more might give away that Tommy Lee'd been going with me to get a drink from the spring in between Sunday school and preaching service. "You best put that away before I tell Mama." I figured that ought to keep him from asking any more questions.

"Snitcher!" He jammed the slingshot down into his pocket, turning his back to me at the same time. That was fine with me. We were nigh to town and I wanted to look around anyways.

Everything was closed down since it was Sunday. About everybody went to church too, except the Snodderlys and the Youthers. Of course not all the people round here went to our church. Some were Free Methodists—their church was just west of Jordan's Bend—and others went to the Church of God that was meeting in a building on the edge of town. It used to be another general store, but since the Depression the store had moved out and the church people moved in.

We turned down the road that led to our church, passing the syrup mill on the way. Seeing it made me think of molasses and suddenly I was hungry again. *Wish I'd eat that biscuit,* I thought to myself. I could see the Pursers' wagon and Nellie's wagon was there too. Verna Mae's house was so close that they walked, and of course Merry Jo just walked too, seeing how the parsonage was right next door. When I spied Tommy Lee's wagon I smiled. Wouldn't do atall for him not to see my hair done up all fancy.

Daddy pulled up Old Mean Dean underneath a tree and then him, James Junior, and Andy jumped down. Andy went running off towards church, but Daddy turned to help Mama and James Junior helped Granny Mandy climb down. I was ready to jump down by myself when

James Junior come round to the back of the wagon and held up a hand for me.

For a moment I hesitated, and James Junior urged, "Well, come on young lady. You be lookin' so fine this mornin'. Ain't no call to risk messin' up that pretty hair."

I took his hand, feeling his other muscular arm go round my waist and lift me all the way to the ground. I felt so honored and special, like a princess or something out of King Arthur's court that I'd read about. But then come a jumble of feelings wishing that he hadn't done it as I suddenly remembered again that this was the last time—for how long?—that he'd be going to church with us. How I was going to miss times like this when James Junior took pains to do something so fine for me! I knew if I looked in his eyes I'd tear up for sure, so I just muttered, "Thank you, James Junior," staring down again at my feet, like always.

He tugged lightly on my hair but didn't say no more. That was another thing James Junior was right smart about—knowing when my feelings were tender.

We walked on up the steps and into church. It always felt so different from the everyday schoolhouse when we young'uns were racing up the steps, coming in shouting and shoving in response to Miz Travis ringing the bell. On Sundays, instead of running up them steps, we walked more slowly, deliberate like, respecting the knowing that on this day, this was God's house. Preacher Morgan always arranged the benches like pews and he placed a pulpit up front. We had a few hymnals which he'd always put here an' there, and then he'd move the piano up front by the pulpit. Miz Morgan played the piano for us, and Merry Jo was getting better all the time. She played sometimes when we were passing the plate. I always enjoyed hearing her play, wishing that I could play too.

I nodded to Merry Jo then; she always set on the front bench with her mama. I looked around quickly for Nellie and Verna Mae, giving each of them a smile too. Of course I had already spied out Tommy Lee. He was the first one I'd looked for, but I couldn't let him see that. Or anybody else neither.

The Harrises were setting on the other bench in the front row. They set there so's Miz Harris could hear better, but generally her and Mister Harris both just fell asleep. The Pursers were just over from us, with Earl and Daisy in between them. In front of them poor Uncle Evert and Aunt Opal were already struggling to keep Jessie, Eugene, Billy Ray, and Baby John Evert quiet. Them boys were a handful.

When we sat down, I moved in between Andy and James Junior. Although I wasn't especially wanting to sit by O.A. (he couldn't never set still and was always wiggling), I did want to set by James Junior. Mama was on the other side of James Junior, and I knew she'd want to be there too.

The whole church always met first for a few minutes to sing and pray for opening exercises, and then we'd break into two groups for Sunday school: adults and young'uns. The real little ones would stay with their mamas, but us older girls would keep an eye on the others. Since it was nice today, I reckoned we'd probably go outside.

"Good mornin'!" said Mister Hickman, Verna Mae's daddy. He always led the singing. Mister Hickman didn't sing so good, but he was loud.

"Let's us sing 'Rock of Ages, Cleft for Me.' Page one hundred and twenty-one. Miz Morgan?" Miz Morgan began playing an introduction, Mister Hickman started waving his arms round in the air (they were never in time with the music, though), and then we all began to sing.

I glanced over at Tommy Lee and was embarrassed to note that he was looking at me too. We both looked away quickly, and I could feel that red color flowing up from my neck again. I decided that I'd best be concentrating on singing this here song.

> *Rock of Ages, cleft for me,*
> *Let me hide myself in Thee;*

Do the others find as much needin' in these words as I do? I thought to myself.

> *Let the water and the blood,*
> *From Thy riven side which flowed,*
> *Be of sin the double cure,*
> *Cleanse me from its guilt and power.*

We moved as one body with the rise and fall of the melody. I can't rightly say that we sounded good, but there was a yearning in our voices that gave that hymn a different kind of beauty.

> *Not the labors of my hands*

We knew about laboring for sure, all of us. And the Depression had only made our hard lives even more uncertain; we could work choring from morning 'til night and still not have enough to feed young'uns.

> Can fulfill Thy law's demands;
> Could my zeal no respite know,
> Could my tears forever flow,

I glanced over at Mama and saw that she was barely moving her lips. And she wasn't looking at the hymnal or Mister Hickman. She looked to be staring at the wall. Or through it.

> All for sin could not atone;
> Thou must save, and Thou alone.

Mister Hickman kept on waving his arms, and Miz Morgan was still playing. But I could feel something that I didn't quite recollect noticing before. *We really were singin' as one.* Sure, we were Uncle Evert singing all them notes like they stayed on the same note; and we were Mister Hickman, singing too loud; and we were Miz Smith, Nellie's mama, singing with a high-pitched warble that hurt my ears; and we were even Daddy's steady bass, rich and pure in its deepness. But we sang as one because the needing we all knew and felt in that hymn pulled us together.

> While I draw this fleeting breath,
> When mine eyes shall close in death,
> When I soar to worlds unknown,
> See Thee on Thy judgment throne,
> Rock of Ages, cleft for me,
> Let me hide myself in Thee.

We drawed out the last line and held "Thee" while Mister Hickman ended our singing with a big flailing of his arms. There was yearning in this room all right for heaven and hiding and soaring to worlds unknown. We were each and every one different and separate. But our yearning and hope for them comforting words made us one.

"The government people has called a town meetin' tomorra night." Preacher Morgan's announcement slashed at my thoughts like Mama's knife, snatching away any comforting feelings. "Reckon you'll all need to be attendin'." Most everybody sat forward to catch his every word, anxious to hear what this was all about.

"What they be snoopin' round here fer? What they up to, Preacher?"

Mister Buchanan, the miller here in Jordan's Bend, shouted out his question from the back of the room. Nodding of heads and mumbling from the whole crowd followed.

"Don't know nothin' more'n you all do. Only know they wants us to meet here tomorra night at six o'clock. We'll be a-ringin' the bell 'bout then."

"They didn't say nothin' more atall to ye?" This come from Tommy Lee's daddy.

"No, sir. Reckon we'll all have to wait to find out. Now let's be a-prayin', and then we'll be dismissed for our Sunday school classes. The young'uns'll be meetin' outside seein's how nice it is."

When we'd been dismissed, me and Andy moved on outside with the rest of the young'uns. Me, Merry Jo, Nellie, and Verna Mae all set together on a quilt that Merry Jo had brought. We gathered some little'un's on our laps and settled down to hear our teacher, Mister Smith, Nellie's daddy.

The time seemed to be crawling by, and I couldn't think on our lesson atall. I kept watching a bird fly by, or hearing a cricket chirping somewhere in the nearby creek, or feeling a bug biting somewheres. Little Anna Ruth Dickerson was setting on my lap fidgeting too, but I reckon I wiggled more'n she did.

When Mister Smith finished, he excused us to get a drink from the creek. I drifted away from Merry Jo, Nellie, and Verna Mae, although I kept ahold of Anna Ruth's hand since I was supposed to be keeping an eye on her. Tommy Lee was already by the spot where he always helped me to get a drink, and I went over to him.

"Hey, Anna Ruth! You be parched?" Tommy Lee helped her by cupping his hands full of the cool water and offering her the first drink. She drank it eagerly and then giggled.

"Thankee, Tommy Lee!" She covered her mouth coyly and giggled again.

Is ever gal in this county moonin' over Tommy Lee's eyes? I wondered to myself, feeling right aggravated.

I knelt down, making right sure that it wasn't dirty so I didn't muss up my Sunday dress and then waited for Tommy Lee to help me too. He looked me right in the eye the whole time he scooped up a handful from the creek, but I quickly looked down. Gals round here that weren't forward or mean didn't return them kind of looks; that gal wouldn't be clever atall. I took a few swallows and risked glancing up at him again. He was staring at my hair now.

"Yer hair's different." He cleared his throat. "It's right pretty that way." And then Tommy Lee looked away too. We were both embarrassed, and I knew by the feeling of it that I was blushing just the same as him.

Anna Ruth was pulling at Tommy Lee's sleeve. "'Nother drink! 'Nother drink!"

"Sure 'nough, Anna Ruth," Tommy Lee answered, obviously glad for the interruption. He scooped one more handful for her and then got a quick drink for himself, wiping his mouth on his sleeve when he'd finished. "We best be headin' on in now, less you want 'nother, Rachael?"

I shook my head with certainty. I wasn't about to risk him looking in my eyes like that again.

We took our time heading back into church. I made sure Anna Ruth found her mama, and then me and Tommy Lee give each other a kind of "see you later" smile. I was hoping we might get to see each other after church; I was counting on everyone staying awhile to talk about the town meeting.

When we come inside, seemed like everybody was already talking about only one thing: that meeting. Some were whispering behind cupped palms; others were getting plain excited, raising voices like them Yankees were right there to be hollered at. Daddy was talking low with Uncle Evert and James Junior, but Mister Hickman put a quick end to all the talking by shouting out the name of another hymn. Everybody quieted down and headed for their seats, but all the questions and uneasiness just seemed to hang in the air. We all were fretting about what them Yankees were up to, that was certain.

We always had a song service first, and Mister Hickman generally had us shout out our favorites for singing. Then Preacher Morgan preached. Sometimes it seemed awful long to me, but no matter how long he preached or on what passage, there was always a chorus of *amens* from several of the men. Some of them just seemed to say *amen* whenever Preacher Morgan stopped to catch his breath. But Daddy wasn't like that. He always listened to Preacher real close like, and when Daddy said *amen*, I could tell it was a point that Daddy took to heart.

When we'd sung nearly a dozen hymns, Preacher Morgan come up to the pulpit. "Our Lord," he began praying, "please help us now as we seek to understand Thy Word. Only Thy Word has the answers for all the questions that we be askin'."

I heard several *amens* from round the room.

"Help us to be puttin' Thy Word to work too. 'Tain't doin' us much good just settin' on them pages, not bein' used in our daily livin'."

More *amens*, only louder.

"We be askin' Thy Holy Spirit to teach us today. And we be mighty thankful for all that Thou hast given to us."

The *amens* weren't quite as forceful this time.

"In Thy name, A-men." Preacher cleared his throat a moment and then went on, "Now, let's us be turnin' to First Corinthians twelve." Our family owned one other Bible that Daddy brought to church, and since it also was well-worn, I watched Daddy gently turn its pages to the New Testament passage. He held it over for Mama and James Junior to see too.

"I'll be readin' this here chapter; you all follow along." He cleared his throat again and began to read, "'Now, concernin' spiritual gifts, brethren . . .'"

I found myself daydreaming, looking out the windows and wondering what dinner was going to be like—James Junior's last one before leaving tomorrow morning—when I suddenly noticed Preacher Morgan reading something that sounded so familiar.

"'For as the body is one, and hath many members, and all the members of that one body, bein' many, are one body: so also is Christ." I was thinking hard on that when later he went on: "'There should be no schism—'"(What did that word mean?) "'— in the body; but that the members should have the same care one for another. And whether one member suffer, all the members suffer with it; or one member be honoured, all the members rejoice with it. Now ye are the body of Christ, and members in particular.'"

I sat there in amazement. This was what I had felt when we were singing before—knowing we were all different, and yet one, somehow. I just couldn't believe that I would be thinking on the same thing that Preacher would be preaching on.

"You can see how the good Lord give us all different gifts," Preacher Morgan was saying. Then he started listing off the different ones and how each one was needed. When he come round to the front of the pulpit and began pointing out his foot—and how his foot might say it wanted to be a hand instead, or else it just plain didn't want to be part of Preacher Morgan's body—most everybody started laughing right out loud. Then he went on about maybe his ear wanting to be an eye, but then how would he hear the dinner bell ringing? Or how would he smell Miz Morgan's good cooking if everything was for hearing? Point being, and Preacher made it good, that every member was needed. Different too. And it wasn't right for one to be wanting to do what another was doing, because what everybody was doing was important.

"We can't be sayin' one ain't as important as 'nother. No sir," he went on.

Again there was a chorus of *amens*.

"Says right here that them that are more feeble or less honourable or less comely ain't less important. Maybe in our eyes. But not in the good Lord's."

I saw Granny Mandy nodding her head in agreement. Glancing over at Mister Harris, though, I seen that the only nodding he was doing was putting his chin on his chest again. Miz Harris seemed wide awake though. I reckon she perked right up when Preacher was talking about hearing.

Then Preacher Morgan started talking about that word *schism*. "We all be a-knowin' what that be 'bout—the backbitin', fussin', gossipin', and arguin' that ain't no help atall to bein' one body here at Jordan's Bend Church. We's s'posed to be carin' for one another, not hurtin' each other!"

Amens come from all over the church. And this time I noticed that Daddy said *amen* too.

Preacher Morgan went on, saying, "We should be so carin' that when one of us suffers, we all suffer! Say that Mister Buchanan here had a fire at his mill—heaven forbid!"

At that, Mister Buchanan shouted, "Amen!" and everyone laughed again.

"But say maybe he did have a fire," Preacher said. "What should we be a-doin'?"

He paused just a minute, and I was afraid someone might say *amen* in the silence.

"Why, we need to be helpin' him, that's what! We need to have our fine women folk bringin' in meals for his family. An' we need our men to help him rebuild that there mill. We all need to be carin' in ever way we can!"

I stared out the window again for a moment, pondering over what I would do to help the Buchanans, and then I started in daydreaming about all I would do for the Arnolds if they was to have troubles. Then before I knew it Preacher Morgan was praying, and I jerked my head down right quick. Mama didn't spell daydreaming in church.

As we walked out everybody always shook hands with Preacher Morgan, telling him what a good sermon it was. I saw Mister Harris pumping the preacher's hand good, exclaiming that it was one of his best ever. We all knew—Preacher too—that he probably didn't hear no more than the *Let's turn to* and the *amen* at the very end. Most folks gathered into small groups, and I heard talk about the town meeting again. Mama and Daddy lingered awhile, but really not long atall. Mama was anxious to get on home and get that special meal of chicken fried up for James Junior. So me and Tommy Lee didn't get to talk, and the ride home seemed ever so much longer—and bumpier—than the ride into town.

That Sunday dinner was a special one with all the fixings—taters, gravy, biscuits, and beans. But we all were mostly quiet, and I can't say that anything tasted good because nothing seemed to have any taste. I remember thinking to myself that maybe my taster done said it wanted to be an eye or something and when it couldn't, then maybe it just quit being a member of my body.

Afterwards we set on the porch by the breezeway and rocked. Seemed that was as much doing as we could manage, setting and rocking. Every time I'd give a push on that old chair, I'd try to recollect my dream, but the feelings seemed to be the only part what was left. I fretted on James Junior's leaving, and then I'd hear Mama's words over and over again in my head. *They's* changes *a comin'*. So I set, rocking, worrying, stewing.

When I eventually drifted off to sleep, I dreamed once again. But this time I saw James Junior working a cornfield, cutting at the tallest stalks you ever seen with a knife that caught the light of the sun flashing something powerful in my eyes every time he slashed at them stalks. He'd pause now and then, admiring it. I fretted over him, knowing how razor sharp that knife was. And I thought about grabbing at James Junior, keeping him from getting cut bad. But I didn't do nothing. Just stood there watching him, shielding my eyes from the bright glare.

3

The dark is sound against my ear,
Is loud with clatter of my fear.
I hear soft footsteps padding near.
I, who have fed, will be the eaten,
Whose dinner will I sour or sweeten?

The dreariness of that Monday morning hung over us like the rain that poured steadily, drumming in an even patter on our old wood-shingled roof. The fog was thick and heavy, feeling like it set right down on my eyelashes. I reckon I squinted through most of my choring, partly because of the steady rain and partly because the fog did seem to be pressing my eyes closed, making my eyelids feel so heavy.

I was setting at the table eating my breakfast when James Junior came into the kitchen. He'd dressed in his Sunday clothes, and we all stared at him as he moved to stand before Mama. His white shirt, not nearly as crisp as it was yesterday, was still obviously starched and stiff round his neck. The tie he wore with broad brown and gold stripes was stiff too; it hung straight down, not bending atall with James Junior's movements. His suspenders held up what must be scratchy-feeling pants, since they were made out of coarse wool. But Mama had ironed them too, making the creases in them as sharp as Daddy's were. I figured them creases must be important to Daddy and Mama. And James Junior had worked on shining up his old oxfords, although I knew the bottoms couldn't be helped much. They were worn clean through in both the soles. I'd seen him put some cardboard from an old box in them the night before. In his hands he held his straw hat with the black band. The rain from a few weeks ago had ruined the straw, causing it to make a crackling sound as he pressed it nervously between his fingers. Today's steady rain wasn't going to help it any more neither. He looked at Mama intently, and I knew as sure as anything that he was seeking her approval. For how he looked? Or for his going?

Mama stood, glancing up at him in the eye for just a moment before she concentrated on his tie, reaching to straighten the knot and the collar of his shirt. "Reckon ever man needs a woman to get his tie tolerable neat like. Ain't never knowed yer daddy to get it right yet." She tugged at the collar and then adjusted the knot, smoothing the tie against his shirt. "I knowed you said them government people'll be givin' you workin' clothes, but I can't help wonderin' 'bout the washin' an' ironin' of 'em." Mama kept fooling with his tie, pulling at it as she talked. "This here shirt's good quality; needs a body who knows how to wash it just so with the right amount of starch. 'Tain't never scorched it none neither."

James Junior stood straight and tall and still, like he was standing for the pledge at school of a morning. He dropped his arms to his sides, one hand still gripping his hat. I noticed he was staring over the top of Mama's head towards the wall, and he was blinking his eyes again and again. My eyes began to fill, and soon I felt tears run down each cheek. They tickled as they made a path towards my chin, but I didn't wipe them away. I wanted to feel them.

"Don't know how them Yankees'll do washin' and mendin' yer clothes, fixin' meals that prob'ly ain't fit for a body to eat." Mama kept on touching him here and there, smoothing his shirt or straightening the sleeves or his suspenders. "If you be needin' more clothes, you jest say so in yer letters an' I'll get 'em to you somehow an' . . ." Her voice caught and suddenly stopped.

James Junior looked at Mama for only a moment, and then he wrapped his long, muscular arms around her, hugging her protectively to his breast. He rested his cheek against the top of her head, and I saw one brown wave move gently from his breath against her hair. Mama just stood there a moment until finally she pulled her thin, firm arms up around James Junior's waist, fiercely returning his hug. And then she pushed away from him and moved to do up the breakfast dishes. James Junior followed her every move with his eyes. "You all best be headin' on into town. I'll do up these dishes, Rachael. Seein's how it's rainin' so, you an' Andy be needin' to hitch a ride on the wagon with yer daddy an' James Junior."

I looked over at Daddy and he nodded. I'd never seen Daddy cry before and he wasn't now, but his face was chalky white and blank. He got up, pushed in his chair, and collected his hat and gun for the trip into town. "Be home 'bout dinner time, Miz McKenney, after I deliver the mail. Anythin' you be needin' in town?" I couldn't believe how even his voice could sound when his face said otherwise.

"No, reckon not." Mama worked quickly at the sink, never looking up to meet Daddy's eyes. "You young'uns got yer lunch pails? James Junior, ye got yer dinner?"

Me and Andy said "Yes, ma'am," and James Junior picked up another pail, balancing it on top of the box of clothes he was toting along with him.

"We'll be a-goin' then," Daddy said. But we all just stood there hesitantly, waiting for Mama to do something.

"Mama?" James Junior said her name softly, questioningly. He stood there, with his box, lunch pail, and hat in hand, waiting. She did not look up at him. "I'll be writin' letters. Promise. I'll send the first 'un soon's I get settled." Mama scrubbed at a pot with the luffa gourd while James Junior took a deep breath and let it out slowly. Then he put his hat on his head, glimpsing into Daddy's mirror on the windowsill. He pinched the hat into shape as best as he could, pulling it down slightly onto his forehead. "Well, best not be late." Yet he lingered a moment still, glancing nervous like at Mama.

Ain't you goin' to say nothin', Mama? I thought to myself. *James Junior's all but begged you to say somethin' encouragin' to him!* My heart ached to see the look on his face as he kept staring at her.

Daddy finally strode across the room, holding the door for me and James Junior to go on out. James Junior hesitated only a moment more and then he walked through. Andy had gone to fetch the wagon and was waiting out in the rain, his old hat dripping all round the rim. James Junior stopped and looked back over his shoulder towards the door once more and then he climbed up into the wagon's front seat with Daddy. The rain continued to fall as we huddled into the wagon, and we slumped down and hunched over in our attempts to keep from being soaked. It was useless though. I knew we'd all be good and soaked by the time we got into town. As soon as we were moving down the rutted drive, I looked back up to the cabin and saw that Mama was standing in the doorway. One arm hung limply at her side while the other held open the door. She appeared to be moving her lips, but I couldn't tell what she was saying. "James Junior, Mama's standin' at the door," I said to him, reaching to tug on his already soggy sleeve.

He jerked his whole body around quickly, and I saw the rain trickling down through that cheap hat, plastering his hair to his forehead and soaking his newly shaved cheeks. "Mama? I love you, Mama!" he shouted through the fog and downpour.

Again her lips moved, but I couldn't hear her reply. Whatever it was she said and whether he understood Mama or not, it was enough for James Junior. He smiled and then waved.

When we turned onto the road, Granny Mandy was standing there in the pouring rain waiting for us. She'd put a large quilt over her head and peeked out from underneath it to look up at James Junior. "Made ye some fresh gingerbread cookies. Thought ye might be needin' somethin' extry." She handed them up to James Junior, waving off his thanks. "'Tain't nothin' to mix up a batch of 'em. Get on now. God be with ye, James Junior." She pulled the quilt high up over her head and then stood watching us too. Daddy urged on Old Mean Dean and we slowly ambled on our journey again. I could see Granny Mandy and Mama, both staring after us, still as statues. The rain dripped off the porch roof down onto the muddy dark red ground, following several newly made gullies zig-zagging down to the road. One of them came right down to where Granny Mandy stood, hunched up underneath her quilt. I kept staring at Mama, Granny Mandy, and the rain gushing down them gullies until we rounded a big bend and our homestead was no longer in sight.

The rain soon soaked my straw hat and the rest of me too. None of us talked atall; we just sat quiet like in our misery. Even Andy wasn't saying nothing. Up the road a ways we caught up with Earl and Daisy and so we stopped to let them climb into the wagon with us. They chattered about this and that for awhile, but both caught on that it wasn't a day for jawing and were soon quiet. Seemed like even the everyday sounds that should be coming from the woods and pastures were silent today. All I could hear was the steady patter of the rain.

As we drove into town it looked like things were moving slow like there also. Mr. Hickman was just opening up and there weren't very many wagons about neither. Miz Hickman was sweeping dirt and dust out the door (didn't she know everybody would just be trudging it all back in today soon's it turned to mud?); when she saw us she waved us over. "You be leavin' today, James Junior?" Miz Hickman asked. She stayed inside the doorway since a steady leak from the porch's roof dripped just outside the door.

"Yes, ma'am. Daddy's takin' me over to Crawleysville. Then I catch the bus to Chattanooga."

"Gettin' yer trainin' in Chattanooga, then?"

"Yes, ma'am."

"Don't let the big city corrupt you, son!" This advice come from Mister Hickman. "'Specially don't let them Yankees learn you none of their bad ways! Wouldn't trust 'em a lick if I was you!"

"I only mean for 'em to learn me 'bout takin' care of this here land, Mister Hickman. Reckon I can take what them Yankees knows and use it to our good."

"Didn't never know a Yankee what did somethin' for our good," Miz Hickman said, shaking her head. "But I reckon if you've a mind to, you needs be doin' jest that." She leaned heavily against her broom and sighed. "Take care, James Junior."

"Thank you, Miz Hickman. Nice visitin' with you, Mister Hickman."

James Junior and Daddy both tipped their hats and then we rode on through town, saying *hey* to anyone we passed. Not many were setting around town like usual since the rain was still coming down steady. Except for old man Snodderly. He was George Snodderly's daddy and hadn't worked a lick since he was born, some said. Now he was nigh unto eighty, just a nubbin' of a man, and about the only thing he ever done was keep the town's bench warm in front of the post office. And some said even that was a chore that tired him since he snored most the day!

When we passed him on his bench Daddy started right in to chuckling. "Daddy, what you be laughin' 'bout?" Andy asked. Andy'd been watching something across the road and hadn't even noticed old man Snodderly.

"George Senior's 'bout the onliest man I know can sleep right through a Tennessee downpour. And snore louder'n one too!" Daddy shook his head and laughed again. "Wonder if he could outdo a real crackin' thunderstorm too?!"

We all laughed then, and the relief of laughter felt so good to me. I hadn't even realized until then how tense every inch of me was. When Daddy turned down the road to the schoolhouse and I switched positions to get up, I found that my feet were plumb asleep. I started rubbing them hard, twitching with the tingling feeling in them. I reckon I'd sat in the same position all the way into town, all drawed up into a tense ball. No wonder my feet were feeling so poorly.

Daddy called out, "Hold up there, Dean!" and pulled us to a stop. He turned to look at me and Andy. "You two best be sayin' yer good-byes to James Junior. Won't be long 'til that school bell be ringin'."

James Junior jumped from the wagon—just missing a big old mud puddle—and come round to the back. O.A. jumped down next and, throwing back his small shoulders and holding up his chin, thrust out his hand in a dignified way. I know Andy was meaning to act and look like a full-growed man, but the sight of him standing there—soaked nigh to the skin, rain dripping all around the brim of his sorry-looking hat and overalls with holes showing two scraped, bruised, and scratched-up knees—my heart melted for the still little boy in him that cried out for James Junior's respect.

I saw James Junior's shoulders move up and down in what must've been a big sigh, and then he reached out to give Andy a good, firm handshake. "Take care of Mama for me, will you? She be needin' another man round the house now. I know you be the man for the doin' of it."

Andy nodded his head, his eyes so intent and serious on James Junior's. They released hands, and Andy looked at him for a moment more before turning towards the schoolhouse. But he hadn't got but a few steps when he come tearing back, jumping up into James Junior's waiting arms. I could hear O.A.'s muffled sobs against James Junior's chest and was glad now for the pouring rain; hopefully it would hide Andy's wet cheeks. I knew he wouldn't want anyone in school to know he'd been crying. And then just as quickly as he'd come back, Andy pushed out of James Junior's arms and, wiping his eyes good on his sleeve, walked resolutely towards the steps into school. This time he did not look back.

Then it was my turn. James Junior lifted me down, and I again fancied the feeling of being held by him. When he set me down, though, he didn't let go. Instead he held me in his firm, muscular hug, and I held on as tight as I could—trying to memorize the feel of his arms about me, the smell and feel of his starched shirt against my face. I had to make this hug live a long time in my mind; I wanted to be able to call up the memory often, so I held on as long as I could.

James Junior gripped my arms and pulled me away from him so he could look me straight in the eye. "I don't want you to be frettin' none 'bout that dream of yers. Bein' a teacher someday. I aim to see it true. Don't let go yer dreams, Rachael." He hugged me to him once more and then pushed me away, suddenly turning to climb back up with Daddy.

"See you to home later, Rachael," Daddy said. "Come on now, Dean. We'uns got a ways to go yet." He slapped the reins, sending tiny sprays of water off Dean's back.

They turned the wagon around and slowly headed out, getting bogged down now and then in the heavy mud. But they did move on, and I stood and watched them go just like Granny Mandy and Mama had done. Only now I was the woman watching them until they were out of sight. The rain was still dripping onto my hat. But I didn't feel it any more.

The day dragged on just as slow and steady as the rain kept on coming down. Every time I had a chance to daydream, I thought on James Junior, wondering just where he was and how he was doing now. Miz Travis must've noticed I wasn't concentrating much, but she didn't say anything. I guess since everybody was slow like on account of the rain, I wasn't no more noticeable than anybody else.

When Miz Travis let us out for the day, we all had to walk home since Daddy'd already delivered the mail earlier in the afternoon. It was mostly a fine drizzle by that time, but it sure got a body just as wet. My blouse and skirt were both clinging to me by the time we were just east of town.

And the creeks—land, were they ever up and flowing swift! Possum Trot come clean up to my knees; it was a trick to balance on them slick rocks while I was holding up my skirt, lunch pail, and Daisy Purser to boot. Once I got across I thought to myself that I didn't rightly recollect why I was so bothered about falling. If I had I couldn't of got no wetter'n I already was.

As soon as Daisy and Earl headed on home, Andy reached out and grabbed my sleeve. "Let go, O.A.! I ain't in no mood for foolin'," I told him, impatience clearly evident in my voice. He jerked his hand back down quickly and stuck one finger in his mouth. O.A. had the bad habit of biting his nails. Seemed like mostly when there was dirt crusted all over them too. "An' take that dirty finger outta yer mouth! You'll be gettin' worms for sure." After making a face at him, I turned and walked towards the house when Andy grabbed me once more.

"Can I jest ask a question? I ain't knowin' who else to ask." The rain had become merely a fog by now, but Andy's hat still drooped noticeably as he anxiously looked up at me. He kept glancing away towards the road.

"This best be important, and you better make it quick." I gave him an impatient glare. "Mama ain't goin' to spell us bein' late."

Andy dug one toe into the mud, turning his foot this way and that to make the hole deeper. Clearly he was working up his courage, but I wasn't in no waiting frame of mind. "O.A.!" I hollered.

"I jest want to know 'bout some things, that's all."

"What things?" I was about ready to shake them out of him!

"Well." He took a deep breath. "Why's Mama so tolerable put out with James Junior?" He wouldn't look at me while he was asking, but now his big green eyes studied mine intently.

"Mama ain't put out, Andy. She's hurtin'."

"Hurtin'? For James Junior's leavin'?" He looked at me in disbelief, and I nodded. "But why's she so ill with all of us? James Junior 'specially?"

"She ain't meanin' to be ill. That's her way of showin' the hurt, that's all."

"Is all gals thata way?" Andy screwed up his face with alarm.

"Naw. I ain't."

"Ha! Iffin that ain't the biggest fib I ever heared!"

I gave him another stern look. "I'm needin' to get to my chores if you ain't got no more to ask about than that."

"But I still ain't understandin' why Mama be so hurtin' 'bout James Junior leavin'. You'd think he was a-goin' off to war or somethin'. He ain't, is he?"

"Ain't what? O.A., you ain't makin' no sense atall."

"Goin' to war. James Junior ain't goin' off somewheres to fight, is he?" Andy's eyebrows shot up and his eyes opened wide. He looked as excited as he did frightened by this prospect.

"Where in God's land would you be gettin' that idea? I do declare, O.A. 'Bout the onliest things you think on is scufflin' an' fightin'." I turned to walk up our hill. Far as I was concerned, our jawing was done.

"But Mister Hickman says he done heared on his wireless how everthin's—now how was it he put it?—brewin' in Europe." Andy followed along beside me, only he was hopping from one rock to another (we had a whole passel of them that lined our pathway), balancing and teetering as we went.

"Brewin'? Is he talkin' 'bout coffee or people?"

"Rachael!" O.A. suddenly stopped, sliding off one of the bigger rocks—into an even bigger puddle—and folding his arms across his chest. I stopped then too, folding my arms the same way to mock him. "Mister Hickman says he jest heared them Germans are aimin' to build a *Luftwaffle*." He lifted his chin like Preacher Morgan does when he's preaching on sin. Ours, of course.

"A what?"

"A Luftwaffle. Means a air force! An' that Hitler says he ain't goin' to abide that treaty no more. Says he's goin' to build him all sorts of guns an' all too. An' mebbe that means they's goin' to fight Austria, them wireless people says."

"Andy, I don't rightly reckon Mister Hickman or you heared right atall. Ain't no such word—luftwaffle?—as I've heard tell of and there ain't no call to be frettin' over what ain't happened yet. Or what ain't goin' to happen!" By now I just wanted Andy to be quiet before Mama caught wind of any of this. That'd be just what she needed—to hear Andy talking about James Junior going off to fight in a war. "'Sides, what's Germany and Austria got to do with the United States of America? They's clear on the other side of the ocean. Or ain't you been listenin' to your geography lessons?" Shaking my head at him, I walked on again. "This ain't no more'n nonsense, Andy." I turned to face him once more and put my wagging finger right up to his freckled nose. "And you ain't to breathe one word of this to Mama, understand? If you do, I'll, I'll . . ."

"You'll do what?" Andy put his hands on his hips now, squinting up at me with pure meanness popping out. Now I'd made this a dare and that wasn't what I wanted at all. O.A. wasn't one to ever miss taking a dare.

"Well, 'tain't what I'll do. It's what Mama'll do. She'll be a-frettin' an' hurtin' and then be ill at all of us! Is that what you be wantin'?" He let his arms fall down limply to his side. That was a good sign that I was winning this one. "You was already stewin' on Mama bein' ill. You goin' to scare her even more talkin' 'bout Germany an' wars an' fightin' an' such?"

Andy pondered this a moment, chewing on that dirty fingernail again. He avoided my eyes and then said, softly, "Reckon not."

"Swear?"

Even more softly, "Swear." And then the rain started in to drizzling again.

"Now you done it. We been standin' here jawin' when it weren't rainin' and now it's done started up again. Now we both'll be chorin' in the rain!" I tugged my hat down farther on my head and trudged on up the hill, stomping through most every puddle I come near. *If I'm goin' to get even wetter chorin'*, I thought to myself, *I might as well enjoy splashin' through some puddles.*

When I looked back, Andy was still standing there—finger in mouth as he gnawed on a nail, drenched clothes clinging to his thin, small body, mud splashed clean up to his knees, and wet hair plastered to his forehead under the sad-looking dirty straw hat. I felt a moment of pity for him and stopped again, sighing. *Were all little brothers such a trial as mine?* Made me think on picking blackberries. No matter how tight I pulled up my socks or wore long sleeves or kept out of them bushes as much as I could, them chiggers always were finding a way to bite me. Of course those bites were also in the very worst of places and nothing on God's green earth itched like a chigger bite. O.A. was just like them chiggers. And now he'd done bit me again!

"Andy."

He looked up at me, still chewing on that fingernail.

"Are you frettin' 'bout James Junior goin' off somewheres? Other than the CCC, I mean?"

He studied something far off in the hills, squinting. "Reckon so. Just ain't seemin' right somehow. They's too many changes an' I don't like 'em. None of 'em."

Changes. That's just what Mama'd said! "I know, Andy. I don't like changes neither. But there ain't nothin' I can be doin' 'bout any of them." He was blinking right hard again. Wanting desperately to console him, I muttered, "Andy, I ain't changin'."

He turned to me with hot anger flashing now in them green eyes. "Oh yes, you is! You be 'bout all growed up! An' you're pinin' to be goin' to some silly high school! You can't wait to leave me just like James Junior done!" He spit out the words at me, his whole body shaking with the effort. "Go 'head an' leave! I don't care none! Don't need James Junior! Surely don't need you neither!"

"But Andy, that's only growin' up. I can't help that none!"

But now it was Andy that was done jawing. Trudging on up the hill, he stomped angrily through mud and puddles, deliberately splashing that muddy water as high as his small feet could make it go. Finally he shot back, "I said I don't need you none!"

I watched him stalk away, noticing how his shoulders slumped and his head hung low. My heart ached to go after him. I was wishing I could pick him up and kiss him like I always used to do when he was a little one. But Andy wouldn't want kisses no more; he was too big for that. Besides, I knew that kisses couldn't heal that kind of hurt. And I couldn't make the changes to stop coming neither.

During supper Andy was sullen and quiet. He didn't talk atall hardly until Daddy mentioned going to the town meeting. Then we both pleaded with Daddy to let us go too. At first Daddy insisted that this wasn't for young'uns, but then when we promised to just stand quietly at the back, he decided there wouldn't be any harm in it. So once me and Mama finished doing up the dishes, we all piled into the wagon again. We gave Mister and Miz Purser, Earl, and Daisy a ride and Daddy stopped to collect Granny Mandy too, but she said that all the rain was bothering her rheumatism and we went on without her.

Fortunately the rain had stopped by now, but fog was settling in right thick. Sometimes the fog would just hunker down in the valleys, crouching down here an' yonder, but this one covered everthing like a heavy quilt. Coming home would be a might troublesome. Daddy would probably have to just let Old Dean find his way.

Daddy and Mister Purser talked most the way about planting the crops, the weather and signs, and how long the growing season would be this year. Daddy told him again how glad he was to have a sharecropper who was so clever and hardworking. Miz Purser squeezed Mister Purser's arm then; I figured she must've been right proud of him.

Andy was still being sullen, but Earl and Daisy were sure chattering to beat the band. They were seeing haints hiding around every bend out in the fog or hearing buggers howling just behind us. Daisy'd squeal every time Earl'd hold his hand over the side of the wagon. He'd grab it back up, swearing that he'd done seen something and that it touched his fingers for sure too. Then Daisy'd squeal again, and Earl would cackle. I was getting tolerable tired of this game when we finally turned into the schoolyard.

There was a big crowd. Seemed like about everybody in Jordan's Bend was there that night. The schoolhouse would be fairly packed. Mama and Daddy went right in; Daddy told me to keep an eye on Earl and Daisy (they were going to be a handful) and showed us young'uns where we should stay back out of the way. Me and Andy both leaned against the bookshelves and eyed each other. "Wish you'd quit yer sulkin'," I said to him.

"I told you they was too many changes." He nodded towards the government men up front. "An' they's bringin' more. Ain't goin' to be to our likin' neither. Granny Mandy said so."

I was going to ask Andy just what Granny Mandy'd said when one of the men—a skinny one with beady eyes peering out from thick horn-rimmed glasses—started banging on Preacher Morgan's pulpit with a thick ruler. Most people stopped talking, but then they started in to whispering. Using Preacher Morgan's pulpit was bad enough. Pounding on it—a Yankee outsider!—was nigh to blasphemy! The widow Campbell was setting just in front of us, and she was fanning herself furiously with one of the church's straw fans that had "Morgan's Funeral Parlor" printed on it. I could see Miz Smith whispering frantically in her ear, but all the widow done was purse her lips and fan harder. This here meeting had just started and already it promised to be right interesting!

"Can I have it quiet, please? We'd like to get started right on time as we have much to discuss this evening."

The whispering tapered off except for Mister and Miz Harris. Since she's so hard of hearing, Mister Harris had to practically yell in her ear. And Miz Harris hollered all the time anyways. Guess she thought everybody else was as hard of hearing as she was.

"What's he sayin'?" Miz Harris was asking. She leaned towards Mister Harris, squinting her eyes like she was hoping that would help her to hear better.

Mister Harris put his mouth to her ear. "He said to get quiet!"

"Well, iffin he'd stop a-bangin' on Preacher's pulpit, I could hear 'im tolerable better!"

Several people around them chuckled then, and the man banged the pulpit again. I don't rightly know if he heard Miz Harris or not, but if he did, he didn't think it was funny atall. His face was red and flushed looking to begin with, and it was getting redder all the time. And them eyes seemed to be getting beadier too.

"Now, my name is Dr. John Sherman," (the whispering started in all over again when he said that name) "and this is Dr. Robert Whitaker." He paused, clearing his throat, and gave the whisperers an impatient glance.

"Did I hear 'im say *doctor*?" Miz Harris asked, and Mister Harris nodded. "Why them Yankees sendin' us doctors? They think we be feelin' poorly?"

"I ain't. You feelin' poorly?"

"Eh? What'd you say?"

"I said, ere you be feelin' poorly?"

"Land, yes. My rheumatism be actin' up again an'—"

Bang! Bang! Dr. Sherman glared in the Harrises' direction now. "As I was saying, Dr. Whitaker has degrees in agricultural engineering and crops and soil science from some of our country's finest universities. I am a civil engineer."

Miz Harris leaned towards Mister Harris again. "What was all them words?"

"I'll be durned iffin I know!" Mister Harris shook his head slowly. "Cain't repeat 'em iffin I cain't even say 'em. An' I ain't met a Yankee yet what was civil."

"What's that?"

"I said, he said he's civil!"

"Ain't no civil Yankees!"

"That's what I'm sayin'!"

It wasn't no time to be gigglin', but I felt a grin come over my face just the same.

Mister Sherman kept on talking. "I suppose you're all very anxious to find out why we're here." He cleared his throat again, as if he had something right important to say. "The government is most concerned about your part of this great country. This economic depression has hit us hard all across the United States. But your government wants to help you. With the flooding that destroys your crops nearly every year. With the poor condition of your soil. With your lack of electricity for any modern conveniences. And we hope to accomplish all of these goals with a major project we call the Tennessee Valley Authority."

I whispered to Andy, "That's what James Junior was tryin' to recollect! And the car—'member its license plate? *TVA!*" Andy nodded, screwing his face around again. He obviously remembered, but he didn't look none too pleased about it.

Behind the government men was a huge map mounted on a stand. Mister Sherman moved over to it and pointed to Jordan's Bend. "This is Jordan's Bend and here's the Tennessee River. If we keep following the river way back upstream," he said, sliding his finger up the map, "to the rivers that feed the Tennessee—the Clinch, Holston, French Broad, Little Tennessee, and Hiwassee—we find that all of these areas have the same basic problems that you do."

Mister Sherman lifted another map over top the other one. "This map shows basically the same area of the South, but you can see that these are plans for construction—construction of a whole system of dams, lakes, and waterways to control the Tennessee. When all these dams are built, you will no longer experience yearly floods. And we can provide electricity to you for a fraction of the cost that the local electric companies want to sell it to you for. Finally, the CCC boys," (both me and Andy looked at each other at this point, and I felt a sudden sharp pang of loneliness for James Junior) "they and Dr. Whitaker will train you farmers how to refurbish your soil by analyzing it and putting the nutrients back in that flooding and years of corn and cotton planting have sucked out. We'll give you fertilizers that will enrich that soil once again. And finally, we're going to plant trees and teach you to rotate crops, putting much to pasture, so your soil will be fertile again. Now, what questions do you have at this point?"

Uncle Evert raised his hand right off. "So what's the government be wantin' fer all this? Last time the Yankees come through here with a Sherman, they didn't give us nothin'. Nothin' but trouble that is!" Several chuckles and *amens* were heard around the room. "Didn't give no handouts then; just took. And we ain't be wantin' no handouts now. I know I fer one ain't goin' on no relief!"

This time the *amens* were hollered. I noticed that Daddy was nodding his head too.

"Sir, we're not giving any 'handouts' as you call them. We will, however, be offering jobs with good pay and excellent training. We'll need good, strong, reliable workers to build these dams. It will be hard work. You'll earn your pay, I guarantee it."

"Now why should we be a-listenin' to you all?" Mister Harris shouted out, suddenly standing up and looking around the room at folks. "Who ere you be, to be comin' round heres like this, tellin' us what to be doin' with our land?"

Miz Harris was nodding her head, mumbling, "That's right, that's right," under her breath. She must've heard him fine this time.

"Sir, have you lived here all your life?" Mister Sherman asked.

"Not yet I ain't."

Chuckles rippled round the room; Andy even started in to laughing right out loud until I poked him one in the ribs.

Mister Sherman lifted one eyebrow, pushed down the other one over a squinted-up eye, and frowned right hard at Mister Harris. He plainly didn't appreciate Mister Harris' humor any. "I'm sure you're quite familiar with your land, sir, but Dr. Whitaker has spent many years studying the soil too and what it needs to produce a good harvest. He'll address questions to that effect in just a few minutes. Now. What other questions do some of you have for me?"

Then Daddy spoke up. "Ere you be plannin' to put a dam round here?"

His question startled me. I hadn't even thought of that possibility while listening to all of Mister Sherman's plans. Seemed like something that big would need to be a ways from here, not in Jordan's Bend. The room suddenly got much quieter, and Mister Sherman looked down at Preacher Morgan's pulpit, squirming around a bit. "This area will soon become one of the most beautiful places in all of Tennessee."

"Already is!" I think Tommy Lee's daddy hollered that one.

"Yes, sir, that is true. But soon it will have a huge, gorgeous lake. And remember what I said: no more floods plaguing you every year. And electricity! See, the power that is generated from water going over a dam can be turned into electricity that you can use for electric lights, stoves, even refrigerators, radios!"

"What's a friger-a-tor?" Andy whispered to me.

"It's like a springhouse. Keeps things cold."

"Why we be needin' 'em when we already got springhouses, then?"

"Don't know. I only know Granny Mandy's is the best place anywheres to be on a hot summer's day."

Andy nodded in agreement. "Can a body set in one of them friger-a-tors?"

"Don't reckon so. Ain't likely big enough."

"Then what good is they?"

I shrugged my shoulders at him. Then me and Andy were surprised to hear Daddy's voice again. "You still ain't rightly answered my question. You be plannin' one round here. Where?"

"To tell you the truth, sir, we're still surveying the whole area. The boundaries are still being determined. But you bring up a most important part of this meeting. When we build a dam, it stops up the water to form a lake, as I said. And that lake will permanently flood a good deal of land."

"What land?" This question sounded frantic, but I couldn't tell who asked it. I just know that whoever it was reflected my feelings too. And Mister Sherman sure took his good sweet time answering it. Everybody was dead silent. Waiting.

"As I said, we're not for certain just what land will be flooded yet. But yes, it will be someone's land. Many of you will be involved." The panicked-sounding whispering started up again now. "Let me assure you, however," Mister Sherman's voice suddenly got much louder as he talked over the whispering and emphasized his point, "your government—and that's why Dr. Whitaker and I are here—plans to take care of you and help you in every way we can. We're going to pay top dollar for every acre of land that we must use for this project."

Mister Harris leaned over to holler in Miz Harris' ear, "I see any Yankee on my property, the price done just doubled!"

"And for those of you who must move," Mister Sherman continued—or tried to, because then the murmuring increased to plain talking out loud. "For those who must move," he shouted over all the racket, "the government plans to help relocate you with all the assistance we can provide."

Mister Snodderly stood up then. "Move? I ain't movin' nowheres, nohow, never!" he shouted, shaking his dirty fist at Mister Sherman.

"Now sir, you don't know yet if the government will even be asking you to move, do you? And besides, I believe when you hear the mighty fair price the government will be paying for an acre, you may change your mind quickly. We'll be helping you to pick out new farms, even building new homes and barns if they're needed. Who in here wouldn't like a brand new cinder block house—no flimsy wood one—with electric lights too! Wouldn't you like a house like that with electric lights, sir?"

Mister Harris shook his head and hollered to Miz Harris, "Only a addle-brained Yankee would run a 'lectric line a fer piece so's George Snodderly could have 'im a light bub!"

"What's that?" Miz Harris asked.

"A light bub! He be talkin' 'bout stringin' a light bub fer Snodderly!"

"Snodderly? He ain't got nothin' worth seein'!"

"That's what I'm sayin'!"

"When will you know them what's land is to be flooded?" Daddy asked. His words sounded strained and clipped.

"Soon. Within this next week." He turned to look over at Mister Whitaker. "Dr. Whitaker and I will be visiting personally with those of you who will be directly affected by this. We want to assure you again that everything will be fine. And we want to answer any questions that you may have." More rumbling and muttering came from around the room. "I know that I haven't been able to completely answer all of your questions tonight. Since we're still in the planning stages yet, I can't do that. But we'll be holding a meeting every Monday night from now on for as long as we need to. So hopefully we'll be able to answer even more of your questions next week."

"So we's meetin' here again next week?" Mister Hickman asked.

"Yes, sir. And now Dr. Whitaker needs to speak to you about how he's going to help you farmers."

Mister Sherman stepped back, and Mister Whitaker moved up behind the pulpit. "Good evening, ladies and gentlemen, girls and boys." Mister Whitaker's voice was smooth sounding and pleasing to the ear somehow. He had a full head of wavy, dark brown hair streaked with gray (quite a difference from Mister Sherman's bald one), and his eyes were as soft as Mister Sherman's were sharp. I liked Mister Whitaker better right off. "I know this has been a difficult and possibly alarming evening for you. Again, I just want to reassure you that we are here to help you in any way that we can. We want to make this time of change as easy for you as we possibly can."

There was that word again. *Change.* Out of the corner of my eye I could see O.A. staring at me with them green eyes of his wide open in alarm, again with that "I done told you so" kind of expression. But I wouldn't return his look.

"Dr. Sherman and I are here because your government—and I do mean *your* government—cares about each of you here in Jordan's Bend. Please come to us at any time to ask questions or seek help. That's exactly what we're here for. You can find us at the motel when we're not out with the surveyors.

"Now, I'd like to take some time to talk to you about how we're going to help you farmers improve your land and therefore the crops that your land produces. I'm sure you've noticed that for several years now, your corn rows are getting sparser."

"Not McKenney Way corn!" Earl hollered. Everyone around us

chuckled, but I reached out and grabbed Earl by the arm right quick and give him a stern look. Daddy'd put me to watching him, and I knew he wouldn't be happy with me letting Earl interrupt again.

"Earl, if you don't hush," I whispered frantically through clenched teeth, "I'll take you right outside and give you a switchin' like Miz Travis does! You hear?" I give his arm a firm squeeze to make sure he knew I meant it too.

He narrowed his eyes at me and pushed out his lower lip. But at least he didn't say anything more.

"An' it's out east of town a piece," Preacher was saying. Giving Earl a talking to had made me miss some of what was being said, but I assumed Mister Whitaker had asked where McKenney Way corn grew. Knowing Daddy, he wouldn't speak up about it, so Preacher Morgan must've explained where our rich soil was. "That bottomland grows 'bout the most corn per acre round here, I reckon."

Mister Whitaker just stared at Preacher Morgan for a spell, not saying nothing, and then the whole room got strangely quieter. I noticed the widow Campbell had stopped her fanning; she was just holding it straight out like, pointing it towards Mister Whitaker. Miz Harris was leaning so far forward in her seat that she looked about ready to fall on her knees. Glancing around the room, I noticed that everyone seemed to be straining forward, waiting on Mister Whitaker to say something, anything. And then Preacher Morgan cleared his throat right loud like. Mister Whitaker turned front ways again, looking up towards the ceiling and stretching his arms straight out from the pulpit that he clutched in front of him with both hands. Seeing his shoulders slowly go up and down, I could tell he took a good deep breath before he said, "Sorry. I was thinking about something else for a minute there." He took another quick breath. "Now, we were talking about the soil, weren't we?"

No, I thought to myself. We—you—were talkin' 'bout McKenney Way corn! If I was 'lowed to ask a question, I'd surely be wantin' to know what yer thinkin', Mister Whitaker.

"There are many things that we plan to do to help you," he continued, not hearing my silent pleadings atall. "First of all, we'd like to choose one of you farmers for a demonstration farm. For supplying the use of your farm as a test area for the county, we'll give you free fertilizer and help you improve your land."

"What kinda fertilizer? And what you aimin' to do?" Mister Smith asked. He sounded awful suspicious of Mister Whitaker.

"The fertilizer is called metaphosphate. Some people say it looks kind of like hoarhound candy. But you wouldn't want to eat it, though, because it is a concentrated fertilizer. One that we've had good success with. We get it from right here in Tennessee. Middle Tennessee, that is. After refining the metaphosphate at Muscle Shoals, Alabama, we'll be using it to help your soil here in east Tennessee. As for the land, well, we want to try several different things. First of all, we'll want you to put more acres to pasture with a cover crop. Much of your soil is tired. It needs a rest and that fertilizer to get well, just like someone who's sick."

I remembered Daddy using those very words to describe the Harrises' property.

"And how you figure we be goin' to feed our young'uns? Cain't feed my brood clover fer dinner!" Mister Youther lived a good bit east of Jordan's Bend, and he wasn't fooling when he said brood. Them Youthers had a whole passel of young'uns—twelve already and another on the way.

"Clover isn't the only cover crop, sir. And as a matter of fact, we're hoping many of you will discover another cover crop that does sell. And Northerners especially like it."

Mister Whitaker had everyone's attention now. We were all interested in selling; that was a fact. And if them Northerners were willing to pay good money for it, we were listening.

"And what might that be?" asked Tommy Lee's daddy.

"Strawberries!" Mister Whitaker paused a minute, grinning. Most everybody looked to be shaking heads slowly in disbelief. "Strawberries don't rob the soil of its nutrients like corn or cotton do, and they are a good cash crop! We hope many of you will give them a try this next growing season."

The whispering picked up again then. Miz Smith was jawing furiously in the widow's ear, but the widow never answered back that I could tell. She was too busy fanning herself again. I reckoned that Mister Whitaker hadn't rightly convinced anyone about them strawberries just yet.

"Back to the subject of the demonstration farm," Mister Whitaker continued. "I do hope many of you will apply for this opportunity. You farmers will decide which farm is best suited to be chosen, and then my team and I will need to do surveys on it, analyzing the soil's contents—and its needs—and also checking land use and drainage. Could be you'll need to put strawberries in some of your cornfields and give other fields a rest for a year or so."

I kept glancing around the room, wondering who might apply and who'd be chosen. *Would Daddy apply?*

"But there's one thing I'll tell you right now," Mister Whitaker went on. "And that's this: whoever is chosen may not do as well that first year, or maybe even the second. But then I can guarantee that he'll start seeing excellent results from our work. That land will begin to produce again like it used to. No, I'll say that it'll be even better!" He paused a minute, looking around the room to nod at the men. And here and there I noticed a few heads slowly nodding back at him. Daddy's was among them. "Next week we'll talk more about applying for this demonstration farm. But even if you're not the one chosen by your neighbors, we plan to help all of you in other different ways. For instance, we want to begin working on the problem of malaria."

I winced when he said malaria, seeing as how Mama was here. Malaria had taken both my brother and sister when they were just babies. Mama doesn't spell talking about it atall.

"Mosquitos carry the disease from one person to another, and those mosquitos breed in stagnant water—marshes, swamps, any pools that don't have water flowing through to keep them clean. We plan to spray with a dust called Paris green and hopefully eliminate a good deal of the mosquitos' breeding areas."

Mister Whitaker looked around the room again. He seemed to be measuring our reactions to what he was saying. Considering he was an outsider from the North, I thought he'd done tolerable good.

"What's that he's sayin' 'bout Paree havin' green skeeters?" Miz Harris was hollering in Mister Harris' ear.

"Aw, Mary! He ain't sayin' that atall! Said he's goin' to spray our swamps green. To kill the skeeters."

"Swamp's already green!"

"Well, I's jest tellin' ye what he's a-sayin'!"

Andy rolled his eyes at me and grinned, but I quickly put my finger to my lips, giving him the "hush!" sign. I didn't aim to get Earl and Daisy started in to giggling again, and besides, I didn't want to miss what Mister Whitaker was saying.

"The Tennessee Valley Authority will also help Jordan's Bend by providing a community-owned refrigerator, a library that will eventually become Jordan's Bend's own . . ."

A library! In Jordan's Bend! I could feel my stomach tighten in excitement at just the thinking on it.

". . . health services for our employees that you'll use too and expand upon, maybe eventually building a hospital right here." Mister Whitaker leaned over the front of the pulpit, raising one arm and pointing down just like Preacher Morgan when he gets to shouting and waving his arms around. "You'll have electricity all over this county, and just think what that means, ladies!" His eyes opened wide, and he grinned at Miz Morgan setting in the front row. "Dr. Sherman already mentioned refrigerators. How would you like an electric stove? No more messy wood ones! And electric lamps. No more kerosene! The possibilities with electricity are wonderful and nearly endless!"

I noticed that nearly everybody seemed to be leaning forward again, straining to catch every word Mister Whitaker said. But this time we were listening because this was exciting! *Would Jordan's Bend really be gettin' all them wonderful things?*

"And lastly," Mister Whitaker continued, "don't forget about that beautiful lake. Jordan's Bend Lake, as a matter of fact. Already has its name before its even built. Our corps of engineers will make it almost as lovely as one made by God. Remember I said almost now! We don't pretend to be able to create anything like what God's almighty hand can do, but I will tell you one thing." Mister Whitaker stopped talking and walked around to the front of the pulpit. Folding his arms across his chest, he looked over the room several times, meeting folks' eyes here and there. It were so quiet that I could hear the widow moving that fan back and forth. And when Mister Whitaker started in to talking again, he didn't have to holler like that Mister Sherman done. He spoke right slow and soft like.

"When that dam is finished and the lake begins to fill up, forming small islands here and peninsulas there . . ." Mister Whitaker pointed left and then right, just like he was already seeing them things. And every head in that room followed just where he was pointing, pretending and trying to see them too? "Beaches that way for swimming and deep banks for fishing to your heart's content. And when the sun peeks over a cloud and shines on that water, reflecting and sparkling in your eyes, well . . . I tell you. Maybe there won't be much difference at all from one made by God's hand. Sure takes us a lot more trouble and time," he said, grinning again. "Can't do it in one second like He could. But the end result may be very pleasing to us all." He paused again, unfolding his arms and putting his hands into his pants pockets. "Thank you, everyone, for your time and patience. Dr. Sherman and I will look for you here again next week. Good night." And then turning round, he and Mister Sherman started in to gathering up their things.

Of course the quiet during Mister Whitaker's speeching immediately erupted into loud talking all around the room. Daisy and Earl were both trying to jabber in my ear at the same time, and I didn't rightly hear a word they were saying—partly because they were both jawing at the same time and partly because I didn't want to listen to them. I wanted to hear what other folks were saying.

"Lake's good fishin'. Daddy done tol' me so!" Earl was hollering, tugging on my arm so he was sure he had my attention. "He done said we's goin' to get a lake right here in Jordan's Bend! Ain't that somethin', Rachael?"

I glanced around the room, wondering where O.A. had took himself off to already. If he hadn't disappeared, Earl would be pestering him and not me, most likely. "Well, Earl," I said, "I s'pose so." I kept looking around, watching for Mama and Daddy. "But I'd be one for waitin' to see just where they's goin' to put all of that water. You wouldn't want it to be a-floodin' this here church, now would you?"

Earl looked smug. Motioning that he wanted to whisper in my ear and grinning like a dog what just ate the slop left over from a hog killing, he said, "Iffin that means they ain't no schoolhouse neither, that's surely all right with me!"

I shook my head at him in exasperation, noticing Daddy out of the corner of my eye. "There's my Daddy, Earl. Daisy, come on now," I said, grabbing for each of them with a hand. "We best be headin' that a way. I reckon Daddy'll be anxious to get on to home. Fog's kindly bad tonight."

Daisy shook off my hand, saying, "I ain't that little. Don't rightly think I'll get lost at the schoolhouse!" She crossed her arms in front of her, looking at me defiantly.

"I ain't sayin' you'd get lost. I'm only tryin' to get you headed where I'm aimin' to go!" I started nudging Daisy towards the door now. If I couldn't drag her out, I'd push her! "'Sides, Daddy done told me to keep an eye on you an' Earl, and I aim to do just that. Now come on!" I felt more and more frustrated. This needless bickering with Daisy was keeping me from hearing folks' comments about the meeting, and I still hadn't spotted O.A. either.

As we moved on out the door, most people seemed tolerable excited. Whether that was anxious excited or happy excited I couldn't rightly tell. Seemed to be a mixture of both—just like I felt. I could hear Mister Snodderly hollering above everbody; he was still saying something about not ever leaving his land, seeing how it was the best in the county. *Don't that sound just like him*? I thought to myself. *That ground of his ain't growed corn worth nothin' for years now, but ask him to maybe move and suddenly it's the richest soil in this whole United States of America!*

I caught snitches of the widow Campbell still fussing about them Yankees banging on Preacher's pulpit, and Verna Mae's folks was gushing on how this was certainly going to help business at their store. Miz Hickman was already listing off all the new things they'd have to order. Of course Miz Harris was still hollering, trying to make out what had been said and what was being said by everybody now. Didn't seem to me that she was getting neither one atall. I could hear her mumbling something about them "shiftless Yankees runnin' a e-lectric light bulb line through Snodderly's swamp that were already green!" Mister Harris looked like he plumb give up explaining.

Daddy, Mama, and Mister and Miz Purser were not far ahead of us. They were talking softly among themselves as they walked towards the wagon. I could see Andy was already there hunkered down in the back, knees pulled clean up to his chest and straw hat pushed way down over his face. He didn't look to be in no mood for jawing, that was for sure. Just then I saw Daddy turn around, looking for me, Daisy, and Earl, I assumed. "We's comin', Daddy!" I hollered. We squeezed around the folks who were gathered here and there and then climbed up into the back of the wagon.

"Everybody in?" Daddy asked. "Can't make out much o' nothin' in this fog."

Miz Purser glanced back at us before sayin', "All noses is counted!"

"Let's us head on home then," Daddy said. "Been a long day, ain't it, Miz McKenney?" The weariness in Daddy's voice alarmed me, and I looked at him with concern.

Folks were gathered around all over the schoolyard, still talking about the meeting and all that the men had said. Daddy had to maneuver Old Mean Dean around groups of folks standing everywhere. Some were even waving Mama and Daddy over to talk, but Daddy told them it was late and the fog was getting mighty thick. Seemed to me, though, that Daddy wasn't jawing for other reasons. Daddy was the type that, when he was really studying on something, he was one for thinking, not talking. He never was one to jaw. When Daddy had something to say, he'd thought on it awhile. And it was worth hearing too.

When we were just on the other side of town, Mister Purser looked over to Daddy and asked, "Well, what you be makin' o' all this? Gives ye a might to be considerin', don't it?"

The sun had already set behind the trees, and the fog was moving in all around us, so it was getting harder and harder to see anything. But I could tell that Daddy looked at Mister Purser and nodded. He was silent then for a good while, and I was beginning to wonder if he was going to say anything atall when he finally answered, "Yes sir, it does give a body a heap to think on." Putting the reins in one hand, he reached up to take his hat off and run his fingers through his hair. "I had rather be thinkin' on my farmin'—gettin' the hay stacked for dryin', plowin' up my cornfields in time for plantin', an' seein' to that sled what's broke. Don't reckon I got the time for thinkin' on all o' this too." Dean was slowing down a good bit so Daddy put his hat back on and held onto the reins with both hands again. "Come on now, Dean. Fog's thick, but you be knowin' the road to home." Giving him a gentle nudge (didn't seem like none of us could ever really light into Old Dean, unless he was being especially stubborn), he asked, "Ain't you anxious to settle down for the night?"

"I surely know I am," sighed Miz Purser. "Long past my turnin' in time."

I heard a slight snoring sound then and turned around to discover Earl all curled up in a tight ball next to me, sound asleep. His lips were slightly parted and damp curls were clinging to his forehead. I reached out to touch one cheek, and he immediately grinned in his sleep. *How can he be lookin' so innocent like?* I wondered, shaking my head at the change from Earl at the meeting to this Earl.

Daddy and Mister Purser were quiet again. About all I could hear was the steady clop of Dean's hooves against the rutted road, little Earl's soft snoring, and the constant droning of the tree frogs' chorus somewheres out there in the heavy fog. *How on earth can Earl fall asleep with so much to think on? And how can Daddy just set it all aside, decidin' not to think about it? Ain't anybody else's thoughts a jumble like mine, tumblin' this way an' that over top one another, hollerin' to be spilled out?*

I settled back against the side of the wagon, sighing. If Daddy and Mister Purser weren't going to talk no more, I decided I might as well find a comfortable spot like Earl had. Daisy was cuddled against her mama and looked to be nearly asleep too. "Is you still awake, Andy?" I whispered. *Even talkin' with Andy is better than this awful silence,* I thought to myself.

His head moved, but all I heard was a grunt.

"I said, is you awake?" This time I poked him in the ribs too.

"Ain't in no mood for jawin'," he grumbled from beneath his hat.

"Take off that hat and talk to me a minute! Just tell me what you thought 'bout the meetin'." I stared at him, waiting for a reply. But when he still wouldn't say anything, I quickly decided on a way to get some kind of a response from him. I snatched up that old hat.

And then he moved all right. Moved right after me and latched onto the other side of that hat. At least having him tugging on it made him have to look at me. Without hardly moving a muscle on his rocklike, stern face, O.A. whispered me a warning. "Let go my hat! Now!"

"Answer my question and I'll let go right off!" We were pulling on that hat something awful. It wasn't in none too good a shape to begin with, and we weren't doing it any more good atall. "And if Mama or Daddy sees us, we's both goin' to get it!" I held onto the brim fiercely, giving him the meanest stare I could.

He eased up just a bit on the pulling. "What question?"

I took a deep breath in exasperation. "The meetin' tonight. What you be thinkin' 'bout it?"

"Done tol' you. Changes. Nothin' but changes. Don't like it none."

"But Mister Whitaker seemed right nice, don't you think? I reckon he wouldn't do nothin' mean. Changes can be good, Andy."

"Huh! Seems to me a body could see the daylight through them smooth-talkin' words. Now let go my hat!"

I looked at him in amazement and then slowly released my hold. Andy snatched up his hat, retreated quickly to the other side of the wagon, and plopped back down, again mashing that hat down over his face. I knew it'd be a waste of breath asking him anything more. Besides, he'd just give me something else to stew over. *Why didn't Andy like Mister Whitaker? He seemed right kind to me.*

The fog was all around us now. Looked about like our wagon and us what was in it were the only thing there was in the whole world. Down right eerie feeling it was, except for the tree frogs' familiar rhythmic hum. I looked left and right, then ahead and back. Nothing but fog so thick that you wanted to be grabbing at it to gather it up out of the way. Daddy wasn't hurrying Old Mean Dean any now, because Dean was the onliest one that could find our way home. He was taking his good sweet time again, but I was right glad. There were too many gullies just off this old road to be hurrying anywhere.

When we passed Granny Mandy's, I squinted over that way with longing. Couldn't see nothing but the fence next to the road that went round her truck patch. But oh, how I ached to be setting in front of her fireplace, rocking in one of her chairs and spilling out all them thoughts that were about to make me crazy. The hurt and worry of James Junior's leaving. These Yankees and all they were doing—and going to do. The changes Mama and Andy were talking about. Granny Mandy could always make sense of what was bothering at me.

The next morning the sun had a time coming out. Burning off that layer of fog took awhile, but the sun finally won the scuffle. The breeze smelled so fresh and new with the scent of its sun-washed cleanness and blooming spring flowers. After I'd gathered up the eggs in my basket, I tucked it over my arm so I could pluck a few bright blue violets from around the stones that formed the pathway to our breezeway. Seemed like me and Mama both needed something to cheer us up, a distraction to help keep our minds off James Junior's empty place at the table this morning.

Coming in the door to the kitchen, I held up the violets, saying, "Look Mama! Ain't they pretty?"

Mama glanced over at them and nodded. "Why don't you put 'em in my granny's cup, Rachael."

I placed the basket of eggs by the sink and then moved to the safe to fetch the cup. We kept all kinds of special things there so they wouldn't get broke—or more broke, since nearly everything we owned showed signs of being chipped, worn, or had at least one part missing. But that didn't matter none atall; long as it was from kin, it was special. As I reached in and took out the cup, with my finger I carefully traced the outline of the pink rose painted on it. The delicate pattern always fascinated me. Then, putting a bit of water in it and breaking off the stems of the violets to even lengths, I placed them one by one into the cup. I took it over to the window to admire it in the bright sunlight.

"Mama, tell me again 'bout the cup." I knew by heart the whole story of how it come from her granny, but I loved hearing her tell it anyways.

Mama pushed the pans to the back of the stove and, after wiping her hands on her apron, moved to the window beside me.

"It were my Granny Dickerson's," she said, taking the cup from me and placing it gently in the palms of her hands. Seemed like my eyes just couldn't get enough pleasuring in its soft colors and delicate lines and the beautiful blue of the violets. "She used to tell me how it come all the way from England in a big ship. 'Twas used for afternoon teas when they would make tiny sandwiches to go with their tea." Mama lifted the violets to her face, and then closing her eyes, she took in a deep breath of their sweet scent. "Seems they'd set an' talk a spell, restin' a bit."

"Restin'? They had time for settin' down in the afternoon?"

Mama sighed. "Seems they did."

I stared at her rough, worn hands holding the delicate, white china cup. Then glancing up at her face, I noticed that she stared beyond the cup out the window to . . . where? A home in England with ivy climbing up the brick with pink rose bushes blooming just outside the front door? To a parlor with a tea service set at a cherry table, and a fine sofa and chairs decorating the room? Studying Mama's face with its firm, high cheekbones and her well-defined, almond-shaped eyes below beautifully arched brows, I wondered to myself, *Isn't that where she's really belonging?*

And then I noticed again her red, chapped hands touching that fragile cup. Suddenly the roughness of our kitchen with its constant smell of lard for frying mixed with the smell of sweat, the sound of Mama's taters sizzling in the skillet, the sight of our plain, unfinished furniture, and the feel of that puncheon floor under my feet—all of that come rushing back, pushing out any seeing of what might've been, should've been?—beyond our window. Out of reach.

Mama jerked like she'd woke from a dream. She handed me the precious cup of violets. "Best be gettin' back to work. Ain't got no time for standin' here dreamin'. Put the cup on the mantel, Rachael. It'll be out o' harm's way there an' still easy for the seein'." She moved back to the stove and her cooking, wiping her brow with the back of her hand.

The change in her—and me—made me feel out of sorts for a moment. And here I was thinking and wondering and dreaming all sorts of silly things again. How I wished I could ask Mama if she'd ever done them things. *Or am I the onliest one?*

"Daddy tell ye the chicken boat come in?" Mama asked, breaking into my silent worries.

My eyes lit up with excitement. "No! When?"

"Heared tell 'bout her comin' last night. She ought to be in for sure this mornin'."

I thought about the big steamboat that come down the river several times every year. She was old, worn down, and dirty with grime, but we always looked forward to her coming because it was like a floating general store carrying all sorts of goods. Wondrous goods! And since the chicken boat could travel on down the river to bigger cities so quick and easy like, the men on the chicken boat were right eager to swap them goods for our produce, meat, and eggs and such, whatever we had plenty of just then. The general stores here in town didn't give us near as much for swapping as the chicken boat did. I started into washing up the eggs, knowing they'd give me even more if they were clean and fresh looking.

"I seen you gathered up the eggs already," Mama said. "You milked the cows yet?"

"Yes, Mama."

"How many eggs you get?"

"Let's see . . . two, four . . . ten, fourteen today! And countin' yesterday's, I think we got nearly four dozen all together! What you be needin' me to buy?"

Mama sighed. I knew she never liked to think on what we were needing. Especially since it seemed like we were always needing something and had no money to buy it neither. "Best be gettin' some kerosene. Won't be long before it'll be right warm lightin' a fire of a evenin'." I helped Mama by holding open the warming doors while she moved the biscuits up from the oven. "An' you be needin' some blouses seein's how you've 'bout outgrowed ever one you got. Ain't goin' to be able to use no more flour sacks neither. Got to get us some yard goods."

"How much kerosene and yard goods you be wantin'?"

"Get two gallons o' kerosene. It be ten cents a gallon at the Hickmans' so's you be knowin' how to dicker. Then swap for whatever yard goods they'll give ye. Should get least two yards, I reckon."

I felt a rush of excitement again. *Two yards. Mama oughta be able to make two blouses for me with that*! I thought to myself.

"Oughta have a bit left over for stick candy. Whatever ye get, save half for Andy, you hear?"

"Yes, Mama. Thank you." I thought about the stick candy and what a treat it'd be, but a grape Nehi sure sounded better. I shook off that idea though, knowing one bottle of Nehi cost a whole nickel.

After Daddy'd read from the Bible (he was still reading from the Psalms) and we'd finished breakfast, I helped Mama do up the dishes and then went over to Granny Mandy's to see if she was wanting to go to the chicken boat with me. She looked a bit tired but said though her rheumatism was still paining her, it was better. Since she wasn't needing anything, I headed on out the door, promising to come over later in the evening if I got my chores done early enough.

Me and Andy hitched a ride into town with Daddy. Andy was still put out with me, and especially so when he heard I was getting out of school and going to the chicken boat too. He pulled that old hat down over his face again, so I teased him that I'd plumb forgot what his face looked like anymore seeing how all I ever saw was that old hat. He didn't appreciate my teasing much.

Daddy pulled Old Dean up to the post office, and then I headed on down the main road through town to the river. Soon as I passed Verna

Mae's house I could spy the chicken boat. She wasn't putting out pillars of black smoke from them big stacks right now, but she was still mighty dirty looking all over. The big wheel in back looked so rickety that I wondered how it could ever go around well enough to push her on down the river. And though I was sure she used to be some sort of color, now I could best describe her by saying she just looked dull. Gray maybe. But mostly dull. Didn't make no difference, though, and I smiled to myself. Even though she looked awful, she still looked beautiful to me!

I skipped the rest of the way to the gangplank (Nellie and Verna Mae would've just had fits if they'd caught me skipping, scolding that I was certainly past acting like such a young'un) and nearly jostled the eggs in my excitement. I frantically checked them to make sure I hadn't broken none. *You best be settlin' down,* I lectured myself. *You won't be swappin' for nothin' if you bust them eggs*!

"Mornin', Rachael."

I looked up to see Miz Smith, Nellie's mama, coming down the gangplank. "Good mornin', Miz Smith! Ain't it a fine day for the chicken boat to come?"

"Reckon so, though seems any day would be a fine one to me." I nodded in agreement. "Yer daddy an' mama say anythin' 'bout the meetin' last night?"

Her question brought back sharply all the uncertainties I had felt hovering over me. I glanced up at the sky, squinting at a cloud that had suddenly cut off all the bright sunlight. "No, they didn't say much atall. I guess they's waitin' to see what's goin' to happen. Daddy ain't much for jawin' on somethin' 'til he's done thought things through right well. Guess he's still studyin' on it all."

She laughed, but not a real laugh. I never did like the sound of laughs like that. "Last night folks surely wasn't waitin' to jaw on it! Most everbody were talkin' 'bout them Yankees and what they's up to—no good, prob'ly! 'Specially since everbody knows Yankees don't know manure from molasses." She pointed a finger at me, jostlin' her basket of purchases around. "Mister Smith says not one of 'em is settin' one foot on our land, now I can say that for truth! 'Course now, iffin they was to do all them good things they's promisin'—buildin' a fine lake an' all. An' what was it they's sayin' 'bout pickin' one farm for demonstratin'?"

I opened my mouth to answer Miz Smith, but that's as far as I got. Talking with Nellie's mama meant you spent most time listening and precious little time talking. And just because she'd asked you a question wasn't meaning she'd be waiting for no answer neither. I figured I might as well just set back and listen a spell.

"Well, I done tol' Mister Smith, I said, just these here words now, 'Ain't no better farm to be usin' than this here Smith farm!' An' I can say that for truth too! Plenty folks I was speakin' to last night was right agreein' with me. Mister Smith be one fine farmer and our land's got tolerable good soil too. Folks in this county be choosin' a right sound farm iffin they be choosin' us. But I best be headin' on home with what I done traded for. Can't stand round all day, wastin' time. Good day, Rachael!"

"Bye, Miz Smith." I watched her go, noticing that she'd only toted her basket a few steps when she latched onto Miz Buttram, asking her about the meeting. I figured she were jawing on it enough to even up for Daddy's silence. And then I laughed to myself—a real laugh!

Looking around, I saw people moving about everywhere. Seemed like every inch of that whole boat was covered with either folks or goods of some sort. I lingered by the ready-made clothes awhile, not daring to touch anything, but I sure enjoyed looking at them. The added touches of ribbons, bows, tiny buttons, and metal zippers were so tempting to feel and explore with my fingers that I kept clutching my basket tighter and tighter just to keep my itching fingers busy. The shoes were most interesting too. There was even a pair of bright blue ones—the same color as them violets I'd just picked. Was I having a time picturing them on my feet!

Couldn't help wandering over to the candy counter neither after noticing the icebox with a sign that said, "Drink Nehi and Coca-Cola, 5 cents!" That "Co-Cola," as we called it, was fairly new to Jordan's Bend. I hadn't had any yet, but Verna Mae'd told me she thought it was tolerable. She didn't think it was good as a grape Nehi though. I didn't see how anything could be better'n a grape Nehi.

There were all kinds of newfangled things for the kitchen too. Kitchens that had electricity, that is. There were electric mixers, toasters, waffle irons, orange juicers, and a stove that was the prettiest shiny white. I reached out to stroke my fingers over its smooth surface, shaking my head at the difference from our grimy black wood stove. I studied on a percolator for a spell, wondering what all them separating parts did and just how they all worked. One of them even promised to make coffee and toast at the same time. A "perc-o-toaster" it was called. I was thinking that me and Mama could fix Daddy biscuits for many years coming for the asking price of nearly twelve dollars.

They even had one of them refrigerators. Verna Mae's mama had a icebox, but it needed a block of ice in the compartment at the top of the cabinet and Verna Mae had to empty the drip pan all the time too. But this white one (it was shiny like the stove) didn't need a block of ice or drip pan. It was a genuine electric one with a motor that drove the "compressor." At least that's what the advertising sign said. Also said it was made by B.H.T. (wonder what them letters stood for?) and it had a round, funny-looking thing on top called a "radiator." It was mighty small compared to our springhouse, but I couldn't help but think I wouldn't be missing running to that springhouse when it was so cold outside that Mama's dishwater'd freeze as soon as she flung it out the back door.

I was leaning way over, feeling around the refrigerator's legs and the bottom of its door (*How could it feel warm outside and yet be cold on the inside? Didn't make no sense atall.*) when I suddenly noticed a right familiar pair of feet next to mine. I jerked straight up to look right into Tommy Lee's eyes. Tommy Lee's doe's eyes.

He grinned at me. "You figurin' on climbin' in there somehow? Or maybe you be lookin' for where the spring comes in?!"

"Ain't thinkin' no such things! Well, not just them things." I felt my face redden again. Why did I always have to do that when Tommy Lee was with me? "I was wonderin' though how such a thing could be warm on the outside and yet cold on the inside. Don't make much sense to me," I said, shaking my head in bewilderment.

"Easy," Tommy Lee said, leaning back against the refrigerator and crossing his arms.

I tucked the basket of eggs farther back by my elbow and then crossed my arms. "Ha! You don't know neither!" I challenged him.

"Do so. See this rope here? Called the electric cord." He pointed it out to me and where it went. "Fits into what's called a outlet. That's where this refrigerator gets its 'lectricity. Goes through this here cord into the refrigerator an' the machine in here makes it cold." Tommy Lee crossed his arms again, looking at me importantly.

I could feel myself screwing up my face just like O.A.'s always doing. "Tommy Lee, none of that makes sense. How's this here old chicken boat gettin' 'lectricity?"

"Look up there." He pointed to wires overhead that stretched from a pole on land over to the boat. "Comes right through that there wire."

"Oh." I still wasn't convinced about the rest though. "But how can 'lectricity go through all them wires an' cords an' such?"

"Just does. Like happened to Ben Franklin, 'member?"

"'Course I do! I recollect that story from when we was just little'uns!"

I knew he was just teasing me, but I still wasn't about to admit that Tommy Lee knew more about this here refrigerator than I did. "Well, how can the machine in this refrigerator make it cold in there? Ever machine or engine I've ever knowed gets mighty hot, not cold!" Tommy Lee started in to fidgeting a little, and so I just kept right on going. "Ain't you never been round Mister Hickman's truck when he just come back from Crawleysville? Top of that hood's so hot you could fry a slab of ham on it! So why don't this machine get hot too?" Now I leaned back and crossed my arms. Guess I'd just showed him!

We just stood there and eyed each other awhile. I knew I was concentrating like anything on what Tommy Lee was going to say next, and I was sure he was doing the right same thing. For once I was determined to—and was sure I already had—outsmart him.

Suddenly Tommy Lee dropped his arms and shrugged his shoulders. "Guess you be figurin' right! Can't be cold in there! Let's us go look at somethin' that works." He reached for my arm and started pulling me towards another section of the chicken boat.

"Now wait a minute here!" I struggled to stop without getting in the way of other folks. "'Course it has to work, for goodness sakes! Them government men was even talkin' 'bout gettin' one for Jordan's Bend. They wouldn't've done that if the thing didn't work atall!" Folks were pushing around us and pretty soon we were moving right along with them, like we didn't have no choice in where we were going. Except for the fact that Tommy Lee was still pulling on my arm.

"Nope. Engines gets hot, not cold," Tommy Lee threw back at me over his shoulder. "You be right, Rachael. Must be like a oven in them things."

I looked away from where we were heading for a moment to study on his face. He looked right serious, and I was getting just plain aggravated now. "Tommy Lee!" I pushed over to the side of the aisle for a minute and turned to face him eye-to-eye. Putting both hands on my hips, I then gave him the sternest look I could muster up. "Them refrigerators gets cold inside! Now that's all they is to it! You hear?"

The grin started slowly, beginning in them eyes of his first, I guess. They started in to twinkling, and then his eyebrows seemed to ease on down a bit. Finally, the corners of his mouth started in to pulling just barely until he went ahead and let loose, giving room for a grin to move all over that ornery face of his. "Tol' you so! I always did like a gal who was a-arguin' for my side! Jest like my daddy says though." He rolled his eyes and sighed. "Sometimes you got to convince the gal that you's on the same side!"

I threw back my head and laughed at him. "Ain't no fair though. You tricked me!"

He took my hand then and guided me around displays of goods and folks packed in everywhere. I was still giggling when I asked him, "Where are you takin' me, Tommy Lee? Or maybe I should be sayin' draggin' me? If I break these eggs—"

"You jest hang onto them eggs for a spell more. We's jest headin' right over here to my most favorite place on the whole chicken boat!"

"And where's that? Are we headin' back to the refrigerators?!"

Tommy Lee glanced at me and grinned again. "Why no! But we is goin' to somethin' that keeps things cold. De-licious things cold!" His eyes were dancing with excitement, and I couldn't help but laugh at him again.

When we rounded the corner I spied the candy counter and the Nehi sign once more. Tommy Lee pulled me all the way up to the counter with him and announced loudly, "We'll take two grape Nehi's please." He dug around in his overall pocket a minute and then plunked two nickels down on the glass.

The man behind the counter fished two bottles out of the icebox and, after flipping off the caps, handed them to Tommy Lee. Peering at us over the top of his glasses and scooping up the coins, he said, "Thankee, sir. Enjoy them thar refreshin' drinks."

"Thankee to you, sir!" Tommy Lee said proudly. He handed one to me, bowing and touching his straw hat. Of course I had to giggle again at him. There wasn't no helping it atall!

We both lifted our bottles to take the first sip, and the sweet taste set my cheeks to tingling so much so that it was near to hurting! "Tommy Lee, ever since I started out to come here today I been thinkin' 'bout a grape Nehi." I stared down at my feet again, avoiding looking into his eyes. "I don't know how you knowed that I sure been wantin' one. And it tastes ever bit as good as my dreamin' on it. No, even better!" I paused for just a minute to catch my breath. "Thank ye." I glanced up at him with a note of seriousness about my eyes, and then just as quickly I looked away when I felt that unwanted knot in my throat. In just a matter of a few minutes Tommy Lee'd made me feel excited, frustrated, stubborn—to the point of being angry!—purely joyful, full of laughter and fun, and now so special. *Is this what livin' with the man you love is like?* I asked myself. *Could I stand feelin' them things over an' over all the time? Or does a body fairly burst for all the feelin' of them?*

When I'd gathered enough courage to look at him again (after thanking the good Lord that Tommy Lee couldn't hear my thoughts), he smiled at me and nodded his head. "Let's us go over to the railin' an' drink our Nehi's there. Be kind o' fun to look down in the water."

I followed him again through a good number of folks. The chicken boat was getting busier and busier so I knew I better be swapping my eggs before too much longer. Mama'd expect me to do some looking, but she wouldn't spell my wasting too much time—or letting these here eggs spoil right in my basket.

Tommy Lee finally found a spot along the side where there weren't no folks pushing to get here and there. He looked out over the water and, after taking off his straw hat, rested his elbows on the railing. "Water's mighty muddy lookin' today. My daddy can tell how much rain we've done got just by lookin' at the river." Tommy Lee squinted his eyes and rubbed his chin, drawing my attention to the stubble of whiskers that was sprinkled there. "I'd guess . . . um . . . a good inch and a half done fell yesterday." Then he looked at me and winked. "'Course that's what our rain barrel was holdin' this mornin' too!"

I grinned back at him, putting the basket of eggs safely by my feet and leaning over the railing too. It felt smooth to my skin, and I wondered how many folks before us had leaned over this railing the same way. "They's somethin' special 'bout watchin' them tiny waves lappin', ain't they?" I took another sip of my Nehi and sighed for a sudden longing to just set here and stare—the whole day maybe. "Been too long since I visited Lookin' Point. That's my place where I go to set an' watch an' think."

"I climbed up my shagbark hickory this mornin'. Had me a good thinkin' on that meetin' last night." Tommy Lee stared at the muddy greenish-blue water, not even blinking in his concentrating. He pushed back that lock of hair again, out of pure habit, I was sure.

"Daddy wouldn't say much atall last night. Didn't speak on it this mornin' neither." I spilled out everybody's responses in a rush. "Andy said you couldn't see nothin' but daylight through their Yankee words, and Miz Smith said this mornin' that they wants to be the demonstration farm."

Tommy Lee suddenly looked over at me. "What do you think 'bout it?"

I looked away from them searching eyes of his to the safety of the Tennessee's meandering. "Can't rightly say, Tommy Lee. My thoughts is such a tumble that I—I just don't know!" I realized I couldn't even put to words all my confusing thoughts. "'Course I ain't never trusted no Yankee. Ain't likely to start now. But I liked Mister Whitaker. I think. At least, somehow I want to." I shook my head in frustration at myself. "Shucks, Tommy Lee. I ain't makin' no sense atall. I s'pose I just want things to stay the same. No, go back to the way they was. With James Junior to home. And Mama not seemin' so far away all the time. You know, in her thinkin' like, and sometimes Daddy can't even seem to reach her!" I took another drink before asking, "Is them Yankees really goin' to do all them things they said?"

"Yes'm. I reckon so."

"But . . ." I stopped, realizing I was beginning to put words to things I didn't even want to think about.

"But what?"

"Oh, nothin'. Just somethin' O.A. keeps on sayin'."

"Andy has a way o' knowin' when someone's measurin' his corn in their basket."

His words startled me, and I felt my stomach tighten. "He says they's changes all round us. Too many. Too quick like."

Tommy Lee didn't say anything as we both stared at the water below us. He finished his Nehi, holding it upside down a good while to get every last bit of the sweet drink. And then suddenly he rared back and threw that empty bottle as far as he could down the muddy water. It made a soft *splunk* sound when it hit.

"Why'd you do that? You know that man what sold it to you'd buy it back. Or yer mama could use that bottle for sure!" I looked at him in amazement, waiting for his reasoning.

"This here Tennessee River's been goin' by this piece o' land for years an' years. No tellin' what all she's seen come an' go this way." He nodded to the quickly disappearing bottle. "I reckon that bottle'll change this riverfront—how it looks from here—for 'bout one minute. An' then this river'll be on her way jest like she was before I throwed that tiny ol' thing in." He stood up straight and looked intently at me, pushing back his hair again. "This here river ain't changin' none, Rachael. Not really, no matter what them Yankees does to her. Reckon we got to think 'bout all what's happenin'—'bout us what lives here in Jordan's Bend—the same way."

I nodded to him, feeling pulled into his thoughts by them doe's eyes. And I wanted to believe him. Oh, I did.

The sounds of folks dickering brought me back to my needing to get my choring done. I leaned over to pick up my basket. "I best be swappin' these here eggs and headin' to home. What are you be tradin' for?"

"Me an' Daddy was lookin' at the tools when I seen you comin'. That's when he give me the money for the Nehi's. Said ever man ought to buy his gal a Nehi."

I felt myself blushing something awful at the mention of "his gal" and looked away from Tommy Lee in embarrassment. *Does everone think on me as Tommy Lee's gal?* I wondered.

"Well, I best be goin' 'bout my business. You figure yer daddy still be round here somewheres?" I looked off into the crowds of folks moving about, wondering who else might be on the chicken boat this morning. It surely looked like most everybody in the whole county was here.

"I reckon he's still lookin' at the same axe head we was interested in before. Daddy always studies on things a good while before he trades." Tommy Lee plopped the straw hat back on his head again. "Be seein' you at school come tomorra. Bye, Rachael."

"Tell your daddy I said *hey*." Tommy Lee was already on his way before I remembered to add, "And thank ye again for the Nehi!" I caught one last glimpse of him waving at me before the crowds swallowed him up. I smiled to myself, recollecting the fun we'd had and the reassuring talk. And then I set my feet to moving on myself, heading for the dairy and produce stand right off.

I did well with the swapping, getting the kerosene and two and one-half yards of the prettiest yard goods. One yard was plain white, but the other one and a half yards had tiny light blue flowers all over it. I was sure that Mama'd be pleased with it, and I moved on to the candy counter once again with excitement.

After I'd picked out some saw logs and peppermint candy, I tucked the candy in my basket, pushing it way back on my arm, and picked up a gallon of kerosene with each hand. It took some adjusting to get everything situated just so, but finally I felt ready to set out and I headed on down the gangplank. I turned back to look at the chicken boat once more, wishing I could spend the whole day wandering her decks, exploring her treasures. *But wishin' doesn't get the needin' to be doin' done,* I could hear Mama lecturing. So without another glance back, I resolutely set out. Again I saw several folks I knew, but I only took time to say *hey*, exchange a few words about the Yankees (seemed that's all anybody was talking about today), and then moved on. I figured I'd been gone long enough. Mama'd be put out if I didn't get home before she noticed there was more chores to be doing.

I walked along the path by the road, enjoying the lovely spring weather, listening to the birds chirping, and spying flowers shooting up everywhere. I wanted to explore everything like it was brand-spanking new this morning! I lifted my head to smell the freshness in the air (*was that honeysuckle I was smellin' already too?*) and then I moved off the beaten path a bit to enjoy the soft clover against my feet. I waved at folks as I passed by, exchanging *heys* with Mister and Miz Harris again. I could hear Miz Harris hollering "Eh? What's that?" long after I'd gone round the bend, and I chuckled to myself for a good while.

I stopped for a spell, putting down the gallons of kerosene to stretch out my fingers and rub out the aching where the handles of them kerosene jugs ate into the palms. Then, readjusting the handles and hugging my basket to me, I caught sight of the Nehi bottle again and that set me to grinning from ear to ear. *Tommy Lee's gal? Tommy Lee's gal.* I let it echo back and forth in my mind. "Tommy Lee's gal," I said right out loud finally, and then giggled. *That sounds so fine*, I thought to myself. *Right fine!*

When a bluebird fluttered by me, I followed it with delight. I've always been partial to watching bluebirds just to gaze at the amazing brightness of their blue, but today it seemed even more beautiful. As I stared at the glorious color, drinking in its beauty, I kept glancing around for the mama. Bluebirds are like redbirds in that they most always fly together. *I wonder if they're buildin' their nest?* I thought to myself. The less colorful mama lit in a redbud tree before flying on up the road, the papa soon following. I smiled at them, silently wishing them as much happiness as I felt today. And then all the loveliness around me just fell away to nothing as I saw what was parked off the road ahead, just beneath the glorious splashes of blue of the disappearing birds.

The TVA car was setting on our property.

4 *This is not hell, nor say I damn.*
I know not who nor why I am
But I am walking with a lamb
And all the tears that ever were
Are gently dried on his soft fur.

I couldn't say how long I stood there, staring. Seemed it took forever before the ground beneath my feet come together again so I could walk on it. Surely it had fallen away to nothing for a spell. I looked down at it, stupidly, almost expecting it to be moving at least, unsteady at best. *You needs be gettin' to home, Rachael,* I told myself, trying to bring myself back to my senses. *Walk!* I ordered.

I concentrated on putting one foot in front of the other, focusing on the familiar and therefore comforting feeling of the soft clay squishing between my toes. But as I kept staring down at my feet, memories of the last time I stared at my feet come rushing back, making tears push to spill out. *Oh, Tommy Lee,* I cried inwardly, *promise me you's right. Promise me them changes won't make no difference! Promise me the changes won't make no real changes!*

When the bumper of the hated car came into my line of seeing, I stopped. *Don't have to mean anythin',* I reassured myself. *'Course. That were it. They's only here to look over McKenney property 'cause of what they heared last night—that it's the best soil here 'bouts. And they's wantin' a demonstration farm, like Miz Smith said. Only it's goin' to be our farm what's to be doin' the demonstratin', not the Smiths'!* Closin' my eyes a minute, I took a deep breath and then walked around the car.

"Hey, Rachael."

I started at the voice, recognizing Granny Mandy and yet wondering how I could've been so deep in my thinking that I hadn't even noticed her. She was leaning against her fence, a hoe in one hand; she'd obviously been working in her garden. "Hey, Granny Mandy." I tried to tuck away all them worries, concentrating on making my voice sound easy. "Been workin' your truck patch, I see."

She shifted her position at the fence, turning slightly to glance over to the garden. "Blessed weeds. Never could understand how they can be growin' in one day what takes ever other plant a week or more. Cursed with stubbornness, they is." Granny Mandy nodded her bonnet towards the TVA car. "Speakin' on stubbornness, seen them Yankees drive up here. Headed right up to be pesterin' yer mama an' then she rung the bell fer yer daddy to be comin'. Don't them Yankees know a body's got better to do of a day than set round an' jaw with the likes of them? What they be wantin' anyhow? Ever Yankee I ever knowed be wantin' to take somethin' from us." She narrowed her eyes, frowning at the offending car.

"Might be they wants to help us, Granny Mandy. They was speakin' of a library. Right here in Jordan's Bend. And they's talkin' 'bout electricity in ever home!" I knew I was running on and on, but I couldn't hardly stop myself. I suppose I was trying to convince myself too. "I seen the prettiest electric stove on the chicken boat; I can just imagine how beautiful it would look in Mama's kitchen. And—"

"Hep us? Land's sake, child!" She smacked her hand on the rough paling fence. "Ain't no Yankee what ever said he was a-goin' to hep us Southerners but didn't swindle, rob, an' then plumb lick the jelly jar clean in the end! 'Sides, I ain't a-pinin' fer no e-lec-tric-i-ty"—she hitched up her nose and strung out the word like she was handling one of John Evert's messed diapers—"no more'n I'm a-wantin' a tel-o-phone. Only a fool Yankee'd be itchin' to have him a bell in his house that any other fool in the whole U-nited States could ring!"

I had to grin at her reasoning, but I wasn't giving up on convincing her just yet. "Mister Whitaker was at the meetin' last night, Granny Mandy. An' he were right nice. You would've liked him. Mister Sherman too." I winced as soon as I said that name, knowing what Granny's reaction would be, sure as anything.

"Sherman! Now iffin that name don't tell ye somethin', Rachael, then ye be believin' what the thievin' Yankee said when yer grandaddy caught him stealin' his most favorite mule!"

Now I knew no Yankee had ever tried to steal anything from my grandaddy. For one thing, Grandaddy would've shot his head off before the Yankee had a chance to mutter anything. So I smiled at her again, knowing one of Granny's tales was coming again for sure. "What'd the Yankee say, Granny Mandy?"

"Said he were only stealin' the bit an' bridle. Weren't his fault they just happened to be a mule inside 'em!"

We laughed together, and I suddenly knew how much I needed her teasing. Seemed like Granny was always telling a story just when a worry that was growing inside me was about to take root and grow like the nettles always do. Nasty plant, those nettles.

"Good tradin' at the chicken boat?" she asked, eyeing my basket and kerosene.

"Yes'm. Swapped my eggs for two gallons," I showed her, lifting up each one in turn and then setting them back on the ground. "An' a whole two and a half yards of these here yard goods, Granny Mandy. Ain't they pretty?"

She looked at the material and nodded, saying, "Best not touch it. Got mud clean up to my elbows, I reckon. Them blue flowers'll look right nice on ye, Rachael." Then she spotted the empty Nehi bottle and candy. "Land, you done even better. 'Nough left over to get candy an' one o' them Nehi's too. You been sweet-talkin' them what's on that chicken boat, gal?!"

I felt myself blushing again under Granny Mandy's teasing grin. There just wasn't any way out of this one. "Tommy Lee bought it for me."

"Well, now. That be right nice!" Her eyes seemed to go all soft and warm for a moment as she looked at me. "I recollect the first time my James Henry brung me somethin' special when he come courtin'. Was a bouquet of his mama's lilies tied up with a ribbon. Kept that ribbon in my Bible for so many years it plumb fell to dust. I can still recollect its color though. Rose-colored pink it was." She touched my hand lightly. "You keep that bottle. It's a special 'un." Standing up straight again, Granny Mandy grabbed the hoe with both of her weathered hands. "Best be gettin' back to my weedin'. Ain't about to pull themselves out o' the ground. Tell yer mama I said *hey*. Oh, an' tell her too I said not to feed them dogs 'til she sees if them Yankees is stayin' fer supper!"

Laughing at her once again, I called out, "'Bye, Granny Mandy," and then waved at her as I started across the road. Dreading to turn and see the hated car and then especially fearing what was being said up at our house, I dallied longer than I should. Finally I gave myself another order to *Walk*! and quickly scurried up the path to the kitchen. It was near dinnertime, and I knew Mama'd already be at the stove.

Just as I was reaching for the door, I heard Mister Whitaker's voice. I froze, arm raised, completely in a quandary over not wanting to hear, to walk on in, or to be caught eavesdropping like a young'un. The problem was settled for me when I heard Daddy and Mister Whitaker's voices fade as they walked towards the breezeway and on out the front door. Slowly and cautiously I eased open the door, cringing at its familiar creeking sound.

I saw Mama right off. She was bending over the stove, stirring what looked to be a kettle of pinto beans. "Hey, Mama. Got us some fine goods this mornin'." I set the kerosene by the back door—they were getting tolerable heavy in my hands and it surely felt good to plunk them down for good—and then I set the basket on the table. I peered out the door to the breezeway, noting Daddy standing outside still with Mister Whitaker. "Um, seen Mister Whitaker was here." I took a deep breath. "Is he wantin' somethin' from us?"

Mama moved over to the table, lifting the yard goods from my basket and holding them up to examine the cloth. "Jest come to say he be droppin' by after supper tonight. This here be a fine choice, Rachael. Over two yards is it, too?" To my answering nod she appeared very pleased. "Make you fine blouses, it will."

"But Mama, is Mister Whitaker comin' to see us? What's he wantin'?" Normally I would have been excitedly showing everything I had to Mama, but her attention to the yard goods only frustrated me when I felt so anxious about the Yankee and his coming here.

"Don't rightly know. Reckon we'll find out tonight." I fidgeted, watching Mama fish around in the basket some more, and then she pulled out the candy and the Nehi bottle. "Rachael! Jest where you be gettin' the money to buy a Nehi? I declare, child, we's strugglin' for every penny an' you go an'—"

"I didn't, Mama! Tommy Lee done bought it for me!" Tears instantly stung my eyes, and I blinked them back. Memories of Granny Mandy's reaction to the bottle compared to Mama's flitted across my thoughts, and again I swallowed hard to keep from crying.

Mama let the bottle drop back into the basket, sighing as she let it fall from her hands. She rubbed the back of her neck, closing her eyes as she did so. I kept glancing from her face to the Nehi bottle, fearing to catch her eye. "Seems too much is pressin' these days, Rachael. I don't always be . . . don't be measurin' things as they really is, as I know they would be. I should've knowed you wouldn't've done such a thing." She looked over at me, searching my face for understanding, it seemed. "Twas right kind o' Tommy Lee to do that. You have a nice time with him on the chicken boat?" She went back to her cooking, stirring the beans once again.

"Yes, Mama. I weren't expectin' the Nehi atall," I assured her nervously. "And the chicken boat had so many excitin' things to look at. I had such fun until, well, until I saw the Yankees' car settin' by the road. Mister Whitaker didn't say nothin' 'bout why he's comin' here?"

"No. Yer daddy asked him, but he said he'd rather explain it all tonight when he come." We heard Daddy come in the door then, and we both turned to him, questioning silently, waiting.

Daddy shrugged his shoulders. "Ain't sayin' nothin' jest yet. Said him and that Mister Sherman would both be back 'bout seven o'clock."

"Did you invite 'em to supper?" I asked, knowing him and Mama most likely had.

Daddy nodded to me as he pulled out his chair at the table and set down. "Said they's much appreciatin' the invite, but wasn't wantin' to bother us none." He looked into me and Mama's concerned faces. "Ain't no sense frettin'. Prob'ly no more'n wantin' to talk 'bout farmin' an' the soil an' all. He did ask a good many questions 'bout our soil. Them beans ready yet, Miz McKenney? Sure smells good!"

I fetched bowls and spoons for us and then opened the warming oven's doors, knowing Mama must've made cornbread too. I cut the cornbread while Mama served up the beans. "Mister Whitaker was askin' 'bout our soil then, Daddy?" I asked. "Do you s'pose he's wantin' us to put in for the demonstration farm?" The hope and relief I felt spilled over, making that cornbread smell better'n any I'd ever served up before. Suddenly I realized just how hungry I was.

"Could be. Don't rightly know if I'm interested though. Have to be thinkin' on it." I put a big piece of cornbread in Daddy's bowl, and then Mama ladled beans on top of it.

"What am I a-thinkin'?" Mama said. "Nearly forgettin' the chow-chow. Can't eat beans without it. Rachael, run an' fetch some from the springhouse."

"Yes, Mama. Be needin' anythin' else?"

"Don't reckon so. Jest hurry back so's yer daddy's food don't get cold."

I rushed out the door, letting it bang behind me, and run for the springhouse. When I opened the door, the rush of cold air washed over me, making me close my eyes a moment in the pleasuring of the feeling and smells there. The jars of chowchow were stored on a shelf, and I snatched up one quickly.

I had firmly shut the springhouse door behind me when I happened to glance down the hill to the road. Mister Whitaker stood next to his car, a map spread across the hood. He was bent over it, one hand appearing to be tracing a line across the paper. When he looked up my way, I quickly hid behind a bush, not wanting him to see me staring. Then peeking out cautiously, I saw he was folding up the map and climbing back into his car.

Why's he lookin' at a map? An' what's it to do with our farm? My thoughts tumbled over one another again, pressing at me for answers, easy answers. *Well, you'll be knowin' them tonight,* I told myself. *Like Daddy said, ain't no sense frettin' 'bout it now.*

When I'd set down to dinner with Daddy and Mama, we prayed together, Daddy asking for God's hand of protection on James Junior. And then he asked for wisdom and understanding for the work that Mister Whitaker and Mister Sherman was about to do. I'd thought on hating them (because they're Yankees and all); I'd thought on fearing them (though I wasn't even ready to put thoughts to the whys of it); and I'd thought on liking them (on account of helping farmers and the library and all). But I surely hadn't thought on praying for them. Don't know that I could put it to words like Daddy was doing. Or if I even wanted to.

"Rachael, I be needin' you to work the garden after dinner," Mama said, passing me the slaw.

"Granny Mandy was weedin' hers when I come by."

"Almost forgot," Daddy said. "Mister Whitaker wanted to know if Granny Mandy were kin. Said to ask her to come by tonight too." A grin spread slowly over his face when he added, "Asked if she could be leavin' her gun to home too!"

"What'd you tell him, Daddy?" I asked, knowing Granny Mandy were of a mind to do just what she wanted to do.

"I tole 'im ever since I could recollect, Granny Mandy done reminded me what was to be the doin'. 'Tain't never been the the other ways round that I know of!"

"You reckon she'll bring her gun?" I knew I was sounding like Andy, anxious for a scuffle.

"If Granny Mandy comes, she'll be a-totin' that gun."

"If she comes?" Mama asked. "Ain't she wantin' to know what them Yankees is up to?"

"She done tole me they's up to no good. Once Granny Mandy's made up her mind 'bout somethin', ain't nothin' goin' to change it." Daddy held out his bowl for Mama to ladle in some more beans. "'Sides, ain't likely to get Granny Mandy in the same room's a Yankee. Last one tried to step foot into her cabin ended up treed!" Daddy grinned again, shaking his head.

"Treed!" I glanced over to Mama, and she was smiling too at the memory. "Tell me the story, Daddy!"

He scooped up a big spoonful of cornbread and beans, but he paused a minute and looked over at me. "Revenuers come lookin' for stills. Don't rightly know all what happened, but yer grandaddy told me Granny Mandy had the revenuer treed by the time he got there. She were standin' under the tree, starin' up at 'im through the sight o' her gun." Daddy started chuckling. "The way yer grandaddy told it, it was days before the poor man'd come down outta that there tree too!"

I grinned at the thought of it, picturing Granny treeing Mister Sherman or Mister Whitaker. Wouldn't that be a sight! "Do you reckon she was the most riled 'cause he were lookin' for stills on their land or 'cause he was a Yankee?" Suddenly my imagining didn't seem so farfetched. We'd like to never hear what Mister Whitaker had come to say if Granny sent him up a tree!

Daddy shook his head. "Hard tellin'. All I be knowin' is, she ain't fergot it yet."

"Ain't never goin' to neither," Mama added.

I needn't have fretted over it any; Granny didn't so much as poke her nose—or the end of her gun—out her front door when Mister Whitaker and Mister Sherman parked their shiny black station wagon at the bottom of the hill that evening. A sick feeling come over my stomach, seeing it setting there again. Just didn't rightly fit in next to Mama's truck patch, the paling fence, and several rusted old tools scattered round here and there. Anything shiny and black seemed to be belonging in town somewheres. Or maybe on the chicken boat. But not on McKenney property.

The two men slowly picked their way up the hill. Daddy was waiting for them on the breezeway, keeping Ezra and Nehemiah still but certainly not quiet. They were carrying on something awful. Mister Whitaker and Mister Sherman kept glancing back towards their car like they were reassuring themselves it was still there. If Ezra or Nehemiah moved one paw off that porch, I figured we'd most likely be doing our talking while they were setting in that car and we were staring at them through the windows.

Stopping a good many steps short of the porch, Mister Sherman asked, "I assume those dogs will let us onto your porch and safely through the front door?" His beady eyes, peering through those thick glasses, glanced from Daddy to the dogs and back again to Daddy's unwavering gaze. He held a worn brown leather briefcase which he nervously rubbed between his hands.

While Daddy nodded yes and said, "Them dogs'll do whatever I be tellin' 'em to, whatever I'm a-needin' 'em to do," I noticed one of Mister Whitaker's eyebrows go up. Mister Sherman just kept on twitching nervous like as he stepped onto the porch, but I was sure Mister Whitaker hadn't missed Daddy's hint. Just the slightest smile lit on Mister Whitaker's face as he reached out to shake Daddy's hand. I smiled too.

"Mr. McKenney, this is Dr. Sherman," Mister Whitaker said.

Reaching out to firmly shake his hand, Daddy answered, "Recollect Mister Sherman from the meetin'. This here's Miz McKenney and these are two of my young'uns, Rachael and Andy. My eldest's off workin' with the CCC."

"He is? Well, that's wonderful!" Mister Whitaker's face lit up at the news. "Then he's learning many of the principles that we'll be teaching and putting into practice right here in Jordan's Bend."

Daddy motioned towards the rockers on the porch, and they all settled into them. Both men removed their citified hats (that's what Granny Mandy called anything what wasn't straw and worn), and Mister Sherman put his briefcase next to his chair. I set down on the porch itself, letting my bare feet dangle just above the packed dirt around the cabin, but O.A. was in one of his stubborn moods again. He leaned up against the house, tugging that old hat brim way down over his eyes like he most always did anymore. Ezra and Nehemiah come rubbing up against me right off, pestering me by pushing their noses under my hands for petting.

"Well, I s'pose that be fairly true," Daddy went on. "But McKenney men been handin' down how to tend this here soil for many a year now. This piece o' land be gettin' richer an' producin' more crops 'bout ever season. Soil needs carin' an' feedin' same's a newborn babe, I reckon." Daddy rocked gently as he shifted his steady gaze from Mister Whitaker to Mister Sherman. "Been learnin' my James Junior them same lessons. If that CCC can learn him even more, that be fine."

"Just what soil preservation techniques have you been implementing, Mr. McKenney?" Mister Sherman asked, then quickly corrected himself. "Umm, let me rephrase that. What have you been doing to your soil?"

Once again I bristled at the suggestion that Daddy was so uneducated that he couldn't even understand what Mister Sherman was asking. I glanced at Daddy, expecting to find anger written about his eyes, but all I saw was weariness there and something else. *Was he guarding himself somehow?* I stared down at Nehemiah and rubbed his ear to hide my frustration. *Didn't Daddy never have a need to show these Yankees he was the wisest man anywheres around these parts?*

"Been restin' fields, like you was sayin' last evenin', ever since we been tendin' this here property. Sometimes move crops around; sometimes we'uns just plain let a field go to grass for a year or two. Always knowed she'll grow better if she gets a rest."

Both Mister Sherman and Mister Whitaker looked surprised. I suppose they was plumb disappointed that Yankees hadn't thought up everything in this whole world like they were thinking. I smiled again, smugly. Glancing up at Andy, I noted he was grinning too, but as soon as he saw me looking at him he cleared his throat and put that familiar pout back on.

"Where did you learn to do these things, Mr. McKenney? I don't believe we've met anyone else in this part of the country who does that." Mister Whitaker leaned forward in the rocker like he was anxious to catch Daddy's every word. Maybe he'd finally recognized the worth of my daddy.

"Bible tells us 'bout restin' the land, Mister Whitaker. The good Lord knowed what He was tellin' way back when. Reckon He still does now."

"The Bible?"

"Says in the book of Leviticus that God done tole the Israelites they was to rest the land ever seventh year. Called a Sabbath Year." Daddy continued to rock slowly back and forth, and he kept his gaze steady upon Mister Whitaker's face. "Wasn't to be doin' no sowin' nor prunin'. That were God's year. Now the fiftieth year—she were somethin' special. The year of Jubilee!" Daddy grinned and nodded his head. "That were a time of liberty for God's people the likes of which Southerners ain't seen since Yankees done decided they couldn't keep their noses out of the South's business!"

A slow, answering grin spread across Mister Whitaker's face, but Mister Sherman looked plumb put out. He fidgeted in his rocker (the poor man didn't even know how to do them fine rockers justice) and then pulled the briefcase up onto his lap. "Now Mr. McKenney, those stories from the Bible sound quite interesting, but you know as well as I do that this is rich bottom land that gets flooded almost every year. And when it gets flooded, your land receives nourishment—nutrients, minerals, and fertilizers—from the hills above you." Mister Sherman's flighty hands poked and pulled at the briefcase's lock until it grudgingly come open. He rummaged around inside the briefcase and continued, "Scientific knowledge proves that this land is rich merely because of where it's located."

I squeezed Nehemiah's ear in my anger, and he whined, causing everyone to suddenly glance at me and then the dreaded red to rush up my face. Looking down in my embarrassment, I noticed the differences in Daddy's and them Yankees' shoes. Daddy's were rough and muddy and just nigh to wearing clean through. The big rounded toes pointed up because they were too big for him. Like all store-bought things, you took what was there and what you could afford. Mister Whitaker and Mister Sherman had shiny new brown ones with thick soles yet. But I noticed—with pleasure—that McKenney mud was clinging to them fancy shoes too.

Daddy rocked just a bit faster, but otherwise he seemed to not even have noted Mister Sherman's rudeness. He gave him a level stare again, saying, "Well, I ain't be ignorin' what the good Lord done put into the cycles of the seasons neither, Mister Sherman. But I reckon too that you'd have to be admittin' that my great-great-grandaddy done picked him one fine bit o' land." Daddy paused just a minute and took his eyes off Mister Sherman's to look towards the sloping ground by the river. "Yes'm, McKenney soil been blessed a good many ways. All by the Lord."

"I think it was blessed to have McKenneys put upon it," Mister Whitaker said firmly, crossing his arms over his chest and resting them there.

I felt a knot of warmth in my stomach spread outward, rushing to my toes, wrapping round my heart, and ending in a flush of pleasure that most likely was plain as day on my face. *Mister Whitaker did understand,* I thought to myself, the delight causing me to draw up my knees and give them a hug against my chest. *Surely he's goin' to ask Daddy now to be considerin' our homestead for the demonstratin' farm!*

For a moment all the sound we listened to was the creaking of our rocking chairs, a woodpecker's even rattling against the rotten old oak tree down by the river, and Mister Sherman shuffling papers around inside that briefcase. Finally he pulled out what he'd been searching for and handed them to Mister Whitaker. Daddy glanced at them and then leisurely looked back towards the river. I studied on his face a minute again, anxious myself to find relief there. But this time Daddy's feelings were hidden to me. Whatever he was feeling was tucked deep inside.

"Mr. McKenney, first I just want you to know that we intend to make this part of the country one of the most beautiful places in the United States. I can and will make that promise to you; this county will be enjoyed for generations to come for its beauty."

Daddy nodded. "Reckon she's right pretty already. Don't know that man can improve on what God done said was good."

Mister Whitaker grinned and answered, "You're right. Let's say we'll bring this land back to what it used to look like. Before it was stripped of its beauty by years of overproduction. Agreed?"

Again Daddy nodded.

"To accomplish this, we're going to offer you some wonderful privileges, Mr. McKenney." He leaned forward in the rocker now, looking intently from Daddy to Mama and back again. I felt my eyes follow his every move. "Your future and your children's futures will be greatly benefitted by what we're going to do for you. A better home. No more cold winds whistling through thin wood walls. How does brick or stone or cinder block sound to you? And electricity. We mentioned that at the meeting last night. Can you imagine having lights come on with a tug on a chain?"

Mister Whitaker pulled an imaginary chain hanging in the air. Me and Mama watched him intently; O.A. still had that hat pulled down, but the front crease of the brim was pointed in Mister Whitaker's direction. But Daddy—Daddy was still rocking easy like and staring towards the river. *Was he searchin' for somethin' down that way?* I noticed the woodpecker again.

"How about heat at the turn of a button on an electric stove?" Mister Whitaker went on. "No more cutting wood, carrying it inside, putting it into the firebox, and waiting for it to catch. All sorts of electric appliances. There's just no end to the benefits from having electricity—some we can't even imagine yet."

I felt myself being caught up in his excitement, wondering what it would be like to have all them things like I'd just looked at on the chicken boat. *Would I like havin' one of them refrigerators right in the kitchen? Would Mama ever use a electric stove? Granny Mandy grumbles about using that "newfangled wood stove," as she calls it still.*

"As we said the other night too, we're going to see everyone in Jordan's Bend benefit from this project." Mister Whitaker began listing them by counting them out on his fingers. "Library. Medical services. The infant mortality rate here must be improved." To Mama's questioning glance he explained, "Deaths of newborns and young babies must be diminished. We want to see qualified doctors here—and a hospital—to save many that would otherwise die." He moved to the next finger. "Improved schools." I leaned even closer, anxious to hear what he was meaning by this. "This area is in desperate need of catching up with the rest of the country's school systems. It's hard to believe that you don't even have a high school yet. We hope to see one begun as soon as possible."

I noticed Mama and O.A. both glance over to me for a moment, but I didn't acknowledge either one of them. I couldn't take my eyes off of Mister Whitaker's. *A high school. Here in Jordan's Bend*! My mind seemed to be spinning in endless circles as it tried to bring together all the meanings of it: *I could attend. I could become a teacher. I wouldn't have to be leavin' Mama or Daddy or Andy. Or Tommy Lee*! Now I was finding it hard to be setting there much longer. Instead, I wanted to be jumping up and shouting out the joy of it—a high school! The woodpecker was silent now, but a chorus of sparrows was singing somewhere in the distance. Even the birds were singing out my joy!

In my excitement I'd missed some of what Mister Whitaker was saying, but I knew it couldn't have been anything near as wonderful as what he'd already said. I hugged my knees once again and concentrated on his words. "So you can see, Mr. and Mrs. McKenney, that we really do want what is best for you and for this community. We're here to help and assist you in any way possible." He glanced from Daddy to Mama and then to O.A. and me with a real kind of caring look on his face. Mister Sherman wasn't looking at anything except his feet. Something that Granny Mandy'd once said—about not putting trust in a man who wouldn't look you square in the eye—flickered across my mind. I was glad that Mister Whitaker faced Daddy square.

"Mr. Sherman, give these fine folks the exciting news," Mister Whitaker continued, after setting back in the rocker once again and staring off to where Daddy'd been looking.

I hid my grin behind my knees. *He was goin' to say it now. Our farm had been chosen*!

"But Bob, surely you'd rather . . ." Mister Sherman straightened up and clutched the arms of his rocker.

"No, Dr. Sherman, I believe you're better suited for this. And they'll be directly under your supervision—although I'll be helping out, of course." Mister Whitaker rocked gently back and forth as he calmly handed the papers back to Mister Sherman. The persistent woodpecker had started up once more. It reminded me of the way Uncle Evert sings. Always on one note, the same note.

Mister Sherman cleared his throat and fidgeted with the papers again. His eyes kept shifting from Mister Whitaker to the papers and back again. *Cowardly nubbin' of a man*! I fumed to myself. *You can't even be spittin' out the words you be needin' to say. Don't make no sense atall that you can't be tellin' us 'bout this demonstratin' farm.*

And then I noticed Daddy's eyes narrowing, and I saw the same look on his face what I'd seen so many times before, the same accusing and knowing gaze that could make Andy squirm and look so frazzled that even his shadow appeared to have holes. It was the stare that said, *I know. You might as well be 'fessin' up.* "Spit it out, Mister Sherman," Daddy said coolly.

"Umm, well, you see here, Mr. McKenney," he finally said, pointing to one of them papers. "This is a map of the proposed dam and lake behind it. Well, the boundaries of this lake are such that . . . such that . . . well, you'll just have to move elsewhere, you see. Your whole property will be flooded and under water." He stopped abruptly then. And the silence was filled only with the sounds of Mister Whitaker's even rocking and the woodpecker.

His words had flown at me, slapping my face and sending the pain of it racing down my whole insides. And then a dark, heavy fog come, making my thinking slow; it was like back-bending choring to just place one thought after another. My mind slowly took apart the words and then put them back together again. *They were just words! How could there be so much pain in the mere hearin' of 'em?* I remembered the morning at breakfast when I'd wanted to grab Daddy's words out of the air. *What was it that Daddy'd said?* I couldn't think sure enough to remember anything. But again the pain of them was still in my memory so sharp like. When had words become living, breathing, hurting things of themselves? *Move? Move elsewhere?* Were those the words Mister Sherman had said? They weren't possible!

"Move? Mister Whitaker, surely you ain't meanin' for us to be leavin' our home an' land?" Mama's question sounded of disbelief. Like she was sure she hadn't heard them words right either. She totally ignored Mister Sherman and instead looked to Mister Whitaker for the explaining.

"Yes, Mrs. McKenney, that is what Dr. Sherman said. He may not have given you the news as gently as possible; we government men are not known for our ease with words, I'm afraid." He chuckled, and Mister Sherman flinched. "That is the gist of our message for you tonight. But remember what we said about helping you in every way—"

"Help us? How can you possibly be doin' that? Can you be movin' this here rise what I've watched Mister McKenney stride over for chorin' ever day since I married him so many year ago? Can you move this soil what were so rich an' good that it made a corn the whole county named McKenney Way? Can you move the memories of birthin' two babies what died in this windblown wood cabin as you call it? Can you . . ."

"Go inside, Mae." The sound of Daddy's voice was hollow. And ever so empty. Mama closed her mouth in a grim line, but she noticeably lifted her chin as she rose from the rocker and reached for the screen door. Andy jumped off the porch and took off running towards the upper pasture. "Andy!" Daddy called, but then he didn't say no more.

"Let him be," Mama said softly. She pulled the door closed behind her and disappeared inside the cabin.

Suddenly the vague memory of the forgotten dream nagged at me. Wasn't there something about Yankees being in our truck patch? *Oh, Mama!*

"Gettin' late. Got work needs doin'." Daddy rose from his chair and put his hands in the pockets of his overalls. Ezra and Nehemiah rose too, moving towards Daddy protectively.

"Yes, I suppose it is getting rather late, and we have to be up bright and early in the morning. We'll be visiting others tomorrow." Mister Whitaker cleared his voice. "I'd appreciate it if you didn't say anything to your neighbors just yet. Dr. Sherman and I would like to give them the news ourselves." Daddy didn't give him a response; he just kept staring towards the river. Mister Whitaker picked up his hat and rubbed it between his fingers. "We'll be needing to come again to discuss moving. How much your place is worth, where you'd consider going, and all sorts of logistics, um, details. Lots of new experiences coming your way, Mr. McKenney. Exciting changes."

Changes! Here was the dreaded word again, coming from *Yankees*.

He placed his hat on his head, smoothing the brim and squeezing the front crease. "Good night now. I assume you'll be holding those dogs."

"Them dogs only bother them what's aimin' to hurt this family. Funny how they can sense a varmint's intentions. Better'n I do." Daddy turned to stare at him until Mister Whitaker looked away and then began making his way down the hill.

"Good night, Mr. McKenney." Mister Sherman touched his hat and followed Mister Whitaker. They both picked their way hurriedly, never turning to look back at us. Ezra and Nehemiah growled softly, but they didn't leave Daddy's side.

"Daddy? Are they really meanin' what they's sayin'?"

"Reckon so."

"But how can we . . . ?"

"In the mornin', Rachael." The weariness in Daddy's voice made my heart hurt even more. "I best go speak with yer Granny Mandy. You stay here an' keep a lookout for your brother. Yer mama might be needin' you too." I stared at Daddy's wide, solid back as he took those long strides down our hill. The silence of the woods—even the wood-pecker had left off—mocked the sounds of Daddy's footfalls.

Seemed I felt so weak that I couldn't even begin to think on getting up, let alone doing something. My thoughts were jumbling over each other, trying to find the reasons and whys, seeking and desiring order in my world again. The fog that was setting over my thoughts had made everything so confusing. One thing only was plain: the nauseating sickness that kept coming over me in waves like the Tennessee lapped up against the shoreline. *You were wrong, Tommy Lee. Even the great Tennessee's goin' to be changed. This ain't no bottle driftin' by to interrupt her for just a short spell; these changes are goin' to make the flowin' tide of my life different. Forever.*

I thought on the Psalms Daddy'd been reading of a morning. They'd seemed real to me then, full of promise and comfort for whatever troubles the future might be bringing. But now those words seemed empty. *These* were just words! There wasn't no living nor breathing in them! *God, why're You doin' this to us?*

Daddy come out of Granny Mandy's cabin just then. He stood right still with his hand on the closed screen door a minute. I wondered if Granny'd called him back and he was about to open the door again, but then he didn't move any. He just stood there a moment staring up at the sky—*Is Daddy askin' God why too?*—and then walked on up the hill with those same familiar strides.

When he reached our cabin he hesitated, grabbing one of the poles supporting the porch. I stared at his fingers, knowing how much I loved the strength in those hands. They were so strong and—how can I be putting it?—could always take away my worrying. When Daddy was holding my hand, there wasn't anything that I was afraid of. For just a moment I yearned to run to him, aching for Daddy to hold my hand so tightly that all them new fears would go away. But I was even more frightened to try. *What if he held my hand and I was still afraid?*

He leaned heavily against the pole. "Yer granny said to tell you she's aimin' to make fried pies." He barely glanced at me before going on, asking, "Seen Andy yet?"

"No, Daddy. I s'pose he's down by Lookin' Point."

He nodded and then reached for the door. "Reckon Granny Mandy's wantin' yer company. Don't be late. School tomorra." His short sentences sounded cold. Seemed like he was dismissing me like the ringing school bell dismisses us at the end of the day.

"Yes, Daddy." Now that Daddy'd gone in, Ezra and Nehemiah come to me for attention and petting again, but I shoved them off angrily.

They'd suddenly become nuisances, like everything else around me. *Who'd be wantin' to pet some old dogs? And why should I even be gettin' up off this old porch? Might as well just be settin' here. Ain't nothin' nowhere worth doin' nohow*! Both of them set down and looked at me like they were waiting to play fetch. "Let me be!" I hollered at them, and they finally sulked off, tails tucked.

I stood up, kicking rocks out of my way until I come to some of them violets. These I put my bare foot on and stomped as best I could, rubbing my heel on them, smashing out their beauty into the soil. "Won't be no violets here no more! Them Yankees goin' to drown everthin' round here. Might as well start destroyin' everthin' what's here right now!" All the way to Granny Mandy's I continued kicking, smashing, and stomping on anything in my path. I knew I was acting like Andy. But I didn't care one whit.

When I come to Granny's door I rapped on it right hard. "Ain't no sense to be bangin' on that door, Rachael. I knowed ye was fetchin' to come." I opened the door cautiously, ashamed at my temper and yet still too hurting inside to really care. Seemed like my hurt and anger were like looking through Granny Mandy's windows. They were real old and the glass in them changed the way trees, grass, people, just everything really was when you looked out through them. Cleaning them didn't help any. I'd even tried squinting, but that didn't help neither. Nothing did. I knew I was peering out at everything through my anger and hurt and they were changing the way everything looked. But nothing could help that neither.

"Fetch a few apples from under the floor, Rachael," Granny Mandy said. She was busying about the kitchen, getting out knives, bowls, a rolling pin, and the fixings to make fried pies. I realized that I hadn't even thought about her reaction to the news. I glanced at her out of the corner of my eye, but I couldn't see any difference in her. She was just going about her living like always, it appeared.

I lifted up the small door in the floor that covered the place where Granny Mandy stored her apples every year. It was just a small, dug-out hole, but somehow it worked right well. Granny's apples kept there nearly a whole year. I picked out four big ones and then settled the door back into its place. After washing off the apples, I started into peeling them. Granny was busy mixing up the dough for the crust.

"Ain't got much to be sayin' tonight, hmm?" Granny asked. I stopped peeling a minute to watch her mix the flour, shortening, and water. Her crusts were the best in the whole county, far as I was concerned.

"No." It came out barely above a whisper. And sullen. "Granny Mandy, how can they . . . ? What are we goin' to do?"

"Do? Why, we's goin' to keep on doin' what we's been doin' on this here land for the past many a year." She worked at the dough, kneading it to the right consistency. "Plowin', plantin', weedin', harvestin', eatin', growin' older ever year." She turned and winked at me then. "And ornerier ever year too."

"But Granny Mandy, they's sayin' we's got to be movin'!"

"Yer grandaddy brung me here as his bride. Birthed six young'uns in this cabin; buried four."

I remembered Mama talking about her babies too. *Is that part of what makes a woman's home her own? Birthin' babies there?*

"Worked this soil right along with yer grandaddy and daddy all these years. Buried yer grandaddy next to my young'uns in the McKenney plot. Now yer Daddy says the high an' mighty U-nited States government's goin' to flood these here hills. I's sayin' I ain't goin' nowheres. Them Yankees want me out, they's goin' to have to float me out."

I smiled just a fleeting moment at her stubbornness. And even though with most folks them might be only words, I could sure picture my Granny Mandy sticking to them. She'd be meeting them Yankees at the line of her property with that shotgun she toted round on her hip.

"Ready to be mashin' them apples yet? Be sure'n get all the core out." She moved over to her cupboard and then come back with sugar and cinnamon. "Go 'head and mix it the way you like. I know you be favorin' more sugar'n I do."

After putting all the peeled, cored apples into a bowl, I mashed them with a fork and then added cinnamon and sugar—a extra good amount of sugar. Somehow it felt comforting to be making these pies. They were a familiar part of my memories of times spent in this cabin. Like a favorite quilt with squares of remembered materials, making fried pies was a comforting part of the pattern of my times with Grandy Mandy. *Would we be makin' more fried pies in the years to come?* I watched Granny Mandy take a small amount of dough, roll it into a small ball between her palms, and then put it on the table. She picked up the rolling pin and rolled it out into a small circle.

"Get the skillet a-heatin', Rachael. I's 'bout tastin' them pies a'ready!" she said, nodding towards the skillet pushed to the side of the wood stove. "Lard's right here. Get it meltin' kindly good."

I scooped a good amount into the skillet, knowing we needed a fair amount to make them good and crispy. I checked the fire, noting that it needed a bit more wood. Then, after putting another piece in through the eye and making sure it'd caught good, I placed the skillet over the flame. Granny Mandy had worked fast, spooning the apple mixture onto several rolled out circles and then after folding them over, she'd pressed the edges down with a fork. "Poke a few holes in 'em, Rachael, an' put 'em in the skillet. Won't be long now!"

Placing them in the skillet produced that familiar sizzling sound and then before too long, the most delicious smell. I closed my eyes and breathed it in slowly. "They smell wonderful, Granny Mandy. How did you know that makin' fried pies would help me to be feelin' better?"

"Didn't know fer sure. Knowed they'd be makin' me feel better! They's somethin' 'bout fried pies too, ain't they? Jest thinkin' on 'em can make me hungrier'n a red-headed woodpecker with a headache!" She winked at me again and I smiled at her, loving her, knowing how much I was needing her wisdom, her caring, her way of sorting through what was bothering at me and throwing it away.

When the pies were done we set down to enjoy them with mugs of coffee. We talked about the weather, our gardens and what they'd be growing soon, school, and the chicken boat. She even asked about Tommy Lee. But we didn't talk about the Yankees. I ate until I was too full to eat a bite more and then felt the worrying fog come over me again. I slumped over the table and drew circles in the spilled flour.

"How'd yer Mama be takin' in the news?" I took a deep breath, dreading to talk about the Yankees. Knowing we needed to.

"She was askin' them how they was goin' to be movin' all her memories. When she spoke 'bout my brother and sister what died, well, then she didn't say no more after that."

"And Andy?"

"He run off. Most likely still down to Lookin' Point."

Granny Mandy sighed. That was the first I noticed that this "mess"— that's the way I thought of all these changes in my mind now—was weighing on her too. She wasn't dismissing it as easily as I'd supposed.

"Now tell me 'bout Rachael."

I turned to look into her eyes and then quickly looked away as tears threatened to come from the caring I saw there. *How can she be so concerned for me when she must be hurtin' and angry at this mess too? And how can I begin to answer her, puttin' into words all that I feel inside?*

"I don't know that I can say, Granny Mandy. I only know that I keep askin' God why. Why ain't He stoppin' them? Don't He be carin' 'bout us no more? Don't He love us . . . ?" I stopped, not knowing if pouring out my thoughts like this was good or not. *Would sayin' out my anger like this make God do more bad things to us?*

Granny Mandy got up from the table and went to look out her window. I watched her with curiosity, wondering what she was thinking now. "Cloudy tonight. Fetch my lantern there, Rachael, whiles I get my sweater. You need one too?" she asked, and I nodded my head yes, knowing normally I would've brought one but didn't because of my heedless tantrum all the way down the hill.

"Where we goin', Granny? Are you frettin' 'bout Andy?" I took a sweater from her and snuggled into its cozy warmth. It smelled like Granny Mandy—a mixture of spices, spattered grease from frying, and sweat from choring. I loved that smell. "He'll be goin' on home soon. Andy ain't growed up 'nough yet to be out late past dark. He's still scared of haints."

"Ain't goin' lookin' fer Andy. You be right. Andy'll be headin' on home when he's done sorted things out." She opened the door and we walked outside. When Granny'd closed the door behind us, shutting off the glow and warmth of her fire, I shivered, feeling a rush of cool, lonely fear. "We's got doin's of our own tonight. Come 'long this a way."

We walked side by side, me holding the lantern out in front of us to light the way. Granny was right; it was a cloudy night. I couldn't find a star or trace of moonlight anywhere. We took the path that led us to the river and the woods that grew along there. The rock that we'd named Lookin' Point was to our left, but Granny Mandy pointed me to take the right fork when we come to it. I thought we were heading to the river, but soon Granny nudged us off the path and we were walking through the woods themselves now, pushing up piles of dead leaves and twigs with our feet. A familiar damp, woodsy smell drifted up to my nose every time we took a step. What wasn't familiar was the shadows that appeared here and there from the glow of our lantern. I knew this place like the back of my hand in the daylight, but everything looked so different in the shadows of the night.

I held the lantern more firmly, trying to keep it from wavering this way and that with every step. I was hoping them shapes out there would stop their shifting with the glow's moving. But that didn't help any. Everything still looked different. Nothing looked familiar. And my stomach was beginning to jump about the same as them shadows did.

At least there wasn't even the hint of a breeze blowing to move the branches of trees around too. It was one of them nights when everything was still and silent. No owls were hooting. Even the tree frogs hadn't started up their rhythmic croaking sound yet, so the woods always seemed unnatural quiet like when they were silent. I didn't particularly like the tree frogs' sound; it kept me awake sometimes listening to them croaking all together and then getting their rhythm all mixed up and then back together, repeating that over and over again. Like to drove me crazy sometimes laying abed of a night. But even that sound was familiar. And anything familiar was welcome on a night like this one.

"Over here, I'm a-thinkin'," Granny Mandy said, directing us towards her right. "Hold the lantern up a mite higher." She peered out into the glow of the lantern, finally nodding her head and nudging us farther. "There she be," Granny whispered, in a voice that revealed excitement—and awe. "Set the lantern down here."

I put the lantern down on the ground and searched hesitantly for whatever it was that Granny was looking for. "What is it?" I whispered back, feeling my stomach tighten even more. I'd never known nothing to give Granny Mandy pause.

She leaned over an old, rotten stump, feeling round the bottom with her hands. Walking all around it, she stepped gingerly—tenderly?— glancing this way and that like she was afraid of what she might be stepping on. "They's fairies in these woods. Cain't you feel 'em watchin' us?"

The flickering light of the lamp made strange shapes in the distance again, sending a shiver down my back. I snuggled farther into Granny's sweater, tucking it up round my neck. "I know I been feelin' mighty strange, Granny. Is that 'count of the fairies? Where is they?"

"They's everwhere! Cain't see them. They sees *us*!"

I shivered once again, glancing around for the sight of eyes staring back at me. "What are you lookin' for? The fairies?" Granny was still moving around the stump, feeling here and there.

"Tol' ye, cain't see fairies 'cause they ain't wantin' ye to. But sometimes, if ye catches a night just so and the fairies is willin', ye can see . . . " Suddenly she pushed over the stump, announcing, "This!"

I gasped in complete awe at the sight before us. Glowing blue-green lights—a beautiful color the likes of which I'd never set eyes on before—filled the hole where the stump had been. They moved and shimmered in a unnatural sort of way, dancing to a magical tune—a fairy one? The lights caught my eyes and held them, entranced and captive. Seemed I just couldn't drink in the beauty of them fast enough. "Oh, Granny." I swallowed once to recollect my wits. "What is they?"

"'Tis foxfire, child," she said with a hush, getting down on her knees before the glowing lights and never once taking her eyes off the wondrous sight. I knelt beside her as quietly as I could, since it seemed like we were kneeling before a fairy throne.

"Heard tell of foxfire from Daddy before. But I didn't never . . . didn't never imagine it bein' this beautiful." The jumping lights held our eyes still; seemed there wasn't anything else in the world existed just now but them. They looked like a small city—or a castle covered with jewels that the fairies had built. Had the fairies just scampered off, leaving a celebration that only little people know of? Was that why the lights seemed to be dancing joyful like still? Or did the lights come from way below the earth, just barely twinkling out and teasing us with the wondrous glow that was caught and contained down there?

"'Tis the fairies' fire, it is. Ain't like ours—red-yellow and hot. The little folks' fire is a right curious thing. Deep green. Deeper blue. And coolin'." Granny Mandy stretched one hand out over the foxfire, but she didn't touch it. The lights seem to flinch at the moving shadow of her hand.

The more we stared at the curious glow, the more puzzling it was to me. "Granny, how can it seem so bright and glowin' and at the same time be 'most hard to see? I keep blinkin' my eyes—to make sure it's still there. Seems to be movin' and—how can I put it?" I was struggling to find words for the curious sensation. "I think it's tryin' to dance away from us, keep us from seein' it somehow. I know that don't make no sense, but . . ."

"You's makin' sense, child. Foxfire ain't natural, ain't meant to be seen by big folks like us, really. 'Tis barely of this world, Rachael. Meant for the other world. The unnatural one." Her voice grew even softer. "Some people cain't never see foxfire. 'Tain't meant to. Cain't reach a bit into that other world to catch a glimpse of the wondrous."

Catch a glimpse of the wondrous. Her whispered words echoed through my mind. I knew we were seeing something right special. Mysterious and magical. "I can understand why you can be seein' it, Granny Mandy." Granny'd always had a sense of wonderment about her, like her "seein'" that the whole county had respect for. "But why me? How come I can see the foxfire?"

"You's special, Rachael. Got the wantin' in ye to be touchin' that other world. Some don't even be a-knowin' it's out there. Others ain't got the courage to try'n reach for it." We both continued to stare at the foxfire, I suppose never daring to look into the other's eyes for fear it might snatch us back to the big folks' world.

"Special? I don't feel special, Granny Mandy."

"How do ye be feelin'? Put it out there in words so's ye can be a-lookin' at it, testin' it for what it be."

I paused a minute to gather up and think on all those feelings. The beauty of the glowing lights seemed to give me courage, saying, *We're here. We're from the other world. And if you can see us, you can be looking at that other world deep inside yourself too.* "I feel sick inside. Like Mister Sherman and Mister Whitaker—especially Mister Whitaker—done took all the meanin' to life right out of my insides, Granny! Ain't nothin' left in there to make me want to go through the things of daily livin' no more. Don't want to be goin' to school. Doin' chores. Cookin'. Eatin' even."

"Ye eat them fried pies." There was a touch of humor in her voice, and I smiled silently upon the dancing lights.

"I guess it's the doin' for all the tomorrows that stretches ahead of me like somethin' to be dreaded, Granny Mandy. Just as soon set here and stare at the fairies' fire forever."

"Cain't do that, Rachael. The little folks' world—the unnatural world—ain't meant to be lived in. Not by us. Not yet."

"Then how do I be livin' in our world, Granny Mandy?"

"By knowin' the foxfire's here. Livin'. Glowin'. 'Tain't goin' out like our fire. Never."

"But it ain't what's real! Mister Sherman and Mister Whitaker's real! Them what's forcin' us to move's real!"

"No, Rachael. That's where ye be mistaken." She stretched her hand out over the foxfire again, making them blue-green lights shimmer and dance even more in her shadow from the lantern. *"Them's* what's real! When ye be thinkin' on what's the meanin' for livin', what's natural and touchable—" Granny suddenly reached outside the stump and grabbed up a fistful of McKenney soil, holding it out to me "—this here ere only a passin' thing. The unnatural, what's not a-comin' from this ol' world, that becomes the real!"

I nodded slowly, the meaning of her words just barely touching my understanding. I think my mind was catching what she was saying. But my heart wasn't ready on account of the anger and hurt that was still pushing out everything else.

"From now on ye'll be a-knowin', Rachael, that the foxfire be here. Ye won't be seein' it whenever ye want. It won't be lettin' ye into the other world so easily. *But it will be here.* And ye must be believin' that."

"And what will knowin' it's here say to me, Granny? How will it help me tomorrow when I can't be seein' them pretty lights, when I'm not starin' into them like I am right now—and believin'?"

"Ye'll know that God is real. And lovin' ye. Don't make no matter what no Yankees say or do. What anybody else be sayin' or doin'. Ye'll be knowin' what God be a-sayin' ere the only thing what's real in this ol' unnatural world!"

We continued to stare at the sight for some time yet, not saying anything. I was trying to fill up my senses with the hope of remembering every color, shimmering glow, and dancing joy of the fairies' lights. Time passed, but I didn't recollect knowing how long we knelt there until finally Granny Mandy slowly and silently rose. I got up too, regretfully, and helped her carefully replace the rotted stump. The beautiful city winked out of sight, hidden once again. *Would the fairies return, resumin' their celebratin'? Or, the magic gone—intruded upon by us big folks—would they settle down to sleep, plannin' to dance once again tomorrow night?*

I picked up the lantern again and led the way, easily knowing the path back to Granny Mandy's cabin now. We still clung to the silence; I know I wasn't wanting to lose the feeling of awe that still hung about me. Talking might break that spell. Strangely, Granny clung to my arm, like she wasn't sure of the pathway or her footing. I'd never knowed her to be setting out for anywheres without knowing exactly where she was going and walking—head high—just that way. I glanced at her now and then to see if something was bothering about her. But the lantern wasn't giving off enough light to see her face. The dark, cloudy night was hiding anything I might've seen there.

When we reached her cabin I held the lantern as best I could over the steps and yet Granny Mandy stumbled, grabbing at me for support. "Granny, you be feelin' poorly?" I asked her, concerned.

"Land no, child. Jest plumb wore out, that be all." Her voice sounded drained. Seemed like it was an effort for her to even talk. "Jest bring the lantern on inside fer me, an' I'll be fine."

Opening her door let the light from her fire shine out into the darkness, but the fire had gone down a good bit. "I'll just get your fire goin' better, Granny, and then I'll be headin' on to home. Anythin' else needs doin'?" I quickly grabbed up some of her wood, placing it over the red embers and stirring it round a bit with the poker.

Granny Mandy sat down in her rocker, watching the catching flames and moving back and forth in a even rhythm. "I's jest fine, Rachael. Be settin' here jest a spell afore I be a-headin' to bed." She continued to stare at the fire, rocking. "'Night now."

I moved to kiss her wrinkled cheek. Didn't usually give Granny Mandy a kiss good night, but this night hadn't been usual atall. "'Night,

Granny Mandy." She didn't look up at me but merely nodded her head. I lingered a moment, my uncertainty at her actions keeping me from leaving. *It ain't like her to be actin' this way*, I thought to myself, fretting. "Granny, is anythin' ailin' you?" I asked cautiously, knowing Granny didn't take to sympathy for any paining she might be feeling. She'd always told me a woman bears up under her pain, finding the strength to think it small enough to be living with.

She looked at me then and smiled warmly. "No, child. S'pose it's jest that—how I be explainin' it to ye? Jest that glimpsin' on the unnatural world makes a body my age yearn fer—yearn fer passin' over to it. 'Tain't but right there, ye know." Granny reached out into the air like something was floating there. "'Tain't but right here, a reach away." She kept her hand held out, staring at it like there was something still just beyond her reach.

I watched her with confusion, not understanding her meaning—or maybe not wanting to. And then I grabbed up her aged, gnarled hand in mine, clinging to it, holding it tightly between my two young, still-smooth ones.

"Cain't hold on to me thata way, Rachael." She looked back at the fire, her stare again fixed on the glowing flames. "Best be headin' on home afore yer mama an' daddy be frettin' 'bout ye. I be fine." She breathed deeply. "Jest fine."

I let go of her hand slowly, reluctantly. After opening her door I glanced back at her once more. "'Night, Granny Mandy."

"'Night, Rachael."

For once I purposefully closed a door softly, not wanting the sound of it closing to intrude upon the scene of Granny staring still into her fire. And the way I tiptoed home would've been a right funny sight for a body who'd seen the way I'd stomped down there earlier that same evening.

When I'd curled up underneath my quilt, I reached out one hand to pull back my curtains and peer out into the night. The clouds were clearing now and a few stars were twinkling here and there. The magic was gone now. 'Twas no more a night to be seeing fairies' fire. But when I closed my eyes I could still see it glowing.

The next few days seemed to be dragging by. Mama and Daddy moved through the choring like they were empty. They did everything we would normally be doing—cooking, eating, and doing up breakfast, lunch, and dinner; plowing up fields in readiness for planting; washing, wearing, and re-washing clothes; milking the cows and churning butter; cleaning inside, choring outside. Daddy even read the Bible every morning just like always. But it looked to me like they were just walking through those things; they weren't *living* while they were doing them.

And Andy. Poor Andy. The face he was presenting to the world was madder'n a sore-tailed cat. He hissed, scratched, and bit at anything and everything that come in his path or even those that tried to show him a kindness. But I knew Andy's fury was only a cover for the hurting that he was feeling. He couldn't let no one know he was crying inside, so he wore that mask of anger on the outside.

Every once in awhile Daddy or Mama would say something about moving, but it was like they were talking about someone else, some other family. It was like we were all watching a play up to Chattanooga on some big, fancy stage. We were setting in the audience, watching them actors and actresses acting out their parts. They were the ones that had to leave their home, packing up memories in their minds like you'd pack up dishes in boxes. But the actors and actresses were us! Somehow we were stepping back from ourselves, watching our pain from a distance. I wondered if Daddy and Mama did it to protect me and Andy. Wasn't no reason to do that for me, though; I just kept squeezing my eyes shut tight to see the foxfire.

I visited Granny Mandy every day, and she seemed to be back to her old self. Whenever I'd mention the "mess", she'd just shake her head, generally saying something like "I ain't goin' nowheres" or "Jest let 'em try to move me! My shotgun'll convince 'em otherwise!" Her responses always made me smile. And hope. *Can one determined Granny hold off them Yankees? And if me and Granny Mandy keep believin' in the foxfire, can't that make it so too?*

Going to school was another matter. Every day the whispering increased. Every day it was getting harder to ignore. Me, Verna Mae, Nellie, and Merry Jo hadn't talked about the Yankees atall. We'd watch the others whispering and passing notes, but that subject was something we avoided like the Snodderlys when they come down with measles. We walked around it. We ignored it altogether. And we talked about other things. But we never mentioned the Yankees and what they were doing in Jordan's Bend.

I also ignored Tommy Lee. Don't rightly know why. I guess looking at him made me think on our conversation about the Tennessee and it never changing. I felt disappointed in him even though I knew it wasn't his fault. He was only trying to help me at the time, and he did too. But now it all seemed so skewed and mistaken. I was looking to Granny Mandy and fairies' fire to get me through this time. Tommy Lee hadn't glimpsed the wondrous. I wasn't knowing how to even begin to explain it all to him. And then I asked myself, *Would he even be able to see it? Does Tommy Lee have the gift for reachin' to the other world?*

Friday morning come into my bedroom loft like a gentle whisper. The sun peeked through the window and coaxed me awake, promising a beautiful day. I hurried into my clothes and just before I started down the steps I heard Andy stirring. Poking my head around the quilt, I whispered "Pssst!" at him. Andy quickly pulled his quilt clean over his head, ignoring me. "Remember Mama said she'd be cookin' eggs with all the fixin's this morning since the chickens been layin' right well these past few days. Ain't you anxious for Mama's eggs instead of mush?"

There was no reply atall. Except that Andy scooted even farther down underneath that quilt.

"Andy, I know you be feelin' awful 'bout all this, but you got to believe God! Me and Granny Mandy seen . . . well, we done seen somethin' mighty special and . . ."

Suddenly that quilt come yanking down and Andy's head come popping up. His red hair was still all tousled from sleep, making him look more childlike and innocent than usual. And making me want to protect him as his big sister. "You don't be knowin' how I feel!" he spat out at me. "An' I don't want to be hearin' no sermons, no stories 'bout what you seen, nothin'! Go 'way!" And just as quickly as he'd come out from under the quilt, O.A. went right back down again.

"Andy, I know it's hard for you to be believin' me now, but I'm tellin' you true. I promise you I am! Me and Granny Mandy are workin' it all out. You'll see." I left him then, knowing how he felt even though Andy didn't believe I did. But I had felt that way before seeing the foxfire. I had!

After breakfast me and Andy hitched a ride with Daddy to school. I was carrying a basket of eggs to sell—I'd gathered up a good number again this morning—and so I went into the Hickmans' store first thing. Miz Hickman was working behind the counter when she glanced up and saw me. "Oh! Rachael! Why, how fine to be seein' you today!"

I must've looked at her kindly strange like, seeing as how I was coming in nearly every morning the whole blessed week with eggs. Couldn't for the life of me understand why she was acting like I'd just traveled from the next county or something. "Mornin', Miz Hickman. Got some extry eggs again. Don't rightly know why them chickens be layin' so good lately, but we ain't complainin' 'bout it none!" I laid the basket carefully upon the counter. "Brung two dozen again. And Mama fixed us eggs to eat this mornin' already too."

I noticed Miz Hickman hadn't even looked at the eggs yet. She was just gazing at me, not saying nothing. And for Miz Hickman, that was something fairly amazing.

"Miz Hickman? You feelin' poorly this mornin'?"

"Land sakes, no, child. I be feelin' right fine this day." She leaned towards me over the counter to whisper—but in a loud voice. Which of course didn't make no sense atall. Especially since there wasn't anybody else in the whole store just then. "How's everone out your way? Anyone layin' abed yet?"

I looked back at her in total wonderment. *Layin' abed yet? What on earth was she meanin'?* "We's all just fine, Miz Hickman. Why would we be layin' abed? They ain't nothin' catchin' goin' round, is they?"

"Oh no, nothin' like that." She began lifting the eggs out of the basket, holding them up to the light and checking each one for cracks. "Just that, well, we heard the news 'bout the dam and you all needin' to move an' all, an', well . . . Well, it's just that when the mighty hand of God strikes, seems a body best be countin' his blessin's. Makes them other little problems just plumb disappear in the comparin'. Like Mister Hickman an' his achin' back. Ever time it acts up, I tell him to think on all the places what don't hurt. Oughta make him feel better right off, it should. That's what I do. A body just can't be settin' round feelin' sorry for himself like some does. They's some what lays abed, but not me. That's not for Sarah Anne Hickman. Praisin' God for everthin'—that's what I do!"

I felt the hurt and anger come washing over me in waves again. Only this time come the realization of insult all mixed in too. *Why was she sayin' them things to me? Could she possibly be thinkin' she was helpin'?* Miz Hickman kept inspecting them eggs like she was from the United States government, looking each one over like they'd just come from a sick, scrawny chicken. She did not look me in the eye. I gathered every bit of courage I could and took a big breath before announcing, "Miz Hickman, like I done said, we's all just fine. And everthin'—and I do mean everthin'—is goin' to be just fine too. And I ain't never knowed Daddy nor Mama to lay abed. Never." I paused a moment, and she sneaked a quick glance at me. "Now, if you'll be payin' me for them eggs, then I'll be a-headin' on to school. Verna Mae 'bout ready?"

Miz Hickman walked back towards the door that led to their living quarters and opened it, leaning in a ways. "Verna Mae! Rachael's here!" she hollered. "You 'bout ready for school?" I could just barely hear Verna Mae's voice answering her, and then Miz Hickman come back over to the counter. "Now then, here's your egg money," she said, counting it out into my hand. "Like I done said, you'd best be countin' your blessin's just like I's countin' this here money. Now here's Verna Mae." She gave her daughter a quick pat on the head. "You all be goin' off to school now. 'Member what I said, Rachael. It's right good advice to be heedin' to!"

Verna Mae give me a curious look, but I shook my head. I wasn't about to be repeating what her mama'd just said, figuring it was hurtful enough hearing the first time. I was afraid she'd be pestering me to tell her anyways, but Verna Mae had other news she was most anxious to be telling concerning the Snodderlys. Seems that George Snodderly'd been boasting all over town how he was going to be a rich man. Something about fishing rights and his property. It didn't make any sense to either of us, so we figured he was just jawing to be passing the time of day again. All them Snodderlys were known for that.

We were just coming around the corner and could see the schoolyard when I sensed something wasn't right. There weren't the usual sounds of children playing—laughing, shouting, singing rhymes for skipping rope. And where was everybody? Me and Verna Mae looked around, wondering where everyone could've got off to. And then we heard it down towards the river a ways. Dropping my lunch pail and book, I took off at a run; somehow I just knew it was Andy in the middle of the scuffle, sure as anything.

The passel of children around the fighting boys blocked my way, but I began pushing my way through them right off. I heard someone hollering "Give 'im a good one, Andy!" and another boy was shouting "You's showin' him now, Andy!" When I'd finally shoved my way through to the middle, Tommy Lee'd already got there and pulled the two apart. He had each one by the scruff of the neck, but that wasn't keeping them from trying still to punch the other. Andy was flailing them fists this way and that, and Willie Snodderly was doing the same. Only he was kicking too. Looked to me like Tommy Lee was the onliest one in danger of taking a punch or kick now.

And then I took a good look at Andy. One eye was so puffed already that it was about closed shut. Blood trickled out his nose, and he had cuts and scratches nearly everywhere his freckled skin was showing. The stubborn red hair was tousled like always, but now it had clumps of mud sticking here and there too. One suspender of his overalls hung down, torn, and his shirttail was sticking out all round. And still he kept furiously a-swinging them fists, meeting only air. He looked beaten, rumpled, and so pitiful. I started to rush towards him when Tommy Lee glanced up to see me coming. He looked alarmed and then shook his head just barely, yet so I could see it well enough—*No!* I stared at him a moment, wondering at his meaning when I started towards Andy once more. This time Tommy Lee plopped Andy firmly on the ground, leaning down to stare him eye to eye and stating right firm like, "Andy, that be enough!" He kept ahold of Willie with one hand and give Andy a shove with the other. "Now head on down to the creek and be washin' up them cuts an' all. An' you be doin' this alone like a man, you hear?"

"But Tommy Lee, he—" Andy started in.

"No buts! Head on down to that creek before I whup you good!" Andy give him a scowl—with Tommy Lee not backing down one bit, mind you—and then shoved his way through the children who were still crowded around, intently watching still. Even though Tommy Lee had apparently put an end to their fun, no one was about to leave just yet.

Tommy Lee looked over at me again then, and I nodded my head at him. Of course Andy wasn't wanting his big sister running to him, babying and mothering him in front of everybody. Again Tommy Lee had taught me about caring for someone's feelings. Watching Andy's retreating form as he stomped towards the water, I was still aching to snatch him up into my arms. But I realized now that loving him meant I'd let him trudge towards that river alone.

Willie'd evidently decided to take out all of his anger on Tommy Lee, because now he was kicking and punching in his direction. Tommy Lee just held him out at arm's length, though, and give him a good shake. Willie stopped a minute, surprised at Tommy Lee's strength, I suppose, and then started in to fighting him again. "Willie! Ere you goin' to be stoppin' or ere you goin' swimmin' in the river?" Willie dropped his arms once more, scowling at Tommy Lee something awful. But he kept them dirty hands clenched in tight fists. "I reckon you's measurin' whether I's jawin' or tellin' you true." Tommy Lee scowled right back at him. "You be wantin' to test me?"

"Children! What's going on here?" Miz Travis was running towards us, alarm sounding in her voice. I noticed that once she reached us, she didn't have to move anyone out of her way; young'uns were scattering in every which direction until only me, Tommy Lee, and a banged up, pouting Willie were left. "William! Why, you's nothin' but a mess! Ere you all right? What's happened? Tommy Lee?" She started in to feeling Willie all over, checking for broken bones, I guess. By the looks of him, he'd just been run over by a wagon or herd of horses. Willie just stood there, sulking. Most likely he was reckoning that he was in for it once Miz Travis heard he'd only been scuffling.

"Willie here and Andy had a difference o' opinion, Miz Travis," Tommy Lee explained. "Don't rightly know who done started it, but I ended it."

Finding nothing much wrong with Willie, Miz Travis stood up, dusting off her skirt. She continued staring at him, though, and her expression turned from concern to frustration. "You been scufflin' again, William? Seems to me you've been warned 'bout this enough already!" She glanced at Tommy Lee. "Andy tusslin' with you this time, hmmm? Where is Andy?" Cupping Willie's chin in one hand, Miz Travis tilted his face up to get a good look at his cuts and bruises. The signs of a good shiner were already sprouting under his left eye.

While Willie cringed and wiggled under Miz Travis' inspection, Tommy Lee answered, "Sent him to the river to clean up an' cool off. Here he comes back now."

I turned to see Andy come walking towards us. He'd washed away the blood from his nose and generally splashed water around the middle of his face. But his efforts only left even more obvious smudges of where there was remaining caked-on dirt left behind. His hair had been smoothed down a bit, his shirttail was tucked in once again, and he'd managed to somehow tie up the torn overalls. But that eye! It looked plain awful, swollen clean closed, and he was blinking the other one something fierce. Must've hurt something terrible already.

As he come closer towards us I realized there was something about him that kindly reminded me of Daddy. I stared at him a minute, puzzled. *How could this filthy, dirty, beat-up, ragamuffin young'un look like our tall, quiet daddy?* And then I saw it plain as day. Andy had pulled back his shoulders. And lifted up that chin. He knew he was in for it from Miz Travis. And yet he'd come to her facing square ahead, ready. Suddenly—surprisingly—I felt proud of him.

Miz Travis give a small gasp when she saw that eye. "Andrew! What a mess you be! Land a mercy, never in my life will I understand why young'uns—and men—always be thinkin' that it's fightin' what solves their differences." She turned Andy's face up and examined him too, shaking her head at him. "Andrew, what's your part in all this? Quick now, give me your side and then we'll hear William's."

"Willie told a lie, and I hit 'im. I cuffed him first. Started it I did." Andy took a deep breath and then winced. I winced right after him, reckoning he must've got some sore ribs from the scuffling too. "I'd do it again too. I would."

"You won't be doin' no more scufflin', Andrew," Miz Travis ordered, putting a finger in his face. "Now what did William say?"

"Can't repeat it, Miz Travis. Won't repeat it." Andy closed his mouth then. Tight. I could see his jaw clenching behind the dirt and scratches.

"What's this? I asked a question, and I'm wantin' a answer! Now!"

Andy still stood there, shoulders back, chin up. "Sorry, Miz Travis. Reckon I ain't never disobeyed you before. But I got to now."

Miz Travis turned to Willie. "You tell me what you said. This minute!"

"Didn't tell no lie! Didn't say nothin' but the truth! An' then Andy just hauled off'n hit me, right here!" Willie whined, pointing out his quickly developing shiner.

"And what do you say to that, Andrew?" Miz Travis looked at Andy again, but he only shook his head. "You have nothin' more to say?" Again Andy shook his head. "William, what exactly did you say?"

"Cain't 'member 'xactly."

Miz Travis sighed and put her hands on her hips. "Then tell me what you said as best you can recollect."

Willie dug one toe into the dirt, swinging it back and forth. Then he looked up at Miz Travis like he had the most important speech on earth to be making, only he was taking his good sweet time about it. You'd a thought he was President Roosevelt, lifting up them eyebrows and nose the way he was. "Said that Andy's daddy and mama must've done mighty bad things for God to punish 'em so, losin' their land to the *Yankees*!" Willie sneaked a glance over to me now, squinting them mean eyes like he does. "A good switchin' from heaven, that's what them McKenneys be gettin'!"

No wonder Andy hit him! I fumed, feeling my own hands form into fists and wanting to punch him a good one myself. I took a step towards Willie, but Tommy Lee grabbed my arm. Again he give me a slow, solemn shake of his head. And there was something else about his eyes—understanding? Or was it pity? I shook his hand off my arm. *God, I ain't takin' no pity from nobody. Not even Tommy Lee*!

"Concernin' a switchin'—seems to me you's the one best be worryin' 'bout that, William!" Miz Travis still stood there with her hands resting on her hips. She looked puzzled, like she was totally confused about why Willie would even be saying such a thing. "Now what on God's green earth are you talkin' about William Snodderly? That don't make no sense atall!"

"Yankees goin' to build 'em a dam round heres. McKenneys got to move on account of their whole land's goin' to be under water. My daddy said so. Heared it from Mister Whitaker, he did."

Miz Travis' mouth dropped open. "This true, Rachael?"

I stared down at my feet once again, drawing circles like Willie'd done. "Yes, ma'am." And then, remembering the foxfire, I added, "But me and Granny Mandy ain't give up yet." I looked around at Miz Travis, Andy, Willie, and most importantly, Tommy Lee, announcing, "You'll see. You'll just see."

Miz Travis turned her attention back to Willie. "It might be true that the McKenneys will have to move someday, William, but that does not mean that they've done anything bad like you say. I know sometimes God needs to get our attention and teach us but—"

"That's jest what Miz Smith was sayin' to Miz Buchanan. My grandaddy heared 'em jawin', he did! Everbody thinks Grandaddy's a-sleepin' on that bench, but he's a-listenin'. He hears 'em talkin' an' that's what they done said. So when he done tol' my daddy, then Daddy said—"

"William, I think we've heard enough."

"Well, me an' my daddy's only repeatin' what Miz Buchanan and Nellie's mama said 'bout God tryin' to teach them high an' mighty McKenneys. Daddy says they's like the rooster what figured the sun only come up to hear 'im crow. And they need to be figurin' out what God's learnin' 'em from this."

I'd heard enough. Grabbing Andy's arm I steered him towards where I'd dropped my lunch pail and book. The school day had barely begun, but as far as I was concerned, it was over. Me and Andy were heading to home. Andy shook off my hand angrily and then walked back a ways to pick up his hat, plopping the now even sorrier looking thing on his head. But that didn't make any difference to Andy. He was walking like Daddy again. Shoulders back. Chin up.

"Rachael!" Miz Travis called after me. "I assume you be takin' Andrew on home?"

"Yes, ma'am."

"That be best for today." She give Andy a stern look. "And you be tellin' your daddy 'bout that fightin', young man. Don't rightly think you could keep it a secret from the looks of you. But I expect you to be explainin' it all. You and your daddy both be knowin' that fightin' is not permitted on school grounds! I trust your daddy will remedy this here situation." Looking over to me, she added, "Don't make no difference how ill Willie was meanin' to be. That still be no excuse."

I clenched my jaw right tight before answering, "Yes, ma'am." Then I nudged Andy.

He raised that chin even higher. "Yes, ma'am."

"Tommy Lee," Miz Travis went on, "I want you to march William on home. And tell his daddy that I expect him to apply discipline as needed too. Or I'll be applyin' my switch to any young'uns with a hankerin' to fight. That be clear to both of you?" She give Andy and Willie a glaring look. "Now, 'bout time I get to ringin' this here school bell and start in to teachin' some lessons before the day is wasted clean away. What a mornin'!"

Andy immediately turned towards home. I quickly run to get my pail and book and started after him when Tommy Lee grabbed my arm once again. He had a firm hold on Willie with his other hand. "Rachael? I know you be hurtin' mighty bad, but I just want you to know I understand . . ."

"Understand?!" I snapped back at him. "How can you be understandin' me? Can't nobody be. Nobody but Granny Mandy!" I shook my arm free and run after Andy.

"Rachael!" Tommy Lee called again. There was despairing in the sound of his voice. But I walked on, ignoring him.

The whole long walk home I looked at Andy's back. No matter how fast I tried to run, take shortcuts, or catch up to him, I still saw only the proud line of them shoulders of his. And he wasn't saying anything neither. Not even grunts in response to my questions. Nothing but a angry silence. And so we trudged on home, me following behind and Andy leading. *To what?*

When we come in the kitchen door, Mama looked up, in surprise first and then concern. "Andy? What on earth—yer eye! Rachael, run quick an' fetch a cold jar from the springhouse!" Mama set Andy down to the table, and I went off to get the jar. Seeing how Andy's eye had already swelled shut, I didn't think the cold would help much. But I went to fetch it anyways, knowing Mama would want to do something for Andy.

By the time I come back, Mama was washing off Andy's face with a rag, revealing even more of them cuts and scratches. They had to be stinging something awful, but Andy wasn't saying nothing. He was doing a good bit of squirming around though. "Here, Mama. This one seemed the coolest."

She held it up against Andy's eye, and he flinched backwards. "Set still, Andrew. I know it be hurtin' fine, but this'll help. Who was ye tanglin' with?" Mama's voice sounded stern. But her look was still one of worry.

"Willie Snodderly. You should've seen his face! Cuffed 'im a good one, I did!"

Mama ignored that remark. "Miz Travis send you to home?"

"Yes, ma'am."

"Andrew, ye know better'n to be fightin'. Why was you into it with Willie?"

Andy's face—what I could see of it behind that jar—twisted to the side like he was in terrible pain.

"Andy? You be all right?" Mama asked in alarm.

"I be fine."

"Fine? With this eye so swolled up ye look like ye been tanglin' with the Travises' bull?" She pulled back the jar a minute to get a better look at Andy's eye, winced, and then put it back again. "Now, tell me what the scuffle was about."

Andy swallowed. "Can't rightly 'member."

"Can't 'member? You be lookin' this poorly, and ye can't recollect what possessed ye to get yer face rearranged like this?" Mama looked at him in exasperation. Then she looked at me. "Rachael?"

I knew Andy's dilemma sure as anything. I couldn't repeat it again. I didn't want to say it. And more important, I didn't want Mama to be hearing it neither. "I weren't there when the fightin' started." I'd told the truth. But even telling Mama a half-truth made me look away from her steady gaze.

Just then Daddy come in the door. He looked over at all three of us with surprise and a questioning look. "You all havin' a party, an' I ain't got a invite?!" Daddy joked, moving over towards Andy.

"Hmph! Some party!" Mama muttered. She lifted away the jar a moment, and Daddy let out a low whistle.

"That's a good 'un. Did ye be doin' the other boy justice for it?"

"James Otis McKenney!" Mama said, giving him a stern look now.

Daddy immediately put on a more serious face. "Yer mama be right. Ain't 'lowed to be scufflin' on school grounds. Ye know the rules, Andy."

"Yes, sir," Andy answered.

"Get a switchin' from Miz Travis?"

"No, sir."

"Then we be needin' to visit the shed."

"Yes, sir."

"Who was ye fightin' with?" Daddy asked, pouring him a cup of coffee and settling down next to Andy, studying on his cuts, scrapes, and bruises.

"Willie Snodderly."

"Ye could've picked a body who fights fair."

"Wasn't gettin' to pick who I needed to be fightin', Daddy." Mama moved away, and Andy reached up to gingerly feel the sore eye.

"Guess I can understand that. So then Willie started it?"

"Yes, sir. Mostly. But I done took the first swing." Already Daddy'd found out more'n Mama had. Guess it took another man to be understanding scuffling.

"Said somethin' to provoke ye then?" Daddy took a drink of his coffee and set it down on the table. He stared at Andy intently.

"Um . . . Yes, sir."

"Somethin' what got ye riled 'nough to be fightin' on school grounds. Must've been right mean."

"Yes, sir."

Daddy shifted his gaze towards Mama and then sighed. She stared back at him. "Reckon ye might be wantin' to say what it were?"

Andy cleared his throat and looked down at the floor. He answered softly, "No, sir."

Daddy nodded, saying, "Sometimes things ain't worth repeatin'. Better left unsaid." Him and Mama were still looking at each other. "Best be takin' our trip to the shed, though. I 'spect ye be wantin' to get it over with?"

"Yes, sir."

Andy and Daddy both got up, and I held the door open for them. I noticed Andy's shoulders were slumped downwards now, but he walked on out that door of his own. They weren't but a few steps away when I saw Andy look up at Daddy and proudly announce, "I did him justice, Daddy. You should've seen Willie!" And then Daddy put his arm around him.

"Ye be knowin' what Willie said to Andy," Mama stated matter-of-factly. "'Twas 'bout them Yankees and us movin', weren't it?" I didn't answer her. Just kept staring after Daddy and Andy. "That's just like them Snodderlys."

I turned to her and spit out, "Weren't just the Snodderlys! First thing this mornin' Miz Hickman were tellin' me to count my blessin's. Like all this was just nothin', and I should be happy 'bout it! And Willie was only repeatin' what Miz Buchanan and Miz Smith said. 'God's punishin' them McKenneys' and 'Them McKenneys best figure out what they's doin' wrong so's they can fix what God's tryin' to learn 'em' and 'Them McKenneys is sinnin'.' That's what they's sayin'! That's what Nellie's mama be sayin'! Then Miz Travis was agreein' with them all, sayin' practically the same thing 'bout us needin' to listen to God. And even Tommy Lee . . . he . . ."

I stopped then. The memory of pity in Tommy Lee's eyes was more than I could bear. Shoving open the door so hard that it banged against the outside wall, I went tearing down the steps and headed towards the river fast as I could. Pushing all those hurting memories from today aside, I decided to be thinking on only one thing: the foxfire. Granny Mandy'd said it'd always be there—and always glowing. I needed to see it again now.

I glanced towards Granny Mandy's cabin, but she wasn't nowhere to be seen. The path looked mighty different now than it had that evening earlier this week. During daylight there wasn't any scary shadows nor strange shapes here and there. Instead, familiar trees, limbs, and rocks lined the pathway to me and Granny Mandy's secret place. Our magical, wondrous place. Our hopeful place.

Turning off the pathway to the right, I searched frantically for the special stump. Would I be able to find it? Near panic, I rushed every which way for a minute, losing my sense of direction from that night. *Did we come this way? Or was it more to the left?* Dead limbs and smaller stumps were laying about everywhere, confusing and worrying me at the same time. *Where was it?*

I stopped, tears welling up and threatening to spill over when finally I saw it. Our stump! The one that fairies lived in, just barely in this natural world and giving hope amidst so much hurting. I started to run towards it and then slowed, looking about me for signs of the little people. I didn't feel awed and tingly like the other night, but I decided the fairies might still be here, watching. So, stepping gingerly like Granny had done, I approached it with reverence. And then I knelt down before it, wrapping my arms round it and hugging it against my cheek. In my sudden happiness, I giggled, thinking on how silly I would look to anybody happening by—hugging a stump!

Slowly I eased the stump over onto its side once again. When I had placed it gently onto the ground, I squeezed my eyes shut tight. I wanted to be kneeling right over the hole—that glorious city of the fairies— when I opened them, swallowing in that beautiful sight again. Knowing that it would surely look a bit different in the daylight but anticipating its beauty still, I took a deep breath and then opened my eyes.

My mind exploded with horror at the sight before me. *No! No! No!* it was screaming silently, over and over. The ugly, rotting fungus made me draw back in revulsion. It looked slimey and putrid in its tan and dark brown-colored murky chunks of—what? Rotten, filthy life wasting away.

This could never have looked beautiful. Where was the glorious blue and green? Where had the dancing lights of the fairies' city gone? It was a joke! A mean, ill joke that someone was playing on me! There wasn't any beauty here—no magic nor wondrous nor seeing into the fairies' unnatural world. This was *death*. That's what this was—death staring back at me. This foxfire wasn't only not glowing. It was dead!

I rolled onto my side and, curled into a tight ball, sobbed uncontrollably into the leaves piled about my face. The memory of the glowing foxfire had been the only thing giving me hope for the living. It was gone now. God had snuffed even that out. And the blackness left behind pulled me into the dark with it.

5

And tears that never could be shed
Are held within that tender head.
Tears quicken now that once were dead.
O little lamb, how you do weep
For all the strayed and stricken sheep.

The tears came until there were no more. Yet still I laid there, exhausted, spent, weak. I lifted my hand to wipe the wet from my face and then dropped my arm again upon the ground. Seemed like all the energy I once had for living—breathing, moving, wanting to be going somewheres—had come pouring out of me with all them tears.

A smell of sharp dampness made me move my head, and then I noticed a bit of color among the dull, dark brown leaves. A spring beauty had pushed its way through the ground cover. Pushing myself up, I stared at it a minute, studying on its creamy white petals with deep purple tinting around the center. "Don't be a-mockin' me!" I snapped, commanding it to obey. And then I picked what wasn't belonging there, furiously flinging it away as if touching that stem burned my fingers like fire.

Avoiding any looks in the direction of the stump, I slowly rose to my knees and then to my feet. Every inch of me ached like when we'd finished laying by the corn. Except then everybody'd put aside the hurting to celebrate the day being done, and done well. There was joy mixed with those aches. Only more hurting—of the heart kind—covered me now.

I picked my way slowly along the pathway towards Granny Mandy's cabin. And for probably the first time I could ever remember I was hoping to not be seeing her. When I knew the cabin was within sight, I stuck my hands in my pockets and looked down intently at the ground before me.

"Rachael? You been visitin' Lookin' Point?"

The sound of Granny Mandy's voice made me wince. I sneaked a quick look at her, noting that she was in her truck patch, and then I quickly shifted my gaze down to the ground again. *I ain't goin' to be talkin' 'bout no foxfire*! I thought to myself. "Been down towards the river. Thinkin'." Knowing she could tell I'd been crying, I avoided meeting her eyes. The thought struck me that it was the second time today I hadn't told the whole truth.

"Ye feelin' poorly?"

"Yes, ma'am. I need to be headin' on home so's . . ."

"Ye needs to be comin' here so's yer granny can be feelin' ye. What's ailin' ye, child?" I looked up to see Granny Mandy coming towards me with a look of love and concern on her face. Using the hoe like a staff, she walked as far as the fence would allow and then beckoned me over to her. "Come over here an' let me see ye up close," she ordered.

I sighed, knowing there wasn't nothing to do but obey. Daddy'd said once that he never could hide nothing from her, so there wasn't no cause to even try. Guess it was the same for me. I quickly wiped at my face once more, hoping it wasn't still red and splotchy from crying. Walking over to her, I stood before her, staring down at my feet again.

She took my chin in a weathered hand and moved my face one way and then the other. "I'm a-knowin' jest what ye's needin'. Come 'long now." She turned and walked quickly towards her cabin, dropping the hoe where she'd been weeding.

"But Granny Mandy, I . . ."

She kept walking, her form straight, demanding, not taking to no arguing. Glancing down now and then at her budding plants, she picked her way quickly across the garden and up onto the porch. I sighed once more and then walked around the fence to follow Granny Mandy into the cabin.

Holding the door open for me, she studied on my face with them piercing gray eyes of hers, the intentness causing the lines about her eyes to deepen. I could feel myself squirming under her gaze. "Yes'm, that's jest what ye be a-needin', it is." And then she suddenly moved to her wood stove, pushing a pan towards the front and adding some more wood through the eye. "Ye best run and fetch some fresh water from the spigot, Rachael. Fresh'll work best."

"Yes, ma'am." I still didn't know what Granny Mandy was fixing to cook, but I was relieved anyways. She hadn't said anything about me crying—nor had she mentioned the foxfire—and for that I was surely grateful. Least, I think I was grateful. Daddy'd told us about some of Granny Mandy's remedies from when he was a young'un, and some of them sounded kindly bad. Awful even. Like the time he complained of the itch on his chest and stomach. Granny Mandy'd mixed lard, sulphur, and whiskey and spread it over his whole body! Then another time she was treating him for a bad stomachache and give him a swallow of wine—followed by a dose of Vaseline! Daddy said it done stopped the hurting though. Like to scared it out of him.

When I come back, Granny Mandy was examining the leaves of one of her many kinds of herbs. I leaned over her hands, taking in a deep breath and knew right off that it was sage. It smelled good, reminding me of cornbread dressing and chicken soup.

"Get that water to boilin', Rachael. We's fixin' to make us some sage tea."

I poured the water into the pan and moved it to the hottest eye, the one directly over the firebox. Granny's stove was old, but that didn't mean it couldn't work right well. I knew it wouldn't take the water long before it was bubbling. "Now, we'll put in this sage and let it boil 'til it's right dark colored," Granny Mandy said, picking up a wooden spoon and handing it to me.

"Never heard of usin' sage for tea, Granny. What's it for?" I stirred the water and leaves of sage, wondering what she had decided was ailing me. I was hoping too that this was the only remedy. And that she wasn't planning on adding any Vaseline to this here pan.

"Sage tea's a springtime tonic. Plain to see you's ailin'. And it be spring." She lifted her eyebrows and shoulders. "Oughta be hepin'. 'Sides, it most certainly ain't goin' to hurt ye none." Motioning towards the chairs before the fire, Granny Mandy said, "Pot don't need to be watched. Let's us set and rock a spell."

Reluctantly I put down the spoon and moved to the rocker. It did feel good to be in this familiar place once again, rocking in Granny's rocker, staring into her fireplace. But the cloud of darkness still hung about me. And the foxfire set right down between us, separating us same as a thick wall.

"Reckon they's some reason you be home early from schoolin'. Seen Andy up to the house too." I could feel her eyes on me, but I didn't return her look. "Was they trouble to school?"

"Andy got into a scuffle." The words come out as plain and matter-of-fact like I'd answered a question about geography from Miz Travis. Granny Mandy didn't seem to take no notice though.

"Who was he after?"

"Willie Snodderly." I paused a minute, deciding on whether to add more information or not. "Tommy Lee ended it."

"That be good. Both boys banged up a good bit?"

"Kindly so. Miz Travis sent 'em both to home. And Daddy and O A. already visited the shed." I glanced up at her. "For fightin' at school."

Granny Mandy nodded her head. "Same rule yer grandaddy always had fer yer daddy." She chuckled then. "I can recollect they was days yer daddy jest come up the lane an' headed straightways fer the shed. Didn't bother to come inside nor say nothin'. Jest went straight fer the shed an' yer grandaddy followed 'im in!"

She got up to stir the tea, saying, "She's comin' along just fine. Be ready soon." Once she'd settled into the rocker again, she asked, "So what's Andy scufflin' 'bout? Cain't be gals already!"

I smiled faintly at that. "No, onliest way Andy'd be fightin' over a gal was if someone accused him of likin' one. That'd make him come out a-swingin'."

"What did get him riled?"

I took a deep breath. After already telling Mama once, I surely wasn't wanting to say all them things again. Somehow repeating those awful words seemed to be giving them a right to be said. Like they were true or something.

"Is they hurtin' in the sayin' o' the words?" Granny asked. Her voice was tender. Soft. I remembered Daddy saying about the same thing to Andy.

I looked at her then, wanting to for the first time, searching for the caring that I knew would be there. *She knows me so well*, I thought to myself. *Does she know the foxfire is between us now?* "Yes, Granny. They was real ill things what Willie said. But Willie was only repeatin' what other people'd said. That's what made 'em so mean." I looked back at the fire. "And made Andy so angry. And hurt."

"My daddy used to tell a story 'bout thrashin' the rye." She rocked harder then, and I knew she'd be repeating it for me. "Didn't have no thrashin' machines way back when I was a young'un. So they'd dig 'em a hole in the ground, put a wagon sheet in it, an' then lay a bunch o' poles over that there hole. Then Daddy'd put the rye over top them poles and we'd all beat at it with more poles. The rye'd fall right down the hole onto that sheet. We'd gather up that sheet an' dump the rye into a big ole sack. Only problem was, that rye had plenty o' chaff in it. So, we'd wait til' a windy day come. Then you'd take a handful o' that rye an' pour it into another sack, lettin' the wind blow the chaff right out o' it." She stopped rocking a minute and went through the motions of lifting a handful of that rye and then pouring it into another sack. I watched her intently, puzzled.

"I'm not understandin' you, Granny. What's the thrashin' got to do with Andy's fightin'?"

"Well, my daddy used to tell me that folks' jawin' was like rye what had chaff in it. 'Ye need to be throwin' the whole handful o' them words to the wind,' he'd say to me. 'See what's rye an' what be chaff. And then let the chaff blow away.'" She threw her arm up into the air once more, watching imaginary chaff blow away. And then she looked at me. We stared at each other a minute before she continued, "Think on it a spell, Rachael. Some be rye. Most prob'ly be chaff." She got up to move to the stove once again and then glanced at me over her shoulder. "Let that chaff blow 'way!"

I could hear the advice from Miz Hickman, words of gossip from Miz Buchanan and Miz Smith, and then the agreeing from Miz Travis repeated in my head. *Us McKenneys wasn't sinnin'!* my mind shouted. *And we don't have to be countin' it a blessin' that the Yankees is tryin' to take our land! But could God be tryin' to teach us somethin'? Teach me somethin'? Is this the rye among the chaff? How was I to know the diff'rence?*

Granny Mandy come back over to me with a steaming cup of the tea. "Here. Now be sippin' this. I put in a heapin' spoon o' honey, knowin' how you like a good bit in everthin' else. Springtime tonic it is. Works right well too." She stood before me, watching.

"Ain't you goin' to drink some too?" I asked her.

"I ain't feelin' poorly. You is," she pointed out.

"Did you put anythin' else in it?" I asked warily, glancing around the room for her case of medicines and homemade remedies.

"Jest the honey. Come on now, take a sip. 'Tis a soothin' drink."

I lifted the cup to my lips, breathing in the gentle, caressing aroma of the sage. Letting the first sip set in my mouth awhile, I pondered over its effect a minute. Granny Mandy was right. It was good. And soothing. "'Tis a fine tea, Granny. Thank you for makin' it for me."

She smiled then and set down in the rocker. "Good. Iffin it weren't hepin' ye, I were goin' to add a little somethin'. To hep it a bit." She give me one of them teasing smiles and her gray eyes twinkled.

"What's that?" I asked suspiciously.

"Cain't say."

"Why not?" I took another sip of the hot tea.

"Count o' it takes away the 'kick' what makes a body get well if it ain't a secret."

"But Daddy said you once give him Vaseline for a stomachache. He knew 'bout that and it worked."

"Weren't the Vaseline what made him better." Granny rocked back and forth in an even rhythm, shaking her head and giving me a smug look. "Done tol' you, they's got to be a secret ingredient to make a body better."

"Well, then, if it weren't the Vaseline, what was it?"

"It were what I added to the wine." Those eyes were really gleaming now. "Kerosene!"

"Kerosene!? Are you tellin' me that to this very day Daddy don't know that you give him kerosene?"

"Cain't tell 'im—you neither! He might be comin' to me again some day fer my famous cure for the stomachache!" Granny Mandy started into chuckling, and then I was laughing with her. "'Sides, kerosene's s'pose to be fer curin' the cough. I only added it to be makin' sure my remedy had a secret ingredient." She chuckled again. "Iffin I'd knowed it would've worked so quick like, I'd o' added that drop o' kerosene to ever cure I give yer daddy!"

Thinking on me and Granny's secret made me smile until I looked at the glowing embers of the fire again and was reminded of the other secret we'd recently shared. *Will I ever be able to look at a fire again without thinkin' on the cool, blue glow of the foxfire? The foxfire that had lied, mocked, and cheated me?* My smile faded, and I became silent again. The only sounds were the steady creaking of me and Granny's rockers and the occasional soft crackling of the fire.

"Ye were sayin' that Andy were angry an' hurt." Her words were an intrusion upon the cabin's quiet. I frowned. "Seems to me Andy's not the onliest one who be angry and hurtin'."

"I ain't angry," I insisted, stubbornly.

"Rachael, ye be fairly burstin' with it! Yer anger come stompin' up that path from the river right in front of ye—meetin' me long before ye did!"

I looked at her in amazement. "I ain't angry, Granny Mandy! I'm just hurtin' so terrible bad that I can't . . . I can't . . ."

"Ye cain't see no end to it. And it's threatenin' to drown ye in the depth o' it. The sun's gone dark an' the moon an' stars ain't goin' to shine no more. Ever." Granny Mandy stopped rocking as she leaned towards me, looking as though she was straining with every breath. Her skin seemed to be stretched taut over her face and her eyes mirrored my pain. *My pain? Or was it her own?* She leaned back in the rocker again. "On account o' the dark has come. The dark."

Granny Mandy stared into the fire, and I stared at her. *How does she know? How can she be explainin' exactly how I'm feelin'?* "What do you mean by 'the dark,' Granny? Oh, I feel it. But what is it?"

"'Tis yer anger. And ye need to be admittin' that ye be angry before ye can begin to see beyond the dark."

I sighed. "I reckon I am right put out with Willie. But not nearly as much as with Verna Mae's mama and Nellie's mama and Miz Travis, for the mean things they was sayin'. They's the ones I guess I'm most angry with. Or maybe the Yankees. They's really the ones I'm thinkin' so ill about."

"No they ain't." Granny voice was gentle and yet firm at the same time.

"They ain't? Then who?"

"Need to be lookin' deep inside ye, Rachael. Ye needs be answerin' that fer yerself." I thought a minute about the times I'd been angry lately—when Mister Sherman had first talked with us and upset Mama so. And when I stomped down the hill to Granny Mandy's, mashing all the flowers along the way. I recollected when I first saw Andy's pitiful, beat-up face and then heard Willie's whining excuses for fighting. And then there was the foxfire. Of course I was hurt and angry about the foxfire.

Granny's words cut into the silence again. "Ye be arguin' with people, Rachael, but who ere ye truly blamin'?"

The answer fairly burst out of me. "God!" I sobbed out. "'Tis all His fault! Wouldn't none of this be happenin' if He wouldn't let it be so!" My tears come pouring out once again, running down my face, stinging my already chapped and raw cheeks. Granny let me cry awhile before she softly said, "I ain't goin' to give ye no reasons an' whys fer all this, Rachael. Seems to me Job's friends—an' some friends they was—already done tried that. All they done was make everthin' worse."

I sniffled and wiped at my face. "Like Miz Hickman, Miz Smith, and Miz Travis?"

Granny Mandy nodded. "Let's us be lettin' that chaff blow 'way. What I am goin' to be tellin' ye is that ye needs be seein' yer anger at God fer what it is. Lettin' it out. Settin' it free. Gettin' on." She paused a minute. "Most folks don't want to be admittin' they's angry with God 'cause they's afeared then He'll get angry back at 'em. But God's anger ain't like ours, Rachael. He's bigger'n that. His anger's towards *sin*, not people. Not His lambs. You's one of His lambs . . . an' He's a-lovin' ye, no matter how things may be lookin' to ye."

The tears kept running down my cheeks. When I blinked, the fire seemed to grow bigger and brighter from the tears filling my eyes. "God seems so far away, Granny Mandy," I whispered. "I can't rightly feel Him no more."

"He ain't left ye. Might seem that way, but He ain't. And He ain't put the dark there. That's our doin'." I looked over at Granny Mandy and saw she was resting her head against the back of the rocker with her eyes closed. "When yer grandaddy died the darkness come to me. Stayed fer a good bit until I set down in this very rocker, cryin' my anger an' hurt out to God. Askin' Him why He weren't carin' that I be hurtin' so." I saw one tear move slowly down through the many wrinkles on her aged cheek. "It was then that I was a-knowin' that God weren't way off somewheres, just a-watchin' me hurtin'—not carin' nor nothin'. He were hurtin' with me. Cryin' with me. So's I pictured Jesus settin' right here in this rocker, holdin' me in His arms, lettin' His tears flow and mingle with mine."

I closed my eyes then, resting my head against the back of the rocker like Granny Mandy. And I pictured Jesus holding me, crying with me, caring that I was hurting. More tears flowed down my cheeks for awhile, but then they slowed. And finally stopped. I could still feel the darkness, but it wasn't pushing and pressing at me right now. It had moved off to just beyond my reach. But I knew it was still there, waiting.

We rocked together in silence for some time. Sipping my tea, I recollected that I did feel kindly better now and then started in to worrying that Granny Mandy had snuck something in it after all. I tilted the cup to inspect the bottom and then suspiciously looked around the room for her kerosene jug when Granny's voice made me jump.

"No, James Henry. They ain't lettin' me go jest yet."

Her odd-sounding words sent a shiver down my spine. "What's that Granny? I didn't hear what you's sayin'.'"

Granny Mandy turned towards me then—but with a vacant gaze through glassy, unfocused eyes—like she wasn't even knowing I was there. Her lips were slightly parted, and the heavily wrinkled forehead creased into a confused look. Squinting her eyes as she stared past me towards her quilted bed, Granny said, "Soon, James Henry. Veil's gettin' thinner, passin' 'way . . ."

I jumped up then, knocking my tea to the floor and causing loud clangs as the metal cup bounced across the hearth of the fireplace. Grabbing up Granny Mandy's hands, I knelt at her feet. "Granny," I said breathlessly, "Granny, is you all right? Is somethin' ailin' you?"

She looked down at me then, and slowly a relaxed smile spread across that weathered face. The now clear gray eyes focused steadily on mine. "Why Rachael, what you be doin' at my feet, frettin' over yer granny so? Ain't no cause to be worryin'!" She patted my cheek, shaking her head at me. "Time's gettin' on too. Best be headin' on out to that truck patch again. Them weeds ain't goin' to be hoein' themselves." She squeezed my hands once, brushed them aside, and then putting her hands on the arms of the rocker, pushed herself up. Rubbing the small of her back, Granny Mandy said, "Feelin' it in my bones again today. Rain's comin' this evenin', I reckon."

I still set there on the floor, watching her with concern. "Shouldn't you be restin' awhile yet, Granny Mandy? If your rheumatism's botherin' you—"

"Land, no, child! Iffin I set ever time it acted up, I'd be settin' in that there rocker more'n Ol' Man Snodderly snores on his bench!" She giggled then and walked over to the stove, pushing the pan of tea to the back. "Or I'd be like that rooster what was so lazy that he done waited fer the other roosters to be crowin'. An' then he jest nodded his head!" I smiled at her. She held out the pan towards me. "More tea here for the wantin'. Don't be backwards none."

"Thank you, Granny Mandy, but I best be gettin' on home to see what chores Mama wants doin'." Still worrying about her, I added, "I bet Mama'd be happy to let me weed yer garden for you, Granny. I just need to run home to ask and . . ."

"Rachael—" She turned to me then, putting her hands on her hips. "Iffin I be too old to be weedin' my own truck patch, then ye best be puttin' me in a pine box. Now you be fetchin' yerself home before yer mama starts in to hollerin' fer ye. And come on back later if ye be needin' any more o' my springtime tonic." She winked at me then. "I could make a special batch iffin yer daddy be wantin' some too!"

I stood up and, after retrieving the cup, walked over to her. "Thank you again for the tea, Granny Mandy." I set the cup down on the table. "And if you be needin' any help, you just holler for me, okay?"

"Ain't goin' to be needin' no help, but thank ye anyways, child." She picked up the cup and studied on it a minute, turning it this way an' that. "Don't rightly 'member this handle bein' so banged about. Reckon that don't matter much though. She'll likely hold my coffee good's the queen's china!"

I hesitated about leaving once again, concern for her welling up in me and threatening to spill over. Wanting to grab her up in a hug but afraid to lest it would somehow confuse her even more, I stood with my hand on the door handle, waiting. She give me a puzzled look.

"Rachael, now I'm wonderin' if my tonic done worked or not! You best be comin' back later for a refill. And maybe I should put in a secret ingredient in yers next time too . . ." Her eyes twinkled again, and I smiled at her.

"No, Granny Mandy. I b'lieve it worked just fine the way it is!" Again I hesitated a moment. "Remember, I'll be in hollerin' distance if you need me for anythin'."

"Shoo! I ain't goin' to be doin' no hollerin' less it's at them pesky weeds!" She waved me on, and I went on down the steps and across the road towards home. Glancing back over my shoulder, I saw her still standing there, watching me.

Oh, Granny Mandy! I worried to myself. *I know the foxfire's come between us, but I still be needin' you. How I be needin' you!* I kept seeing her vacant stare and confusing words. *James Henry,* she'd said. *Was she talkin' to Grandaddy? She ain't never done that before!* And then I thought on her not even remembering when the cup fell, denting the handle. *Where had she gone to when that happened?*

The rest of the day I watched over chickens, cows, and mules in the doing of chores; I glimpsed at trees, grass, and the outbuildings as I passed them by; and I looked into the eyes of Mama, Daddy, and Andy as I talked with them. But all I ever really saw was Granny Mandy's face.

Granny was right. On Friday evening the rain had come in sneaking like a fox to the henhouse. And Saturday saw a steady patter on the roof followed by a drizzle that lingered through the night. But the sun come peeking through the lingering clouds on Sunday morning, promising a beautiful spring day. I watched it this morning since I'd been up long before dawn; me and Mama'd been fixing and cooking something feverish to get everything ready for today's after-church social and all-day singing.

We'd made fried chicken and gravy, cole slaw, sweet tater casserole, green beans with Irish taters, biscuits, and my most favorite: Mama'd baked her special layer cake. Smelling those sweet taters cooking made me think on James Junior and how fiercely I missed him. *Could it truly be only a week since that last Sunday together? Doesn't it seem like a eternity of heartbreakin' things have happened since then? And does James Junior know about the dam and what the Yankees are askin' us to do?* Oh, how my heart ached to talk with him.

When I was little, my big brother had been my watchman, my protector, my rescuer. During recess at school, James Junior played games with his friends but somehow still managed to keep a watch over me. Any bullies casting a look in my direction were quickly discouraged by a narrowing squint of James Junior's eyes. He kept the playing of games fair, righted wrongs, and settled the squabbling amongst all us young'uns. I always felt safe when James Junior was running the playground and kindly unsure when he stayed home to help Daddy with the chores. And now he'd left us to be working for the government

CCC, leaving a playground that not only wasn't fair, but was terrible wrong. *Oh, James Junior*, I thought to myself as I lifted them sweet taters into the warming closet, *can't you come home and settle all this just like you done for me so many times before?*

Once or twice this morning I'd glanced towards Granny Mandy's cabin. A sick feeling of fear still washed through me when I thought about her confusion on Friday morning. Granny'd always been so quick and keen; and unlike so many old folks around here, she wasn't hard of hearing, losing her eyesight, nor getting forgetful about things. Oh, I know the rheumatism bothered her a good deal more'n she let on, and she did squint when she was reading. But she could still do her own choring—insisted on doing it—and I imagine she could use that gun of hers to easily hit a Yankee a considerable distance down the road too.

I kept going back and forth between feeling anxious to see Granny Mandy again—and then seeing that there wasn't no cause to be worrying—and feeling afraid to see her and finding out that there was. *What if she's still confused? What if she's worse yet?* The memory of her glassy, unfocused eyes caused me to shiver. I recollected one time when I was fretting over a number of things, complaining to Granny Mandy, and she'd said, "Ye's traipsin' yer worries in front o' ye like a parade, Rachael!" Well, I was parading them again this morning, all right. Marching neatly right in front of me they were.

When I was ready for my bath, Daddy helped me haul the galvanized tub into the kitchen, and I mixed enough boiling water with the cold directly from the spring to make the water tolerable warm. While scrubbing my hair, I was thinking that maybe Mama would help me fix it special again this Sunday. I was hesitant about seeing Tommy Lee; remembering his pitying look made my stomach tighten. But I still wanted to look nice. Just because.

I toweled myself dry and put on old clothes once again so I wouldn't risk getting my church clothes wet when me and Daddy dumped the water from the tub. Mama'd already sewed me a new blouse from the yard goods with the blue flowers, adding a bit of lace what she'd been saving for round the collar. It was downright beautiful, and I couldn't wait to wear it for the first time.

"Daddy, can you come help me empty this tub now?" I called across the breezeway.

Just then Andy come stomping out the other door and into the kitchen, followed closely by Mama. Mama didn't look none too happy neither.

"Since you're here, Andy, you can be helpin' me dump this here water," I said to him. "Grab up the other side and—"

"Andy ain't goin' to be dumpin' no water just yet," Mama said. "Least ways not 'til he's done scrubbed himself in it. From head to toe too! Boy's such a pigsty, why, folks'd be goin' round 'im like the swamp." She folded her arms across her chest, shaking her head at him.

"But he took a bath last night, didn't he?" I asked. And then I noticed the caked-on dirt still all over his face, in his hair, and under his fingernails. "How'd you manage to set in there all that time and not get any of that dirt off you anyways?"

Andy screwed his face over to one side again. And scowled at me. "Done the best I could."

"At what? Keepin' the dirt on?" I teased him. Mama give me a frown then.

"Appears them bruises and black eye ain't takin' to scrubbin' so good just yet," Mama said, helping him undo the suspenders of his overalls. "But a body oughta be thinkin' on that before he was a-scufflin' at school!"

I looked at his face more closely then, noting the many cuts and bruises that were still there, along with the puffed eye. That shiner did appear to be terrible sore. It was in the first stage of the many colors I knew it would go through—blackish and dark blue. And it did indeed fairly shine. Suddenly I felt bad for him, knowing Mama would be scrubbing that face of his without no mercy. Mama didn't take to no dirty faces going to church, sore or no. Poor O.A. was in for it, that was for sure.

"Go on an' get dressed and get yer hair dry, Rachael," Mama said. "Andy won't be in this here tub long. We needs be packin' all this food yet."

I give Andy one last look and, since Mama's back was to me, mouthed *sorry* to him. He only shrugged his shoulders in response, but that was something. At least he hadn't scowled again.

"I'll be down to help you with the food, Mama," I called over my shoulder as I walked out of the kitchen. Up in my room I examined my new blouse, picking it up so carefully and handling it like it was one of those expensive ready-made ones from the chicken boat. Hurriedly I shed my working clothes and then, pulling on the blouse, I buttoned it slowly, enjoying the feel of it against my fingers and skin. Pulling the small mirror off my windowsill, I examined the collar the best I could. The extra bit of lace was so thoughtful of Mama. It looked lovely.

Grabbing up my comb, I began working through the tangled mess of coppery-colored curls. I knew I didn't dare ask for Mama's help now, seeing how Andy's unexpected bath would take up more of her time this morning. So I combed my hair the best I could and then worked it into one long braid. It wasn't special and it sure wasn't what I had been planning on, but it would have to do.

I slipped on my skirt and socks and give my Sunday shoes a quick spit-shine again. Looking at them shoes and then the blue flowers in my blouse, I thought of the beautiful blue shoes on the chicken boat. *Oh, wouldn't they just look beautiful?* I mused. I closed my eyes a moment and imagined them on my feet and Verna Mae, Nellie, Merry Jo—and Tommy Lee too, of course—making over them shoes! Then, jumping up to inspect myself in the mirror once more, I give my hair a quick pat and gingerly walked on down the steps.

Mama was just putting on her hat at her dresser and she looked over at me, motioning me to come to her. That dresser with the big swiveling mirror on top was the prettiest piece of furniture that our family owned, once belonging to Mama's family and toted here in a wagon when Mama married Daddy. It was made of oak, and the carved wood round the mirror was curved beautifully. Something about it always made me want to rub my hand along them graceful curves. The dresser drawers had pretty handles that Mama said James Junior, me, and Andy'd loved to pull on when we was crawling babies. I also loved to look at the feminine things that she kept setting there on top—her silver brush, comb, and mirror set (though they weren't real, since the silver plating was nearly completely worn off the handles), a china hair dish that was chipped, and two empty yet still pretty perfume bottles. All those things fascinated me, so I stood there pleasuring in the looking at them, waiting on Mama.

"Quick now," Mama ordered. "Take down yer braid."

I gave her a puzzled look but did as she asked. "Ain't we needin' to get all that food packed up?"

"Yer daddy and Andy's seein' to it," she said, picking up her brush and working it through my thick hair. Then she opened her top dresser drawer and pulled out a light blue ribbon—one that exactly matched the blue flowers in my blouse.

"Mama!" I exclaimed. "Where did you get that? It's perfect!"

"Found it with my box of special things where the bit of lace was. Couldn't believe myself how perfectly it matched. It were made for wearin' with this blouse, Rachael." Her face lit up with excitement as she gathered up my hair like she'd done last Sunday and then tied the beautiful bit of blue around it. She placed her hands on my shoulders then, and we both admired the color as I turned my head one way and then the other before the mirror. "'Sides, it be important for us McKenneys to be lookin' fine today. Holdin' our heads up high." I noticed her chin lift just a bit as she said that.

"You mean because of the Yankees and all?"

She nodded her head. "No matter what happens, Rachael, us McKenneys will be facin' our troubles square, just like we always done." Mama squared her shoulders to the reflection in the mirror, and I watched as a determined look come over the set of her fine features. "My mama used to be sayin' they was two kinds o' southern women— them what whined and pouted over their troubles and them what set to doin' what needs doin'. Wasn't that they wasn't afeared, mind you. But they had what my mama called character. An' courage to be facin' troubles. You'll be facin' everbody with a new blouse and ribbon,"— she looked at me and smiled faintly then—"and Andrew'll meet 'em with a *clean* bruised and battered face. Now, let's us see how yer daddy and Andy done with the packin'."

Mama turned to head towards the kitchen, but I stopped her a minute. "Mama, thank you for the beautiful blouse and the ribbon. They make me feel very . . . very special. And more courageous too." She reached out and touched my cheek, giving me another quick smile.

When we went out onto the breezeway, Daddy was calling, "Whoa there, Dean! We ain't loaded up the gals yet!" He looked over at us then, holding onto the reins with one hand and waving the other at us. "Come on, you two! Everthin's loaded a'ready and Old Dean here's a might anxious—smellin' all them fine dishes of yers, I reckon, Miz McKenney. Andy, help yer mama an' sister up."

After Mama'd climbed up to the seat beside him and I settled in the back of the wagon with Andy, Daddy looked back at us and frowned. "Don't rightly know if we'll be makin' it to church on time. Might not even get any further than this here spot."

"Why's that, Daddy?" Andy still fell for Daddy's teasing sometimes, biting at his bait like catfish bit on a calm, easy evening.

"Old Dean's nose ere prob'ly goin' to just follow them pleasin' smells comin' from the back of the wagon, takin' us round an' round an' round in circles. I recollect if we's lucky, we might git 'im to stop in 'bout a week or so!"

"Oh, Daddy!" Andy sighed, knowing he'd been taken again. But me and Mama grinned at Daddy's fooling.

Granny Mandy was waiting for us on her porch, rocking easylike in her most favorite rocker. Anxiously I looked her over from head to toe, noting the faded green felt hat with torn netting that she'd carefully arranged over her forehead, her Sunday-best dress with the big yellow flowers all over it, and her best black shoes that she wore only on special occasions or Sundays. She stood up quickly and easily, no pushing herself up from the arms of her rocker like she'd done Friday. As Old Dean pulled us up to her porch, I saw a grin—and more importantly, a clear look about her eyes.

"Hey, you all," Granny greeted us. "'Pears we got us a right fine day for the church social." She leaned over to pat a box next to the rocker. "Packed me just a few fixin's to be takin' 'long."

Daddy picked it up, letting out an exaggerated groan. "Granny Mandy, the day you be takin' a few fixin's be the day we's all meetin' Jesus fer that big weddin' feast." He offered her his arm and then added, "Then again, I might oughta be changin' my mind on that 'un." Daddy winked at her. "If there's a feast in heaven, you likely be cookin' up a storm for that too!" He placed Granny's box next to ours and then led her around to the front of the wagon, helping her up beside Mama.

Andy leaned over to take a good sniff of the smells teasing at us from Granny's box. "Oh, Granny Mandy! You fixed fried chicken too!" Andy exclaimed. She looked back at us then, smiling. "I'm goin' to be sure an' get some of Mama's and yours!"

"You best be gettin' to the table before Preacher Morgan then; you know how them preachers love their chicken!"

"Why is it preachers be so partial to chicken?" Andy asked her. "Truth tell though, I ain't never noticed Preacher pilin' his plate with no more chicken'n everbody else."

"Didn't I never tell you 'bout the time before yer grandaddy and me was hitched?" Granny Mandy asked us. Me and Andy exchanged glances, shaking our heads. "Well, then. Had us a travelin' preacher way back. Didn't live here to Jordan's Bend an' only come preachin' once ever month."

She shifted a bit on the seat so she could see me and Andy and Mama and Daddy. Evidently she was settling in to talk a good bit, and as Daddy coaxed Old Dean down the road, I smiled contentedly. Granny Mandy was telling us another of her stories. She was fine, and I pushed away all them silly fears that had been bothering at me.

"Well, one Sunday we'd planned a all-day singin' and dinner-on-the-grounds," Granny Mandy went on. Those eyes were dancing and kindly lit up now. "We all was right excited that the travelin' preacher were goin' to be with us that day. So us gals was plannin' to cook us up a feast. The week before the social, somebody passed round the rumor that the preacher fairly craved fried chicken. Fact was, folks was sayin', that were his most favorite an' 'bout the only meat what he liked." Granny Mandy looked back at Andy then, nodding her head at him. "So, 'course I fried me up a chicken. Fattest one o' the lot. Yer great-granny fried up a chicken too, but I'd done a'ready picked the best 'un. Packed it up an' me an' my daddy an' mama set off fer the services."

"Did the preacher eat yours, Granny Mandy?" Andy asked.

She chuckled, shaking her head at him. "Well, ever gal what come was totin' fried chicken. An' 'bout ever gal in this whole county come to that all-day singin' an' dinner-on-the-grounds. They was more fried chicken than ye could ever imagine in all yer borned days! Piles of it, tables of it, a schoolyard full've it! That there preacher eat fried chicken, that's fer sure. But mine? Ain't no way a body could tell what belonged to who with all that chicken everwheres!"

"But Granny," I said, skeptically, "we's had us plenty of socials, and I never knowed ever gal to bring the same dish. They's always plenty of cured ham with red-eye gravy and fried pork chops and roast beef and baked chicken and—"

"Oh, but they's one part o' this here story I ain't tole ye yet." Granny Mandy paused a minute, raising her chin important like and givin' us all a "you best be listenin' close now" look before she continued. "This particular travelin' preacher ain't picked him a wife yet. He were right eligible, as they say, and so tall an' skinny. Why, iffin he'd closed one eye he'd look like a needle. An' such a head o' hair on 'im—thick an' black it were—an' one o' them voices what boomed when he talked. Sent shivers down most folks' spines. Well, I tell you, when everbody heard this fine, eligible preacher were wantin' fried chicken an' they was goin' to be a dinner-on-the-grounds, you can bet they come from far an' wide. Why, I 'magine they was single gals at that there social come from—oh, far 'ways as Cal-i-for-ni-ay prob'ly. And totin' fried chicken, ever one of 'em, they was."

She laughed then, and we all joined in with her. Andy tugged at Granny Mandy's sleeve, though, looking a bit confused. "But Granny, was you tryin' to impress the preacher too? What 'bout Grandaddy?"

"Oh, I recollect that I was wantin' to be bringin' the best fried chicken. But I only said most folks was shiverin' at the sound o' his voice. Not me. No, sir!" She grinned at Andy and then grew more withdrawn for a moment, gazing off to the dogwoods that were in full bloom now, scattering their delicate white blooms across the hillside. "No, they was a soft-spoken man at that there social what was a-stealin' my heart 'way." Granny Mandy grew quiet, and I watched her closely, concerned again. Suddenly she leaned over to look at Daddy. "Reckon Mister Roddy be there today?"

"'Spect so. You be needin' to speak with 'im?"

"Yes sir, that I do."

"Needin' lumber from the mill? Me an' Andy can be makin' whatever ye be wantin'." Daddy was hunched over with his arms resting on his knees as he kept ahold of the reins.

"Thank ye, but I'll be speakin' with Mister Roddy. 'Tain't nothin' much I be needin'." Daddy turned to Mama then, giving her a puzzled look. I saw Mama shake her head at him, answering his look with a questioning expression of her own.

What is Granny Mandy plannin' now? I wondered. *Does it have somethin' to do with them Yankees?* I stared at her awhile again, my mind fretting and stewing over what could be, might be. And then I shook it off, telling myself that by all accounts Granny Mandy seemed fine. She was her same old self and there wasn't no cause to be worrying. And if she had a hankering for some wood for a new shed or chest or something, then there wasn't any reason to be thinking it was anything more than that.

"Nigh to forgot!" Granny Mandy said, slapping one knee and reassuring me again that she hadn't changed one bit. "They's a end to my story too. That preacher didn't see fit to pick ary a gal from our county." She frowned, shaking her head. "Picked 'im one from upstate somewheres we heard. 'Spect none o' our fried chicken suited him! Well, several years later he come travelin' through Jordan's Bend, preachin' for a week o' tent meetin's. By then he'd changed a good bit."

"How Granny?" Andy asked. "Weren't he preachin' with a—how'd you say it?—boomin' voice no more?"

"Oh, he still made 'em tremble! Packed 'em in that tent for them meetin's. Fact is, he were hollerin' out them blessed words louder'n ever!"

"Then how were he changed, Granny Mandy?" Andy was anxiously pulling the telling out of her. He knew—like me, Daddy, and Mama—that Granny was dangling another part of the story in front of us, keeping our attention better'n any schoolteacher ever could've done.

"Why, there weren't no more'n a smidgen o' black hair ringin' round that head o' his." She drew a *U* around her own head, demonstrating. "And the top—land, a body had to shield his eyes from the glare what come off that bald head when they lit the lamps in that there tent!"

"Oh, Granny!" Andy chuckled and scoffed at her.

"That ain't all!" She paused again, and me and Andy both leaned closer towards her so we wouldn't be missing one word. "That preacher could holler up a storm on account o' he most likely weighed nigh to six-hundred pounds iffin he weighed a ounce!" I glanced over to Andy and saw that his eyes were big around as could be. I suppose he was trying to imagine a body that big, just like I was. "Reckon that wife he hitched up to could fry some chicken, all right," Granny continued. "Yes, sir, yer grandaddy said it well, he did. When he seen that preacher he says to me, 'Miz McKenney, once that preacher done seen all them tables o' fried chicken what Jordan's Bend fixed for 'im, well, he didn't never ferget it. He most likely done decided that were a tolerable amount fer his bride to be fixin' ever day!'"

We laughed with Granny Mandy again then, and I was thinking to myself that most likely every time she told that story, the single gals that come got more and from farther away, the amount of fried chicken covered more tables and piled higher, and the preacher—well, he got bigger every time in the telling too!

"So, Andrew," Granny Mandy said, "that be one reason why we be knowin' that preachers be partial to fried chicken. I ain't knowed one yet what wasn't. No, sir, I ain't."

She turned to face the road before us then, her story done. A uneasy silence settled over us all. Me and Andy stared at where we'd been, and Granny, Daddy, and Mama looked ahead to where we were going. I closed my eyes, not wanting to see what was ahead nor behind me. The silence forced me to think on too many things—what folks might be saying at church, how awkward I'd be feeling around Nellie and Verna Mae, and how I was wanting to avoid meeting Tommy Lee's eyes. *Oh, Granny Mandy!* my thoughts cried out. *I want to be believin' you and hopin'—hopin' that you be right and we won't be movin', hopin' that everthin'll be just as it was before. But the foxfire, Granny. There ain't no hopin' in the foxfire no more!*

When we rounded the bend just up from the schoolhouse, my stomach tightened nervously. Glancing over to Andy, I noticed he stared straight ahead, jaw clenched, eyes narrowed, and lips pressed in a grim line. I could see a muscle twitching in his cheek—it moved a particularly bad scratch in and out—and I wondered if he was thinking about what Miz Smith, Miz Buchanan, and Miz Travis'd said. Them words were surely bothering at me still.

Folks were calling *hey* to each other and waving, appearing excited about the social today. When we pulled under the shade of the curvy-limbed oak and Daddy jumped down to tie up Old Dean, a few called to us, but those that had been standing around talking began moving on inside the church. Quickly I glanced around to look for Merry Jo, Verna Mae, Nellie, and Tommy Lee among the groups of folks going up the steps into church. Not spying any of them, I was thankful. And then I remembered Mama's instructions about us McKenneys keeping our heads up today. As Daddy helped me down from the wagon, I glanced over to Mama and noticed the firm set of her jaw and the upwards tilt of that sculptured chin. After smoothing my hair and quickly checking the bright blue bow, I took a deep breath and then raised mine too.

Daddy and Andy carried our boxes into the schoolhouse, setting them with everybody else's in the back. There were piles of them there, and the smells were wonderful. We were all going to be hard-pressed to listen right well to Preacher Morgan this morning with all them smells teasing at us during his sermon.

Granny Mandy, Daddy, and Mama were saying *hey* and *good mornin'*! to folks, nodding and smiling at everybody as they walked up the aisle, with me and Andy following behind. Seemed like everybody'd smile right quick back to them, then turn away even quicker like they didn't have time for any conversation. Or like they were nervous about something. *Were we late?* I wondered to myself. *Could it be past time for services to start and so that's why folks isn't wantin' to talk with Granny, Mama, and Daddy right now? But why is they actin' so nervous like?* Glancing over to Andy beside me, I noticed he wasn't even looking around; instead, he was still staring straight ahead just like he was in the back of the wagon. Seemed like Andy'd drawn into himself somehow, not even admitting that there was anybody else in this here church today. I almost wished that were true.

I could see Tommy Lee out of the corner of my eye, but I didn't look over to him. Didn't have the courage to. And even though I could feel his eyes following me, I kept looking towards Preacher Morgan's pulpit. What would I do when it was time for getting a drink between Sunday school and preaching service? *Should I meet him at the creek like usual?* I wondered. *Could I?*

Once we were seated, Mister Hickman come up front, announcing, "Good mornin' everbody!"

A chorus of *good mornin's* come from all over the church in response.

"The good Lord done give us a be-autiful day for this here all-day singin' an' after-church social!"

Amens were shouted by several.

"So how 'bout we be liftin' our voices in praise by singin' 'When I Can Read My Title Clear.' That's a favorite, ain't it?"

Amens again.

This hymn was one I usually enjoyed singing, but this morning I seemed distracted by Mister Hickman's singing (was it extra loud today or was it just my imagination?), and his directing (I could swear he didn't manage once to wave them arms in time with Miz Morgan's steady rhythm at the piano), and his fixed smile (all I could see was Miz Hickman's shaming smile while she was telling me to count my blessings).

Still, that last part made me close my eyes when I was singing it. I suppose because I was seeing it different than I ever had before.

> *When I can read my title clear*
> *To mansions in the skies,*
> *I'll bid farewell to every fear,*
> *And wipe my weeping eyes;*
> *And wipe my weeping eyes,*
> *And wipe my weeping eyes.*
> *I'll bid farewell to every fear,*
> *And wipe my weeping eyes.*

I felt tears pushing at my eyes again, thinking on saying good-bye to more fears than I could even count. And then quickly I opened my eyes, concentrating once again on Mister Hickman's loud voice and flapping arms. I wasn't about to let anyone see that I was hurting.

Before I was ready—*But would you ever be?* I asked myself— Mister Hickman dismissed us for Sunday school. The young'uns were to go outside again and so I searched for Anna Ruth. When I spied her clutching onto Merry Jo's hand, I glanced around to see if I needed to hold onto another young'un. Feeling a light touch on my shoulder and turning around, I looked right into Tommy Lee's eyes.

"I had me a feelin' you might not be wantin' to meet me at the creek after Sunday school today, but I'm most anxious for you to be there, Rachael," he whispered intensely. After I hesitated, glancing to see if anyone'd heard and then worrying about what folks might say if they had, he pleaded, "Please, Rachael. It's right important, or I wouldn't be askin' you to."

There wasn't no saying no to the look on his face and the entreating in those eyes. I nodded and then hurried outside, avoiding meeting his look anymore for now.

Merry Jo was sitting on a quilt with Anna Ruth, and she motioned for me to join them, patting the place next to her. Anna Ruth giggled and then reached up to grab my hand. "Come set with us, Rachael. You an' Merry Jo's my most favorites!"

I grinned at her compliment, knowing that every week whoever she was setting with was her "most favorite."

"Hey, Anna Ruth. Hey, Merry Jo." I set down gingerly, just like I would be picking my words.

"Are you all right?" Merry Jo looked at me with loving concern, reaching out to touch one hand. I glanced away quickly, not wanting her to see in my eyes what I was truly feeling.

"Why, I be just fine. Why wouldn't I be?" I asked her, taking a deep breath and looking for Verna Mae and Nellie. "Where's Verna Mae? And Nellie?"

"They's comin'. They was goin' to help their mamas move some of the food down by the creek, for keepin' it cool." Merry Jo's gaze shifted in that direction. "There they come now."

Turning, I saw Nellie was toting her youngest brother and Verna Mae had the littlest Buttram girl by the hand. They spread a quilt a good ways away from us and settled down on it just as Mister Smith started in to teaching. *Wonder why they didn't come set with me and Merry Jo?* I asked myself. We nearly always set by each other during Sunday school.

When a few minutes had passed and they finally looked my way, I waved to them, hesitantly. Nellie waved back and Verna Mae nodded to me, but it all seemed so forced, so strained. *Are they avoidin' me? Why does everthin' seem so unnatural like?* I wondered. *Why can't things just be the way they was? I don't want no changes!* Realizing I was sounding just like Andy, I concentrated on Mister Smith's lesson. At least, I tried to.

He was teaching us the creation again this Sunday, reviewing the days we'd already studied ("What did God create on the very first day? That's right, Jessie, He made light and darkness. And what did God call the light and darkness? Raise yer hands iffin you know now!") Young'uns were anxiously waving their hands this way and that in the air, eagerly and proudly shouting out correct answers. Even Anna Ruth answered one that Merry Jo must've whispered in her ear.

I stared at Mister Smith grinning and asking and then wondered at the girls and boys grinning and answering, feeling like I was watching Andy and cousin Jessie throw a ball back and forth, back and forth. I wasn't playing though; I was only watching. And then an incredible sadness come over me, reminding me of grieving for something lost. *I ain't misplaced nothin'*, I said to myself scornfully, wondering what had come over me now. But the feeling persisted, nagging at me until I searched to put a name to it, see a reason for it. And then just as suddenly as the feeling come over me, the reasoning for it flashed across my mind.

It was my thinking on God. Or what was left of it. *No!* I cried out silently. *I ain't stopped believin'. I could never do that!* But somehow, sometime, somewhere in all this mess of changes and hurts and anger, it seemed like my faith—least ways like it use to be—was missing. I'd lost it!

Panic pushed thoughts this way and that through my mind as I tried to make sense of it all. I knew that I couldn't even remember a time when I didn't believe in Jesus. I'd prayed to Him every night for as long as I could remember, and all them Bible stories, like the creation, were as real to me as everything around me—this here schoolhouse, the bright, friendship-patterned quilt I was setting on, and the soft clover, budding trees, and clear blue sky around me. I never doubted the Bible stories or anything in God's Book, just like I always believed God took care of His own—blessing them and supplying for their needs and protecting them from bad folks and always, always answering their prayers. My prayers.

But now every thing I'd held onto—as proof that God loved me, Rachael, proof that God was real—was gone! Lost! He wasn't blessing us McKenneys nor supplying for our needs nor protecting us from bad folks, and He most certainly wasn't answering any prayers of mine. I still believed in God—that He was real—but yet it seemed like all those things that were telling who God was and what He should be doing— those were lost. I suppose it was a feeling like I was right in the middle of Possum Trot Creek and suddenly the bridge was yanked from underneath me, leaving me standing in midair. There wasn't nothing under me no more.

While Mister Smith's voice kept drumming on, sounding like the annoying buzzing hum in the background of the Hickmans' radio, questions of my own pounded in my mind, one after another. *What is this Sunday school lesson meanin' to me now when us McKenneys are hurtin' so? Is knowin' God created the heavens and the earth goin' to keep them Yankees from stealin' our land? Is it goin' to keep folks from sayin' mean things? How is the lesson this mornin' goin' to help me atall?* The questions accused and demanded answers, but there wasn't any.

Worse yet, I couldn't be telling nobody I was asking such fearful things, not even Granny Mandy. *What am I to be doin' with questions what have no answers?* I asked myself, panic causing me to hear my heart beating, feel it pulsing and pounding against my chest. *What do I do with questions what ain't even got no right to be asked in the first place?* The realization that there wasn't no end to my questioning—that they were going to be chasing circles forever—pressed right down on me until my head ached and my shoulders slumped.

Mister Smith kept on quizzing everybody ("What did God create on the sixth day? Yes'm! Ain't that wonderful!") Young'uns were excitedly waving hands to answer. I looked over to Merry Jo and Anna Ruth, noting how they were grinning and waving their arms. And then I stared down at my hands, holding them palm up. They were empty. There weren't any answers there. No excitement for knowing anything. ("And then what did God do on the seventh day?!")

I stared at the faces of all those young'uns—excited, happy, laughing young'uns hollering out them answers to the Bible story. Young'uns I grew up with. How and why was it they'd all suddenly become strangers? I didn't know them. And they didn't know me. *God, my faith done fell away somewheres. I've lost it. I've lost it!*

I shut my eyes tight then, focusing not on the words to a song and not on Mister Smith's questions, but on Jesus. Setting here—right here beside me, like Granny Mandy'd taught me to. I pictured Him believing in me even when I couldn't be believing in Him like I use to. *Yet how could I be believin' in Him and yet not believin' at the same time? Would He love me even then? Could He?*

A gentle touch on my hand caused me to suddenly open my eyes. Merry Jo and Anna Ruth were both staring at me, bewildered like. Clyde Travis, setting just over from us, leaned over and teased, "Mister Smith been done prayin' fer nigh to a minute a'ready, Rachael. You been sleepin' an' snorin' like Mister and Miz Harris always does!"

"Wasn't sleepin'!" I grumbled at him, my voice sounding short and curt.

Turning my back to Clyde, I spied Anna Ruth shaking a pudgy finger at me. "Rachael not good! No, Rachael not good." Then she smugly looked up at Merry Jo, seeking praise and bobbing that head up and down. "Anna Ruth good! Anna Ruth knows God made fishes," she said importantly.

Merry Jo looked over the top of Anna Ruth's head, giving me a sympathetic look as she smoothed the little girl's curly hair. "Now, Anna Ruth, just 'cause Rachael ain't answered no questions don't mean she don't know the answers. I reckon she knew ever one. Ain't that right, Rachael?"

They both stared at me, waiting on me to agree and to be—what— agreeable? Like Rachael always is, of course. But I wasn't of a mind to do them things. Not today. Not now. "Reckon I don't be knowin' nothin' 'bout anythin' no more." I got up abruptly and, glancing towards Merry Jo and Anna Ruth once more, noticed Merry Jo's mouth drop open in astonishment. "Do know I don't want nobody makin' excuses for me nor givin' out sympathy like the government hands out relief!"

I turned and walked quickly towards the creek then, feeling like I was escaping from the words I was leaving behind me. Purposefully staring down at my shoes so I could avoid meeting everybody's eyes, I headed for that creek so fast that I was nigh to out of breath when I got there. Tommy Lee was waiting on me, setting on the bank with his feet dangling above the water. I stood beside him a moment, trying to decide on whether I should set down with him or just keep on sulking and walk a while when he pointed to the ground beside him. "Ain't no mud here. Yer skirt won't be gettin' dirty if you set here a spell."

It ain't my dress I be frettin' over! I fumed to myself. *It be facin' you, Tommy Lee—or Merry Jo or Verna Mae or Nellie or—anybody*! I stewed for a bit more, shifting my weight from one foot to the other, until finally, taking a deep breath, I plopped down beside him. *Reckon I can't avoid talkin' with everbody forever,* I thought. *But I ain't goin' to be talkin' 'bout no Yankees just now! And I certainly don't be wantin' no more pity nor sympathy*! Glaring at the creek water rushing by, I suddenly remembered the last time me and Tommy Lee had talked while we were staring at water. On the chicken boat. And that had been such a wonderful day. Only that was—before. I frowned and glared at my shoes instead.

"'Member the other day when Andy and Willie was scufflin', and you said only yer Granny Mandy could be understandin' you? Well, you's wrong, Rachael. You's wrong!" He broke a twig that he'd been holding and tossed both pieces into the stream. We watched them float downstream a moment before the silence between us demanded that I say something.

"How could you be knowin' what it feels like—havin' some Yankee to tell you to leave your land?" I asked him accusingly, angrily. Stopping a minute to catch my breath, I blurted out, "Don't even myself be knowin' all the feelin's that be runnin' through my heart, changin' and explodin' and catchin' me unawares. Just now I were watchin' everone anxiously answerin' all them questions 'bout the creation, and I just couldn't . . ." I paused a moment, picking my way carefully. "I couldn't understand why they was so happy, and I didn't see no reason atall to be so excited or interested when everthin's so terrible bad and—"

"I weren't answerin' no questions," Tommy Lee said, breaking into my rush of words. His voice sounded flat, empty. I looked over at him for the first time then—really looking at him—and the strain about his eyes was the same one I'd seen reflected back at me in the mirror so often lately. I saw tired, weary hurt in them. He sighed deeply. "Cursed Yankees done told us we has to move too, Rachael."

"Oh, Tommy Lee." I instinctively reached out my hand to him and then shyly pulled it back, shaming myself for being so consumed by my own grief that I hadn't even noticed his. A crushing pain pulsed through me again. For Tommy Lee? For me?—as I experienced again the feelings from when Mister Sherman first told us McKenneys? Or was the pain for both us and how this would change the path of our lives, leading us away from each other? *If we was both to move, then what would happen to us—me and Tommy Lee?* We both sat silently until I found the courage to speak. "I'm sorry for blamin' you and for not knowin'," I said softly. "Makes me think on how much I been lookin' on everthin' only through my eyes. Selfish like." My mind raced on then to even wider circles. "Is they others? They must be! Who else you reckon them Yankees be plaguin'?"

"Don't rightly know yet. Daddy's thinkin' prob'ly yer mama's kin— Les and Evert Dickerson."

I gasped. Of course! The Dickerson land butted right up to McKenney property, and I hadn't even thought about that. "I wonder if Daddy and Mama been thinkin' that too—or if Daddy's even spoke to Uncle Les and Uncle Evert already. What are they goin' to do with all them young'uns and . . . What are we all goin' to do, Tommy Lee?" I looked over at him then, and he looked back at me with despair hanging over them eyes. I'd never seen his eyes look that way before. There wasn't any light in them.

"My mama were settin' in her rocker next to the fireplace when Mister Sherman told us. Rachael, that were four days ago. And she still be a-settin' there. Ain't got up atall what I seen her."

"She ain't tendin' to you and yer daddy? She ain't cookin' and cleanin' or anythin'?"

"Just sets there. Rockin'." He looked away then, blinking them eyes and rubbing his nose against a sleeve. There was a smudge of wet showing when he dropped his arm listlessly back to his side.

"Ain't she eat nothin'?"

"Daddy feeds her . . . like . . . like she were just a little'un . . ." Tommy Lee's voice dropped away to a whisper and then drifted off completely, blinking out like the last ember in the fireplace.

Slowly I lifted one hand, reaching out to lightly touch his. Tommy Lee's hand wasn't as rough and calloused as Daddy's yet, but it wasn't boyish feeling still like Andy's neither. The manliness that was coming was hinted at there—the fingers being firm and sturdy already from milking and other choring and the brownness of them showed he'd been working the fields a good bit already this spring. I moved my fingers over his hand hesitantly, lightly, afraid to show him how much I loved him and yet desiring that he know. *Could he feel my caring through my touch?*

He turned his hand over then, taking mine in his firm grasp. I felt small the way his hand took in and enclosed the whole of mine. We didn't look at each other—nor have a need to be saying anything—but for a good while just kept staring at the creek water hurrying by, pushing past us on its way to the Tennessee. A bobwhite and its mate called and answered in the distance. *Bob-white!* And then from a ways up the creek, *bob-white!* in response. Most always I'd be trying to fool them birds, whistling out a *bob-white!* call myself to see if the male'd answer me. But not this morning. There was something tender and special about hearing them call, searching for each other when at the same time me and Tommy Lee were setting there—searching for each other in a different way?—with my hand in his.

"Yer folks stayin' for the social and all-day singin'?" Tommy Lee's voice broke into the spell. Talking about church suddenly made me aware of where we were, so I awkwardly took my hand away from his grasp.

"Yes. Mama and Granny Mandy cooked up enough to feed . . ." I stopped then, realizing that Tommy Lee'd said his mama hadn't been cooking atall. "Are you stayin'?"

"Can't. Need to get on home to Mama."

"Maybe she'll be up and around by the time you get back. Maybe she'll be much better," I said hopefully.

"Maybe." But his voice was flat again. Turning towards me, his eyes swept from the top of my head (the blue bow?) to the collar of my new blouse. "Noticed yer hair again. And yer blouse. New, ain't it?"

I smiled at him then, loving him even more for noticing when he was toting around so much hurt and worry. "Mama made it from the yard goods I bought on the chicken boat. And she had this ribbon in her box of special things." Suddenly I realized Tommy Lee hadn't said that my hair or blouse were pretty. But he didn't need to. The light—not much, but just a bit of a glint—had returned to them eyes.

"Um, we be needin' to get on back, Rachael, but I aim to say somethin' to you first." He stopped and, rubbing his hands up and down the worn knees of his coarse Sunday-best trousers, glanced up towards the sky. I could feel a tension in him that reached out to me, causing me to feel anxious too. I nervously smoothed out my skirt, picking away bits of grass and seed that were sticking here and there. "Don't rightly know what's goin' to be happenin' round here, but I'm still hopin' somehow that them Yankees'll come to their senses an' let us be an' then Mama'll be fine again . . ." His voice faltered then and he stopped a minute, clearing his throat.

"Granny Mandy's hopeful too, Tommy Lee. Seems like if all us folks in Jordan's Bend just said *no* then they'd have to stop this mess, wouldn't they?" I could feel just a spark of hope in me still, even though the dark was still hovering and the deadness of the foxfire pressed at my memory.

"Heared they's havin' 'em another meetin' tomorra night. S'posed to be one ever Monday night, folks's sayin'." Tommy Lee looked over at me. There was a deep crease in his forehead, and he'd drawn his eyebrows close together. He shook his head slowly back and forth, saying, "Don't know 'bout folks comin' together, sayin' *no*."

"Surely they would!" I said, the certainty of it making me feel surprise at Tommy Lee's doubting. "Everbody round here looks up to my daddy and yer daddy—and Uncle Les and Uncle Evert. When folks hears what—"

"They know a'ready. Don't take long for news to fly round this county, and they ain't—" The bell started in to ringing, calling folks to the preaching service. I stood up and dusted off my skirt again, suddenly realizing I hadn't even got a drink and that I'd be good and thirsty long before Preacher Morgan was through.

Tommy Lee stood up slowly too, and we looked at each other a minute, suddenly shy and nervous again. "Got to jawin' an' didn't finish what I started in to sayin'." He looked away again, and I saw a muscle twitching in his firm-shaped jaw. Sighing and pushing back that everpresent lock of hair from his forehead, he said, "Don't rightly know what'll be happenin' to us, meanin' my kin and yer kin. But one thing I promise you, Rachael." He looked me straight on then, and his eyes—what were they now? not just alight again—they were nigh to blazing with feeling and fire. "Even if we's separated for awhile, I aim to take you for my wife someday. 'Count of—'count of I ain't never been able to see nobody else. All I ever seen was thick red hair, flashin' green eyes, sprinkled freckles," (he grinned when he said that) "and the teasin' smile what makes up Rachael." His eyes had followed his descriptions, caressing me and holding me so that I daren't even breathe. He gave me one last longing look, and then he was gone, running towards the schoolhouse.

Putting my hands over my heart and closing my eyes, I just stood there a minute, putting to memory the words, the way he looked and sounded when he spoke them, and the feeling of hearing them said by Tommy Lee. And then I took off running for the preaching service myself, hoping and praying I wasn't so late that folks'd be staring after me.

Fortunately, the last group of folks was just going in the door when I come to the steps. I touched my blue bow with one hand, making sure it hadn't come untied, and then smoothed my hair a bit. Glancing down to my skirt, I checked once more to make sure all traces of grass were gone, and then finally, I took a deep breath. Hopefully, I looked as calm as usual, even though my heart was still pounding.

When I sat down next to Andy, Daddy and Mama both give me a look—Mama's with raised eyebrows. Andy smirked at me and whispered, "Thought you might be cuttin' services for sparkin'."

"I never . . . !" I began, and then stopped when I realized Andy was back to being O.A. again, trying to goad me into an argument.

"Then how come yer cheeks be red an' all flushed like?" he teased.

"They ain't!" I said, putting my hands to my face and feeling the heat rise then. "Least ways, they weren't 'til you started in to pesterin'!" Andy just grinned at me, enjoying my squirming.

Miz Morgan started playing "We're Marching to Zion" on the piano then as Mister Hickman stepped up to the pulpit again. I didn't feel right singing atall, like I was being a hypocrite or something. Used to be that I'd sing right enthusiastic and then look over to Mister and Miz Harris, looking down my nose at them when I was thinking on how they'd go right to sleep soon's Preacher started his sermon. *Now here you be singin'*, I thought scornfully, *and yet you won't be a-listenin' like you should neither—'cause you ain't believin' the same as you use to. Ain't believin' like you oughta be. You done lost it, remember?* I chided myself, bringing a wince to my face. I sang right soft then, barely moving my lips.

When we'd finished, Preacher Morgan come up to the pulpit and made some announcements, including one about the meeting here again tomorrow night. I glanced over to Uncle Les and Aunt Opal, trying to see if their reactions said anything about what they were feeling. But they only glanced at each other for a moment and then looked back at Preacher Morgan. Uncle Evert's family always sat two rows behind us, and much as I wanted to, I didn't dare turn round to look at them. I was way past the age of a young'un who was still squirming round during services, and Mama had always been extra strict about us setting still.

"All week long God's been layin' on my heart to be speakin' on His will," Preacher Morgan began. "So if you'd all turn to Genesis thirty-seven in the Good Book, let's us take a look at Joseph's trials—and how God sent them trials to shape him into the man what God wanted him to be. Them sufferin's was God's will!"

The *amens* started already. I swallowed hard, wondering if Preacher Morgan knew about the Yankees telling us to move. *'Course he knows,* I said to myself, remembering the look in Merry Jo's eyes. There was pity there, I was sure of it!

"First off, we're knowin' how Joseph's brothers sold him into slavery. Can any of you think of anythin' much worse in this whole world than bein' betrayed by your own kin?"

"No, sir!" echoed across the room.

"But did Joseph complain?" Preacher Morgan asked us, jabbing one long pointed finger in every direction, meeting eyes across the room.

"No, sir!" again. I felt myself hunching down lower in my seat.

"And then Joseph was taken into old Potiphar's house, where the missus tempted him and tricked him. But Joseph were innocent, weren't he?"

"Yes, sir!"

"And yet still he were thrown into prison! That were God's will!" Preacher Morgan pronounced it in a booming voice, and I wondered if it was anything like the preacher in Granny Mandy's story. "Then did he rail against his God?"

"No, sir!"

I could feel guilt moving over me like a coverlet, threatening to smother me. *How was he seein' into my mind, knowin' what I was thinkin'?*

Preacher Morgan's words broke into my thoughts, asking, "An' then what 'bout when that chief butler forgot Joseph? Didn't Joseph stop believin' in his God then?"

"No!" come from everywhere.

I closed my eyes in shame then. *But preacher, how can I stop feelin' what I'm feelin'? And how do I keep from askin' them questions? Tell me them things. Help me!*

"Didn't he stop trustin' Him none?"

"No!"

"Weren't he angry with everbody—and 'specially his God?"

"No!"

An unexpected ruffle of noise in our row caused me to open my eyes and I glanced over to Andy, expecting to see him fidgeting or something. But Andy was setting still—glaring at Preacher Morgan he was—but setting still. And then I noticed Granny Mandy setting with her Bible closed on her lap, drumming her gnarled fingers against its worn cover. Leaning over just a bit so I could see her face, I saw that she'd closed her eyes for a spell too, but she wasn't sleeping. She'd drawn her thin, parched lips into a grim, straight line—and I knew that positioning of Granny Mandy's mouth and jaw. She obviously wasn't none too pleased about something. None too pleased atall.

Preacher Morgan's shouting and pointing went on for some time. I caught bits here and there concerning more about God's will and that the good and bad were for us to be accepting and praising Him for. Just like Joseph. And that the only way to respond to suffering was to praise Him, he said. The words moved over and around and against me, shoving up against me until I felt bruised and battered by them. *Why am I thinkin' again that words is alive?* I fussed at myself. *'Cause you be knowin' they are!* my mind shot back in answer. *Words has a power of their own. Folks can fling 'em out there to hurt. And bruise!*

When he was finished and we were bowing for prayer, I leaned over and glanced at Granny Mandy again. She'd stopped drumming her fingers, but her mouth was in that same grim line. And now that everyone's eyes were closed for Preacher Morgan's prayer—except mine, of course, since I was peeking at Granny Mandy—them gray eyes of hers were open too.

Several *amens* followed Preacher Morgan's when he finished, and then folks broke into excited chatter. Most of the women folk headed for the food at the back of the room, directing the men to carry out tables for placing under the shade trees outside. Granny Mandy, Daddy, and Mama stood talking for a minute, and I saw Granny firmly shaking her head.

"Rachael," Daddy called, motioning me towards him.

Walking over to them, I noticed a stubborn tilt to Granny Mandy's head. Like the line of her mouth and jaw meaning she wasn't pleased, I recognized that positioning of her head. It meant you weren't going to be changing her mind. Period. "Yes, Daddy?" I asked, looking from Granny to Daddy.

"Yer granny says she can't be stayin' for the social. Needs to get on to home." Daddy sounded right tired. "You go 'head an' take Old Dean. Me an' yer mama an' Andy can hitch a ride with the Pursers later."

"Yer sure you not be feelin' poorly?" Mama asked, reaching out to lightly touch Granny Mandy's arm. "Ere you needin' us all to be goin' home with you?"

"Land no! Just feelin' a need to be settin' in my rocker by my own fire today. Time for thinkin'. That's what I'm a-wantin'." She glanced at the groups of folks gathered here and there, laughing and jawing as they carried armloads of food outside. "Cain't be hearin' myself think round here. And I ain't in no mood for shoutin' at Miz Harris the whole day neither. Plumb wears a body out." She looked Mama square in the eye and then Daddy. "Don't ye be frettin' none! A old granny be 'lowed to be settin' by her fire now an' then. Me an' Rachael'll be fine. Have us a nice ride home. We'll just take us a bit of my fried chicken to eat on the way. You all just have a fine time."

"I'll be boxin' you up some dinner then," Mama said, heading towards the back of the room. Glancing over her shoulder, she added, "Rachael, ye make Old Dean mind, ye hear?"

"Yes, Mama."

Me and Daddy looked at each other and grinned. "Yer mama ain't learned yet that, in the first place, a body don't be makin' Old Dean mind on account of, and this ere the second place, a mule has to be havin' a mind to make 'im mind! Ain't that right, Rachael?"

"Yes, Daddy." He'd told that bit of fooling for about as long as I could remember, but Daddy still enjoyed the telling and it still brought a grin from me—especially considering Mama kept on starting the whole thing by continually warning me to make Old Dean mind. You'd thought she would be wise to Daddy by now. "Are you ready to be goin' then, Granny Mandy?" I asked her.

She studied on the room again, obviously looking for somebody. "Need to be speakin' with Mister Roddy. Ye seen 'im 'round anywheres?"

"I s'pose most the men folks be outside settin' up the tables, Granny. You be wantin' me to find him for you?"

Granny Mandy shook her head. "Best if ye be findin' yer mama an' help her to boxin' up that chicken. I'll be meetin' ye outside in jest a bit."

She walked towards the door then, her head tilted up and her step firm. Once again I noted how Granny Mandy never strolled nowhere; nor did she pick her way hesitantly. She walked everywhere with purpose and like anyone who might be meeting up with her had best be ready to give account—or be moving out of the way. *'Cept for the night of the foxfire,* a small voice reminded me. I grimaced at the memory, quickly pushing it away from me.

"You be mindin' missin' the social an' singin'?" Daddy asked, weariness returning to the tone of his voice.

Remembrances of our last singing passed through my mind. I recollected Mister Hickman asking for favorites and folks good-naturedly racing to shout theirs out first. Lots of folks had sung solos and there were duets, trios, quartets (even me, Verna Mae, Merry Jo, and Nellie sung "Rock of Ages" together), and all sorts of choirs. James Junior and Daddy sung with the men; me, Granny Mandy, and Mama with the women; and Andy had been part of the children's choir—along with every other squirming young'un. We had us banjos, fiddles, and the piano, of course. Merry Jo had played "Amazing Grace" with the fanciest flourishes; we clapped so much when she finished that she played it again. But even though all those memories were from just late last fall, they seemed years ago. And as excited as I was then to be joining in with folks and singing them songs with rejoicing and pleasure, today I was most anxious to be going on home.

"Ain't botherin' me none, Daddy," I told him honestly. "Tommy Lee a'ready headed on home, and Nellie and Verna Mae seem sorta—I don't know—like they's avoidin' me or somethin'." *And you's avoidin' Merry Jo!* my conscience reminded me.

"You gals been scufflin' like Andy?" he teased.

"Ain't been arguin' if that's what yer askin'." We walked slowly towards the back of the room. The women folk had already moved all the food outside and the schoolhouse was empty now. "No . . . I don't rightly know how to be puttin' it even. It's like they was tryin' on purpose not to meet my eye. And I wondered if they was late goin' out for Sunday school just so's they didn't have to be settin' with me."

"Reckon that might be of yer imaginin'?"

"Maybe." But I doubted that. Things between us weren't right—besides just me and Merry Jo. I could sense it.

"Well, I reckon yer mama's 'bout fixed up yer dinner by now. Be watchin' the road round Possum Trot Creek on yer way home. Spring rains done washed holes deep 'nough to 'bout swaller the wagon an' you and Granny Mandy 'long with it."

I grinned up at him again. "Yes, Daddy. I'll keep a lookout for 'em."

We walked down the steps together, gazing over the groups of folks gathered here and there, laughing, talking, enjoying each other. Suddenly I realized that I'd been aching to go home ever since I first walked into church this morning. I just wasn't belonging here today. I closed my eyes a moment, silently thanking Granny for saving me from what would've been a long, hurtful day.

"Well, be seein' you later then," Daddy said, putting his worn hat on his head. He took time to position it just so and then moved off to a group of men standing under the shade of one of the huge oaks that circled the schoolyard.

I searched for Granny Mandy, looking for signs of her green hat or yellow flowered dress. Finally I could pick her out standing next to Mister Roddy; they were over to the road, a good ways apart from the rest of the folks.

"Rachael, here be yer dinner all ready," Mama called, beckoning me towards the tables of food.

Walking over there, I took in a deep breath of the wonderful mixture of smells, closing my eyes and pleasuring in what they were promising. The tables were nearly overflowing with good cooking. Tempting me were platefuls of crispy fried chicken (of course—just like Granny Mandy said there'd be!), juicy pink cured ham and red-eye gravy, fried ham with brown gravy, pork tenderloins (they were my favorite), and fried and baked pork chops, to mention just a few of the main dishes.

And then there were sweet tater casseroles (the thought of James Junior brought a quick dart of pain), fried apples oozing with cinnamon and sugar, sliced onions and green beans, sauerkraut, slaw, fried taters, creamed taters, cornbread, and biscuits everywhere (plus jams, jellies, and gravies to go on them), and then there was the desserts! Oh, the desserts! Every sort of pie, cake, cobbler, and fruit was piled on one table, beckoning and teasing at the young'uns that were anxious to be at them. Most of them were pointing at their particular favorites, bragging about how they were going to eat a whole pie or a whole cake. I smiled at them and then walked over to Mama, where she was busy sorting and putting out more food still. We might be poor and, according to President Roosevelt, in the worst depression this here country had ever seen, but when it was time for a social in Jordan's Bend, we cooked. And plenty.

Mama placed a box in my arms, saying, "Best be eatin' right off before this here spoils. You reckon ye can eat whiles hangin' onto Old Dean?"

"Yes'm, Mama. You know Old Dean ain't never in no hurry to go nowheres, even to home. Reckon he could get there all by himself anyways, just like he done the other night when the fog was so thick. Don't be worryin' none," I reassured her. "Me'n Granny Mandy'll be just fine." I spotted Merry Jo, Nellie, and Verna Mae then, helping just a few feet away at another table. And I watched them, one by one, notice me and then quickly turn away, not saying *hey* or nothing. An aching pain passed through my stomach.

"Don't be frettin' over it so, Rachael," Mama said, obviously noticing my reaction to my friends. "They's havin' a tolerable hard time knowin' what to be sayin' or doin' just now." She gazed past me, and I looked at her in amazement.

"How's that, Mama?"

"Folks don't know how to be actin' towards us just now. They's nervous like . . . 'fraid prob'ly." She sighed. "Reckon they'll be adjustin' to everthin' kindly soon." The look about her eyes was weary, like Daddy, but also—what was it? One of fear? In Mama?

I wanted to ask her more—about why on earth folks would be afraid—but I knew Granny Mandy was probably waiting on me by now and besides, this wasn't the place for talking about those things. Mama smoothed some escaping wisps of curls back behind one ear and patted the neat bun at the back. Then she raised her chin. Just a little, but it was noticeable. "Ain't responsible for how others be; am for how I be actin'. Best be gettin' back to servin' up this here food." She checked the apron that she'd brought to wear, straightening the front to cover and protect her Sunday clothes the best it could. "Be seein' ye later, Rachael."

"Bye, Mama." I watched her walk away with the same assured steps that Granny Mandy had taken. Only I was knowing that Mama wasn't feeling that way. *I'm right proud that you be my mama,* I thought to myself.

Walking towards our wagon, I called *hey* to everyone I passed. They all greeted me with the same nervous responses and then turned away. Once I'd catch somebody's eye, they'd shift their eyes away right quick—like they were pretending they hadn't seen me, it seemed. Hands would go jerking up to cover their mouths or folks would push back hair, men would take off and resettle hats, women would smooth skirts. Anything it seemed, to be avoiding jawing with me a spell. *Am I only imaginin' it?* I asked myself. *But even Mama said folks was nervous and afraid. That doesn't make any sense though. Why would us McKenneys make folks nervous? Why would they be fearin' us?*

Granny Mandy was standing by the wagon. "Ready to be goin'?" she asked. At least Granny looked me right in the eye.

"Yes'm. Got us some fine eatin' here too, I reckon," I said, holding out the box to show her. "Mama packed it, so what's in here'll be a surprise for us both. And after peerin' over them tables of food, I'm sure knowin' it has to be delicious, whatever it be!" After untying Old Dean, I helped her up onto the seat and then climbed up after her. "Come on now, Dean. Daddy's says you ain't got no brains to be able to be mindin' me, but we'uns do need to be headin' to home." I give the reins a good slap, and he ambled on up the road into town and then slowly took us through the still mostly deserted Jordan's Bend.

Once we were on the other side of town, Granny Mandy opened the box. "Land but don't them fixin's smell good!" Granny exclaimed. "Let's us pull over to the side here and set us down on the grass by that pretty dogwood for a spell. Fine food like this needs eatin' slow like." Her eyes were brimming with excitement—sort of like a young'un that had played hooky from school.

"But Granny, I thought you was right anxious to be gettin' home to your rocker and fire." I pulled up on the reins, stopping by the side of the road. "I thought you was wantin' to be spendin' time alone to—"

"Wasn't as anxious to be goin' to as I were to be leavin' behind. I were wantin' to get away from bad preachin' an' spineless folks! Now let's us climb down so's we can be enjoyin' this here good cookin'!" And without even waiting on my help, Granny Mandy nearly jumped off the wagon and headed for a small patch of shade under a dogwood in full bloom.

Remembering a quilt that we always kept in the back of the wagon, I took it with me and spread it out for us to sit on. And then me and Granny Mandy excitedly explored the box's contents together. On top was some delicious-looking fried chicken. "You reckon it be yours?" I asked Granny Mandy, winking at her.

She shrugged her shoulders. "Might be some from that preacher wife I done told you 'bout. I hear she fries up a dozen or so hens ever Sunday. 'Course, all them be mostly for her husband."

"Oh, Granny," I said, shaking my head at her before turning my attention back to the delicious smells coming from the box. "Look—Mama's put in a couple of tenderloins! Don't they look delicious? And there's sweet tater casserole and some of Miz Harris' blackberry pie!" Me and Granny was like two young'uns on a Christmas morning, tugging and pulling surprises out of their stockings hung over the fireplace.

"Here's some o' the widow Campbell's gritted bread and a big ol' piece o' Lena's pound cake!" Granny Mandy looked up at me and grinned broadly. "Me an' you's goin' to eat like kings, ain't we?! And, I might be addin', with the best company this here county's offerin'! Now let's us be sayin' that blessin' an' get to it." We bowed our heads then as Granny said, "Lord, we'uns be mighty thankful for this here good food Ye be providin' for us. An' I be thankin' Ye for Rachael too—the bestest company any granny could be askin' for to set down to dinner with. A-men. Now let's us eat!"

I giggled at us both as we ate, getting sticky sweet tater casserole on our chins and dropping bits of fried chicken and gritted bread on our laps. But I didn't know when a meal had tasted nearly so good nor been so pleasuring to eat. A soft breeze caressed us, keeping us cool and gently swaying the branches of the dogwood's blossoms above our heads. Clouds drifted by, sometimes winking out the sun's rays and then allowing it to shine over the field around us once again, pointing out the gently waving grass. Somewhere honeysuckle was blossoming too, since the distinct smell of the blooms was floating along with that breeze.

Sadly, the box wasn't nearly empty when I was too full to eat any more. "Can't be puttin' another bite in my mouth, Granny Mandy, even though I sure be wantin' to finish off this here blackberry pie. How 'bout you? Anythin' else you be wantin'?"

"I'm clean full an' 'bout to bust too, I'm 'fraid! How come it seems a body always gets full faster when they's delicious fixin's like this? Iffin I had mush I reckon I could eat all day an' not feel satisfied!"

We packed up what was left over and folded up the quilt. I hated to be leaving that place, knowing that the peace I'd felt wouldn't be coming with us. It was a fleeting thing, belonging to this place and time only, and I felt like I was folding it up and putting it away with the quilt—or else leaving it behind on the square of pressed-down grass where me and Granny Mandy had been setting. I glanced back at that patch longingly as we walked towards the wagon.

"Granny Mandy, why weren't you wantin' to stay for the social and all-day singin'?" I think I asked not only to be knowing Granny's reasoning, but to be understanding mine as well. After I'd helped her climb up into the wagon and then got in myself, she answered, thoughtfully, "My daddy use to say, 'Don't be walkin' in tall weeds in chigger season.' Seems to me that be right good advice."

I urged on Dean and then looked at her with puzzlement. "Well, I know that them chiggers'll eat a body up, but I don't rightly understand what else you be sayin', Granny."

She took a deep breath and then let it out slowly. "Them folks today at church was like the tall weeds, Rachael. An' the things they be a sayin'—an' sometimes maybe not sayin' with words, but with their eyes—them's the chigger bites. Yes'm, they's bites all right. Mean ones too. My daddy were right. Ain't no need to be lookin' to be bit."

"You mean I wasn't imaginin' them things? Was folks avoidin' me? You too? And Mama—she were sayin' 'bout the same thing too."

"What'd yer mama say?"

"Said folks was nervous around us. And afraid. Why would they be fearin' us, Granny Mandy? That don't make no sense."

"On account o' the changes."

There was that hated word again.

"You see, Rachael, folks don't know what to be sayin' or doin', so they don't be sayin' nothin' atall. They be avoidin' us. Like we'uns got the leprosy or somethin'. An' it's like they's fearin' them changes'll jump on them somehow too. Like they'd catch the leprosy. That's what they's afeared of." She paused a moment, straightening that faded green hat to shield her face from the sun the best it could. "An' folks is 'fraid o' sermons like the one we done heared this mornin'. Harmin', hurtful preachin' it were. An' ye be knowin' I don't take to tearin' into the preacher ever Sunday, chewin' up his words whiles chewin' on Sunday dinner."

"But folks was sayin' *amens* all the time."

"Ye be knowin' good as I do that some folks be sayin' *amen* in they sleep. Heared Mister Harris shout thata way jest last week—right in the middle o' the biggest ol' snore. Hollered *amen* so loud even Miz Harris heared him, deaf as she is. Seen her jump clean off'n her seat, I did."

I giggled at Granny's story, figuring she probably wasn't exaggerating—too much. "Preacher's sermon today made me feel guilty," I admitted to her, feeling guilty in the telling even now. "Kept scootin' further an' further down in my seat."

"'Member we done talked 'bout anger, Rachael. God don't want us to be tryin' to hide it from Him. Ain't no sense to that since that only be a-hurtin' us. Don't be sinnin' with that anger, though, but see it for what it is—admittin' it—an' then be done with it! 'Sides, how's Preacher knowin' what Joseph felt? Bible don't say." She stared straight ahead as she talked, nodding her head now and then. "Reckon Joseph were jest as human as me an' you. Surely he must o' felt angry. Difference was, Bible do tell us what he done with it. Decided to be trustin' his God." She looked straight at me when she said that. "An' the purpose o' the tellin' 'bout Joseph ain't preachin' on anger anyways; be to show us that God be faithful. He'll be doin' jest what He says He will. That be the point!"

Granny Mandy's wisdom most always hammered at me, causing me to then work hard to understand and take it in. I thought a minute before asking her, "But how could Joseph keep believin' in Him, Granny Mandy? How could he have that kind of faith?"

"On account o' he didn't believe what was goin' on round him. Them things—'specially the bad, terrible bad—don't be tellin' us who an' what God be. Only the Bible be tellin' us true 'bout what our Lord's like. Cain't b'lieve sickness. Dyin'. Drought. Bein' poor. Bein' hungry." She stopped then, catching her breath. "Nor Yankees what tells a body to leave his homestead what he's loved for so many a year. Things like them says, 'God don't love you no more.' But that ain't true!" Granny Mandy reached out to touch my face then, pulling me round to look straight at her. "An' don't you be b'lievin' that. Be knowin' that God loves us McKenneys! Loves you—no matter what you may be a-thinkin' all them other things says!"

She kept her hand against my cheek a minute, staring deep into my eyes with her intense gray ones. *Is she tryin' to let her believin' flow into me?* I wondered. Then she removed her hand, turning to look up the road once again. "Granny Mandy, is it possible to be believin' and yet not be believin' at the very same time? It don't make no sense, but . . ."

"'Course it do! Here, give me them reins a minute. Ye be lookin' up the gospel o' Mark. Mark, umm, let me think on it a spell . . . Mark nine, I b'lieve 'tis."

Granny's Bible was even more yellowed and frayed than ours was. I handled it carefully, turning the pages with care. "Here's Mark nine. What am I lookin' for?"

"Find the story 'bout the daddy an' his young'un. Sick young'un. Needin' healin' by the Lord Jesus."

My eyes skipped quickly down the page until I come to the part Granny was talking about. "Here 'tis, I think. Want me to be readin' it to you?"

"Yes'm. Read it to both o' us."

"'And one of the multitude answered and said, Master, I have brought unto thee my son, which hath a dumb spirit; And wheresoever he taketh him, he teareth him: and he foameth, and gnasheth with his teeth, and pineth away: and I spake to thy disciples that they should cast him out; and they could not. He answereth him, and saith, O faithless generation, how long shall I be with you? how long shall I suffer you? bring him unto me. And they brought him unto him: and when he saw him, straightway the spirit tare him; and he fell on the ground and wallowed foaming. And he asked his father, How long is it ago since this came unto him? And he said, Of a child. And ofttimes it hath cast him into the fire, and into the waters, to destroy him: but if thou canst do any thing, have compassion on us, and help us. Jesus said unto him, If thou canst believe, all things are possible to him that believeth. And straightway the father of the child cried out, and said with tears, Lord, I believe; help thou mine unbelief.'" I stopped then, for the hearing of those words was like a refrain being sung again and again in my mind.

"Say 'em again, Rachael."

"Granny?" I hadn't heard her over the music in my head.

"Say them last words again."

I looked down at the verse, but I didn't need to read it. The words were my prayer now. "'Lord, I believe; help thou mine unbelief.'"

"Now. Can ye be b'lievin' an' yet not be b'lievin' at the same time?"

"This here man did." I pointed out the words. "Even tole Jesus so—askin' Him to help the part of himself that were unbelievin'."

"Reckon ye can be doin' that too?"

I nodded, still listening to the words repeating in my head.

"What happened to the young'un?"

"Oh, I recollect that part. He were healed."

"Reckon the daddy could be a-trustin' Jesus to be healin' him too?"

"Heal him? He weren't ailin' like his son were."

"'Tain't the same, no. But weren't he jest as much in need o' the good Lord's healin'?"

I sat in silence for a minute, thinking on the meaning of what she was saying. "Am I ailin', Granny Mandy?"

Softly Granny Mandy answered, "Be for ye to be sayin', Rachael. Ye and the Lord, that is." Glancing over at her, I saw that she'd closed her eyes. She looked so peaceful, setting there like that. "Seek Him out, Rachael. Tell Him." Even more softly she said, "He's a-waitin'."

We rode the rest of the way in silence. Only the steady sounds of Dean's plodding, the creaking of the wagon wheels, and an occasional peeping of a redbird broke into the hushed stillness. Once Old Dean had lumbered into Granny Mandy's yard, I helped her get settled into her cabin, making sure she was comfortable by the fire. Then I headed on up to home.

I kept busy nearly the whole day, doing my normal choring and then extra for Mama and Daddy, even Andy. I know Mama didn't rightly approve of me doing extra—it being Sunday and all. But she didn't stop me and the working and sweating felt good somehow, keeping my thinking on those things: hoeing, cleaning, chopping wood. But even concentrating on all that choring didn't stop that one cry from sounding in my head, repeating until it seemed to be ringing like the dinner bells across the hills. *Lord, I believe; help my unbelief*!

And that was the only prayer that I could be putting to words when Mister Roddy come to Granny Mandy's the next day, plodding up the road in his big wagon, making a delivery from his lumberyard. I watched, feeling like the very life was draining out of me, as Mister Roddy carried into Granny Mandy's barn one simple white oak box. A casket.

6

Your living fur against my hand
You guide me in this unseen land,
And still I do not understand.
The darkness deepens more and more
Till it is shattered by a roar.

Weeks passed. And with them had come too many signs showing that Mister Whitaker and Mister Sherman weren't just talk. The government people had been busy—building new roads ("access" roads they called them, for getting to their construction sites), dynamiting (I enjoyed the crash of thunder, but hearing those awful booms in the distance all day long was terrifying), and driving by in the strangest newfangled machinery of every kind. From Mister Whitaker we learned that they were called bulldozers, dump trucks, steam shovels, concrete mixers, pan scrapers, and turnapulls. Daddy said a body needed to write a dictionary just to keep up with the naming of them, let alone to be knowing what mischief they were up to.

The road at the bottom of our hill was the same, but soon as you got near to town, it widened a good deal and had rock covering the whole of it. Them big trucks'd come through town and then head on down that access road to the construction site. Seems they were slowly working to move a mountain, deciding it wasn't put in the right place to begin with. When Granny Mandy heard about that she carried on for more than a week, insisting that where God done put a mountain, that's where the Good Lord intended it to be staying. She'd even threatened to set smack-dab in the front row of their next weekly meeting. Said she was going to tell them that God was kindly lucky to have them right intelligent Yankees for fixing what the Lord Almighty made all wrong. Me and Daddy set to talking her out of it while Andy kept egging her on all week. But then when two days of steady rain threatened to bring a spring tide and wash away Granny's garden—and caused her rheumatism to act up a good bit again too—she decided even fussing at them Yankees wasn't worth going out of a night like that. So me and Daddy give a sigh of relief.

Daddy'd tried explaining to Granny Mandy that they were digging from the hillside to move the dirt where it could help the crop watering down the river a ways—clear on the other side of the dam. Called the whole doings irrigation. 'Course they were digging the hill out in the first place for where the dam would set. One day me, Daddy, and

Andy'd watched a steam shovel scoop up piles of dirt and then plop them right into the back of that dump truck. From where we were setting, it looked like a huge critter that was eating at that hillside, taking bites out of it. Much as I hated all the Yankees were doing, somehow it were still fascinating to watch them big machines.

Once they were further along, Mister Whitaker'd promised to take us on a tour, showing us all the work they'd done. I was looking forward to seeing the sights—all them huge machines moving and rearranging a mountain—and yet I was right disgusted with myself for wanting to. Seemed I was just like what Granny Mandy called a "no good, fork-tongued politician—a body what talked Democrat and lived Republican." I hated that dam, but my curiosity drew me to it like hounds howling and panting after a treed coon.

I checked in on Granny Mandy nearly every day now, anxious to know she wasn't ailing. And though I'd fretted about that casket a good many days before I had the courage to ask Daddy about it, he told me to not be worrying so. "Yer Granny's gettin' on in years," Daddy'd said. "A body gets to wantin' the casket made an' waitin'. Ready. Makes 'em feel better somehow, knowin' everthin's settled. Don't mean Granny Mandy's lookin' to be laid out," he reassured me, and then added with that twinkle in his eye, "an' I reckon she's stubborn enough to be outlivin' us all. Yankees 'specially!"

Granny Mandy went about her choring with as much energy as ever, but I did catch her talking now and then to someone—someone who seemed just beyond my seeing. I didn't hear her say *James Henry* no more, but still, the ease that'd come about her face, the relaxing of her firm, bony shoulders, and the eager way she leaned forward then—towards what I couldn't see—made me tense with fretting for her. *Could she really be seein' my grandaddy?* I'd ask myself, over and over. *Or is she slowly goin' simple in the head, like old Miz Evert done, talkin' out of her head the whole long day?* When Miz Evert died, her kinfolk grieved. They wept. But I saw the relief in their eyes.

So I avoided thinking on Granny's "spells," as I started calling them, just like I pushed away all recollections of the foxfire. It seemed years ago that we'd gone to that magical place, when the joy and wonder of it wrapped me in a blanket of hope. Those feelings were gone. I couldn't touch them anymore. And yet at the same time, it seemed like only yesterday that I was gazing at that foxfire, on account of the pain being so close still. I wondered if I'd ever be without the crushing hurt of disappointment, the despairing from childish dreams washed away, the grieving for the lost imagining that there was another world out there, an unnatural one turned upside down to become the real. That pain was always hovering beside me, brushing up against me and yet just out of sight—like a bird what wings by out of the corner of my eye and yet when I turn to look at him, he's flown away already. Those hurting feelings were baiting me just the same: when I turned to face them square, they moved out of sight too. I couldn't see them, couldn't grab ahold of them, couldn't fight no enemy what wouldn't meet me face to face. Instead, it was like waking up of a night, not knowing what it was that roused you in awful fear, making your heart pound so and your breathing come quick. But still you knew—knew for certain—there was something just out your window. You can't see it. But you know it's there. In the dark.

James Junior's letters were a ray of sunshine into the gloom of these past weeks, and every day I eagerly looked for another one from him. Mama'd read them out loud at the dinner table while me, Daddy, and Andy leaned over our plates, not wanting to miss a word. His first letter come two weeks after he'd left; it nearly run over with excitement as he described all he was doing. After taking classes on such things as the soil and crops from the TVA men, the government had sent him and the rest of the CCC boys farther north, where a dam was just finishing up being built. It was James Junior's job to work with the farmers, learning them all about feeding the soil with metaphosphate. "Makes a man 'bout want to eat it, on account of it lookin' just like hoarhound candy!" he'd joked. I remembered Mister Whitaker saying about the same thing. James Junior was also learning farmers to rotate crops and plant what Mister Whitaker had talked about putting in here: strawberries. They'd planted a good share of trees, too, that being something James Junior particularly enjoyed.

I couldn't rightly believe all the exciting things James Junior described that were there at the dam site for the using by anybody. He talked about the classes they were offering: learning machinery, math, and woodworking for a few. But the best thing James Junior wrote about was the book truck. "A library on wheels" James Junior called it, and "anybody can go get him a book to read—right off'n that there truck!" The TVA'd built better schools (like they were promising us here too), playgrounds, and a big building called a auditorium. Inside was a gymnasium for playing games and even a theater, he'd told us. They weren't showing any of them exciting films from Hollywood like what me and Verna Mae'd read about, but instead James Junior enjoyed watching moving pictures that were educational—for free!

James Junior had arrived at the dam site just as they were finishing.

Since he hadn't heard the news about us having to move yet, him describing how the land and water looked—"amazin' beautiful" he'd said—was hurtful to hear. "I stood watchin' whiles they let the first water over the spillway," he wrote, "and as the spray sailed up into the air, the prettiest rainbow you ever saw shined through that mist." He carried on about how the locks were so interesting to watch and that the lake was right peaceful looking, blue as it was and lapping gently up against the shoreline. "They done stocked it with bass and trout too. Daddy, you, me, and Andy would sure have us a time fishin'!" There was excitement in James Junior's words, but Mama's reading drowned it out, making them sound empty. Like a promise that you knew wasn't going to be kept.

Soon as James Junior got word about us needing to move, he was terrible anxious to come on home to help. But Daddy sent a letter off to him right quick, telling him to stay put. "Yer gettin' a right fine education there," Daddy'd written, "and that be the best thing you can be doin' for all of us just now. Stay there as long as they's work for the doin'." After that, James Junior didn't say any more about coming home, but he started sending more money in his letters.

At school we were all busy preparing for Children's Day, practicing songs, recitations, and plays. It was nearly a month away yet, but seeing as how it was so important to everyone, we were hard at work already picking out poems, practicing singing, and writing plays. Us older ones were writing a play about the pilgrims and the first Thanksgiving. Andy was terrible jealous, wanting to be a Indian and use his slingshot. But Miz Travis had assigned him a poem already; Andy was to memorize and recite a good bit of Longfellow's "Evangeline." According to Andy, it was awful, and reciting a poem wasn't nothing like being a "mean, nasty, scalp-huntin' Indian—one what could set fire to a Yankee's tail an' send 'im runnin'!" Andy's complaining surely didn't help his mood none. He'd been walking through his days in a sulk. Now he added a scowl.

Me, Merry Jo, Verna Mae, and Nellie were all speaking to each other, but we weren't the same as before. Seemed like we tiptoed around each other, avoiding any talk about the dam and instead keeping to talk about the weather and crops and such. Most days I'd read during lunchtime, shutting out what was going on right around me to escape to another world—the worlds of Charles Dickens or Jane Austen or Emily Brontë. Eventually it seemed like the characters in those books were the real people. They lived and breathed and cared about others, while the folks that were moving around right in front of me didn't care none. So they weren't real. Least ways, I didn't want them to be, and I surely wasn't about to let them know what was going on inside of me.

One day I told Granny Mandy that talking with Merry Jo and all the rest of them was like talking with Yankees. I made sure they didn't know any more than what I was saying to them, what I was putting out there for them to see. I wasn't about to let no Yankee know me. And it was the same way with most folks around here now.

Merry Jo give it a try though. She'd at least meet me before school, asking questions, giving me advice, and attempting to encourage me. But I didn't want to hear no "God's in charge, Rachael" and "Just trust Him. Everthin'll be fine!" or "The Good Lord knows what's best for you. This ain't bad! He's doin' this for yer good!" I think I felt sick to my stomach every time she come out with another one. But what made all those sayings especially bitter sounding was that I'd said the same things before to other folks that were hurting. Repeating empty words, I was. And if they were empty before, they were right dead now. So when Merry Jo talked, I just closed up, same as I did with everybody else. Eventually Merry Jo give up trying too.

I mostly dreaded going to church. Us "lepers" (ever since that first Sunday I'd sarcastically called all of us that were going to be moving by that nickname)—the Pursers; Mama's kin, Les and Evert Dickerson and their families; the Harrises; the Owens; and Tommy Lee's family— all of us sought out each other while most everybody else avoided us, on account of catching whatever it was they thought we had, it seemed. Oh, folks said *hey*. They talked about the crops and the weather and gardens and such. And then they'd get right nervous acting, not knowing what else to be saying. They'd start in to shuffling feet, backing away, avoiding meeting eyes, twisting hands, tucking back hair. Funny how'd they'd all do them same things. It got so that I wouldn't hear a word what folks was saying because I was waiting for them to start in to shuffling. By the time they did, I'd nearly break out laughing. When I told Granny, she surely laughed too. Said we ought to be calling it the "Leper's Jig"!

There was one person who didn't back away from me, didn't do any silly dance. He didn't give me empty words. And he didn't offer mere "appearances," holding back his real feelings and thoughts. Instead, he give me his trust. Tommy Lee. We spent time together most every afternoon, meeting up by Blackberry Bluff. From there we watched the slow tearing apart of our land by the government men—trees cut down and hauled off (how could they cut down a oak so quick and cold like, not seeing its stately beauty?), rich soil picked up and carried elsewhere (weren't they knowing it belonged here, in this fertile valley?), small outbuildings knocked down and moved off already (weren't all outbuildings meant to be left alone, bending in and rotting away right slow like until they became part of the land once again?). Most couples that were promised shared their hopes and dreams with each other. But as me and Tommy Lee watched everything familiar—and loved because it was familiar, belonging to Jordan's Bend—as we saw everything killed, destroyed, hauled off, we talked about what couldn't be, grieved over what would never be.

Sometimes he took my hand in his. We didn't need to say words then. Times Tommy Lee mostly reached for me was when he was talking about his mama. She still sat in her chair, rocking and staring into the fire. Mister Arnold fed her, changed her clothes, combed out her hair, washed, and tended to her like a newborn babe—caring for all her needs with a gentleness Tommy Lee said he'd never known before in his daddy. When Tommy Lee'd talk about her, his voice would go all soft and tender. But then while he was talking, he'd wrap them strong fingers around my hand, squeezing tighter and tighter. I so needed strength and courage from Tommy Lee. But those times when he'd draw up my fingers inside of his palm, clutching at me, it seemed, I'd ask myself, *Is Tommy Lee pullin' strength from me too?*

After a while the government men destroyed Blackberry Bluff, so me and Tommy Lee moved upriver a ways, farther away from the hated dam. And then we moved farther upriver from that spot, too. Seemed like them Yankees were chasing us, teasing us—right mean like, though. Once they'd "caught" us, they'd parcel out what was supposed to take the place of our homesteads. As if any other places could be like our homes!

One day we talked about how we thought they were treating us just like hogs. Most folks around here let their hogs roam wild over the hills, allowing them to fatten up on whatever they can find to eat. But now and then, we'd go out into the hills hunting for them, listening for the ringing of the bells that we'd hung round their necks. Once you hear them, you start in to calling for them—and they come a-squealing too, since they knowed that we was bringing corn and salt. Feeding the hogs now and then like that keeps them from going wild. If we was to let them roam all the time, we'd never be able to get them to come to us, let alone catch them when it's time for a hog killing.

Me and Tommy Lee figured them Yankees were calling for us like we were hogs, offering us a different kind of corn and salt: new homes, schools, libraries, and the like. And I reckon they were figuring too that we'd come running and squealing for what they were offering. Keeping us tame and happy they were, since they were planning a killing, sure enough. Ours.

And so the days and weeks passed. I concentrated on the familiarity of daily living, finding a comfort in milking cows, churning butter, fixing dinner, tending to the garden. In these things I found a measure of peace. I suppose that was why I was looking forward to corn planting day this year. Working hard and seeing benefits for the choring was something I'd always enjoyed. But as the men discussed the soil, the weather, and the signs, finally agreeing the time to plant was here, I was anxious to be working that soil. Was I wanting to be sweating out my hurting? Or escaping from it?

The sun lost the race with me that morning, for I was up long before it was. Groping around in the dark for my working clothes, I pulled on my old slip and blue gingham dress, hoping I wasn't missing doing up any buttons. To please Mama I run a comb through my hair (though I probably made more tangles than I took out), worked it into a long braid, and then snatching up my straw hat, I tiptoed down the steps, thinking Mama and Daddy might still be asleep. But soon as I reached the bottom step, the sounds of Mama feeding wood to the firebox told me otherwise.

"Thought I might be wakin' before you and Daddy this mornin'," I said, smiling at her. "Guess I ain't never goin' to get to this stove before you do though!" I handed her more wood until she signaled that the box was plenty full.

"Corn plantin' day makes yer daddy's eyes pop open 'bout the same time the rooster beds down for the night, seems to me." I watched her nudge the wood this way and that, moving it around to catch fire good. "Ain't no more sleepin' once he's awake. There," she said, standing up straight once again and closing the door to the firebox. "That oughta be fine for bakin' up a double batch o' biscuits. Thought I'd make plenty for later, too, seein's how everone's goin' to be right hungry come dinnertime. Andy up yet?"

"Didn't hear him stirrin'. Reckon he will be soon though."

Mama nodded. "I be needin' him to chop wood this mornin'. 'Bout to run out."

"I could do it, seein's how I'm up already and—"

"Choppin' wood be Andy's chore," Mama interrupted. "Ain't you got enough to be doin'?" She give me a puzzled look with that deep line creasing between her brows. We moved about the kitchen as she talked, fetching a bowl and all the fixings for making biscuits. "Can't even recollect how many times of late me or yer daddy be findin' Andy just a-settin' in the barn, not doin' nothin' but sulkin', wastin' the good Lord's day." She glanced up at me a moment, exasperation and concern showing in them eyes. "And you be always lookin' for more chorin'.''

Mama suddenly stood still, looking up to stare at the flames licking at the fresh wood in the fireplace. "Yer daddy ain't of a mind to be switchin' Andy, feelin' for his hurtin' like he is. Same time, it ain't right to let 'im grow up to be no sorry person neither!" Dumping a fair amount of flour into the bowl, Mama began measuring in the baking powder and salt. I'd seen her make biscuits probably hundreds of times before, but it still fascinated me to watch how easily the soft dough appeared from the working of her able hands. "Seems like them Yankees done turned our lives topsy-turvy, changin' us all in ways what I never seen comin'.''

"But you knowed changes was comin'," I said softly, remembering too well the night I'd laid in bed listening to Mama and Daddy talk.

"I knowed." She stopped working again, giving me a fiercely protective look that startled me. "But then I were only tryin' to be preparin' myself for what was comin', hopin' my thinkin' on it would make whatever it were a mite easier. Didn't knowed it was to be anythin' like this, reachin' out its stranglin' fingers to touch my littlest young'uns—you an' Andy!" Mama worked the dough with her strong hands, using the wood spoon to push and turn it with every word she spoke. "Some day you'll be havin' little'uns, Rachael, and you'll be knowin' the fear o' wonderin' when to let 'em feel the pain o' this world—and when to pull 'em into yer arms, protectin' 'em.''

Mama reached up to touch me then and I felt the soft, dry flour against my cheek. "Ye be a woman now, Rachael. I know ye be feelin' the pull of love from Tommy Lee, and that be a part o' growin' that warms the heart." She looked deep into my eyes then, talking to me not as a mama to child, but woman to woman. "But ye must also be facin' the pain o' us leavin' this here land like a woman, not runnin' from it by doin' Andy's chorin' an' James Junior's chorin' an' this an' that 'til ye can't feel no more atall for bein' so tired." Pulling her hand away and then evidently noticing the smudge of flour, she lifted the edge of her apron to wipe away the mark. "Andy'll be just fine. He's made like yer Granny Mandy. More stubborn'n a chigger bite what's rubbin' against yer waistband.''

Mama stopped again a moment, gathering her thoughts, it seemed. "I heared tell that Miz Arnold's still doin' poorly. I know that must be right hard on Tommy Lee.''

I nodded to her, feeling the heat rising up my face. It was different when Tommy Lee talked about her, but here with Mama—and the two of us picturing Miz Arnold just setting in that chair—made me feel terrible embarrassed. To avoid looking at Mama, I absentmindedly pumped myself some water, drinking in its cooling taste in quick sips.

"Rachael, ye needs to be facin' pain square. Can't hide from it, or ye be hidin' from life." Looking at me then, she didn't ask any questions, but her eyes were searching mine for answers. I looked away.

"Granny Mandy's leavin' us too. Slower'n Miz Arnold, but she's leavin' us just the same." My words were cold, cold as the water from the pump, and they hung low in the silence like willow branches in a steady rain.

Mama's arm jerked suddenly against mine, splashing water on my skirt and knocking my mug to the floor. Again the sound of a tin cup banged into the silence, and I hurriedly reached to grab it, frantic to stop the clang that brought back the disturbing memory of Granny Mandy.

"What ere you sayin', Rachael?"

She clutched at me, her fingers smearing the flour all over my arm. *Had she even noticed the spilled water? Heard the loud clangs of the bouncin' cup?*

"Granny Mandy's talkin' to Grandaddy. I've heard her a-doin' it." Once I started putting words to my fears, it seemed there wasn't no stopping them. They come pouring out, sounding mean in the plain way I listed them off. "And the casket."

"What casket?"

"Granny's got her one. Ordered it from Mister Roddy the day of the all-day singin'. I seen it come the very next day. And Daddy said it were only 'cause she's gettin' on. But it ain't so. I know it's more'n that. On account o' she took me to see some foxfire over to the river, tellin' me it were from another world. And then I seen it later and I know it's nothin' but a dead, rotten stump an'—"

The door creaked as Daddy opened the door to the kitchen, causing us both to jump. We hadn't even heard him coming up the back steps. "What's this? What's rotten? Why, you two look like you done seen a haint! Have I gone all white an' disappearin' or somethin'?!" He moved to the sink to wash up, giving us a puzzled look still.

"We was just talkin' 'bout some old foxfire, Daddy." I quickly went to open the back door, excusing myself with a quick "I best be gettin' to my chorin'. They's plenty to be doin' today with the corn plantin' an' all."

I ran down the steps, letting the door slam behind me. *Why did you say them things?* a voice demanded. Regret come over me in a whole clamor of voices, spilling over me in waves. *Why did you tell Mama 'bout the foxfire? That was between you and Granny Mandy—the beauty of it and the horrible truth of what you'd discovered! That was yer secret!* Running now for the outhouse, I stubbed my toes on rocks, slipped on wet grass, and nearly fell down in my panicked hurrying. And yet I didn't really notice any of them things. All I knew was the dreadful accusations that were flashing through my head, causing a pain that quickly moved to my stomach, making me feel terrible nauseous. *Why, oh, why was you goin' on 'bout Granny talkin' to Grandaddy?* the accuser demanded. *What will Mama think now? Will she be tellin' Daddy? And then what will they do? What have you done, Rachael?*

Reaching the outhouse just in time, I flung the door open and leaned over the hole, emptying everything in my stomach in a painful, violent purging. When there was no more to come and my retching brought only dry gasps, I feebly straightened up, using the hem of my dress to wipe away the tears and sweat that covered my face and had dripped down my neck and soaked the collar of my dress. And then I stumbled outside, holding onto the walls for support like a weak cripple before I sunk to the ground.

After closing my eyes a few moments, I opened them to see the morning sneaking over the hills. The sun was just beginning to send out its first rays, and the dew clung to everything in tiny drops. I could see the drooping coils of spider webs hanging everywhere—each strand covered with them shimmering drops of dew, making them look like the fanciest, tiniest glass designs. Nature's designs. *God's designs,* an inward voice told me, a voice that had taken in Sunday school learning for years and years.

God? Did we ever really meet once—me and You, God? I asked Him, the words so clear in my head it seemed they were spoken out loud. *Or was You merely a name I give credit for makin' this world, and sendin' the rain, and givin' me love and happiness?* The questions came pounding through my head once more, but they weren't accusing. And they weren't even demanding no answers just now. Instead, they were more of a offering, a time to place them out there before me. Before God—if He really existed and was wanting to be listening.

Will I ever be knowin' You again like I done before? I begged silently. *Will a day come when I look at a spider web, seein' it shimmer in the mornin' dew and know that the Good Lord done the designin', done made the beauty?* I stopped a moment, putting a hand to my breast and feeling the heavy pounding of my heart. My chest ached so, and the work of putting the feelings into thoughts and the thoughts into questions made my breathing come in straining, labored efforts. *Will I ever be believin' that the God what made that bit of beauty is the same God what's lettin' Miz Arnold decide to stop livin', what's lettin' my own granny slowly leave me, and what's lettin' me feel pain like I never knowed a body could?* I asked. *Can You still be a lovin' God if You's allowin' me to hurt so?*

As the questions spilled out, it seemed like I was arranging them in my mind—feeling them, knowing them, setting them in their proper places. Made me think on dusting Mama's dresser. After taking off all the delicate things she keeps there and rubbing that top until it's good and shiny again, I carefully put back the crocheted doily, the silver mirror, comb and brush set, the perfume bottles, and the china hair dish, arranging them just so. It was comforting, feeling the familiar shapes in my hands, putting them back in their proper places—the places where they were supposed to be, the places where they belonged. Was this what I was feeling, finding solace in finally putting those questions out there to my God? There weren't any answers. No answers atall. But was this what Granny Mandy was meaning about putting your anger out there to God so you could be seeing it, knowing it for what it was?

And then one last question come rushing out, demanding its place among the delicate grouping of words I was arranging before me in the dew-sprinkled morning. The shock of what I was thinking—what I'd already admitted to Mama—finally moved from vague rumblings about my head to form words. *Is it true? Is Granny Mandy givin' up?* Seems as though it was creeping over her right slowly, like I'd told Mama. Granny hadn't quit altogether. She wasn't setting in no rocking chair all the time. But wasn't it appearing that she'd decided to give up, same as Tommy Lee's mama?

Noticing the feel of the wet grass soaking through my skirt, I rose to my knees and pushed my thoughts away from tomorrow and its frightening worries back to today and its insistent needs. Standing up, I slapped at the back of my skirt, brushing off the grass clinging there. Once more I saw all those questions laying out before me—not demanding, but pleading they were. And then I put one more grouping of words among all the others, knowing it too, finding its place in the arranging. I could hear Granny Mandy's voice joining in and repeating with mine, crying softly, *Lord I believe; help my unbelief!* It was enough for now.

I went about my chores then, moving through the chicken house and rousting the hens so rough like in my hunting for eggs that they were squawking at me something terrible before I was done. Just as I was leading Eenie, Miney, and Moe into the barn for milking, Andy suddenly stuck his head in, lighting out at me, "Don't need you to be doin' my chores!"

I tripped, causing Moe to get squirmish and give a good bump against me, which banged my knee a good one against the stall. "Ouch!" I cried out in pain. "Andy, they ain't no cause to be startlin' me and Moe like that!" I said angrily, rubbing the hurting knee. "And besides, I weren't—"

"Well, I ain't askin' for no help an' I ain't wantin' none neither!" And then he disappeared as quick as he'd come, before I could even tell him that I wasn't wanting to do his chores for no reason but that working—hard choring that made me sweat—kept me from worrying. Kept me from hearing all those questions pound through my head over and over again.

I gingerly felt my knee, knowing a good bruise would be showing there soon. "Moe! You just done that on purpose!" I grumped at her, grabbing up and angrily jerking her rope to lead her into the stall for milking. "I best speak to Daddy 'bout renamin' you Meanie, seems to me." She glanced back at me with a blank, innocent like look. "No, I'm changin' my mind already 'bout that. We best be namin' you Willie. After Willie Snodderly. That's the same look he gives Miz Travis ever time she's caught him in another of his pranks!"

At least Moe didn't give me any problems with the milking, and Eenie and Miney was as easy like as usual. Carrying the pails of milk towards the back door, I paused a moment before going up the steps. *Will Mama or Daddy ask me more 'bout Granny Mandy? What should I be sayin' if they do?* Again, there weren't any answers coming, so I took a big breath and headed on up the steps.

Daddy was setting at the table, the family Bible opened before him. Mama put the last of the fixings on the table and Andy stood at the sink, washing up. I set the milk pails down and waited for Andy to finish. He glanced over to me, favoring me with another of his scowls. "You two be ready yet?" Mama asked. "Yer daddy's fixin' to read and this here food's fixin' to get cold."

"Comin', Mama," I answered, splashing water over my hands as I glanced nervously her way. She didn't say anything about Granny Mandy, but I noticed the quick, jerking movements of her hands. And Daddy was awful quiet, concentrating so on his Bible reading. Maybe they were dismissing my outburst as not worth fretting over. That I was carrying on about nothing. I set at my place at the table, avoiding meeting anyone's eyes by staring at my empty plate.

"Thought I'd be readin' from the book o' Isaiah this mornin'," Daddy said. "Seems to be fittin' our needs just now—what with it bein' plantin' day an' all. This here's from chapter forty." He paused a moment, taking a breath, smoothing the page, and then adjusting the Bible so he could see it best in the weak morning light. "'To whom then will ye liken me, or shall I be equal? saith the Holy One. Lift up your eyes on high, and behold who hath created these things, that bringeth out their host by number: he calleth them all by names by the greatness of his might, for that he is strong in power; not one faileth.'"

Daddy always began slow like, but as the words moved him—and the sound of his voice grew deeper and stronger—he read more quickly and with confidence. "'Why sayest thou, O Jacob, and speakest, O Israel, My way is hid from the LORD, and my judgment is passed over from my God?'" Looking up from my plate to once again watch Mama's movements, I noticed that she was clutching a rag with one hand while the other rested by her plate in a tight fist. Her eyes were closed and that deep crease was still between her delicately arched brows.

"'Hast thou not known? hast thou not heard . . .'" Daddy's voice rose with the questioning, demanding an answer. No, he was expecting an answer, knowing it was coming from the sound of trusting peace that were in his voice. "' . . . that the everlastin' God, the LORD, the Creator of the ends of the earth, fainteth not, neither is weary? there is no searchin' of his understandin'. He giveth power to the faint; and to them that have no might he increaseth strength.'"

I couldn't take my eyes off Mama's hands, seeing how they were ever so slowly relaxing. The rag was mostly resting lightly in the curve of her fingers now. And the other hand was opened, palm up, like she was waiting for it to be filled with something. "'Even the youths shall faint and be weary, and the young men shall utterly fall: But they that wait upon the LORD shall renew their strength; they shall mount up with wings as eagles . . .'"

Wasn't Daddy's voice soaring with them eagles even as he read just now? Closing my eyes like Mama, I pictured the majestic birds—and Daddy's voice winging on the breezes with them.

"'They shall run, and not be weary; and they shall walk, and not faint.'" Silence followed. Finally I opened my eyes to see Mama setting there with hers closed still, the crease that was between her brows completely gone. Daddy was staring at her, a look of such tender caring showing in his features. And then Mama opened her eyes, knowing instinctively that Daddy was looking at her, I suppose. For she opened her eyes to be looking into Daddy's like . . . like there wasn't nowhere else on earth to be looking.

They stared at each other for just a passing moment, but in that instant of time I saw my daddy and mama like I hadn't never known them before. It was like they were pulling strength from each other, sending it back and forth in waves that was so powerful a body could might near feel and see the air moving between their eyes. They were speaking to each other, sure as anything, and yet they weren't saying nary a word. Weren't needing to. Even I knew what they were feeling was beyond needing words—and ever so much more powerful.

Finally, Daddy's eyes twinkled just a bit and he nodded his head—so slight—before Mama broke the pulling and giving between them, turning her gaze to Andy. Her voice sounded abrupt against the silent speaking I had just seen. "Will you be sayin' the blessin', Andy? 'Member to be askin' the good Lord to give us strength for the workin' today."

I closed my eyes again, expecting Andy to start in right off like he usually does—since he's always so anxious to be shoveling in food fast as a slick Yankee salesman can talk. But an awkward moment passed, and then I could hear him fidgeting round in his chair. "Lord," he began, whispering in a voice so soft I could hardly hear him, "we be needin' Yer help to be believin' that You will be helpin' us today. An' 'specially tomorra."

My eyes flew open in amazement. Andy was praying it too, sure as anything. *Lord, I believe; help my unbelief!*

The tone of his voice changed suddenly then from tender to gruff, and the rest of his clipped words come out in a rush. "Thank Ye for this food. Help us today with the plantin'. Amen."

I got up then to pour our coffee—again wanting desperately to keep my hands and mind busy—while Mama served up the ham, biscuits, and gravy. Andy started in to eating like the house was afire, letting the hot gravy drip down his fork onto the table since he was trying to take a bite of biscuit bigger'n a full-growed bear could eat. Mama corrected him, giving him a stern look and telling him if he wanted to eat like the hogs we would just as soon put a bell round his neck and send him out to the hills with the rest of them. But mostly we each ate in silence, probably thinking on the needs of the day, most likely feeling the worries of our uncertain future. Whatever each one was knowing inside, we were keeping it to ourselves.

When we were done, me and Mama done up the dishes together, not finding much to say except what was needed to put the kitchen right again. It was just a usual morning breakfast together. No different from any other. And yet it wasn't the same.

Seemed to me that this morning was like reading the end of a book, finding out how everything would be coming out. Mama'd been right about Andy. He was going to be fine. And I'd seen the strength that Mama and Daddy could give to each other—a strength that was like the spring that was feeding Granny Mandy's springhouse. Coming from way down somewhere in the ground, its supply was always sure. And endless. I learned that morning that Daddy and Mama's spring was the Bible, giving them the courage and strength to be facing whatever was ahead for us. The words in the Bible weren't just words to them; they believed them words. Because they were knowing the God what wrote them.

But I was fearing for Granny Mandy. Every time I looked at Granny, all I really saw was Miz Arnold. Setting. Silent. Miz Arnold'd surely become a prisoner; the walls were her rocker—and her decision to not be living no more. Granny Mandy was still living, but was she slowly moving backwards in time, finding life in what was and couldn't be? Would she be moving her prison walls closer and closer until she couldn't even be seeing me no more?

And who was this me that Granny Mandy should be seeing? Seemed I wasn't even knowing who that was. What was happening inside of me? What about the questions concerning the future—about God— that were droning through my head? This morning's "book" talked about Mama, Daddy, and Andy, but it didn't say anything in its ending about me. For me and Granny Mandy, the words were still being written.

Once we finished up, me and Mama put on our straw hats before going out. We knew we would be needing them soon as the sun was above the trees that grew along Dogwood Creek, taking with it the last of the shade and leaving us toiling and sweating in the boiling sunshine. We were just about to head up towards the field, toting hoes with us, when we heard Granny Mandy's voice calling to us.

"Hey, Mae! Rachael! Don't ye be a-settin' out fer that field without me! Ain't never yet missed no corn plantin' day, an' I ain't 'bout to this year neither!" We waited for her, watching her climb up the hill. She used her hoe like a staff again, planting the end on the ground with every step, but still she walked with as much energy as any young'un I knew. On her head she'd put a bright yellow bonnet, and underneath that wide brim Granny Mandy's eyes sparkled with excitement. "Land, what a day!" she exclaimed, stopping a moment, putting her hands to her hips and staring up into the nearly cloudless sky. "Good Lord done give us a fine day for plantin'!"

I smiled at her, feeling her enthusiasm spread out to draw me in. "Don't appear your rheumatism's botherin' you none today, Granny," I teased.

"What rheumatism?" She winked at me. "Best be gettin' on to that field. Corn cain't put itself in the ground." And then she turned and headed on up the hill, setting a good pace for me and Mama to follow.

"I recollect yer Great-Grandaddy McKenney tellin' 'bout the first year they done cleared this piece o' land," Granny Mandy said, nodding towards me. "He always said this here field o' new ground"—Granny always said *new ground* like it was only one word—"was the richest soil he'd ever knowed. 'Course they had to work it terrible hard first." The day was already promising to be a hot one. Stopping just a moment to catch her breath, Granny drew a sleeve across her upper lip, and Mama reached up to wipe her forehead of sweat, pushing back a dark curl and tucking it under her hat.

"I s'pose if we'uns be tempted to complain today," Mama said, "we best be thinkin' on all the trees an' underbrush an' roots that John and Mary McKenney done took out that first year."

I nodded. "Must've been trees thick as molasses here. Can't hardly believe how ever year still Daddy has to be grubbin' this ground, diggin' out stubborn sprouts from where them trees use to be. Daddy told me the Harrises ain't had to do no grubbin' for years."

"Harris land be dyin', Rachael," Granny Mandy said, the sadness in her voice seeming to slow the liveliness of her pace. "Ain't no topsoil left to speak of. Done been washed 'way into the Tennessee by 'bout as many spring tides as they is hungry skeeters after a young'un at the swimmin' hole on a hot summer evenin'. That soil ain't gettin' fed ever year like McKenney land is." She stopped again suddenly, putting a hand to the small of her back. "Like it was." Granny Mandy turned around then, facing the river and slowly looking over the whole of the McKenney property. We were standing at the top of a quick rise and we stood staring out over most of the valley from here.

My gaze followed Granny's. "Is they really goin' to flood all this?" I asked, although I wasn't really asking Granny Mandy or Mama. It was yet another of them questions that wasn't made for the answering. "How can them Yankees cover it all with so much water, buryin' the rich soil and the things that be growin' here, the hills and the valleys, the years of work that McKenneys put into this land?"

Mama sighed before she said, "Ain't just us, Rachael. It's the Arnolds. And the Harrises, Youthers, and Pursers. Yer Uncle Les and Aunt Samantha and Uncle Evert and Aunt Opal." She stared out towards the Tennessee, pulling the brim of her hat down over her forehead more and yet still squinting her eyes in the bright morning sun. "Everbody what's lived off o' this here land's worked it. Worked it hard. And if a body's worked it 'til he sweated, then they'll be a sore grievin' over leavin' it."

"I would think the Harrises'd be right glad to be leavin', seein's how their land be so poor," I insisted. "If they can get a better farm somewheres else and—"

"'Tain't so, Rachael!" Granny Mandy interrupted, looking at me with alarm lighting her eyes now. "I thought you'd be knowin', understandin' 'bout this here land. It's the years of toilin' an' sweatin' what ties a body to yer soil. Ties 'im same's blood binds kin to kin!" She reached down and grabbed up a handful.

Then suddenly I remembered the day we were planting the garden, the day when Granny'd told me about the soil being red because of the Indians' blood spilt on it. I remembered how I'd held a clump of dirt, squeezing it between my fingers. *Had the Indians been tied to this land once too? Did they shed tears for the leavin' of it?*

"Look here—an' be lookin' right close like." Granny Mandy held the soil out for me to see, cradling it in her aged, gnarled palm like a precious thing. "Yer kin's been here since nigh to eighteen hunnert. That be well over a hunnert years that a McKenney been workin' this land. Once one was gone an' laid to rest over to the family cemetery, they'd done left more'n memories behind 'em." She squeezed the soil tightly in her hand, wrapping her fingers around it until I saw her knuckles turn white for the straining. "They done left their sweat in this here land, Rachael." She opened her hand once again, and all three of us stared at the rich dirt. "Cain't you be seein' it? Cain't ye?"

I hesitated, not knowing if she really wanted me to answer. But then she looked up at me, her eyes questioning, searching mine, waiting. "Umm, I don't . . . Can't rightly see it, don't reckon," I said, my words tripping over each other. *Does she really see our kin's sweat? Oh God, is this another of her "spells"?* I glanced over to Mama for help, but she continued to stare at the clump of soil, her look blank. "I s'pose that's why we be favorin' the feel of it in our hands," I offered, searching for words that would be pleasing her. "An' why we tend to be rubbin' it between our fingers, appreciatin' the cost our kinfolk paid."

Granny Mandy tipped her hand slightly, letting the dirt slowly trickle to the ground. We stood watching until it was all gone, and then we stared at the empty, extended palm. "Ain't only blood an' sweat a-drippin' onto this land, mixin' with the soil, becomin' so much a part o' this here dirt that they ain't but a few of us what can see 'em any more." She relaxed her arm then, letting it fall to her side, and whispered, "They's tears spilt in this soil too."

The hurting in her voice made me look up to her face then, and I saw a tear slowly making its way down the pathways of the deeply wrinkled lines of one cheek. There was only the one, and when it fell onto the collar of her dress I looked away, embarrassed that I'd been staring at her so.

"My rheumatism be actin' up again this mornin', James Henry." I started at the name as if somebody'd slapped me. Looking back at Granny Mandy, I saw such a change in her from when she'd come nearly skipping up our hill. Now her whole body sagged, with her shoulders drooping and her head hanging limp. Even the brim of the bright yellow bonnet hung low over her face. "I reckon it be best iffin I head on back down to the cabin to be restin' just a spell. Come dinnertime, I'll be fit as a fiddle again." Then Granny Mandy turned to Mama, reaching out for her like she was blind. "Mae?"

Mama immediately grabbed onto her. I could see panic in Mama's eyes. "Yes, Granny Mandy?"

"My child, but you look frightened! Ain't no cause for alarm! You's knowin' this rheumatism won't be keepin' me down fer long." She patted Mama's hand and brushed it aside. "I'll just be restin' fer a spell. Send James Henry on to home fer dinner. Ain't nothin' hungrier'n a man what's been plantin' the whole mornin'!" She turned to walk away, but hesitated a moment, saying to me, "Rachael, you be workin' might near hard 'nough fer both us now, you hear?"

I nodded dumbly. "Granny, how 'bout if I just walk you on down the hill an' make sure yer settled in your cabin—"

"Land sakes, no! A spell o' the rheumatism ain't no cause to be escortin' me to home. I can find it fine, I reckon." She chuckled before adding, "Ain't lost it yet!" And then she worked her way back down the hill ever so slowly, leaning heavily on the hoe's shaft, taking small, stiff, jerking steps.

"Ain't you two comin'?" we heard Daddy holler then. Turning, we saw him on the other side of the cornfield. Andy was with him, waving his hat back and forth in the air at us.

"We's comin'!" Mama hollered back, and then she started towards him.

I hurried along beside her, often glancing up at the worried look on Mama's face, seeing the familiar deep crease was back again. "Mama, did you hear what Granny Mandy said?"

"Said her rheumatism be actin' up again."

"I know, but I'm meanin' what else she said."

"'Tweren't nothin' else." Mama's response was quick, and curt. When she talked like that there wasn't no sense arguing with her.

"But I mean when she talked to Grandaddy. To James Henry. She said it! Didn't you hear her?"

Mama dropped her hoe, reaching out then and grabbing for me. Each strong hand took ahold of one of my arms, squeezing them tight in her grasp. I could feel the bones of her fingers pressing against the bones of my arms, she held them so firm. "Didn't no such thing happen! An' don't you be sayin' such nonsense to yer daddy neither. He be havin' 'nough for thinkin' on; we ain't goin' to be worryin' him with this!" Mama let go of me then, and the sudden release of pressure against my arms felt strange, tingly. Snatching up the hoe, she trudged on towards Daddy and Andy.

"But Mama . . . " I hurried after her, my anxiousness causing me to stumble over the clumps of turned earth beneath my feet.

"Now you be listenin' to me, Rachael." Mama's stern words come out quick, sharp, demanding. "Yer Granny Mandy be of strong southern folk. Time an' time again she knowed the pain o' livin' in this sin-filled world. Yer daddy weren't borned yet when she lost three young'uns to the typhoid. Nursed 'em for days before they died, listenin' to 'em cry out in pain."

I hadn't known how Daddy's brother and sisters had died. Hadn't thought to ask. Now I pictured Granny Mandy hovering over them, tending to them, wanting to cure them as she had cured so many others so many times. *Oh, Granny Mandy!*

"Only the eldest—William—survived the typhoid. Come through it fine. An' yer granny told me how she rejoiced, she did. Praisin' God for savin' the one, not blamin' Him for takin' the three."

Mama's voice caught for a moment, but her rush of words kept coming.

"An' then it weren't but a month after William was up an' around when he fell out o' the hayloft, breakin' his neck! Can you imagine that?" Her voice was shrill, frantic sounding. "He lived through the typhoid only to be dyin' in a queer, horrible accident!" And then Mama stopped, staring at me, holding my eyes just like she'd done my arms—with the same fierceness and again, making me feel the pain. "But yer granny survived. Ere you hearin' me? She survived! Granny Mandy come through it even stronger than before, facin' the world with courage—and faith! Yer Granny Mandy ain't givin' up, Rachael McKenney, she ain't. She can't!" Mama drew away from me suddenly, a look of terror on her face. Putting both hands over her lips, she whispered once more through trembling fingers, "She *can't!*"

Mama closed her eyes—saying a silent prayer?—and then she strode swiftly across the field towards Daddy once again. I picked up her hoe, following behind her, staring at the soil we so swiftly trod upon and passed over. Clutching a hoe tightly in each hand, I rubbed my thumbs back and forth, back and forth over the smooth wood. Mama's terror-filled cry echoed through my head. *She can't. She can't. She can't!*

"Don't be sayin' nothin' 'bout this to yer daddy," Mama said softly. The sudden calm in her voice was striking, leaving me dumbfounded. "Best thing for us to be doin' is work—a good day's work o' tendin' to this here field. You hear me, Rachael?"

"Yes, Mama." We walked the rest of the field in silence. Mama stared straight ahead, her shoulders square, her head high. I stared down at the ground, toting the hoes in her wake.

"Me an' Andy be right pleased you be joinin' us," Daddy greeted us, winking at Mama and giving my hat a teasing tug. "Good, cheap help be as hard to find as a honest Yankee!" He grinned at us, waiting for us to smile back at him. "Now, me an' Andy already done finished a dozen rows, hoein' an' diggin' in the corn as we went." Daddy nodded towards the ground, saying, "I know me an' James Junior usually done all the hoein' before plantin' day, but they ain't too terrible many weeds. If everbody can work his swith"—by that Daddy was meaning the distance between us as far as our hoes could reach—"then I b'lieve we'uns'll be finished with the plantin' by evenin'."

Daddy handed me and Mama each a sack of corn which we hung around our necks. "Now, you be recollectin' that them kernels should be dug in 'bout ever three foot. An' we'uns always plant five, knowin'"—and then Daddy recited the bit of verse he said every year:

> One for the ground squirrel,
> One for the crow,
> One to rot,
> And two to grow!

"An' then when the corn's knee high," Andy broke in, "we'll pull up the big'ns so to give the little'ns plenty room to grow!" He gazed up at Daddy then, obviously pleased with himself for remembering Daddy's other favorite bit of yearly teasing.

We set to work then, each of us taking a row on the west side of the field, working our swiths until we come to the other side. And then we'd turn around and work back the other way. Eventually the sun came up over the trees, beating down on us, making shadows that bent and moved and worked along the rows with us. When it was time to be stopping for dinner, we were surely glad that the widest part of the field was done—seeing how it was shaped like a big *V* since Dogwood and Springtide Creek come together, forming the outlines of this fertile piece of land. The field that grew McKenney Way corn.

Me and Mama went to fix dinner, but first I run down to see to Granny Mandy. My heart was fairly pounding when I come to her cabin door. "Granny? Granny Mandy, you feelin' poorly still?" I called to her, peeking anxiously through the screen.

"Rachael! Come on in with yerself. I's jest sippin' some o' my remedy fer the rheumatism." Entering slowly, cautiously—since I was still afraid of what I might find—I walked towards Granny Mandy. She was setting in her rocker, sipping from a tin cup with a steaming liquid in it. "Set yerself down an' rest a spell. An' hep yerself to my remedy." She nodded towards a kettle on the stove. "Don't reckon it'll hurt ye none, an' it might even hep ye a mite today too, seein's how your muscles must be achin' from all the hoein' I s'pose you already done."

"How are you feelin' now, Granny? Is the rheumatism painin' you still?" I ignored her request about trying the remedy, recollecting too well what she'd give to Daddy. Pulling the other rocker up close to her, I set down. And then I searched her eyes—for clarity? focus? for proof she was living with us, now?

Granny Mandy reached out and patted my knee, noting my searching. "I be jest fine, child." She smiled at me, gently, giving me the look of a wise, understanding elder learning the ignorant young'un. "Ye needs be knowin' that pain sometimes makes a body act in ways that might not be, well, familiar to ye." She searched my face then with her caring eyes. "Ere ye understandin' me, Rachael?"

"I think so. I'm tryin' to." I paused a moment, gathering courage to ask the question that was pressing at me something fierce. "Granny, are you meanin' your rheumatism pain?"

"Why, 'course I is, child! That's why I be sippin' this here remedy, ain't it?" She grinned at me again and then patted my knee once more.

"Now, fetch ye some an' come set a spell. Tell me how the plantin's comin'."

"I best not, Granny Mandy. Mama's needin' me to be helpin' her with dinner, and then I'll be headin' back on out to the field. We's comin' 'long fine though. Daddy says we just might finish the upper field by evenin'." I stopped, watching Granny rock gently back and forth. She stared into the fireplace, closing her eyes whenever she sipped of the hot liquid.

"Ye be a big hep to yer mama and daddy. Reckon ye best be gettin' on back to work. This here remedy works like it always does, I oughta be fit an' ready fer plantin' this afternoon too."

"Oh no, Granny! You just stay here and rest and—"

"Rachael, I done tole you that I ain't yet missed no plantin' day! Have ye done fergot 'bout my remedies—an' how they work iffin they's a secret ingredient in 'em?"

I searched her face again, concern for her frightening me once more. "Granny, how can they be a secret ingredient in this remedy if you made it?"

She stood up then, gingerly, with no signs of the jerking, stiff movements of this morning. Walking over to the stove, she said, chuckling, "Well, I done mixed up my apple cider vinegar an' strained honey like always. An' then I let it come to boilin' before I closed my eyes, reached up into my cupboard here o' jars o' spices, grabbed up a jar, throwed in a pinch o' whatever it were, an' then . . . well, then I shoved that jar back in the cupboard before I could see what it were. See there!?" she asked, them eyes alight with laughing at herself. "Now ain't this here remedy done got its own secret ingredient?"

And then we laughed together—laughed for this moment, for all the other times in the past when Granny's humor had put aside my fears, for all the times in the future when I'd be so needing her teasing to get me through the pain. *Oh, Granny Mandy!* And then the unanswered question flashed across my mind. *Is it really the pain of rheumatism that's making you do those unfamiliar things, or is it another kind of pain—the painin' felt of the heart?*

The silent question took away my joy, sobering me as quick as the laughter'd come. "I best be headin' on to home. Is they anythin' I can do for you before I go?"

"Thank ye, Rachael, but I be jest fine. This here remedy an' the comfortin' o' my fire be workin' right quick. Tell yer mama and daddy that I'll be hepin' this afternoon, sure 'nough."

"I'll tell 'em. You keep restin' yerself before then, will you?" I pleaded with her.

"I's restin'! Got to finish this here remedy, don't I? An' a body cain't sip it without the hep o' a good rockin' chair beneath 'im!"

I smiled at her, looking her over once more from head to toe, attempting to reassure myself that she was fine. "We'll be lookin' for you later then, Granny Mandy."

"Sure ye don't want to be takin' no remedy with ye?" Granny nodded towards the kettle, winking at me.

"No, thank you! They's no tellin' what you done put in there," I teased, shaking my head at her. "Bye, Granny!"

I run up to the house, banging open the kitchen door and making Mama jump from the sudden noise. "Rachael! Ever time you come in this kitchen like that I wonder if you ain't no older actin' than Andy!" She shook her head at me. "How's Granny Mandy feelin'?"

"Seems much better." I washed my hands and then started setting the table. "She's sippin' her remedy for the rheumatism an' it appears to be workin'. Says she's goin' to help with the plantin' this afternoon." Mama didn't look up at me. I didn't look at her neither. We were both knowing that Granny's spells—and Mama's insistence that we weren't to mention them—was between us plain as day.

"Prob'ly be good for her to be workin' a spell. Not too much, mind you, but jest 'nough to be workin' out the soreness in them joints. Yer Granny knows that. Too much settin' an' rockin' ain't good for a body." Mama glanced up at me then and our eyes met for just a moment. A picture of Miz Arnold, setting in her rocker, set in my mind's eye. I could feel the flush going up my face before Mama quickly looked away. Discomfort was written on her face too. "Take them biscuits out o' the warmin' oven an' then go fetch some honey from the springhouse. An' after that," she called after me, since I was already out the door, "after that you can be ringin' the bell for dinner."

We ate mostly in silence, hungrily devouring the hot food, knowing we were needing it to give our bodies the strength to work again. I was tired, feeling the all-too familiar aching about my shoulders and back, wishing I didn't have to go back to the planting. And yet at the same time, I was wanting to grab up my hoe again and dig in the rest of my sack of corn. There was good in finishing what was started—finishing the planting in a long, hard day's work so that a body was tired enough to fall into bed, going to sleep soon as you stretched out. Wasn't time to be laying there thinking. Worrying. Hearing the questions over and over again. At least in sleep there was escape from the questions.

The next morning, the sun caressed my face, waking me with its warm touch against my skin. Opening my eyes—and then squinting them against the morning rays—I sat up slowly, feeling the aches still from hoeing and planting. I looked over towards Andy's bed. He was already gone. *How late have I been layin' abed?* I asked myself, moving gingerly to slide my feet to the floor. Every move reminded me that I'd put in a good day's work yesterday.

Reaching to get my blue gingham, I stopped, puzzled, and then had to chuckle. *You really did 'bout fall into bed last night, silly!* I told myself. *You done fell asleep without even gettin' out o' yer clothes!* I stood up then, stretching, rubbing and pulling out the sore places. *Maybe yer 'bout ready for some of Granny Mandy's remedy by now too, sore as you appear to be!* I mumbled to myself.

I walked to the window, looking out towards Granny Mandy's cabin. Amazingly, she was already out working, hoeing her truck patch. Her yellow bonnet bobbed in the sunlight. I shook my head at her. She'd worked most of the afternoon with us yesterday, hoeing and planting her swith as fast as me and mama. And now she was out there working again while I was just getting out of bed, complaining to myself about my aching back. *Granny, oh Granny, are you goin' to be fine? Is Mama right? Are you goin' to survive, Granny Mandy?*

"Rachael? Is you up yet?" Daddy called to me from the bottom of the steps.

"Yes, Daddy!" I run to the top of the stairs, terrible embarrassed to be caught abed so late of a morning. "I'm sorry I slept so late, Daddy. It ain't like me an'—"

"Rachael, they ain't no cause to be frettin'. You was plumb tuckered from a hard day's work."

"But still, Daddy, I . . ." I stopped, suddenly taking in that he had on his Sunday best trousers and shirt. "Why are you dressed for church? This ain't Sunday, is it? Did I plain forget what day it be?" Each question had come tumbling out after the other. If it was Sunday, I knew I had to be moving awful quick if I was to be ready in time.

"No, Rachael!" Daddy grinned up at me, shaking his head. "It ain't Sunday, and you ain't goin' to school today neither. I reckon this'll be somethin' like a holiday for you an' Andy. Mister Whitaker be takin' us to see the dam today. Said he'd come to drive us in his car. Give us the 'grand tour,' he called it. Reckon you'll be a-likin' that?" Daddy run his fingers through his hair, nervous like.

I come down a few steps to where me and Daddy was eye to eye. Setting down and hugging my knees to my chest, I asked, "Daddy, do it make sense to be hatin' somethin' awful and yet at the same time be so curious 'bout it your insides is cravin' to see of it?" I paused a moment, trying to find the words for all the mixed-up feelings inside of me. "And then you be feelin' guilty 'bout wantin' the very thing what you's hatin'?"

"Ere that how you be feelin' 'bout seein' the dam?"

"Yes, sir."

"Don't know if it makes sense." I looked away, feeling embarrassed then. "But I do know that's 'xactly how I be feelin' too."

I leaned towards him, and Daddy pulled me tight against his broad, firm chest, wrapping his long, muscular arms around me. Nuzzling my face against him, I listened to the steady, rhythmic pounding of his heart, finding comfort in its regular beating. I breathed deeply, taking in and pleasuring the smell of Daddy—a mixture of animal smells, sweat, shaving cream, and Mama's soap from the laundering of his shirt. Here, security become a touchable thing—because whenever Daddy wrapped his arms around me, pulling me into the protection of his embrace, I wasn't afraid of anything. Long as I was there. And only as long as I was there.

Daddy took ahold of my arms then, pulling me away from him so he could look me in the eye again. "Well then, what ere you thinkin'? Do you reckon me an' you can be toleratin' this here trip today—an' maybe even be enjoyin' it just a bit?"

He grinned at me, waiting for me to smile back. I nodded, and then he reached out to tug on one of my curls. One of my tangled curls. I jumped up, putting both hands to my tousled head and nearly shouting, "Land sakes! What time is it? And me such a mess! What time is they comin' for us?"

Daddy chucked at me. "If you jest get to movin', I reckon you'll have plenty o' time to be prettyin' up. Them Yankees think mornin' means might near to noon almost!" He turned to go back towards the kitchen but first added over his shoulder, "Yer mama says to come on an' take yer bath. The tub's all ready and waitin' for you. I wouldn't want my gals to be goin' off on no sightseein' tour with . . ." The rest of his teasing was lost as he got closer to the kitchen, and I headed back up the steps to gather up clean clothes.

Frantically I snatched up my new blouse and a skirt, socks, and my shoes. The shoes needed another spit-shine, but there just wasn't time for that this morning.

Much later I was just finishing tying up my hair when I heard Ezra and Nehemiah raising a ruckus and then Mister Whitaker hollering down to the road. Grinning at my reflection, I mused, "Them Yankees is right scared of tame dogs. What on earth would they be doin' if they was to come upon a mountain lion or a bear?"

Daddy opened the door for me, answering, "I s'pose they'd run clean back to where they done come from." He wrinkled his brow a moment, like he was studying on something serious like. "Reckon we ought to rustle us up some wild animals?!"

"Rustle up what?" Andy asked, interrupting our laughter. I noticed Andy'd put on his Sunday clothes for our tour too, and even his hair was combed and slicked down.

"My, but don't you look fine!" I teased him, nodding towards his wet hair. "Ain't you wearin' that hat what looks like the hogs done fought over it?"

He scowled back at me, ignoring my question. "Rustle up what?" he asked Daddy again.

"Oh, me and Rachael was just teasin' on them Yankees bein' so afeared o' Ezra an' Nehemiah. Holler at them dogs to git back up here, Andy, an' then tell Mister Whitaker we be comin'." Daddy leaned towards the kitchen, calling, "Miz McKenney, you be 'bout ready?"

Mama come out then, appearing flustered as she hugged her pocketbook to her with one hand while she nervously straightened her hat with the other. "Ere it crooked? I leaned over to look inside the oven an' it come nigh to fallin' in!"

"Looks fine—but I don't be thinkin' roasted hat be tastin' nearly as good as it looks a-settin' on yer pretty head!" Daddy glanced over at me and then looked down the hill towards Andy. He'd already climbed into Mister Whitaker's car and was waving at us from one of the windows. Ezra and Nehemiah sat dutifully on the breezeway, although every inch of them was straining towards what they considered a prime trespasser setting on their territory. In between panting with them long tongues hanging out, they were whining something fierce. And every time they'd whine they'd first lick them tongues all the way round their mouths, sending drips of slobber spraying everywhere. Me and Mama walked gingerly around them while Daddy reached down to give each one a pat on the head before heading on down the hill. "Stay!" he commanded, pointing towards them with one extended finger.

I giggled as a thought come to me. "You reckon they's lickin' their chops because they's thinkin' how fine Mister Whitaker would taste?"

"Rachael!" Mama scolded. "Ain't no cause to be sayin' such things. 'Specially when Mister Whitaker's tryin' to help us . . . an' even be extry nice, takin' us on this here tour."

"'Sides," Daddy said, shrugging his shoulders, "it's like I done tole you once a'ready. Them dogs know a Yankee only fit for the hogs to eat."

I laughed out loud until Mama looked my way once again, giving me a disapproving stare. Daddy grinned at me until she turned to him too, and then he sobered up right quick, clearing his throat and hitching up his pants. We walked the rest of the way to Mister Whitaker's car without saying anything more. But Daddy did wink at me once. Without Mama seeing.

"Good morning!" Mister Whitaker called to us, opening his door and climbing out. He reached out to offer Daddy his hand and then lifted his hat to Mama. She nodded to him, barely moving her head.

"Mornin'," Daddy replied. Daddy could be right talkative until a stranger come round. Then he rarely offered more'n one or two words at a time, acting as though it fairly tuckered him out to be jawing on so.

"I thought you and Mrs. McKenney could sit right up front here with me." He motioned towards the seat by him. "And then your children can sit in the back. That all right with you?"

Daddy nodded. "Be fine." Mister Whitaker walked around the front of his car and held the doors while Mama and Daddy climbed in the front and I scrambled in next to Andy.

I looked over to Granny Mandy's then—searching for some sign of her—but she was nowhere to be seen. She'd probably run to fetch her gun soon's she heard Mister Whitaker coming up the road. I reckoned she was setting just inside her front window, watching Mister Whitaker's every move through the site of that mean-looking gun she was always toting around when Yankees were anywhere near.

"This here's a fine car," Daddy said, looking all around the inside. I noticed Andy was eyeing everthing too. "It be a Ford?"

"Yes, sir. Ford Sedan. Made in nineteen thirty-four. And she is one fine car except for the lame fuel pump. Crazy thing goes out nearly every two months, just like clockwork!" He rubbed the black steering wheel between his fingers. "Try those windows back there, Andy. I think you'll find them interesting."

"How's that?" Andy asked, excitement making his voice rise. Earlier this morning I'd heard Daddy telling Andy not to be touching anything in Mister Whitaker's car, and now here he was offering for Andy to do the very thing.

"Go ahead and roll your window down and then back up again. See how you like that."

Andy looked at Daddy first, waiting for his nod of permission, and then he gingerly pumped at that handle. A big grin spread clean across his face as the window eased down and then back up, responding to his will.

"Now, try sliding your window back too," Mister Whitaker urged him. "It's a great feature Ford added. 'Clear-vision ventilation' they call it."

Andy pushed at it, but it only moved a inch or two. He paused a minute, screwing up his face. "I like the winder down much better. Can I do that again?"

"Mind your manners, Andrew," Mama said, glancing back at him.

"Please, Mister Whitaker. If it be all right with you."

"Of course you may—and you, too, Rachael. It's a beautiful day for a ride with the windows down."

I caught Daddy's eye then—it being good to always get Daddy's permission first instead of after when you might be in a heap of trouble. And then I carefully rolled down the window next to me, enjoying right off the gentle breeze blowing in my face.

"Almost forgot," Mister Whitaker said, looking over at Mama and Daddy and then peering back at us in that funny little mirror that hung down in front of him. "We're taking another young man along with us. Tommy Joe's his name, I believe."

I suddenly sat up straight. "You meanin' Tommy Lee Arnold?"

"Oh, yes, that's the one. Sorry, I have a hard time remembering all these names sometimes." Mister Whitaker glanced back at me. "Do you know him?"

Andy looked over at me then, rolling his eyes and shaking his head. "Yes, sir. Most folks what live round here know everbody else." I tried keeping my voice even sounding. Inside my heart was racing with excitement at the thought of spending the day with Tommy Lee. The whole day!

"Oh. I suppose that would be true," Mister Whitaker went on. He cleared his throat and straightened his shoulders. "When I lived in New York for awhile in an apartment house, I got to know only one of my neighbors. And that was because we shared a mailbox."

"How many neighbors was you havin'?" Andy asked.

"What? How many lived in the apartment house?" I saw his eyes looking at Andy in the small mirror again. Sure looked queer seeing only them eyes staring at you thata way. "Well, let's see. I suppose there were two hundred or more."

Andy about come clean off his seat. "Two hunnert? In one house?"

"Knowed a feller once what visited to New York City," Daddy told us. "Said the buildin's there was heaped up with so many folks that he had to learn his dog to waggle his tail up an' down since they wasn't no room to be waggin' it sideways."

Mister Whitaker chuckled. "Yes, there are a good number of people in our cities. But you must understand that apartments are big buildings. And they're broken up into small apartments, which are like individual houses of rooms within a big building. Understand?"

Andy frowned. "No, sir, I reckon I don't. Don't see how they can be houses inside o' houses an' then how them folks ain't a-knowin' each other neither. They must be right mean."

Again Mister Whitaker chuckled. "Well, you might be right there. Most people do say that New Yorkers aren't as friendly as you Southerners!"

He drove up the rutted road to the Arnolds' then. Me and Andy bounced around a good bit, it was so rough going. Tommy Lee was waiting for us, setting on the porch in a rocker, looking fine in his Sunday best. He'd even tried combing his hair, too, I supposed. But that one stubborn lock still hung down over his forehead.

"Daddy, Mister Whitaker's here!" Tommy Lee called through the broken screen door. Seemed there wasn't a cabin in this whole county what didn't have rusted, broken screens on the doors inviting in about every fly that come down the river.

Mister Arnold come out the door and walked with Tommy Lee to the car. He moved like an old man, hunched over and bent with the weariness that was setting on his sagging shoulders. After exchanging *heys* with Daddy, Mama, me, and Andy, Mister Arnold then shook hands with Mister Whitaker, who'd climbed out of the car to greet him.

"How's Mrs. Arnold today?" Mister Whitaker asked.

I could feel myself bristling at his asking. *As if you was really carin'!* I thought to myself, indignantly. *And especially when you be the reason the Arnolds is sufferin' so!*

"Same. I cain't be leavin' her." Mister Arnold shoved his hands into his pockets, avoiding Mister Whitaker's eyes and hanging his head, shaking it back and forth. Then he looked back up at Mister Whitaker. "I be appreciatin' yer takin' my boy here to see the dam."

"I'm glad to do it. We'll eat a lunch there and then be back around two o'clock or so. Is that all right?"

"Be fine." Mister Arnold fumbled in one of his pockets, pulling out a few coins. "Got me some change here. How much you reckon that lunch'll be costin'?"

Mister Whitaker reached for the car door, motioning for Tommy Lee to climb in. "Won't take a penny. This one's on Uncle Sam. See you later, Mr. Arnold."

Mister Arnold reached down into his pocket again, pulling out more coins. Suddenly he stood upright, squaring them shoulders and deepening his voice with authority. "Reckon I got 'nough here. Ain't takin' no charity . . ."

"Mr. Arnold, please," Mister Whitaker interrupted. "The government owes you people at least this. It's not much—besides helping everyone get resettled—but it is something that we want to do." He reached out to shake Tommy Lee's daddy's hand once more. "Please allow us to do this."

Mister Arnold glanced towards the cabin. His inner struggling was written all over his features—features that were so like Tommy Lee's. He brushed back a stray thatch of hair hanging over his forehead and then wiped one hand across his mouth. "I reckon it be all right . . . iffin Tommy Lee don't decide to eat like he done this mornin'. Nigh to cleaned us out o' everthin'." He shook Mister Whitaker's hand, giving Tommy Lee a stern look, but Tommy Lee only grinned back.

"Daddy, if Uncle Sam be payin', I reckon I ought to be eatin' my fill!" Mister Whitaker laughed, and Tommy Lee's daddy waved us off, grinning. The smile had transformed Mister Arnold's appearance, making him look years younger. But as he turned to walk back to the cabin, I noticed his head droop once again, the shoulders sagged, and his steps become slow and heavy like he was carrying weights on those shoulders, like he was wading through deep water. The weariness that he was knowing had come over him once more and the aging years returned too quickly.

And then I noticed Tommy Lee staring after his daddy. The same weariness, same heaviness of spirit was reflected in his soft eyes. How I was wanting to reach for his hand, but I dared not. Andy was setting right next to me, and if I was to try to signal Tommy Lee—even to just let him know I was caring somehow—Andy'd be sure to notice. Then there'd be the devil to pay for it.

Mister Whitaker started up the car and backed it carefully down the rutted road. Tommy Lee looked after his daddy the whole time, craning his neck around awkward like just so he could still watch him once we were headed down the road a ways. And then he rested his head against the side of the car, staring out the opened window. Staring at what? *Was he seein' the vine that had wrapped itself round their split-rail fence, the bright yellow daffodils that were bloomin' by the newly-turned field, the stray, mangy dog what was trottin' along the side of the road, its ribs showin' plain and its tongue hangin' out?* I wondered. *Or was he only seein' his daddy still—and the rockin' chair he needs be returnin' to?*

Feeling restless, I rubbed my fingers against the seats, appreciating the softness of the stuffed cushions and yet at the same time noting how irritating the mohair covering could be. It was scratching my legs so that I shifted my weight, pulling my skirt down better so it wouldn't be rubbing against me anymore. Glancing round, I saw how everything was so much shinier than in the Hickmans' old, rusted truck—the handles on the doors, the metal round the windows, and the buttons that were up front near Mister Whitaker. Suddenly he reached out and turned one of them black buttons.

"Ever listen to a car radio?"

"Don't reckon so," Daddy said. Mama leaned away from it like it was a copperhead about to strike her.

"They ain't no radio in the Hickmans' truck," Tommy Lee offered, leaning forward now and looking impressed and interested in Mister Whitaker's. Andy was leaning up against the front seat too, not wanting to be missing anything.

"This is a genuine Philco-Transitone car radio. Worked right well until I got to these mountains. Because of them—causing interference like they do—unfortunately the station doesn't come in too well. And then the station originates from so far away too." He glanced over to Daddy and then back at Tommy Lee. "Comes clear from Chattanooga. But we'll do the best we can." He fumbled with the buttons, making a crackling noise. "This one on the left controls the volume; the other is for finding the station." He moved his hand back and forth between them buttons, turning them ever so slow like. Finally I could just barely make out music behind all them irritating scratching sounds.

"Ah, it's a symphony playing classical music." He stopped talking, straining to hear the music. "Can't quite make out what they're playing. Oh well, I'm afraid there's just too much static today." He turned the left button again, and the sounds stopped as quickly as they'd begun. "Actually, my favorite music is classical." He looked over at Mama and Daddy. "What's yours?"

"How's that?" Daddy asked.

I fumed at Daddy. *He's actin' slow on purpose again,* I thought to myself. *Daddy's knowin' well 'nough what classical music be!*

"Oh, sorry," Mister Whitaker said, clearing his throat.

He rubbed the steering wheel between his hands—hands that weren't atall like Daddy's, I noticed. Mister Whitaker's didn't have no dirt under the nails. They weren't calloused and rough looking. Didn't look atall like they could be baling hay, mending fences, or plowing fields. Instead, they looked soft. Too clean. Too weak. I frowned, thinking to myself, *I reckon his hands is just like some prim an' proper lady's, settin' in her fine house in Chattanooga. I wouldn't be wantin' no man with hands like a lady holdin' mine!* Quickly I glanced over to Tommy Lee's, noting with pleasure how rough and sturdy they were. And remembering how they felt covering the whole of mine too.

"Reckon that be dependin' on what a body calls music." I hadn't heard Mister Whitaker's question; I'd been thinking on his hands so that I'd plainly not even heard him talking. But from Daddy's answer, I assumed he'd asked what kind of music Daddy liked. Daddy took his time talking, staring out the window at the scenes that were passing by. We were traveling on the new graveled part of the road now, and the ride was much smoother. "Of a night, a settin' by the fireplace, I be a-listenin' to the cracklin' o' the fire, the creakin' o' my rocker—an' then the answerin' creak o' Miz McKenney's rocker—the steady drummin' o' the treefrogs, the sounds o' my young'uns sleepin' an' then turnin' in their beds. Why, all them things is music to me, Mister Whitaker. Prettiest music a man ever did hear."

Daddy continued to stare out the window. But I hoped he knew I was smiling at him, seeing how my heart was about to burst. He'd done us proud.

"Um, you know, I believe you're right." Mister Whitaker's voice sounded soft. "If I could choose, I suppose I'd pick that music over a symphony any day."

We'd come to the turnoff that took us to the dam site, and Mister Whitaker had to stop the car at a small building with a man inside it. There was bright, red-lettered "KEEP OUT!" and "DANGER!" signs posted all over the gate that blocked the road and on down the fence stretching as far as I could see. All three of us in the backseat sat forward even more, leaning to see out as best we could. "Seems like we's goin' into a prison or somethin'," Andy whispered excitedly to us, and then he immediately poked his whole head back out the window again.

"Good morning, Mr. Whitaker!" the man in the building called out. "Got some visitors with you today?"

"Yes, sir, I do. I'm going to show them the sights, Tom. Let them see firsthand what we're doing here."

The man named Tom leaned over to peer at us through the car window. He was a short, stubby man with glasses what bobbed up and down on his nose when he talked. "Well now, you folks enjoy yourselves today. You're in for a treat, I tell you!"

He walked over to the gate, working at the lock, then opening the gate wide and motioning for us to drive on through. "See you later, Tom," Mister Whitaker called back to him. Me, Andy, and Tommy Lee all turned around, watching to see if this Mister Tom would close the gate after us. Sure enough, he shut it tight—even hitching up that lock once again.

Andy looked at me and Tommy Lee, eyes wide and alarm showing there. "See? I tole you we was goin' to prison. We's locked in!" he whispered frantically.

"It ain't to keep people locked in, Andy," Tommy Lee whispered back. "They be needin' to keep folks out so's they don't be comin' in an' gettin' hurt or somethin'."

The three of us turned around slowly, anxiously glancing here and there out the windows. Lookin' for—what? Other prisoners, like us? "All I be knowin'," Andy whispered again, "is that we be on the inside. An' the inside be locked in same as folks on the outside be locked out."

Mister Whitaker started in to talking then, instructing us, pointing out this and that. It wasn't long atall before I stopped fretting over that locked gate, seeing how he made everything he spoke about so interesting for us. He may have been a Yankee, and one we most certainly didn't like nor trust. But I was surely terrible curious about everything we were seeing—and everything he could tell us about those things.

"First I want to talk about all the trees that our men have cut down. I know you've noticed that and probably thought awful of us for doing so. But all those trees had to go. If we left them in the lake they'd only die. And then they'd cause boats and barges coming down the river a lot of trouble, snagging them on the bottom. So we used those trees. Didn't just cut them down and throw them away. See how they're used everywhere for walkways, railings, supports for construction, buildings?" Mister Whitaker nodded his head towards an amazing number of buildings that were all round us on both sides of the road. "We try not to waste anything. And especially what was once a beautiful tree."

I saw Daddy nod his head. He never did take to wasting nothing.

"God's creatures an' all o' creation be for us to take," I'd often heard Daddy say. "But God also be expectin' us to use—an' use honest like—what we be takin'."

By now all three of us had our heads stuck out them roll-down windows. Me and Andy were mashed against each other on the one side—and he was most put out with me for crowding him so—but I was determined not to miss anything. I'd never in my life seen so many buildings clumped together before. Cement block ones too. I was just wondering what they were for when Mister Whitaker said, "Later, we'll come back to this area and take a quick tour through it. I want you to see what the men's living quarters look like on the inside." He pointed towards the right and left. "These are where most of the men live. We do have some commuters, too. Did you know that? That a good deal of the laborers working here come from Franklin County?" Mister Whitaker looked over to Daddy, waiting for his answer.

"Knew that one o' Henry Buchanan's boys was workin'. Heard tell that Cain Smith has him two boys over to here too. Reckon I didn't know they was much more'n that." He paused a moment, scratching at his chin. "Does stand to reason though."

"Absolutely. Especially since those boys are not only making decent pay, they're also learning valuable skills. Once this dam is finished, they'll be able to use the skills they've acquired for good jobs elsewhere. We're hoping that a good number of them will follow us to other dam projects since we can use their expertise for a good number of years. Oh! We just passed the combined recreation/educational building." Mister Whitaker stopped the car in the road and pointed towards the window next to my side. "It's back there a good ways—the blue cement block—see it?"

"Are you meanin' that one what looks so big?" I asked, pulling my head back through the window a minute to look at Mister Whitaker.

"That's the one!" he said, grinning at my excitement. "You can't see it from here, but across from it is the library." I turned round again, trying desperately to see it even though Mister Whitaker'd said I couldn't possibly. I could hear him chuckling at my eagerness. "Don't worry! I promise I'll take you through both buildings later, especially since they'll most likely be very important to Jordan's Bend in the near future. As its new school and library. Let's move on. There's something just up ahead here that I want to show you."

Soon as he'd said *library* I knew a tingling feeling in the pit of my stomach. In my anxiousness I clutched at the back of the seat, pressing my fingers against the coarse mohair. And then—not even knowing why, unless it was since I just knew he was wanting me to—I glanced over to Tommy Lee. He was looking towards those buildings we were leaving behind us too, but once he noticed me staring at him, he turned towards me. After brushing his hair from his forehead, he nodded, slow like, deliberate. And then he smiled. *He understands*! my heart was singing. *Is this the same's what was happenin' yesterday between Mama and Daddy*? I wondered. *This knowin', talkin', understandin' without no words bein' said*?

"Now, the next thing I want you to notice," Mister Whitaker was saying, "is the train track just over to your right there. You all know how the train goes just north of town?" We all nodded at him. "Well, we put down a stretch of tracks here so that a train can pull in a load of supplies and then back on out again once it's been emptied. The trains can haul in all sorts of things—big machines especially—that trucks can't. And that's a big help to us. Later I'll show you another stretch of track for a smaller train, a special one that only delivers cement back and forth. I think you'll be real interested in that one too."

We pulled round a bend then and Mister Whitaker stopped the car once more, pulling off to one side. I heard Mama gasp and Daddy let out a low whistle. The scene before me left me openmouthed. Seemed it was more'n I could take in at once, so I just kept trying to swallow it in slowly so I wouldn't choke or nothing. Mister Whitaker didn't say anything, but just set there and stared with us. For now, there wasn't any words he was needing to be saying, no explaining he could do. We only needed to be looking—and trying to be truly seeing it all. I felt like we'd ridden to someplace I'd never ever been before, instead of the place I'd visited countless times since I was a young'un. Coming round that bend was like entering a new world, one completely unfamiliar—and terrible amazing.

There were huge gashes dug into the earth on both sides of the river. In those holes was the beginnings of buildings, huge buildings. In between were walls the like of which I had never seen before neither. Taller'n the biggest trees I had ever seen, they were, and they stretched clean from one side of the river to the other. Giant machines were everywhere, looking like mighty creatures biting at, picking up, and moving great pieces of rock. And then I saw these huge metal contraptions—two of them—reminding me of the pictures Miz Travis had showed us of the Eiffel Tower. Hanging from the top of them lanky-looking things was what appeared to be ropes, but still I couldn't even begin to imagine what they might be for. Train tracks and a small train (was this the one Mister Whitaker had talked about?) stretched alongside the walls, looking almost like a young'un's toy train next to them giant things standing before us.

And the river—or what used to be the river—had been moved! The land in front of the dam area was completely dug down to stone and was nigh to bare; only those big machines moved back and forth across a great sea of rocks. Way over to the other side, by squinting, I could just barely catch a glimpse of what was once such a beautiful stretch of the mighty Tennessee. The workers had somehow routed it around the construction site. Way over to the other side it meandered back, rejoining its original flowing pathway. *What kind of men are these— what can move mountains and rivers? And then build such things as this?* I asked myself. It was a warm day, but I shivered beneath the frightening sight.

Suddenly, while we were still setting there staring, a mighty rumbling come upon us, shaking the very ground and car we was setting in and everyone in it. It had started low like, coming upon us in a sneaking way; you had to listen right hard for what you were already feeling. There wasn't no time to think what to do except grab ahold of whatever was around you. I latched onto the car handle on one side and Andy's arm on the other, but since they were shaking just the same's I was, that surely didn't make much sense when I thought about it later.

And then—why, then come the loudest boom crashing down on our very heads, it seemed, as I had ever heard. I'm sure I gasped, but no one could've heard me—not even me—because of the sound that was moving down on top of us, around us, even through us in waves of thunderous roars, shaking us like we weren't but babes in a cradle. It—whatever it was—had mostly spent itself, but still it lingered. For then the boom echoed across the hills of Jordan's Bend, answering itself over and over again.

Finally, there was silence. Nobody said a word. Didn't even sound like anyone setting in that car was breathing just then. Until Andy, breaking into the sudden, startling quiet and talking in a hushed, awed whisper, asked, "What *was* that?"

7

Lamb, stop! Don't leave me here alone
For this wild beast to call his own,
To kill, to shatter, flesh and bone.
Against the dark I whine and cower.
I fear the lion. I dread his hour

That was the sound of dynamite," Mister Whtitaker explained, drawing his words out slowly. "I didn't realize they'd be blasting today, but what an experience, huh? One I'm sure you'll never forget!" He glanced back at all of us, breaking into a big grin when he saw the looks of fear and amazement on our faces. "I remember a foreman once telling me that, if you're close enough, that sound can rattle your teeth, it jars you so. I do believe he must be telling the truth! Everybody all right?"

Mister Whitaker waited for us to answer, but it seemed like nobody was ready to be talking just yet. I know I was feeling terrible unsure—and like the ground could be moving and rumbling underneath us again any second.

"But it shook the very ground!" Andy exclaimed, a hushed amazement lighting his words yet. He was still clutching at me and Tommy Lee, but soon's he noticed, he let go, jerking his hands back right quick in embarrassment. He give me a scowl and hid his hands under his legs like his hands were to blame for embarrassing him.

"Sure does!" Mister Whitaker said, nodding his head and grinning from ear to ear with—what was it?—pride? "Our workers are moving the very earth beneath our feet, putting rocks and dirt where they'll serve us better. Shakes up everything and everyone around the area they're blasting, too, doesn't it? Yes sir, it's quite an experience for you, quite an experience. How about if we drive on over to the construction buildings now and then one of the men there can show us around?"

"Is them booms comin' again?" Andy asked. I couldn't tell if he was asking because he was scared—or excited.

"Can't tell. But don't worry about them. I've never had one knock me off my feet." Mister Whitaker leaned over and winked at Daddy, winking so hard he nearly pulled up one whole side of his face. And then he glanced back at Andy. "At least, not yet!"

After Mister Whitaker'd parked the car and we'd all climbed out, he guided us towards one of the bigger buildings amongst them that was grouped together. "This is our main construction office," he explained, holding open the door for us. "The main architectural drawings—the plans—are kept here. Other buildings house engineers and all types of workers and their secretaries. Other buildings house supplies, probably every kind of tool and construction material that you could imagine. We've got just about everything here."

The room we'd stepped into was tolerable small, with only one desk and a woman setting behind it. She had a pencil stuck behind one ear and looked mighty busy. And immediately put out with us for intruding. Stopping all her paper rustling for a moment—even appearing to be froze stiff all of a sudden, holding one piece of paper up in the air—she slowly raised one thin eyebrow at Mister Whitaker. Don't know that I'd ever seen a body freeze up in one position quite like that before. "Mrs. Brown, this is the McKenney family," Mister Whitaker explained, nudging us towards her desk. "This is Mr. and Mrs. McKenney and their children, Rachael and Andrew." I noticed Andy frowning at being called Andrew by a stranger. And especially a Yankee one. "And this is Tommy Joe Arnold."

"Tommy Lee," I corrected, without even thinking that it was Tommy Lee's business to be doing the telling.

"Well, what a pleasure to meet you," Miz Brown said, the syrupy-sweet sounding words not matching atall the look on her face. Then she started in to moving once again, shuffling papers around, only glancing up at us now and then. "Is there something that I can do for you?" Turning around, she put her back to us, reaching into a drawer to pull out even more papers.

"Could you tell Mr. Jones that we're here? He's taking us around the site today."

"Of course. If I could just find that pencil so I could . . ."

"It's settin' right on yer ear," Andy said. Mama give him a stern look then, but he only shrugged his shoulders at her. "I's just tryin' to help."

Miz Brown reached for the pencil, raising once more her drawed-on eyebrows (*how was she doin' that to them? had she marked 'em up with that same pencil what was behind her ear?*) and pinching her thin lips together.

"Well, so it is right here. Funny how I could lose it there, huh?" She got up from her chair and walked quickly to the closed door behind her, knocking softly on the door and saying, "Mr. Jones, Mr. Whitaker's here to see you. And he has some locals here with him."

Miz Brown said *locals* about like Andy was usually pronouncing *Willie Snodderly*, making the saying of it sound like the smell of milk that's set in the springhouse too many days.

We could hear a faint, "Coming!" before the door opened and Mister Jones come out. He was a tall man, and lean. Seemed like he had sharp angles sticking out everywhere—his shoulders, elbows, jawline, even the line of his nose. And he had one of the widest mouths I'd ever seen, looking like it stretched from about one ear clean over to the other. He reached out quickly to shake Mister Whitaker's hand and then grabbed up Daddy's, pumping it up and down in a quick, jerking motion. "So who is this you've brought along today?"

"This is Mr. and Mrs. McKenney, Frank. And this is Rachael, this is Andy, and this is Tommy . . . Tommy Lee, right?" Mister Jones worked his way around the room, pumping everybody's hand. I was waiting for him to grab up Miz Brown's too, but he didn't.

"Tommy Leewright, eh? I knew some Leewrights from Columbus, Ohio. Nice people. Any relation to your family?"

"I ain't . . ." Tommy Lee started in to turning red this time.

"My fault! My fault!" Mister Whitaker interrupted, resting one hand on Tommy Lee's shoulder. "His name is Tommy Lee Arnold. Arnold is the last name, Frank."

"Oh. Don't know anybody by the name of Arnold." He shook his head, frowning, and then turned to Miz Brown. Looking over her messy desk of stacked, dog-eared papers, he said, "Mrs. Brown, we're going out to look over the site. Send John for me if you need me. I won't be gone long though. Got those forms finished yet?" Funny how his sentences sounded as sharp and jointed as his bones looked. And it seemed like one of them lanky joints jerked with every word he spoke too. Made him look like he'd plumb come apart if he was to talk like Miz Hickman does.

"I'm trying, sir. There are interruptions"—she nodded her head ever so slightly in our direction—"you know." She looked over to us. "But I do so hope you all have a wonderful time." Miz Brown smiled at us again then. Or tried to smile. What she did was draw up them thin lips—stiff like, they were—and batted her eyes at us.

Mister Jones picked up the strangest looking hat then, placing it on his head. It appeared to be hard metal, like a tin can, and tolerable heavy for a hat. Rounded and smooth on top, it curved down to a brim that stuck straight out all the way around. "These folks'll need hard hats, Mrs. Brown. Are there more in the supply shed?"

"Yes, sir. Ask Bob for some; he'll get them for you." The "smile" was still pasted on her face. It seemed to be drawn on her about the same as those fancy eyebrows.

Mister Whitaker moved to the door, opening it and announcing, "Well, now, Frank. On with the tour!"

We filed out, following Mister Jones, and I wondered if everybody else was feeling like I was—glad to be leaving Miz Brown behind. Mister Jones' walk was a study too: he set out like he was having fits, and at a furious pace. Me and Mama were struggling to keep up with the long strides he was taking. I noticed Andy on one side of him, running like a hound next to his master, not wanting to miss a word Mister Jones said or anything he pointed out, I suppose. Tommy Lee strode along beside Daddy on Mister Jones' other side. Following behind us was Mister Whitaker.

The first place we stopped was the shed that had them strange tin hats. The man named Bob passed them out to us, instructing us that they were "absolutely necessary for our safety." Andy, Daddy, and Tommy Lee plunked on theirs right off, grinning at each other and thumping them with their fists. But me and Mama just looked at them in our hands. I kept feeling how heavy mine was, wondering how silly I was going to look with it perched on top my head. "You best be takin' yer hat off first, Miz McKenney," Daddy said, "or it might be squashin' it flatter'n a pat a butter on a August day in the sunshine." We put them on finally, but I can't say that I didn't feel right silly in the heavy, awkward-feeling thing. Especially having Tommy Lee see me in such as that.

"Look at that!" Andy suddenly cried out, pointing at my head.

"What? Is somethin' the matter?" I asked, frantically reaching for the top of the hat.

"Nah! It's just that . . . well . . . I always knowed you was a hard head!" Andy teased, breaking into laughter.

I give O.A. the meanest look I could, but still I knew it wasn't doing any good; sure as there's at least one stone hiding in a pot of pinto beans, the red started in to creeping up my embarrassed face again, just like O.A. surely knew it would. And this time, it felt flaming hot.

"Ain't the time to be teasin', Andy," Mama said, giving him yet another disapproving look. Daddy was shaking his head at him too.

"Well, then. Come on this way, folks, where I'll be able to point out the sights to you," Mister Jones said, breaking into the awkward moment, thankfully, and motioning us to follow him then. "We can't get too close to the work. That's too dangerous. But you'll be able to get a wonderful view from where I'm taking you."

The hated red was just beginning to cool down when Tommy Lee edged over to walk by me. "Just thought I'd tell you what I was thinkin'," he said, whispering softly, staring down at the ground as we followed Mister Jones. Being able to see only the side of his face, I looked over the curve of his nose, the gentle dip down to his lips, and the firm, sharp lines of his chin. There were amazing sights all around us, but all I saw was the lines that made up Tommy Lee's profile, framed by the rim of an ugly tin hat. "Um, I were noticin' how even a hat such as this'un couldn't hide how pretty you be. I think you look prettier in a dull tin hat than most gals does in their Sunday best." And then he sidled over by Daddy once again. Leaving me with a silly-looking grin on my face now.

As we come closer to the dam area itself, we passed all sorts of buildings, machinery, and men hustling every which direction wearing tin hats and rubber boots. Everyone sure appeared mighty busy. Least ways, they were too busy to stop and say *hey* to us.

Finally we stopped by another fence with a bright red "DANGER!" sign posted on it too. "As you can see, it's a good drop down over the side of this railing here," Mister Jones said, pointing out over the fence with one hand and holding the other out in front of us in warning, keeping us from walking up too quick like. "But if you come right up here to the edge—careful now!—you'll have an excellent view of what we've been able to accomplish so far."

Edging forward cautiously—except for Andy, since he never did have a lick of sense about climbing trees, cliffs, or nothing—we moved up to and leaned lightly against the sturdy wood railing. The sights around and below us were amazing again. I wondered why Andy wasn't asking a dozen questions already and then realized that he was quiet for probably the same reason that I was: because there were so many questions racing through my mind that I couldn't begin to put them all to words.

"First, I want you to look over here to the right," Mister Jones said, pointing at the building on this side of the dam. "Anybody got a guess what this is going to be?"

"A lighthouse. For showin' the boats which way to be goin'," Andy volunteered.

"Well, that's a pretty good guess, young man," Mister Jones exclaimed, reaching over and patting Andy on the back. "There will indeed be lights here, as a warning to boats at night. But there's a lot more involved too. We're mastering this river, showing her who's boss, you could say! Putting locks at each dam site. Then we can manuever boats and barges up and down the Tennessee as we please. Biggest locks you've ever seen. One right down there!" Mister Jones' smile reached from ear to ear again, and he crossed his arms over his chest. He looked as pleased with himself as O.A. does when he successfully—meaning secretly—hit someone with his flip-jack.

Andy glanced over to Tommy Lee, widening those green eyes in alarm. Sure as anything he was thinking on us being in a prison again. Locked in.

"Anybody know what a lock does?" Mister Jones asked, still appearing right pleased with himself.

"Well, I reckon they's them locks what moves water up an' down," Daddy said, putting his hands in his pockets as he leaned against the fence. "Don't rightly understand 'xactly how they works, but, dependin' on whether them boats is goin' upriver or down, them locks lets in water—raisin' the boat—or lets it out, lowerin' it. That be 'bout right?"

"Why, uh, yes, I . . ." Mister Jones stammered. "How'd you know this?" he demanded of Daddy, but then glanced over towards Mister Whitaker. "Robert, you been feeding answers to my students here?"

"Frank, I leaked not one word," Mister Whitaker said, grinning and shaking his head. "You'll soon find—like I did—that Mr. McKenney does a good deal of reading. On a wide range of subjects too." I smiled up at Daddy, knowing deep pride for him once again. But he didn't notice, seeing how he was taken with all the sites below us and staring still at the fascinating lock.

"Well, if I have any questions I can't answer, I'll just defer them to you, Mr. McKenney." Daddy turned his head slowly, looking Mister Jones eye to eye. "That be all right with you?" Mister Jones' smile was still there, and his voice sounded pleasant enough. But there was something about the way he leaned into his question—too eager like. Too anxious. He reminded me of Nehemiah standing over a ground mole's hole, every muscle tensed, waiting for that mole to make the mistake of poking out its head. Once that head popped up, Nehemiah'd pounce on him. Didn't often miss neither.

Daddy merely nodded back at him, but I saw for just one moment the slightest narrowing of his eyes. He always did that when he was sizing up a man. *Wish I knew what Daddy was thinkin'*, I mused, trying to read Daddy's thoughts. But there was one thing I reckoned I did know for certain. If Mister Jones was being like Nehemiah, thinking that he was about to snatch up Daddy, he best think on it again. *My daddy ain't no simple critter, pokin' out his head to be no easy prey*, I thought to myself. *Truth tell, Yankee, you best be careful who be the hunter. And who be the hunted.*

Mister Jones glanced around to the rest of us, pointing down to the lock once again. "See that area right there? That's where the gates will be. You see, the lock lets water in or out by gates opening and closing. Gates operated by hydraulic machinery. Once the lock is operational, we'll be able to raise or lower the water by some fifty-six feet." Daddy shook his head, and Tommy Lee let out a whistle. "After we put in the coffer dams—see those big open steel silos standing all around the site, enclosing it in?—then the next step is to mostly complete these locks. Questions?"

"I reckon I can pick out them coffer dams, but what ere they doin'?" Daddy asked.

"They provide protection, Mr. McKenney. When we first put them down, they're empty. And then we start filling those steel silos with mud and silt from the riverbed." Mister Jones waved bony arms and hands around while he talked, jerking them this way and that to try and show us what he was talking about. "Then we pump out all the water, sealing up any and all leaks. Once we're on firm, dry bedrock, then we're ready to really begin construction. And that's just where our dam must begin, on bedrock, or it won't be much of a secure, sound dam, now will it?"

"Will you be leavin' them coffer dams a-settin' there then?" Tommy Lee asked.

"Just until we finish stage one of our construction, and then we'll move them. First we need to get the locks built, like I said. Then the forms for the base must be put up and the pouring of cement begun. That's what we're doing right now. See the metal forms stretching from one side of the river to the other?"

Tommy Lee nodded his head. I was marveling at how those things towered over us when Mister Jones said, "The forms are quite tall, over a hundred and thirty feet. But I suppose these are like comparing scrub pines to the mighty sequoias when I think about some of the other dams I've worked on. One had forms high enough for a dam rising over three hundred feet!"

Andy looked up at him in amazement. "I can't imagine nothin' that tall."

"Son," Mister Jones said to him, "I can't hardly imagine a dam that big either. Sometimes I just go stare at the blamed thing. Even then I can hardly believe it, standing there gawking at it. Now, see those tall metal constructions?" Mister Jones continued, turning once again towards the work area.

"You mean the ones that look like Eiffel Towers?" I asked, pointing in their direction.

"Exactly! Only they're not quite as pretty, are they? I must say, though, that they're mighty pretty to us since they work so well. They're called stiff-leg derricks."

I repeated the strange name, testing how the words sounded and wanting to be sure and remember them for telling Granny Mandy later.

"What do they do?" I asked, squinting my eyes at them as I attempted to look them over right good.

"Eventually they'll pick up the spillway gates—completely assembled, and therefore mighty big and heavy—when it's the proper time. Yes, sir, those derricks will lift those gates high over the dam and lower them just where we want them."

"Noted them pulleys an' ropes on 'em," Daddy said. "Recollected they was for liftin' things, but didn't figure nothin' quite as big as you's sayin'. Them spillway gates—that what you called 'em?" Daddy said it slowly, questioning Mister Jones, who then nodded. "Is it them what lets the water over the dam?"

"Right again, Mr. McKenney. Depending upon the conditions upstream and down, the amount of rain farther north and south of here—or lack of it—well, all that will determine just how much water we let over the spillway. Those gates allow us to regulate and control what used to be a dreaded yearly occurrence for you folk. Floods. But no more! No, sir, no more!"

Suddenly I was back on that rise with Mama and Granny Mandy, looking out over our valley. Seeing it covered with water. Flooded. *No more floods?* my heart cried, aching to shout it at this Mister Jones. *When you's drownin' McKenney soil forever?*

"Is that the little train you told us about, Mister Whitaker?" Andy asked, pointing to a train that set just under one of those derricks and jerking my thoughts back to the sights below us.

Mister Whitaker leaned over to look where Andy was pointing. "Sure is, Andy. It's delivering cement right now, isn't it, Frank?"

Mister Jones nodded, but before he could say anything more, Andy started in to spitting out questions faster'n a room full of chewing farmers all aiming for the spittoon. "What's in cement? How you be makin' it? Where'd it come from an' . . ."

"Whoa there, boy! One question at a time here," Mister Jones said, grinning at him and resting one hand on the top of Andy's hat. "See that piece of machinery over there, way over to the left? The one with those funny-looking moving belts on it?" We all looked the way he was pointing, searching for a machine with—belts? *Why on earth would a machine be needin' those things?*

"I see it!" Andy hollered. "It's got rocks on them belts. And they's movin'!" I followed the line of Andy's extended arm, finally finding the funny-looking machine Andy was so excited about.

"That's right," Mister Jones said. "Has everybody spotted it? It's called a rock crusher, and those belts are actually called conveyor belts;

they carry the rocks to where they'll be graded and crushed finer down inside the rock crusher. Some even gets so ground up that it comes out sand. Then, Andy, it's all poured into the cement mixer. That's just down here, next to the train tracks." He pointed below us once again. "The cement mixture is essentially made up of those crushed rocks, sand, and water. The mixer keeps it stirred up." He moved his hands round and round in circles. "Keeps tumbling it around so it doesn't harden until we're ready to pour it."

"And then that train delivers the cement to where it's needin' to be poured?" Tommy Lee asked.

"You've got it! This whole project," Mister Jones waved his arm out over the scene before us, "is immensely complicated. And yet at the same time, it's amazingly quite simple. Basics. That's what we do. And, we're using a good amount of the materials that were right here to begin with to construct this dam. We're just moving them around. Rearranging them a good bit."

"You was talkin' on stage one bein' the completin' o' the locks an' them forms. What's the next stage?" Daddy asked.

Daddy stared out over the site, deep interest and sadness showing in the way he squinted his eyes just a bit, causing a creasing of his brows. *Is he feeling that cravin'—and hatin'—at the same time again?* I wondered.

"Stage two includes building and pouring the spillway itself, except for the area nearest the powerhouse. Then we put in the concrete piers, which hold the spillway gates. And we also erect the bridge and install gantry cranes, weighing in at eighty tons each. Tiny things, aren't they?!" He chuckled at his own joking. "Those cranes can pick up the spillway gates which the derricks lifted in, putting each gate in its right spot. Stage three is simply—although I shouldn't say simply, that's quite the misnomer—stage three is finishing up the powerhouse."

Seemed like Mister Jones was carrying on in another language now; I wasn't understanding half of all the names he was using for this an' such.

"Then you already be workin' at this stage two?" Daddy asked him.

"Not quite. We've installed the derricks to help us lift all sorts of heavy equipment. They're quite handy. And movable. See how they're mounted on wheels on those tracks?" Mister Jones pointed towards the base of them things. They were on wheels, all right, but they sure didn't look as if moving them would be so easy like. "No, we're not to stage two yet. We've got more forms to pour and the locks aren't done yet either. But we're coming along. We're coming along." Mister Jones slapped one hand against the fence. "Yes, sir! Right on schedule too!"

"I heared you's workin' right through the night," Andy said. "Is that true?"

Mister Jones pointed out over the site again, only this time he was pointing up much higher. "See those huge lights on top the tall poles? Those come on at night, boy, and then the late shift goes to work. In all, we've got three shifts that give us work time around the clock. Like I said, we've got a schedule to keep to. A tight schedule! Before you know it, we'll raise those gates, letting the river flow through them. Yes, sir, water will be spilling over that dam beginning December first, or my name isn't Frank Jones!"

I'd been holding onto the railing of the fence, but when Mister Jones said *December first*, I tightened my fingers around it something fierce. *That ain't much time*, my thoughts were screaming. *That ain't enough time!*

Seemed like everybody was quiet for a moment from the shock of hearing the day that would change all of our lives. Forever. I noticed Mama clutching at her hat and pocketbook, twisting the handle nervously between her fingers. Andy was staring at the ground, scowling again. Daddy just stood looking out over the scene before us, but I saw a muscle twitching in his firm jaw. And then Tommy Lee took off his tin hat, pushing back a clump of hair that was sticking out from beneath the brim before plopping it back on his head again. His voice cut into the uneasy silence. "What 'bout this here 'lectricity you's goin' to make? Where's it goin' to come from?" he asked.

"The electricity is stored in the generators, but it initially comes from the river itself. The harnessed power of that moving water." Mister Jones looked over to Tommy Lee, and he started using his hands again as he tried to explain the confusing machinery. "See, the water flows in the intake gates—each weighing sixty tons, by the way—and these intake gates control the flow of the water by more gantry cranes. The gates open, letting water through, and when that water comes rushing in, it gets to swirling around, creating such force"—Mister Jones looped his hands around, making circles in the air—"and then, *smack!*" He clapped his hands together then, causing me and Mama to jump. "That water hits up against the five giant propeller blades of the turbine, turning it around to the tune of seventy-five revolutions per minute. And then the turbine rises over two stories above to spin the arms of the generator, which in turn stores the electricity that will eventually illuminate light bulbs, heat stoves, and cool refrigerators all over this county!"

"Sounds right powerful." Daddy rubbed his fingers against his chin. "Terrible powerful."

"Yes, sir, it is. Why, when you're standing way up above in the visitor's room of the powerhouse—separated from that machinery by thousands of tons of steel and nearly half a million cubic yards of concrete—you can still feel the moving vibrations of that turbine under your feet. I once heard someone say that it felt like we'd captured and chained an earthquake down in the bedrock of that dam." Mister Jones looked out over the construction area again. "Yes, sir, capturing and chaining an earthquake—an earthquake named the Tennessee River—that's what we're about!"

We stood there asking questions for some time, wondering at the machines and the men that were working them. Seeing all those things moving every which way, I could see why them hats were so necessary. Although if one of them cables or cement walls or big machines was to fall on a worker, I surely wasn't thinking that little old tin hat would do him much help. Mister Jones did talk about safety, though, pointing out that they had training classes for learning the men, safety committees, and signs posted everywhere giving instructions. They even had some that said, "Caution! Don't Hurry!" Daddy chuckled then, saying that he hadn't met a Southerner yet that didn't know hurrying was just a waste of time anyway.

The buildings for living were interesting to see too. They had comfortable chairs, tables for games, even pictures on the walls (of sights from round the countryside) and curtains at the windows. The cabins were made of sturdy cement block, and were much nicer'n about every home in this whole county.

After that Mister Jones took us to a place they called the cafeteria; a sign there said that you could have "all you care to eat" for thirty-five cents. Regular boarders paid thirty cents. There was Yankee and southern cooking laying out in big pans before us: fruits, salads, vegetables, beans, stew, soup, hot biscuits like Mama's, or Yankee cracked-wheat bread. Andy's eyes were about as round as the plates they put it on once he saw all that food. And although Mama shook her head at him when he started in to asking for a helping of about everything they had, he still ate several platefuls—since Mister Whitaker told him it was fine and that it "certainly is all you care to eat!" Daddy added that he could've cared to eat less though.

The last place we visited was the recreation and education building. From the moment I first reached out to lightly touch its lovely blue paint, it seemed to hold a magical quality, an excitement that lived in those walls; it jumped back into my fingers, sending the excitement running up through my hands and arms, ending in a shiver that scampered across my shoulders.

The first room Mister Jones took us into was amazingly big. He explained that this was called the auditorium; it was where they showed the educational movies, putting the screen for them up on the small stage that was built at one end. I could most imagine James Junior setting there, watching those educational movies he'd told us about. If they weren't showing them films, then the room became a gymnasium for playing games—table games or volleyball, ping-pong (*What on earth is that*? I wondered), basketball, whatever they were wanting to use it for.

There were men setting here and there, drinking bottles of "Co-Cola," playing card games, and jawing. Mister Jones said *hello* to them, shaking their hands (pumping at them again like he'd done ours, looking like he was about to jerk their arms off), and asking them how the work was coming. They seemed friendly enough, but I was most anxious to be moving on to see the library. So I didn't have much use for jawing about building that there lock just then.

Mister Whitaker was the one that finally moved us on, saying something like, "Well, we'd best allow you boys to get back to your game. We wouldn't want to keep you from your leisure activities after a hard eight hours of work."

I could hear Daddy chuckling under his breath as we headed towards what I'd been anxiously waiting the whole day to see. The library.

"Something strike you funny, Mr. McKenney?" Mister Jones asked.

"Well, sir, I was just thinkin' on yer talkin' 'bout workin' for eight hours. I reckon any farmer round these parts be hankerin' somethin' terrible to be workin' that long. Eight hours!" Daddy shook his head, smiling at the thought.

Mister Jones looked right put out. "I see. So what time do you go to work then, Mr. McKenney?"

"Mister Jones, we'uns what's workin' this Tennessee soil ain't be goin' to work. When we get up of a mornin', we's surrounded by it!"

Everybody laughed then—just as Mister Whitaker opened the door to the library. And just as quick as we'd started in to carrying on, we hushed up because of the look that the lady setting behind the desk greeted us with. I reckon she could've silenced even Miz Travis with one glance of that glare.

Mister Jones cleared his throat and then started in to introducing us to her. "Excuse me, miss," he said, addressing the lady in that loud, bursting-with-short-fits-of-words way he talked.

She immediately put one finger to her lips, saying in a soft yet aggravated voice—like she was right put out with us already—"Sir, please. We do operate just like a normal library." She pointed to a sign above her head that said "QUIET PLEASE!" in bold lettering and then to some men setting at desks, holding books. I supposed they'd been reading, but now they were staring at us, taking in the commotion, I assumed. "We do have those who are trying to concentrate as they read. So let's keep our introductions—and interruptions—at a whisper, shall we?" She was a solid-looking gal. Not fat. Not plump atall either, really. Just solid, firm. Even her arms appeared muscular and filled out, her hands strong and capable. I got the feeling right off that she never had no problems keeping her library quiet. Or however she was wanting it to be.

"Oh yes, sorry," Mister Jones said, looking embarrassed. I guessed he must've not been the kind to visit here much, not even knowing the rules. "This is the McKenney family from Jordan's Bend. Mr. and Mrs. McKenney here, and this is Rachael. Over here is her brother Andy. The young man is Tommy Arnold." I smiled at Tommy Lee when he said his name like that—saying Tommy instead of Tommy Lee. Couldn't none of these Yankees get anything right? "And you are . . . ?"

"I'm Miss Stricker, head librarian."

"Head librarian?" Mister Whitaker said. "You mean this small of a library has more workers?" He turned around, taking in the whole of the middling-sized room.

"No, I'm the only one." Miss Stricker cleared her throat. "As such, I'm the head librarian."

"Oh. Of course," Mister Jones said, a slight smirk forming around the edges of his smile. "Now, the McKenney family is interested in . . ." The lady raised a finger to her lips once more, slowly shaking her head at him. Mister Jones' voice had got right loud again. "Sorry!" he whispered, chuckling. "Guess I'm too used to shouting orders at all my men at work. Don't visit libraries much either." I'd surely been right about that. "Anyway, these folks would just like to look around a little bit. Is that all right with you? I mean, if we're all absolutely quiet, of course." He smiled at her, leaning over and resting one arm against her desk.

"Yes, that would be just fine. Please remember, though, that if you remove any of the books, they must be put back in the exact same spot from which they came." She glanced over to Mister Whitaker, ignoring Mister Jones. "We use the Dewey Decimal system here. You understand." Then she looked around the room at us McKenneys and

Tommy Lee again. "So if you can't remember exactly where a book came from, bring it back to me immediately. I'll know where it belongs." Miss Stricker pointed to her left, saying, "The books over there are fiction. If you want to browse through nonfiction, you'll need to go this way. Please ask if you have any questions, and remember . . ." And then she put a finger to her lips again.

I headed right off towards the fiction, walking the aisles and pleasuring in the sight of those beautiful bindings. Even the smell of the books was wonderful, so I stopped a moment, closing my eyes and taking in a deep breath. When I opened them, I looked up to see what books were setting right in front of me. Dickens, Charles, I saw right off, and then excitedly I read the titles of some of my most favorites—*Great Expectations, Hard Times,* and *A Tale of Two Cities.* This was amazing, having all them books setting here before me in one place, just waiting to be read, absorbed, loved! *Could all this belong to Jordan's Bend one day?* I asked myself, excitement welling up inside, threatening to pour out in loud laughter that would surely bring a "Shhh!" and a frown from Miss Stricker.

But as soon as the wonderful thought come to me, a terrible worry came sneaking along with it. *What if this here library does belong to Jordan's Bend some day? And what if we have to be movin' far away to find another farm, far enough away that Jordan's Bend is too far to come for fetchin' books? What good will it be doin' me then?* I tentatively reached out to touch them, caressing the smooth covers, finally finding the courage to be lifting one of them to enjoy the feel of the cover, the pages, the way the pages lightly fanned my face when I let them shift through my fingers. And then I carefully put the precious book back.

"Rachael?"

I looked up in surprise. Seemed I'd forgot there was anything else in the whole world right now besides me and these books.

It was Tommy Lee. "Hey, Rachael. Didn't mean to be sneakin' up like that, but Miz Stricker warned us to be so quiet like." He touched my arm and then quickly withdrew his hand, glancing around to make sure nobody saw him. "Somethin' botherin' at you? Are you all right?" Just as earlier his eyes had mirrored his daddy's confusion and pain, now Tommy Lee's eyes reflected mine.

I glanced at the books again, feeling for them like I did for a good friend. "I s'pose. I were just thinkin' on how wonderful it would be if these were all belongin' to Jordan's Bend someday." I paused a minute because of the sudden lump that come to my throat. "And how awful it would be if we was to move too far away for me to be able to read them. That's all."

Tommy Lee shoved his hands into his pockets. He stared down at the floor. "I know what yer sayin'. Worryin' over what's comin' seems to be doggin' me, no matter what I'm doin' or where I am. Rachael, I . . ." he began, and then nervously peered over at me. He looked away suddenly and sniffed, taking a quick swipe at his nose with the cuff of his shirt. "Recollect I need me some time to think. See things as they is. Do you reckon yer Granny'd be willin' to speak with me? I ain't meanin' to bother her none, but . . ." He reached out to touch the shelf nearest us, rubbing the polished wood between his work-worn fingers.

A sudden sick feeling jabbed at my stomach. Me and Tommy Lee'd talked about most everything these past few weeks, but I hadn't told him about Granny Mandy's spells. *What if she'd be havin' one when he were talkin' with her? What would Tommy Lee do? What would I do?*

"Can't be puttin' no more worries on my daddy. An' of course, Mama, well . . ." He stared hard at the books on the shelf, but I knew he wasn't really seeing them. Nor was he seeing the fear in me just then, so caught up in his own pain like he was. His eyes suddenly shifted over to me, seeking a answer. "Rachael?"

I avoided his gaze, hurriedly reaching out to pick up another book. Any book. I shrugged my shoulders. "You know Granny Mandy. She always be favored to be havin' anyone to come by." I leafed slowly through the book's pages. Didn't recognize the title or the author's name atall, but I concentrated on appearing terrible interested in it.

"You reckon Mister Whitaker'd mind lettin' me ride in his car all the way to yer Granny's?" I could feel his eyes staring towards me still, searching for reassurance, approval. I didn't give him any.

"Reckon not."

"Well. I'll be askin' him then." Tommy Lee was silent for a minute. I leafed slowly through the book, wanting the noise of them pages to put something into the awkward silence between us. He craned his head around, trying to see the title, I supposed. "That particular book be one you's right cravin' to be readin'?"

I abruptly put it back on the shelf, roughly shoving it into the place where it belonged—despite Miss Stricker's warning. "S'pose 'bout ever book's one I be wantin' to read."

"Oh." Out of the corner of my eye I saw him brush the hair off his forehead and then push his hands down into the pockets of his pants again. "Reckon I'll be goin' on outside now. You comin'?"

"In a minute." I could still feel him staring at me. Questioning. I walked slowly away from him down the aisle, lightly brushing the tips of my fingers across the edges of the books. "Just want to look at bit more. Tell Daddy I'll be comin' in a minute."

"Sure." Tommy Lee turned then, walking away from me. I listened to the sound of his hard-soled shoes hitting against the cement floor. Once the footfalls stopped, like he was hesitating. But he continued on until I heard him open the door, closing it softly behind him. Then there was silence once again.

Slowly I let out a long, quivering breath of air. My shoulders slumped, and I leaned against the bookshelves for support. I hadn't even known I'd been so tense, holding my breath like that and all. The sick, nauseous feeling was still there, so I took a couple more deep breaths, hoping that would ease it some. It didn't. I shook my head, berating myself, knowing nothing would. Because I knew thinking on Granny Mandy's spells made me remember the foxfire. And the casket, tucked away in Granny's tumbledown barn. And the dark.

Absentmindedly I reached out to touch them books one last time. Seemed like they had a force that was drawing me to them, pulling me into the exciting stories that I knew were inside those covers, waiting to be revealed in the words. I sighed, pulling my hands away reluctantly. And then, staring straight ahead and not once looking back, I walked past the shelves, past Miss Stricker, and out the door.

Once again we piled into Mister Whitaker's car. Andy asked if he could roll down his window, and after receiving a nod from Mister Whitaker and Daddy, him and Tommy Lee both cranked on the handles. The breeze that come in felt cooling on my face, so I closed my eyes, letting it gently touch my eyelids and caress the wisps of hair about my forehead and cheeks.

When we come to the locked gate and the man named Tom greeted us like before, I opened my eyes to watch him. But soon's we started up—and I could feel the breeze blowing in my face—I closed my eyes again. I suppose I was trying to shut out all the things behind me, pretending they weren't there atall and that the river was all it used to be.

But then my mind's eye started in to seeing things. I saw the cold, vast bareness of the area just in front of the dam, a place that use to be home to a lazy, meandering river. And I seen them ugly machines everywhere, taking gouges out of hills that use to have poplar trees, scrub pines, and blackberry bushes galore thriving on them. I smelled the terrible stench of hot oil, burning rubber, and overheating metal against metal where once the smell of honeysuckle hung in the air. And I heard grinding sounds that made me flinch, high-pitched screeching that caused us to put fingers to our ears, and men shouting, men swearing. Used to be, setting along the Tennessee's bank just there, a body'd hear only the gentle lapping of the river against the shore, the ever-changing melody of the mockingbird and the irritating caws of the crows, and now and then, the *plop* of a fish jumping, leaving lapping circles behind them as the only telltale sign of where'd they'd just been.

Those sights, smells, and sounds pressed at me until I finally opened my eyes, searching for the familiar along the roadside. A sturdy-trunked oak with several small, scraggly looking scrub pines sprouting around it was just off to the side a ways. I stared at that old oak until it was plumb out of sight, and then I expectantly watched for Clear Springs Creek, finding surprising delight in seeing her familiar path over moss-covered rocks and logs scattered here an' yonder. *How many times had I passed this way, never really takin' no care to the things that were breathin', growin', livin' all around me?* So suddenly, the familiar had become terrible dear to me.

Mister Whitaker pulled up the pathway to our cabin and then stopped the car. "It's been a pleasure to escort you folks today," he said, turning towards Daddy and extending his hand. Daddy took his hand in his (about making Mister Whitaker's disappear in Daddy's wide palms and long fingers), giving him a good, sturdy shake and nodding his head. "I hope you had as much fun as I did; I guess I always enjoy showing off our handiwork!"

"Was right kind of you to be totin' us round," Daddy answered. He opened his door to climb out and then helped Mama. I took one last look around the fascinating car and then Tommy Lee and me climbed out the back.

"We's most appreciatin' the ride an' the tourin' of the sight an' the dinner too." Mama straightened her hat and smoothed her skirt before continuing, "You needs be comin' for dinner soon. Let us return the favor."

Daddy leaned over to peer at Mister Whitaker. "Yes, sir. We'd like to be extendin' some McKenney hospitality to you."

"Well, um . . ." Mister Whitaker avoided Daddy's gaze, nervously wiping at a smudge on that mirror that hung down in front of him. "We need to start looking for another farm soon, finding one suitable for you." He glanced Daddy's way, saying, "How about if you stop by my office tomorrow and we'll pick out an afternoon that's good for both of us?"

Daddy took a deep breath, and I noticed his shoulders slump just the slightest bit. He nodded. "Reckon that'd be fine." Seemed like the weariness in the words was touchable. Leaning over even more so's he could see into the backseat, Daddy give Andy a questioning look. He was still setting in the back of Mister Whitaker's car. I suppose he was wanting to stay there long as he could, seeing how fascinated he was with that there car. Still, it wasn't like Andy to be setting still nowheres for that long. "Andrew, reckon you be ready to be climbin' out o' there yet? I recollect Mister Whitaker's got better things to be doin' than set round waitin' on the likes o' us all the day long."

Mister Whitaker chuckled and then reached out to offer Andy his hand. "I admire a man who enjoys the finer things in life, like cars and . . . well, all kinds of modern conveniences! Andrew here will certainly appreciate the benefits of electricity that that dam will bring, won't you now, son?"

Andy stared at his extended hand a moment and then narrowed his eyes. Fairly glaring at Mister Whitaker, he was. "Sir, I thank ye for the ride an' the eats," he spit out. "But I ain't never appreciatin' what you be doin' to our valley. An' you can't be buyin' my favorin' with no rides in this here fancy car, nor no Yankee meals, nor no promises—empty promises they is—neither!"

"Andrew!" Both Daddy and Mama stood looking at Andy with amazement on their faces. Mama's mouth dropped open and I saw Daddy's eyes blinking furious like, but other than that, they just stood there, not moving atall, like they were froze stiff or something.

Andy suddenly jerked open the car door and scrambled out. Leaving the door gaping open and without so much as a backwards glance towards anybody, he took off running, cutting round Mama's truck patch and tearing off towards the woods above the upper pasture, I assumed. I stared after him, noting his red hair flying out behind him and his arms pumping fiercely as he run, dodging round the farming tools and outbuildings scattered here and there. Ezra and Nehemiah come barking after him, excitedly tagging at Andy's heels, and then the three of them disappeared around the cabin and from our sight.

Daddy walked to the other side of the car and firmly shut the door Andy'd left open. He leaned over a bit to see Mister Whitaker eye to eye. "Reckon we be owin' you a apology, Mister Whitaker."

"Oh, that's not necessary, Mr. McKenney. I understand that . . ."

"No, sir," Daddy interrupted. "We'uns ain't toleratin' such behavior. Ain't right." Daddy shifted his weight back and forth and he run a hand through his hair. Clearly this wasn't kindly easy for him to be saying. "Me and my missus be apologizin'. Andrew will be sayin' his too, come tomorra. Reckon tomorra'll be fine for pickin' us a afternoon to be talkin' an' havin' you to supper." Daddy paused a moment, standing up straight and staring towards the upper pasture. I saw the muscle in his jaw working back and forth. "Changes don't be comin' easy for us what lives in these parts, Mister Whitaker. Some folks fights it—like Andrew. Others be strugglin', but though they be pullin' an' tuggin' just like they was in a scufflin' match, they's knowin' an' acceptin' that what's surely to come." Daddy sighed and then continued, "An' then they's the ones what can't . . . they just can't . . ." He stopped, letting his voice drop off to nigh but a whisper.

"We best be gettin' up to the house," Mama said, walking over to stand by Daddy. "We do thank ye for the fine tour, Mister Whitaker." She glanced over to me, expectantly.

"Thank you very much, sir," I said right off, knowing exactly what Mama was expecting. "I 'specially liked seein' the library and all them books."

"An' I thank you too," Tommy Lee put in quickly, walking over to shake Mister Whitaker's hand. "Ain't never seen nothin' like it! All them machines an' what they's buildin' with 'em. Plumb amazed me, it did."

"Glad you all could enjoy the day." Mister Whitaker tipped his hat and started backing out onto the road, but then he stopped a minute, saying, "Don't be too hard on your son. Sooner or later they all come around. People adjust. They have to!" He smiled at us then, a slow, easy smile that dismissed us and all that Daddy'd been saying as careless like as folks that were setting and rocking on a breezeway on a hot and humid summer's evening.

We all watched the car drive off a minute until Daddy and Mama turned and started on up the hill. "Rachael, you best be goin' to Granny Mandy's now," Mama called over her shoulder. "Got chores to be doin' before long."

"Yes, Mama." I started across the road then, with Tommy Lee following. "Don't see Granny Mandy about nowheres. I reckon she could be—"

"Wished I'd said it," Tommy Lee interrupted. "Andy were sayin' truth, he was."

I stopped, looking at Tommy Lee with concern, seeing deep disappointment in himself written about his eyes now. "Tommy Lee, Andy was right hateful. He shouldn't a been sayin' them things."

"Rachael, Andy was *right*! Weren't you hearin' what Mister Whitaker just said?"

"What's that high an' mighty Yankee done gone an' said now?" Granny Mandy, hands on hips, peered at us from around the back of her cabin. "Good Lord done sent you two to be a-hepin' me. Now come on back here an' then ye can be tellin' me what else them government rascals is up to." She motioned for us to follow her and then turned and moved out of our sight again.

I shook my head at Tommy Lee. "Now we's in for it. Ain't no sense in gettin' Granny Mandy riled." My stomach tightened with worry again at the thought of what might happen if Granny should have one of her spells with Tommy Lee being here.

"Is ye comin' or ain't ye?" Granny Mandy hollered.

I give Tommy Lee a pleading look, saying, *Tread careful*! with my eyes and then hollered back, "We's comin'!" When me and Tommy Lee come around the corner I saw that Granny Mandy was busy getting ready to do her wash. Tommy Lee started in to helping with stacking the wood underneath the big, black iron pot while I went to fetch more wood from Granny's porch. "Reckon this be 'nough, Granny Mandy?" I showed her the pile of wood I'd collected near the pot.

"'Spect so. Ain't fixin' to do tolerable much."

"Ain't you usually doin' wash first thing of a mornin', Granny?" I looked up at the sky, squinting and shading my eyes from the sun's glare with my hand. From its distance above the trees near Lookin' Point, I was guessing it was about two o'clock. "Think they's 'nough sun left to be dryin' everthin'?"

"I can take inside whatever ain't dried. 'Sides, Rachael, you must be tetched in the head. Ere you forgettin' what day this be?"

I glanced over at Tommy Lee, saw him shrug his shoulders, and then looked back at Granny Mandy. "Can't rightly recollect anythin' special . . ."

"It's the tenth of May, child! Vine Day! Why, I been puttin' in my cucumbers, melons, squash, and punkins all mornin'. Don't tell me yer mama's done forgot?" Granny Mandy stared at me in amazement and then shook her head. Picking up a bucket of water and pouring it into the pot, she said, "Go 'head an' light the fire, Tommy Lee. She'll come 'long kindly good iffin you blow on her just a mite."

"Reckon Mama did forget. We been gone most the day and—"

"I know where you'uns been. Been off seein' what them Yankees is doin' to God's valley."

"It were somethin' to see, Granny."

Either she didn't hear me—which I doubted—or she ignored me completely. "Tommy Lee, you fetch more water for boilin' in this here pot," Granny Mandy ordered, "an' Rachael, ye can help me start in to liftin' these here clothes out onto the battlin' bench. Once Tommy Lee be done fetchin', I want to hear what them no good Yankees is sayin' now."

Grandaddy had made Granny Mandy's battling bench years ago, most likely when they were newlyweds. The bench was made out of a hollowed out log and was good and smooth now from so many years of washing. At one end Grandaddy'd built a ledge for holding a tub. Granny'd soak the dirty clothes there in cold water and then lift the sopping wet clothes, one at a time, up onto the battling bench. Then Granny'd work the clothes back and forth, turning them every which way with a short, sturdy paddle that Grandaddy'd carved for her. I'd watched Granny Mandy many a time, working her clothes to get them good and clean, turning them over and over with her battling stick.

Once she was satisfied that most all the dirt was out of the clothes, Granny Mandy'd put them into the pot of boiling water which she'd already added soap to. Then she'd stand over the pot a good while, stirring those clothes with the paddle to make sure the soapy water'd worked its way through every bit of the material. When Grandaddy'd made the battling stick, he'd even whittled the end of it to be just like the shape of the bottom of her black pot so the stirring would be easy and smooth like for her. 'Course, it was wore down a good bit, seeing how it had been used for so many years now.

Lastly come the rinsing—which Granny pronounced *renchin'*— and hanging out to dry. We'd carry the steaming clothes by the paddle, dunking them in the fresh water that we'd fetched for the tub at the end of the battling bench. After rinsing them good there, we'd cart them over to a second tub under the water spout and work any lingering suds out. Then we'd hang the clothes on the fence to dry, turning them inside out since they'd dry better that way, according to Granny Mandy.

Tommy Lee toted buckets of water from the spigot to the black pot, filling it to the right level (you could tell just how full to make it from a line that had come to be marked round the inside of that pot) and adding more wood to the fire until the water come to boiling. Once Granny Mandy'd put the battled clothes into the soapy water and started in to stirring with her paddle, she asked, "Well? So just what was this Yankee spoutin' now?"

Tommy Lee was squatting on the ground by the pot, whittling on a piece of wood with his knife. I guess he was wanting something to be working at with his fingers, keeping them busy. Glancing down at my empty hands, I wished I had me something to be doing with mine. "Best back up a bit, tellin' you what come before," Tommy Lee offered. "First off, Andy lit into that old Mister Whitaker."

Granny's eyebrows shot up and them eyes twinkled. "Andy done what?"

"He lit into him. Good too! Told Mister Whitaker he couldn't be buyin' his favorin' by takin' him on no fancy rides or givin' him a free Yankee meal. Or makin' promises like they does. Promises 'bout all manner of things." Tommy Lee glanced over my way and then quickly looked back down at his stick.

"Reckon a Yankee be keepin' his promises 'bout as fast as soppin' wet gunpowder be shootin' yer gun," Granny Mandy murmured under her breath.

"What promises is you thinkin' they ain't intendin' to keep?" I asked him. He avoided my eyes.

"Hard tellin'." Tommy Lee shrugged his shoulders. "Ain't likely they'd just be givin' us them buildin's they's put up for schoolin' an' such."

"The library? And all them books?" I asked.

Still Tommy Lee wouldn't look up at me. "Yankees is known for talkin'."

"An' emptyin' yer henhouse when yer back's turned!" Granny Mandy shot at us, eyes flashing now. "So Andy lit into him, did he?" She made a "hmph" sound, nodding her head in approval. "Reckon he's in fer 'nother trip to the shed. Iffin I'd been there, most likely I'd be due fer a trip there myself!" I grinned at the thought, watching Granny Mandy work hard at her clothes while she stirred them round and round with the battling stick. "Ye still ain't tole me what the Yankee done said."

Tommy Lee looked up at Granny Mandy now, and there was deep pain filling his eyes. I felt a stab run across my chest, seeing him hurting so. "Miz McKenney, he said to pay no mind to Andy or nobody else what was . . . what was havin' a tolerable hard time acceptin' all what them government folks is doin' round here. An' then he was sayin' we's all needin' to be 'comin' round,' as he put it. 'Adjustin'' he says, so careless like." He flung his arms up, waving the stick and knife around in the air. "So easy, he were sayin' it. As if a body could just be hearin' they was goin' to steal yer land from you—castin' you off like they is—an' we would be actin' like some windup toy, noddin' its head up an' down, up an' down, sayin' 'Yes, sir! Yes, sir! I'll come 'round, all right! Everthin's fine!'" Tommy Lee stopped then, but he continued staring up at Granny Mandy, eyes pleading with her, searching Granny Mandy's face for understanding.

"I recollect a gal what lived over to Summit County. Must o' been, oh, forty-odd year or so ago now." Granny Mandy stirred the clothes slower, pulling with her stick as she worked the last of the dirt out of them. She squinted her eyes up in her remembering, like she was searching for the memory. "Lost five young'uns to the cholera, I b'lieve 'twas. Took all she had, it did. An' after them young'uns was buried, well, she set down before her fireplace. An' there she stayed."

"You mean she done like . . . ?"

"She jest set, that's what she done. Poor husband o' hers tried everthin'. Even the preacher come, flingin' Bible verses at her like they was whips." Granny Mandy slowly shook her head, her expression one of disgust. "Knowed other preachers what's done that." Recollections of Granny angrily drumming her fingers during Preacher Morgan's sermon flashed across my mind. "Livin' Word be fer changin' a body from the inside out. Ain't a soul on this earth can switch ye with them words, makin' 'em change ye from the outside in. Them preachers ain't shepherds, carin' fer sheep. They's actin' like lion tamers at a circus, thrashin' ye about the cage with whips!"

"But what 'bout the gal from Summit County?"

"Same thing happened as when any preacher goes to whippin'. 'Twas like she didn't even hear 'im. Like she were somewheres else. In another world."

"Yes!" Tommy Lee stood up, edging closer to Granny Mandy and following her every move. He fidgeted a bit, finally throwing aside the whittled stick and closing up his knife. "But what happened to her?" His voice was soft. And fearful sounding. Like a body that asks a question and don't rightly want to hear the answer, seeing how a unanswered question's better'n hearing a hurtful reply.

"One day, her man'd throwed so much wood on the fire, he made it send up flames what filled the whole of that fireplace, cracklin' an' spittin' so that it sent out sparks. And one o' them sparks landed right smack on her face, burnin' her kindly bad."

Resting the battling stick against her side, Granny Mandy looked up from the pot of clothes and stared off towards the direction of the McKenney graveyard. I felt the all too familiar sick feeling coming again. *Oh, Granny! Are you hearin' Grandaddy again?* Her voice low and husky now, Granny Mandy whispered, "She felt of her face then." Mimicking the same, Granny placed one palm against her cheek.

Without even thinking—or knowing why—I did the very same thing. "An' then she stood up, went 'bout her chores. Never said nothin' 'bout them days she'd jest set. Not ary a word."

Me and Tommy Lee just stared at her a minute. In the silence, you could hear our breathing and the soft crackling of the fire burning beneath the black pot. But even though we weren't talking, the air was filled with words. Unspoken words, forming so many questions. You could nearly feel them moving among us, running back and forth from one to the other. They were there, all right. *But did we have the courage to put sounds to them?*

"But what made her come back?" Tommy Lee's question wedged right into the tension, startling me. I jerked my hand off my face, clutching at my other hand behind my back. "What was it made her get up, Miz McKenney?" The pleading in his voice pulled at her until she finally felt of it. Granny Mandy looked over at him, still resting the one hand against her cheek.

"Cain't ye see? 'Twas the pain brought her back. She let go o' that other world when she was a-feelin' the burnin'. *She let herself feel the pain.*" Granny Mandy suddenly dropped her hand, and snatching up the battling stick, she worked at them clothes once again. "Time to be renchin' 'em. Help me to get 'em to the other tub, Rachael."

Tommy Lee watched us work, his face a picture of someone trying so hard to be grasping at a meaning and not finding it. "Are you meanin' if my mama feels pain—will that bring her back to us?"

"Ain't just that, Tommy Lee." She took a deep breath of air and went on, "Yer mama needs be decidin' iffin she's *wants* to feel the pain. Other world's a-callin' to her." Granny gently shook her head back and forth. "Calls an' pulls at ye 'til ye cain't kindly hear nothin' else. An' the yearnin' comes over ye like . . . like they ain't even nothin' else existin'."

"But why does it feel thata way, Granny?" I dug my fingernails into my palms, making them smart right bad. I wanted them to hurt.

A pair of redbirds peeped frantically in the distance. We all glanced in their direction, searching for what we knew was most likely bothering them. Starlings. They were always stealing birds' eggs this time of the year. The panicked-sounding peeping increased even more until I couldn't stand it, and I closed my eyes against the pitiful sounds.

Granny Mandy sighed heavily. "The yearnin's on account o' they ain't no pain there. No pain."

We worked at the clothes in silence for a while, each of us sorting through all that Granny'd said, I suppose. When we carried the sopping clothes to the second tub under the spigot and plunged them into the cold water, Granny said, "Land, ain't it nigh to freezin' to the touch! Ever notice how this here spring water what's just come from the mountain's so cold against yer skin that it hurts?"

The water was terrible cold, and I remembered that feeling many a time when I'd put my feet in Spring Tide Creek too. I'd yank them out of there right quick when the water was so chilling it set my feet to smarting. Tommy Lee stretched one of his hands down into the tub and nodded at Granny Mandy.

"Feels kindly like a burn, don't it? Ain't that queer like? What's scoldin' hot burns an' what's cold as ice burns." Granny Mandy swished the clothes around in the tub, working at getting all the soap out. But every once in a while she'd glance over towards the graveyard. "The cold burnin'—that be unnatural."

Granny looked over at me then, and the memories of the foxfire come rushing back. The brilliant, glowing, blue-green fairy fire had been cold. But I hadn't touched it. I'd been afraid to. *Would it have burned at the touch*? I wondered. *But that was all nothin' but a dream*! I scolded myself. *You done seen it in the daylight—and it weren't nothin' but rotten wood*! I looked away from her, avoiding the unspoken message I knew she was sending me.

Tommy Lee withdrew his hand then, rubbing it against his britches. "How can that be?" he asked. "Hot and cold feelin' the same. Both burnin'. It don't make no sense atall."

"God give us pain, Tommy Lee. Best be thankin' Him for it, since it be tellin' ye that ye's *alive*! An' ye best be listenin' to what it be sayin' too." Me and Granny Mandy wrung out the last of the clean clothes, hanging them on the fence to dry. "Hot pain pulls a body back to this old world. Cold pain pushes—or draws ye—to the other."

Once more Granny stared over in the direction of the McKenney plot, and then she started walking slowly towards it. I glanced over to Tommy Lee, panic welling up in my throat, cutting off my air and making me nearly gasp for breath. *Why was she goin' there*? *What would she do*? *Oh, God*! *What would she do*? Tommy Lee motioned for me to follow her, but still I hesitated. This wasn't no place for Granny Mandy to be going, not now, probably not ever again. Lord, how I feared that place! No, that wasn't right. It wasn't the graveyard itself I was fearing. It was Granny being there!

"Once ye cross over, ain't no feelin' pain in that other world. Not ary a one," Granny said, glancing back at me and Tommy Lee. She picked up her pace then, walking with a determined step. Tommy Lee hurried to catch up with her, but I just stood there still, dreading that place so that I took a step backwards even.

"Rachael! Come on!" Tommy Lee called, waving one arm at me to follow along. I wanted to stay right where I was, cowering in my fear. But staying here—being all alone—suddenly seemed even more frightening. So I tagged along behind, my feet feeling like sacks of corn I was dragging to be ground.

The family graveyard was over to the opposite side of Granny's property, well away from her truck patch. Me and Andy didn't have no reason to be coming much this direction, and we weren't often looking for no reasons to neither. Weeds had grown up around the fence that went round the whole of it. Daddy'd cut them back now and then with the sickle, but with so much choring to be done, them weeds'd grow faster'n he could ever keep up with them. Granny pushed a tangle of vines back from the latch of the gate and tugged at it until it pulled open.

There was a good number of roughly carved stones sticking up amongst them weeds. We had kin here from a good many years—my great-great grandparents and great grandparents, several of their young'uns that had died in childbirth or of plagues and such, and finally, Daddy and Aunt Hettie's brother and sisters and my own sister and brother. My mind's eye saw Mama then, cradling them clothes up against her breast, rocking them just like there was a real, breathing baby inside. Looking at the rough stones with weeds growing all around, it was hard to imagine they were once real babies.

Granny Mandy headed straight towards Grandaddy's "gravehouse," something you weren't seeing round here so much anymore. But she'd insisted on one for him, though Daddy'd made kindly plain his displeasure. Gravehouses were just that—a house made up of latticework with rough board shingles on the roof. It was supposed to keep the rain from falling on those who'd passed on. Daddy'd kept reminding Granny that Grandaddy wasn't there anymore, that he wouldn't need any protecting from rain, that he was in heaven. Granny Mandy'd argued that she knew all that, but she still wasn't having no rain to be falling on him. "Ain't right not to be buildin' a gravehouse over him!" she'd insisted. And won.

Granny stopped before the gravehouse and reached up to gently move her fingers over the inscription written on the board nailed over the doorway. Burned into the wood with a hot poker, the saying went, "James Henry McKenney, God Bless Him That Lies Here." Daddy hadn't been pleased with the sentiment neither, but that too was of

Granny's choosing. She caressed the words now, tracing one finger through the uneven grooves of his name, just like she was writing it again. Suddenly I felt weak and light-headed; taking a deep, unsteady breath, I realized I'd been holding it ever since we'd stepped inside the gate.

"I be missin' Mister McKenney tolerable much lately," Granny said softly, her words heavy with pain.

I closed my eyes for a moment, wishing that would close off her hurting from reaching to me. *Why was I always thinkin' that closin' my eyes would shut out the hurtin'?*

"Sometimes the loneliness be a-naggin' at me from the first moment I open my eyes of a mornin' clean through to when I be climbin' abed, pullin' my quilt over me of a night."

Granny Mandy closed her eyes then too, but I don't think she was trying to shut out the pain like I was. Seemed to me she was inviting it, concentrating on it, welcoming it. I saw her absentmindedly working at the slim gold band about her wedding finger. "They's times I miss him so much, seems like he might be there iffin I think on it hard 'nough. I can feel his even breathin' against the back o' my head just before we's driftin' off to sleep after a good day's work. Through the night I can feel him matchin' my movin' about—turnin' when I do, a brushin' up against me now an' then. They's simple comfortin' of a night, sensin' that yer man's abed with ye."

I glanced over to Tommy Lee and then immediately looked away in embarrassment and shame. Somehow this was too private, too much between a man and his woman to be hearing now, especially with Tommy Lee. *Why are you sayin' them things, Granny Mandy?* I asked, pleading silently for her to stop. Still, I felt relief in knowing she was only talking *about* Grandaddy. At least she wasn't talking *to* him.

"Wasn't appreciatin' like I shoulda been the comfort—the familiar—of them things when Mister McKenney were with me. Ever since he passed on I be a-workin' at knowin' what them everday things, them feelin's, was like."

Me and Tommy Lee didn't say anything, didn't hardly breathe, it seemed. Making any noise atall would've been like interrupting a whispered prayer.

Granny Mandy stooped down then. She'd eyed something on the ground amidst the tumble of weeds. "Look a here. 'Tis a broken robin's egg! Spotted an' kindly blue, like they always is, an' yet . . . special, ever one I's ever found." She looked up at both of us, eyes smiling, pleasuring in the tiny treasure. Cradling the fragile pieces in her hand, she continued, "Iffin yer Grandaddy was still livin', Rachael, I'd be a-tellin' him 'bout this here egg. He'd laugh at me, a-teasin' at my joy in findin' such as this. An' yet . . ." She closed her eyes once again. I mimicked her, searching for any memories I had of my grandaddy. "An' yet they was a tenderness in him too. I recollect one time he found a baby starlin' on the ground. He'd spied the cat a-worryin' after somethin' an' chased that old tom away. By the time yer grandaddy got to the little thing, though, it were laborin' so hard to take ary a breath. Starlin's be a plumb nuisance; Mister McKenney'd shoot 'em on account o' they gener'ly be chasin' off the other birds or a-stealin' eggs, just like they was prob'ly doin' to them redbirds we heared before. But when that baby drawed its last breath in yer grandaddy's hand, why, he tole me he liked to set to blubberin'.'"

Granny Mandy tilted her hand then, allowing the pieces of shell to fall back onto the ground. Standing up slowly, she stood with her shoulders slumping and arms hanging down at her side. "Yer mama's goin' to be jest fine, Tommy Lee."

Tommy Lee's head jerked up and he stared at her intently. "What's that, Miz McKenney? Are you sayin' my mama's goin' to be all right? Is she goin' to be gettin' up outta that rocker soon? Is she, Miz McKenney?"

"Can't say when. But she will. Yer mama still be wantin' to feel the pain o' this world, though she be a-fightin' it. She ain't really knowed the cold pain. Not yet." Granny Mandy sighed then, and a weariness come over her just as a cloud drifted over us, blocking out the sun. We stood in shadows, feeling the sudden coolness in the air. Somewhere a woodpecker *rat-a-tatted* away, working for its supper. I shivered and then hugged my arms to my chest, seeking warmth of some kind. "I knowed the cold pain." The sudden change in Granny's voice made me wary. "It's a-pullin' at me."

She reached out with one hand, palm up. I took a wobbling step back, nearly tripping and falling in my haste and uncertainty. *Get away, Rachael. Get away!* my mind screamed in fear. *Don't be listenin'. Get away!* But much as I wanted to turn and run, I couldn't. My fears were such that I couldn't do nothing—nothing except stand there, clutching so hard at my arms that they started in to aching.

"I'm so weary, James Henry. Tired o' fightin'. Ain't much left in me to be doin' that no more. I ain't wantin' to be knowin' the pain o' this world no more. The cold pain's comin' to be a friend. See, my hand's a-reachin' for it. It's jest outta reach now . . . jest outta reach. I can 'most touch it. *Almost.*"

Granny Mandy just stood there, straining forward with that arm outstretched, the palm of her hand turned up still. I stared at that empty palm until a slight breeze made me flinch, my cheeks were so cold. Reaching up like I was moving in a dream, I felt of my cheeks, finding them soaked from tears. I hadn't even known I'd been crying.

"Miz McKenney? Hadn't we best be headin' back to see to yer clothes?" Tommy Lee moved closer to stand by Granny Mandy now. Staring deeply into her eyes, he gently took her hand in his own, tenderly cradling it there for a minute until he tucked it into the crook of his arm. "Me an' Rachael best be helpin' you to cart 'em inside now. An' then I need to be gettin' to home, before my daddy wonders where I've done gone off to."

Granny Mandy looked at Tommy Lee blankly, like she wasn't knowing who he was. But she didn't pull away her hand, and she even clung to him for support, leaning heavy like against Tommy Lee as she allowed him to lead her out the gate and away from the family plot. I followed behind them, knowing fear like it was a companion leaning against me.

When we come to the fence that had Granny's clothes and bedclothes draped over it, her step lightened a good bit and I saw her carry her own weight. "Guess my rheumatism be botherin' me again. Bless ye, Tommy Lee, fer takin' pity on a old woman the likes of me! I can't recollect the last time I were escorted by such a gentleman. Makes my achin' bones feel kindly better jest to be thinkin' on the privilege!"

"Miz McKenney, the privilege be mine," Tommy Lee said, grinning at her. "Now, let's us be fetchin' these here clean clothes inside before the sun be a-settin' on us." He glanced over towards the western hills. "Sun'll be a-hidin' behind them hills before we know it."

We gathered up the still-damp clothes, carting them inside and then draping them over furniture so they'd finish drying by the heat of Granny's fireplace. Tommy Lee toted and added more wood, stoking it until it burned tolerable well. He'd even fetched Granny Mandy's quilt for tucking around her and wouldn't think on leaving until she had a steaming cup of coffee in her hands and was setting in a rocker before the blazing fire. Granny had fussed at him, insisting she didn't want no coddling, that she was fine. But still she smiled at Tommy Lee, doing whatever he ordered and finally settling into her rocker with a contented sigh.

While Granny Mandy'd followed Tommy Lee's every move with appreciation and—what was so unlike my granny—easy submission, I'd watched him through doubting eyes, snatching fearful glances at him whenever he wasn't noticing. My shame for Granny's talking to Grandaddy made me want to run and hide from Tommy Lee, but I didn't—only because my bewilderment kept me gaping at him, wondering at his tender care for her. *Hadn't he heard what she were sayin'? Hadn't he knowed she were talkin' to Grandaddy, not about him?*

"You two best be gettin' on home, seein' to yer chores," Granny said. She was resting her head against the back of her chair, rocking back and forth in a even pattern. The floor creaked in a steady, rhythmic response to the weight of her chair. "Go on, get on with you now." She waved us away with one hand, smiling at us once more before raising the tin cup to her lips.

I leaned over to place a quick kiss on her cheek. "You be ringin' your bell now if you be needin' us, Granny Mandy. You know we'd come quick."

"All I be needin' is this here rocker, my coffee, and one more kiss." She pointed to the cheek I hadn't kissed. "On this side! Seein's how my ailin' done got me escorted home by such a gentleman, might as well get kissed on both cheeks by the prettiest gal in these hills!" I smiled at her, shaking my head. But I still planted a kiss on the cheek she offered to me.

Tommy Lee opened the door, and we stepped out into the quieting of the day, the time when even the critters seemed to be settling down, knowing the busyness of the day was coming to an end. There was a restful stillness in the air at this hour, and fortunately, it wasn't terrible hot. Come August, this time of the day'd be sticky and anxious feeling; everybody waits, hopefully, for some cooling to be coming with the evening air. I started walking towards home, hoping Tommy Lee wouldn't be saying anything, wouldn't be intruding into the silence—and peace—of the mood of this time.

"Might as well be spittin' it out." Tommy Lee kicked at a rock in the road.

I sighed, regretting that my moment of peace had been shattered. "Spittin' out what?"

"You know, Rachael. Whatever's been makin' you so jumpy. Ever since we come back from visitin' yer grandaddy's grave you been terrible edgy." He stopped a minute, scratching his head. "No, come to think of it, you started in to actin' queer like before we even visited yer grandaddy's grave. Like you was plumb scared to death of goin' there. Ain't never knowed you to be so afeared of haints and graveyards and such. 'Specially plots what belong to yer own kin."

I avoided looking at him though I knew he was staring me in the eye.

"Don't b'lieve in haints. Ain't afeared of no graveyards. And they ain't nothin' botherin' me. Nothin' atall." Looking off towards the river made the lying easier.

"Rachael, ain't you knowin' I can see through you plain—plain as if you was wearin' a pair o' old shoes what's so fine I can see the wrinkles in yer socks?"

I grinned at his teasing, but somehow that simple bit of fooling caught at my throat and broke down the dam I'd built, letting all the feelings come that I'd held back until now. The tears simply slipped from my eyes, trickling down evenly, following one after another over the same pathways on my cheeks. There wasn't any sound to them. I didn't sob. Didn't even breathe heavy like, gasping for air like I'd done with the foxfire. These tears were silent. Silent in the aloneness and emptiness that I was knowing.

Suddenly Tommy Lee grabbed up my hand, pulling me along behind him as he hurriedly run for the protection of a ramshackle outbuilding that was setting next to Granny Mandy's truck patch. She stored many of her garden tools here, and Tommy Lee quickly scooted hoes, rakes, and everything else out of the way so we'd have a place to set down.

I hung my head in shame, knowing I'd lied to him. Worse yet, I'd pushed him away—not trusting him, wondering at his reasons for being so caring of Granny Mandy, doubting his goodness, and even suspecting him of catering to her like . . . just like them Yankees were buttering up to us. *But the shame!* the voices whispered to me. *He heard yer granny. He knows!*

Tommy Lee reached out and touched his hands to my face, tenderly, gently wiping the silent tears away. And then he just rested them there, cradling my face in his hands. I knew what he was waiting for. He was waiting for me to find the courage to look him in the eye once again. And suddenly I knew too—with all my being I knew—that he'd always be waiting for me, always be loving me until I found the courage to trust him with everything inside of me. Things inside of me that I couldn't find the courage to face alone. Without Tommy Lee's love.

I opened my eyes then, seeing the love there in them eyes so plain. It was just like . . . like he was talking to me when he wasn't saying nothing atall. Didn't need to. And then the memory of Mama and Daddy come back to me again. Setting at the table. Sending the love speaking back and forth in silent waves that were almost touchable. That was right powerful love. And Tommy Lee's love for me was like that.

He took his hands away then, sudden embarrassment making him roughly shove them down into his pockets. He glanced away too, breaking the current between us but not dismissing the love that was there. I felt it still like a quilt that was wrapped about me. I clung to it.

"Are you feelin' better now?" Tommy Lee pushed the hair back from his forehead. "Can't hardly bear to see you cry."

I nodded at him. "It were . . . um, my worryin' 'bout you knowin' Granny Mandy like that. Like she ain't . . . ain't right, and I were so ashamed and—"

"Rachael, how can you be thinkin' that'd make any difference to me? That it would make me think any less o' yer granny? Or of you?"

"But it has to! Didn't you hear? Granny's talkin' to my grandaddy. Talkin' to him, Tommy Lee! When he's dead!"

Tommy Lee suddenly grabbed up both my hands again, squeezing them right hard in his strong, muscular ones. "For weeks now, I been talkin' away to my mama, Rachael. Folks think she's livin'—but she's the same's dead! Am I lovin' her any less? Am I lovin' my daddy less? Are you lovin' me any less on account o' my mama's bein' sick? Rachael, ain't you knowin' it don't make no difference? Listen to me: *it don't make no difference!*"

"It does to everbody else!"

The pain come gushing out of me then, pouring out in waves buried so deep inside that my whole body jerked with the force of my sobbing. But unlike the day I'd cried by the foxfire—so alone, so despairing in the emptiness of my grieving—there was a sharing of these tears, another with me to be bearing the hurting. For Tommy Lee wrapped his arms about me, pulling me close to him, rocking me back and forth, tenderly murmuring over and over, "Oh, Rachael, oh, Rachael . . ."

I don't know how long we set there while I cried out my hurt, but finally the pain was spent. And then I merely rested in his arms, finding such comforting in the warmth of his embrace. He whispered softly against my ear, "Oh, Rachael, ain't you knowin' God's love never changes, never moves, never gets no smaller? I know them others—them what be judgin' us—well, I be knowin' that hurts you. But that ain't nothin' compared to the strength o' the love that's in you—from God. An' Rachael, be knowin' this too." He stopped a minute, reaching up to caress my hair, smoothing it back from my temple, and then he gently tilted up my chin so that I was looking in them eyes once again. "Always be knowin' that God give me that same kind o' love for you. Never-changin' love."

Tommy Lee leaned toward me then, reaching out for me so tenderly, touching his lips to mine. The kiss was soft, like the petal of a dogwood flower brushed against your cheek. And yet at the same time a rushing of feelings coursed through me, making me know every inch of me was alive, leaving me strengthened somehow when Tommy Lee pulled away.

"I know this be meanin' we's courtin' official like. I'm hopin' that be fine with you?" He smiled, and I grinned shyly back at him.

"I reckon if it weren't I'd surely have let you know before now."

"Like you done Clyde under that old crab apple?" He chuckled softly.

"'Spose so. Smacked 'im a good one, didn't I?"

"So hard you knocked down 'bout a whole peck o' apples. An' most of 'em hit 'im on top the head too!"

"A peck! Oh, Tommy Lee, I didn't neither! It were plainly a accident that that apple—one puny apple—happened to fall just then and land smack on his head."

We both giggled, remembering. "'Twas quite a sight, though. I ain't never goin' to forget the look on his face! But I reckon he had a good smack comin'."

"Reckon so."

Tommy Lee cleared his throat and then leaned out of the outbuilding, squinting up at the sky. "'Spect you's feelin' better now? I'm thinkin' we both best be gettin' on to home. Chores needs doin'."

I reached out to him, clutching at his arm. "They's just one thing . . . one more thing I was hopin' you could be answerin' for me." I studied on my hands, rubbing at the calluses from planting day and the many hours of weeding since. "Tommy Lee, it seems like . . . well, when I'm with you or Granny, I can be believin' God, knowin' He's real." I looked up at him then, hoping to find the words I was searching for. "It's like I can feel Him, touch Him almost when you and Granny's explainin' all this . . . all this mess! But when I'm alone, my thoughts is fightin' so, strugglin' to find meanin' or some reason for anythin'. And I can't, Tommy Lee. I can't! An' if they's no reasonin'—no purpose—for all this unhappiness, for Granny's pain . . ." I paused as my throat tightened, thinking on my granny's spells. Softly, so softly, almost so God wouldn't be hearing me, I whispered, "Them times I can't feel God." I shook my head, slowly but deliberately. "Maybe He ain't even there."

Tommy Lee covered both my hands with his and gripped them tightly. Them blue eyes bored into mine, staring nigh to my soul, it seemed. "I swear I'd go to the ends of this here earth for you, Rachael. I aim to be yer husband, an' I mean to be protectin' you from anythin' an' everthin' that might be a-harmin' you. An' I'll be givin' you whatever I can from hard an' honest work." He squeezed my hands even tighter, so that they were fairly hurting now. "But I can't find God for you. Faith ain't somethin' you can be sharin', givin' to 'nother. You needs be findin' Him on yer own, Rachael. I'm knowin' He's there. But I can't be helpin' you to know that. 'Tis between you an' God. Jest you an' yer God. Understand what I'm a-sayin'?"

I nodded. "Understandin' fine." I sighed. "It's the acceptin' part I ain't takin' to."

"My daddy once told me ain't nothin' in this whole world worth somethin' what come easy like." Tommy Lee stared off into the distance. I reckoned he was seeing a rocking chair, setting by a fire. "I s'pose believin' God be 'bout the same way." He stood up then and dusted off the back of his pants. "Now I best be runnin' like fire to home, before Daddy sets to wonderin' if I plumb disappeared somewheres with that Yankee." He reached out and brushed my cheek lightly with the tips of his fingers. A worried look come suddenly across Tommy Lee's face. His lips—which had been so terrible soft just a moment ago—set in a firm, straight line and his eyes seemed unfocused, hazy like. "Me an' you both best be believin' God, not everthin' round us, Rachael. Not no Yankees. No meddlin' neighbors. No spells of yer granny's nor my mama's. Must be trustin' Him in the midst o' pain—the heart-burnin' kind. The kind o' pain what draws a body closer to yer God. Or sends you away, lost." He paused a minute and took a deep breath. "'Bye, Rachael." And then, so softly, "I love you," before he took off running.

I set there for just a moment more, collecting my thoughts, remembering the sweetness of Tommy Lee's kiss and then his frightening words. *I wish like anythin' that he'd lectured me,* I thought to myself. *That'd been right easier to hear, since I could've argued with him, or got angry, or just refused to hear him even, not believin' him.* But the trouble was, I knew he was telling it true.

And then I saw even more as I kept on hearing Tommy Lee's words echoing in my mind: *I can't find God for you. 'Tis between you an' God. Jest you and yer God.* It wasn't that I didn't believe God was real, even though I'd said that to Tommy Lee. I was so angry and hurt that I didn't want to believe, but I suppose I knew He was there just like I knew the blinding sun and pale blue sky and rich, red earth around me was there. I accepted that God was real, but the sudden understanding of my deepest fears made me glance nervously towards the shadows in the decaying shack, and I huddled, cowering and shivering, against the rotten boards of the wall.

God was the one I was afraid of. Terrible afraid.

8

Here is the slap of unsheathed paws.
I feel the tearing of his claws,
Am shaken in his mighty jaws.
  This dark is like a falcon's hood
  Where is my flesh and where my blood?

I knew the name of the dark now. It was my fear of God, and giving it a name was just like naming a little one or an animal or a place or thing. The naming had given it form—a living, breathing thing with rights to *be*. I recognized it, knew it, felt it, knew it was following me like a starving young'un tagging after its mama, clutching to her skirt with a feverish demanding.

There was no escaping from the dark neither. It hovered above my quilted bed of a morning and lay down with me at night. It followed me to school, to choring, and especially to church. Neither Daddy nor Mama nor Tommy Lee made it go away, and it grew even more frightening when I was with Granny Mandy. I didn't know why that was so. And for now I didn't want to think on it, knowing instinctively that worrying over it would make the dark stronger. And even pull at me like it'd done Miz Arnold.

I stopped praying. *How could those hollow, formless words get past the solid realness of the dark?* I asked myself. The dark surely would swallow them up, mocking me for trying to find a way of escape through the dense, heavy cloud that was pursuing me, stalking me at every turn. I didn't set in no rocker, staring at the fire. I wasn't even tempted to. But every place I went, every move I was making, everything I touched, and every person I said *hey* to was covered in gray, touched by the hovering mist of the dark. It was my constant companion, but it certainly wasn't no friend.

That Ford of Mister Whitaker's come to be the same way. After our visit to the construction site, seemed like it was always pulling up by our cabin, carting Daddy on several more trips down the road. Except that what once was a fascinating automobile—all shiny with its new-fangled gadgets what you've never seen the like before—now came to represent all the fear and anger of us needing to move. How I hated seeing that thing come up the road.

Only Daddy went with him too. Mama said she didn't care to be traipsing around in that thing, that she was much too busy anyways. And I wasn't invited. Don't rightly know if I was wanting to tag along or not, but me and Andy's curiosity surely had us to pestering Daddy soon as he come home though. The instant he creaked open the screen door, we'd pounce on him, badgering Daddy with questions like, "What'd this farm look like? Did it have a fine spring? Was the soil good and rich as ours? How far was it from Jordan's Bend? What was the house like? Are we going to have a cinder block one like Mister Whitaker said?"

And somehow every time Daddy managed to give us answers to the questions without really saying anything. He'd shake his head at us, saying something like, "Reckon it be lookin' like a farm" or "Didn't taste no water, but she flowed along just fine" and "Now, you know your mama needs be the one what attends to the house; the mister ain't noticin' what the missus sees. I be lookin' for a place to work, eat, and sleep!" He'd grin at us, passing off the questions and answers like they didn't make no never mind atall.

But when we asked about the soil, then Daddy'd change, so suddenly. Seemed you could plainly see his shoulders slump a bit and a dreariness come over him when he tried to answer those questions. Generally he'd just shake his head, mumbling something like, "Ain't McKenney soil like we've knowed." Understanding how much Daddy valued the land, caring, tending, and knowing it like he knew his very self, I grew anxious over Daddy's obvious concern. His worry over providing for us was something he tried to hide from me and Andy. But I saw it in them green McKenney eyes.

There was some good news. Amazingly, Granny Mandy's "seein'" held true, and it wasn't but a week that went by before Tommy Lee come tearing up the road to our house, shouting and laughing the good news: his mama'd got up out of that rocking chair. That night Mister Arnold was giving her some coffee, and though he was thinking it'd cooled enough for the drinking, it must've been tolerable hot yet. When Tommy Lee's daddy put it to her lips, she started and jerked back, making Mister Arnold splash the burning coffee all over his hand.

"I seen they was a difference in her eyes right off," Tommy Lee'd told us. "Mama was lookin' at Daddy, truly seein' him, for the first time in so long. And then she reached out to him, touchin' his skin where the coffee done spilled and asked, 'Are you hurt? Coffee burned me, but I surely didn't mean to jump so and spill it over you too.'" Tommy Lee'd shook his head, his eyes round with wonder and amazement.

Granny Mandy was to supper with us that evening, so I'd glanced over to see what feelings were written about her face. Those eyes of hers were twinkling like fire, and she smiled, nodding her head. I suppose it was a *knowing* kind of look, one that said this wasn't nothing but what she was expecting.

"And then she went off for the liniment," Tommy Lee went on, "fussin' over his burn and caring for it like . . . like she'd been a-carin' for Daddy these last weeks instead of the other way round." He'd pushed the hair back from his face, letting his hand rest on top of his head. I expect I won't never forget the look that he give us, his voice full of awe as he added, breathlessly, "And she done up the dishes. Just like she done ever evenin'." Tommy Lee glanced over to Granny Mandy then, giving her the slightest nod before he went on, explaining, "I scooted on down here soon's she finished. Didn't come earlier because I were tendin' to her—wanted to watch her ever move—judgin' for myself if she be fine."

"And be she fine?" Mama'd asked, her normally active hands still as she watched Tommy Lee with the same look of wonder.

"Appears to be stiff like. Sore and slow-movin' a bit. But I reckon that come from settin' for so long." He crossed his arms over his chest, pushing his chair back on two legs, and then the biggest, easiest grin come slowly creeping over his face, the most relaxed one I'd seen in some time coming from Tommy Lee. "Otherwise, she's fine. My mama's back home again!"

We'd celebrated with him a good while before he was needing to head on home. And then I walked across the west pasture with him since I was wanting to pepper him with more questions—questions as much concerning Granny Mandy as they were his mama. But there wasn't time, seeing how Tommy Lee was so anxious to get to home. I'd seen worry setting about his eyes once again when he gripped my hands tightly and whispered, "After evenin' chores is done, Mama always be settin' by the fire, sewin' or crochetin' or whatever it is gals does. I'm thinkin' on her settin' in that rocker again and startin' in to worryin' that—well, that she might . . ."

"You's thinkin' she might take sick again," I'd said, understanding his concern. "Go ahead and hurry on to home. I'm needin' to speak with you, but we can talk later this week at practice for Children's Day." He'd squeezed my hands once more before he took off running, jumping stumps, logs, and the fence like they weren't hardly even there. I'd watched after him until I couldn't see him no more, and even then I pictured him running in my mind, knowing my heart was surely with him.

Later that evening I'd asked Granny Mandy about his mama, telling her me and Tommy Lee's worries. But Granny wasn't concerned at all, reminding me that "I tole ye his mama were wantin' to feel the pain, and that be why she come back. Ye needn't be frettin' on it, Rachael. Haddy Arnold done her decidin' a'ready."

At school we'd been working diligently preparing for Children's Day. In past years, I'd be tolerable caught up in the excitement and fun of writing a play and memorizing my lines, composing my own poem for the sharing, or reciting well-known verses by one of my favorite poets. But just like this year was different in every other way, Children's Day was unfamiliar feeling too.

Us older students were writing a play to perform, and working with Nellie, Verna Mae, Merry Jo, and Clyde made school days tense and uncomfortable. Of course, Tommy Lee was in our group too, and I looked forward to being with him every day, sharing our ideas and poking fun as we slowly became Indians and a Pilgrim family that first Thanksgiving. But even Tommy Lee being there couldn't take away the cautious way Merry Jo and Nellie spoke to me—like I was the most fragile china what would break so easily. Or how Verna Mae seemed to either avoid me altogether or else peer down her nose at me, hinting at some more of her mama's "you best be a-hearin' me now" preaching.

Even Clyde was different. Used to be we would tease each other back and forth so easy like, enjoying the baiting and pestering like a brother and sister. But Clyde tiptoed around me now, eyeing my moods, it seemed, and finding them not worth the baiting. *Could it be me?* I'd asked myself, wondering if I'd become so tender or prickly or miserable that it was my fault that everyone was so different now, so difficult. *Am I the one to be blamin'? Or do they sense the darkness chasin' me, the terrifyin' fear that I feel—and shy away from it?*

The day of the program come usual like. There wasn't any glorious sunshine that made me jump from bed eagerly nor was there any thunder and lightning to make it a memorable morning. There wasn't anything different to set it apart, make it special. It was just another day that started with a drizzling rain that gradually sneaked away, leaving a dampness, a stickiness hanging behind like about every other morning in late spring in Franklin County, Tennessee.

We met at school like usual too, only there weren't any lessons today. Instead, everybody brought whatever they could for decorating up the school for Children's Day. We'd made pine cone wreaths to be hanging on the doors, strung popcorn to loop over hooks about the whole room, placed pine boughs and flowers here and there (with bright red ribbon donated by the Hickmans), and scattered several colorful gourds round the room—some with faces drawn on them by the littlest young'uns. We were wanting to show off all the work we'd been doing this school year too, so there were colored and painted pictures tacked to the walls to be demonstrating our artwork and Miz Travis had picked out several examples (at least one from each of us) of neat handwriting, stories, or high marks on examinations to be showing off to our kin. I remember thinking to myself, though, *Plain foolishness, this decoratin'. We's only pretendin' this day be a celebration. Pretendin' same as we's pretendin' to be Indians and Pilgrims and authors and poets. We're deceivers—a schoolroom full of Judases trying to fool ourselves and everbody else round us!* I know I moved through the whole day seeing the bright colors of the pretty pictures, gourds, ribbon, and flowers through a hazy cloud of gray. Made everything look dull.

After supper that evening, Old Dean pulled us over the uneven road to town once again for the program—Daddy, Mama, Granny Mandy, me, and Andy. Granny Mandy seemed a mite quieter than usual, but she'd teased Andy still, telling him his slicked down hair would surely be attracting gals same as "a mule's ear be collectin' hoss flies." Andy'd growled at that, but there was a twinkle in his eye, a dangerous one, seemed to me.

"You all ready for recitin' that poem? Sayin' parts of 'Evangeline,' ain't you?" I asked him, hoping to needle him enough to find out what the twinkle was all about.

Andy looked away from me, staring towards and spying out the Arnolds' farm like he hadn't never seen it before. "Nope," was all he offered. He wasn't about to make my prying easy.

"What do you mean, *nope*? I heard Miz Travis say that's what you was to be workin' on, and you even practiced it yesterday when we was rehearsin'." Andy twitched his freckled nose, sniffed loudly, and then reached up to rub a sleeve across it, from the cuff clean up to the elbow. I shook my head at him in disgust.

"Ain't recitin' no 'Evangeline.'" Then he wrinkled up his nose, just like he'd just stepped in something cutting across the pasture.

I looked at him with alarm then, the understanding of his meaning making me feel awful already for the embarrassment that Mama and Daddy would be knowing. *Andy was plannin' on playin' hooky!* Much as I was dreading this year's program, no thought of not participating had even entered my thinking. Children's Day—even though it was called that and funny as it may seem—was for our parents. We all knew that, and wouldn't none of us think on missing out on showing them what we'd learned this year.

I scooted over next to Andy, putting my face right up next to his. "Andy, you can't be doin' this," I whispered, urgently. "Ain't right. Ain't fair to Mama and Daddy!"

"Ain't what fair?" Andy give me a look like I'd plumb broke fast. Worse even than old Miz Youther'd done when she turned ninety and proceeded to ride to town on her mule, dressed in nothing but her starched nightgown.

"Shh! Don't be hollerin'!" I glanced towards the front of the wagon, worrying that Mama or Daddy might hear. And though Granny wasn't near as sharp of hearing as she used to be, she still had a fine knack for picking up what a body wasn't wanting her to. I whispered, even more softly, "You know what I be talkin' about—playin' hooky tonight, of all the times!"

"Who in thunder said I was plannin' on playin' hooky?"

"You mean you ain't?" I was more confused than ever.

"Was I sayin' so?"

"No, but . . ."

"Well, then, don't be jumpin' about like no skittish flea on a three-legged hound. Didn't say no such thing."

"Then what are you meanin'?"

The twinkle come back again, and I leaned closer to him, searching them green eyes for a clue to the mischief I knew was hiding there. "Miz Travis finally give me permission to be recitin' the poem I were wantin' to say."

"What poem?"

"Ain't sayin'." He give me a smug look. "It's a secret."

"But we done made up the programs to give out. We printed 'Evangeline' next to your name." I remembered that well, recollecting too how it took nigh to forever to write out "by Henry Wadsworth Longfellow" for every program. *Leave it to O.A. to recite a poem by a poet with a name a mile long*, I'd grumbled to myself.

"Done tole you, I ain't recitin' no 'Evangeline.' Now, leave me be awhile so's I can be practicin' to myself."

I sighed in frustration. Knowing that look and the way he'd turned away from me again, I realized there wasn't no more I'd be getting out of Andy just now. At least I felt reassured that he'd be reciting something. I had no idea what and that caused me a bit of concern. But anything was better than Andy's running off, cutting on Children's Day.

We were just coming into town when I frantically checked over my clothes. I was wearing my new blouse again, the one with the blue flowers, and I quickly felt of the collar, making sure it wasn't turned under or wrinkled. Smoothing out my skirt the best I could, I then rubbed at my shoes with the underside of the hem, trying to make the old shoes (how I was wishing they were them blue ones again) shine just a bit. Finally, I gingerly fingered the blue ribbon that Mama had put in my hair, pulling it up again like she'd done so nice the last time. The bow was still fine and I smiled faintly, remembering. Remembering when Tommy Lee had noticed.

"What are you be grinnin' about?" O.A. asked, eyeing me.

"Nothin'!"

Andy smiled knowingly. "Thought so!"

This time, I turned my back to him, but there wasn't much reason to be doing that. We'd just pulled up to the schoolyard and Daddy was easing Old Dean towards the shade of the oak.

"Lookit there!" Andy hollered, pointing a finger towards the road where Mister Whitaker's car set, looking tolerable funny next to the assortment of wagons and horses and such. "Them Yankees is here!"

Miz Travis had told us she'd be extending them an invite, but none of us were expecting that they'd come. Now I glanced anxiously towards Granny Mandy. *At least she hadn't thought to tote along that gun*, I thought to myself. Daddy'd already helped Mama down, but Granny Mandy was just setting there with a right determined look about her jaw, I noticed.

"Now, Mama, they ain't no cause to be lookin' for trouble tonight," Daddy said to her, eyeing the determined look about her chin too. "You can be toleratin' them if yer tryin' hard 'nough. Ain't but for one evenin'."

"Toleratin' Yankees be harder'n scratchin' yer ear with yer elbow."

Daddy grinned up at her, nodding. "Ain't arguin' with that. Only sayin' that depends on if ever itch needs be scratched." Granny Mandy started in to chuckling.

"Hep me down then. Reckon I can be bearin' a itchin' ear fer a short piece. 'Sides, havin' them Yankees here this evenin' might be fittin' after all. Just might be . . ." She turned towards Andy, giving him a knowing look.

While offering a helping hand up to me, Daddy asked, "Now Granny Mandy, what're you an' Andrew up to? You ain't got no plans to be harassin' nobody, is you? Because if you is . . ."

"James Otis McKenney!" Granny exclaimed, putting hands to hips and giving him a wide-eyed, innocent look. I was sure Granny was play-acting to her heart's content, since Andy'd took one glimpse of her and then smirked, stifling back laughter and immediately running off towards the schoolyard where we were to be meeting. "Cain't rightly believe you's accusin' yer own mama of such. When has you ever knowed me to be botherin' Yankees?"

Daddy glanced over to me, rolling his eyes and shaking his head. I couldn't help but to be giggling at her. "Oh, no," Daddy announced grand like, matching Granny's play-acting with his own, throwing his long arms up in the air. "Ain't never knowed you to be pointin' that gun barrel down no Yankee noses nor treeing 'em for hours nor settin' no blamed traps . . ."

I just had to interrupt at that point. "Settin' traps? I ain't heared that story!"

"Now you just never mind 'bout that," Mama ordered. "We ain't goin' to be repeatin' that tale. Never." Daddy nodded his head too, but I wasn't about to forget it, firmly deciding to ask Granny later. She'd tell me—and enjoy the telling too!

Granny walked towards the school, glancing back over her shoulder at us with the same smirk that O.A. wore, swishing her skirts back and forth just like she was a young gal baiting her man. Daddy shook his head at her again, looking like he knew he'd just been caught on that hook. "No telling what yer granny an' Andrew be up to," he whispered to me, rubbing his stubbled chin. "Reckon this evenin' has all the makin's to be tolerable interestin'. Never thought I'd hear myself sayin' such as this, but God help them Yankees!"

I laughed at him, wondering myself what Granny and O.A. were up to. But then I decided, unlike Daddy, that it would be kindly nice seeing them Yankees squirm. *Let 'em fidget like a sweatin' farmer in his new coarse-wool trousers*, I muttered to myself, still chuckling, and then I hurried off towards the back side of the building. All the children were to gather there, where me and all the oldest students were to help organize them, making sure they were lined up correctly. At the proper time, just before the performances were to begin, all of us young'uns were to march in and set in the front rows of the school.

Soon as I rounded the corner, though, I stopped, instant aggravation and amazement causing me to put my hands to my hips. Daisy was bawling at the top of her lungs, with her arms hanging limp at her sides and her tear-streaked face raised to the sky, sobbing something about "Willie done tugged out my hair bow!" Earl was taunting and laughing at her, pointing and slapping at his knee—wasn't that just like a brother?—causing Jessie and Lil' Lester to join in the teasing.

A whole passel of young'uns were gathered around something they were poking at on the ground with sticks, and half of them were rooting in the dirt too, probably spoiling the clean, new clothes I knew mamas had labored over. I could make out something like "Poke him another one, Sadie!" and then squeals of laughter and excitement would follow as young'uns jumped and bounded every which way.

Clyde was up a tree, dangling by his feet from a rotted old limb. *For heaven's sake*, I fussed to myself, *he's a mite too old for doin' such childish an' foolhardy things on a special night like this. And there he is coaxin' Eugene an' Arlin to be joinin' him up there to boot. Like that old limb could be holdin' the three of them*! I shook my head, expecting the limb to break any second and send Clyde to falling right smack on top his fool head. Not that I was thinking it would hurt him much.

And then there was Willie. Covered from head to toe with Tennessee clay, shirttail out and flapping behind him, overalls torn and hair wild and dirty, he was running this way and that, pulling the girls' hair, smacking the boys atop their heads with a branch he was brandishing like some whip and generally buzzing round like an agitated, fuming honeybee that had been caught in a jelly jar. I didn't for a moment doubt that he could be stinging too.

And over top all the carrying on I could just make out Merry Jo's voice, pleading and whining, "Please settle down! Stop yer runnin' now an' set still. You needs be listenin' to me, please!" I knew where Miz Travis was—she was inside, welcoming the parents and showing them the papers we'd tacked up from the past year. But where on earth was Nellie and Verna Mae when they were needed? And most importantly, where was Tommy Lee?

Frantically I looked around, searching for something to make enough noise to capture everyone's attention, and in a hurry too. Miz Travis would be right disappointed in all of us—and especially us older ones—if we didn't get these young'uns settled down right quick.

Just then Tommy Lee come around the corner, toting a dented old pail and the dipper that we kept for drinking down by the creek. I smiled at him, thinking what a right welcome sight he was and shaking my head with amazement. *He'd decided on doing the same thing I had*!

"Welcome to this here Children's Day," Tommy Lee teased, raising his eyebrows and nodding towards the commotion behind us. "Care to be doin' the callin' to order?" He handed me the dipper, bowing like a gentleman and holding out the pail like it was a honored ritual. I giggled, shaking my head at him for only a second before I banged the pail good, making sure I had the sternest, meanest look on my face. A Miz-Travis-at-her-most-provoked look.

That pail and dipper made wonderful loud clangs, and suddenly running feet, wiggly bodies, and all sorts of hollering, blubbering, and squealing come to a stop. Nearly two dozen startled eyes looked over to me and Tommy Lee. Daisy quit her bawling and wonder of all wonders, the clanging had even got Willie's attention, causing him to pause for a moment close enough to Tommy Lee so that Tommy Lee could grab him by the ear.

"Don't let go of him," I warned Tommy Lee.

"Ain't about to," Tommy Lee said, pinching Willie's ear until he started in to whining.

"Now see here!" I hollered, wagging my finger like Granny Mandy had just done to Daddy. "They ain't goin' to be no more runnin' or fightin' or climbin'"—I glanced up at Clyde then, giving him a shameful look—"or nothin' else what Miz Travis wouldn't be havin' durin' school. Is everbody understandin' my meanin'?"

"Sadie's done got her a toad," Anna Ruth announced. "An' she's makin' it hop all over us! We'uns goin' to get warps from it!"

"Silly," Lena scoffed at Anna Ruth. "That's *warts* what you be gettin' from toads."

Giggles and pushing erupted once more so I banged on that pail again. It was certainly going to have a good many more dents once we were through with it. "Hush! Now they ain't goin' to be no more foolin'. Or am I needs be fetchin' your daddies—daddies what's totin' switches?" Willie's whining was the only sound after that threat, and even he glanced over to me with eyes wide with alarm. "Clyde, get outta that tree immediately. Before you bust your fool head." He reached up to the limb and then gracefully swung himself down. I was glad to note that, although he held his head high, his face was redder than a tomater in August. "Merry Jo, how 'bout you take Sadie over to the creek. Seems she's collected a critter what'd be much happier there than amongst this wild group."

Merry Jo'd stood off to the side, wringing her hands, slowly shaking her head back and forth the whole time I was banging and clanging and hollering. *Maybe I am more suited for teachin'*, I thought to myself, proudly. *At least I got the knack for hollerin' at young'uns so they listen to me!* Merry Jo nodded meekly, motioning for Sadie to follow her.

"Daisy, don't want to hear no more bawlin'. Come on over here to me. Ain't no damage what can't be fixed. An' the rest of you young'uns get in line the way we practiced this mornin'. No pushin' now. Tommy Lee's in charge, and he'll pinch anybody else's ear what needs it, believe me!"

Tommy Lee stood by the door, directing and ordering them

young'uns just like I imagined a soldier in the army would, and all the while he was still hanging onto Willie's ear. I smiled to myself when I remembered what he'd said once before when Willie'd done some foolishness that asked for a right good throttling. Tommy Lee had shrugged his shoulders before crossing his arms over his chest, stating matter-of-fact like, "See, with Willie, a body first has to get his attention."

"Daisy, I don't suppose you brung a comb with you, did you?" I asked, shaking my head at the impossible tangle of curls before me.

"Surely did! Mama done my hair awful so's I was . . ."

"Daisy!" I spun her around so she was looking me in the eye. "Now tell me true. Did Willie mess yer hair bow or did you?"

"Willie did! He did! Honest, Rachael!"

"An' what were you doin' when Willie done pulled at it?"

"Well, um . . . I were, um . . ." Daisy glanced away from me and lifted one knee, scratching at it.

"Daisy? The whole truth now." I thought a second and then added, "It's either yer speakin' to me—or your mama."

She looked back at me with wide open eyes and mouth before her little face crumpled up and she started into crying again. Between hiccups and tears I could just barely make out, "Didn't mean to make it all come unbraided! Just wanted it like you does yers—all growed up!"

Impulsively I hugged her to me then, feeling sympathy and tenderness for her little girl desiring. I knew those feelings too. "It's all right, Daisy. We can fix it up good's new, okay? Hush now!"

She hiccuped a few times more. "But will you be fixin' it like yers? With the sides drawed up?"

"I 'spect so. If you'll be holdin' still for me. Can't be fixin' no hair on someone what's fidgetin' ever which way. An' once I get it all fixed, you must be leavin' it be. Ain't goin' to stay right if you keep fussin' with it." Speaking on fidgeting suddenly made me think on Andy. "Daisy, where's O.A. got himself to? He ain't run off, is he?" I asked, panic creeping into my voice. I fetched a hanky from my pocket and wiped her tear-streaked face before turning her round to work on them tangles.

"Nah. He's been settin' over there under the crab apple tree this whole time. Clyde tried to get him to climb up the cottonwood with him, but Andy weren't payin' him no mind. Just marched right over there an' set down." Daisy pulled her head around again to peer up at me. "Ain't sick, is he? Because my mama says I ain't to be round anybody what's got the—"

"Turn your head back round, Daisy. Now I done said you has to be holdin' still. No, O.A. ain't sick an' you ain't goin' to catch nothin' from him neither." I paused a minute. "Unless it's more orneriness." I pulled up the smoothed curls and then carefully tied Daisy's yellow ribbon into a pretty bow. I spun her around once more to face me. "There. Looks right fine too."

"Can't I see it?"

"Ain't no lookin' glasses here. Goin' to have to trust me that you look right pretty."

Daisy stuck out that lower lip for a moment, but then brightened at the thought of something. *Heaven knows what that might be*, I thought to myself. The she looked around for a moment until she'd evidently spied what she was searching for.

"I needs be gettin' in line now." She reached up to carefully touch the bow just about like I'd done earlier in the wagon. I smiled at her. "Thankee for your help, Rachael." And then she took off, skipping to her group at the front of the line.

Tommy Lee was there, keeping all them wiggling, excited young'uns in some kind of order. I watched Daisy skip up and stop before him, and it wasn't but a moment before I saw Tommy Lee start to laugh, catch himself, and then say something back to her, nodding and grinning still. *I'll be needin' to find out what that Daisy was up to*, I told myself. *Hard to say what she was tellin' Tommy Lee now.*

Sadie was back from the creek, pouting and sullen about setting that poor old toad free. Merry Jo had returned with her, but she seemed to be avoiding meeting my eye. Finally my curiosity about Nellie and Verna Mae was too much. Walking through the crowd of young'uns, I lectured Earl to keep his hands to himself, reminded Willie to tuck in his shirt (Tommy Lee'd let go of him finally and tried to fix him up, but it wasn't much use), and cautiously approached Merry Jo.

"Hey, Merry Jo. I ain't seen Verna Mae or Nellie anywheres. Ain't like them to be late for Children's Day."

She nonchalantly smoothed out her skirt and straightened her hair. "They ain't comin'. Both took bad sick with sniffles."

I stared at her, probably looking right simple in my amazement. "Sick? Why, Nellie ain't been sick a day in her life, that I knowed of. And Verna Mae too? Since when has bein' sick kept Verna Mae from performin' in front of folks, showin' off kindly embarrassing like she done on ever other Children's Day?"

Merry Jo shrugged her shoulders. "They's sick in bed, sneezin' and coughin' and blowin' into hankies, the both of 'em. Miz Travis said she were right disappointed they wasn't comin'. I'm to play the piano since we can't be givin' our play."

"What about Tommy Lee? And me?" I paused a minute, glancing round to see if Clyde could be hearing me. "What on God's green earth could Clyde do? Show how he can swing from a tree branch?"

Merry Jo ignored that. "Miz Travis said she'd like to hear you all read your best compositions. You can be pickin' the one you think's best."

I searched her face then, trying to see beyond the easy look she'd pasted there. *Somethin' . . . somethin' just ain't right*, I muttered to myself. "Merry Jo, it just ain't like Verna Mae an' Nellie to miss Children's Day. Why, we been lookin' forward to this for . . . months now, even." Suddenly a new worry struck me and I blurted out, "You ain't lyin' to me, are you, Merry Jo? They ain't really sick—with something terrible bad—are they?"

Merry Jo avoided meeting my eyes, but she reached out to grab up one of my hands. "No, Rachael, they's fine, really. It's just that . . . that when they wasn't feelin' good anyways . . . well, Verna Mae's mama told me she wasn't wantin' to feel even more uneasy like, bein' here."

I could feel the anger rising in me now, threatening to tumble out all over onto Merry Jo. "Bein' here. With me." I stated it bluntly, matter-of-fact like. And drowning in fury.

"Rachael! Merry Jo! Time to help the young'uns to be marchin' in!" Miz Travis shouted over to us, waving her arms about with bubbling enthusiasm.

"I'm sorry, Rachael, but we best go help now," Merry Jo said in a soothing voice, squeezing my hand and then brushing hers softly up against my arm. "We can talk more 'bout this later." She started towards the group of laughing, excited children. "Sadie, get back in line an' march in like a lady now!" she called out.

But I wasn't of a mind to be done talking just yet. I grabbed Merry Jo's arm, jerking her back around to look at me. "Of all the hurt I been swallowin' from everone around here, I reckon this be makin' me choke more'n anything else. You! You done let Verna Mae an' Nellie do this to me—done let 'em be this ill to me! An' you ain't carin' none atall!"

Now Merry Jo's eyes flashed angrily, and though she kept her voice low, there was a force behind them that I could nearly feel hitting up against my face. "Rachael, you's been carryin' yer pain like some trophy before us. Shinin' it, holdin' it up like some idol we'uns should be bowin' down to. Well, I ain't doin' it no more! I seen Nellie. An' I done visited Verna Mae too. Told 'em they was hateful an' that they wasn't no friend of mine no more until they apologized to me and you. But you ain't no better! You ain't lettin' me be yer friend neither. Been pushin' me away ever time I were offerin' you love."

"*Love*? Was it love what caused you to be givin' me all them easy an' simple answers? That ain't love!"

"Ain't you understandin' nothin', Rachael McKenney? It was all I was knowin' to do!" Merry Jo flung her arm out and away from my grasp, pointing it towards the crowd of young'uns and the schoolhouse itself. "All these simple folk, all of them, they ain't knowin' what to do, what to say, how to be givin' you what you need. All they can give is what they know, Rachael. You's askin' more of them than they's able to give!"

Merry Jo moved among the group of children, straightening collars and suspenders, hair bows and braids. And then we could hear her mama pounding out "Pomp and Circumstance" on the piano—the signal for the littlest young'uns to begin marching in.

Miz Travis caught my eye then, in between smiling, nodding, and putting a hand on each shoulder of the young'uns beginning to file through the door. "I'm so sorry, Rachael," she called out to me, shaking her head and giving me a sorrowful look. "You must be terrible disappointed, seein' how this is your last Children's Day and all. And you worked so hard too." She frowned as Willie approached her. "William Snodderly, you are a sight. Hold still while I at least try to clear one clean place on your face!" Miz Travis worked at Willie's face with a hanky, spitting on it and scrubbing at his nose, cheeks, and chin. "What composition are you wantin' to read, Rachael?"

"Um, haven't rightly decided. Can I think on it a bit yet?"

Miz Travis nodded. "Whatever yer pickin' out will be pleasin', Rachael. You've done some fine work this year. Eugene, get yer finger out of Maybelle's ear!" She grabbed up Eugene by the shoulder then, causing him to let go of Maybelle right quick. "Rachael, you seem a mite peaked. You aren't gettin' what Nellie an' Verna Mae have, are you?"

"No, ma'am, I'm fine."

"That's good. Eugene, if you don't keep your hands to yerself . . ."

Glancing up then, I saw Merry Jo staring at me, not saying nothing, but asking me with her eyes, same as if she was talking. And I could see the love for me etched there too, the caring that she'd been offering me all along. Caring that I couldn't accept. Wasn't wanting to. Maybe wasn't able to. Just like Merry Jo and everybody else wasn't able to give what I was needing, seems I was beginning to understand now that even if I could've written it all out in some fine composition, telling the folks of Jordan's Bend just what it was I was needing and wanting—well, even then I couldn't have took it. Couldn't know it. Couldn't let it be touchable and real for me. I wasn't ready to be loved then. *Was I now?*

I helped Miz Travis get the rest of the young'uns through the door and seated in the front rows, noting that Andy went by without any fidgeting, wiggling, or fussing. I wondered at him once again, fretting a moment over what him and Granny Mandy were up to. But my thoughts and feelings were such a jumble that there wasn't any time for worrying over Andy just now. Or time to be sorting through all that Merry Jo'd said—and all the feelings that were arising in me, feelings that left me stripped naked and bare. I resolutely put everything aside that Merry Jo'd said to me, allowing myself to only think on them littlest ones marching proudly up to the front of the room to sing their songs, recite their verses.

Mamas and daddies, grandparents, aunts, uncles, cousins, and kin of all kind clapped and clapped when they were done. Didn't make no difference that Daisy played with her hair bow instead of holding up her picture of the "oceans white with foam" when they sang "God Bless America." Or that Maybelle plumb forgot to sing at all, but instead waved at her granny all the way through the song. Or that Eugene poked at Daisy for playing with her hair bow until Miz Travis had to stop the whole production to make him quit provoking her.

The older young'uns did some skits, read short stories, recited poems, and some even sang or attempted to play the piano. Seemed like they hit more bad notes than good ones, but at least they were trying, so we clapped for the bad notes too.

When it was finally Andy's turn and Miz Travis stepped up onto the makeshift platform to announce that he was to perform next, I sucked in my breath and felt a wearisome knot form in my stomach. "Andrew McKenney will be next on our program," Miz Travis said. "There has been one slight change, though. Instead of recitin' portions of 'Evangeline,' Andrew will favor us with 'Prometheus'—also by Henry Wadsworth Longfellow." She nodded towards Andy, clapping (everybody else joined in then too), and then went back to her seat.

I won't never forget the sight of Andy walking up to stand before us. I swear he'd grown a foot, the way he looked—stretching forward, holding up that square chin, arching his shoulders so tall and proud like. Seemed like most always, Andy'd be sneaking everywhere he went, tiptoeing to either find trouble or to get away secretly after the orneriness was done. But tonight he wasn't sneaking or tiptoeing or walking unsure, like about every other boy and girl had done going up there to perform in front of so many. No, Andy strode up there, purposefully, eagerly, like a *man*. Reminded me of Daddy once again. And Granny.

"The poem I'm recitin' this here Children's Day be 'Prometheus' by Henry Wadsworth Longfellow," Andy repeated. Even his voice was changed. It was deeper sounding, with authority ringing among his words. Seemed like the tone of his voice was announcing, *I got somethin' worth sayin' to you all here tonight, and you best be listenin'.* "It be about the mythical Greek god what give man fire."

Prometheus . . . fire! Now I recollected the story. *But why on earth would Andy be choosin' a poem from classical mythology? An' especially when he ain't never had no use atall for them made-up stories before, and even carried on like the dickens for havin' to waste time readin' them?*

Andy stood up even taller then, and began,

> Of Prometheus, how undaunted
> > On Olympus' shinin' bastions
> His audacious foot he planted,
> Myths are told an' songs are chanted,
> > Full of promptin's and suggestions.
>
> Beautiful is the tradition
> > Of that flight through heavenly portals,
> The old classic superstition
> Of the theft an' the transmission
> > Of the fire of the Immortals!

I clutched the edges of the pew then, straining to catch every word and yet fearing to hear them at the same time. Of all the things Andy could've been reciting, why, oh why was he speaking of *fire*?

And the way he said the words! Andy wasn't just saying them. That didn't begin to describe what he was doing up there before us. No, he was proclaiming them, ringing out those long words and awkward phrases like Andy'd done wrote them himself. Like he knew them. Lived them. *Why, he's preachin' to us more'n Preacher ever done!* I thought to myself, amazement making me stare at my own brother like I hadn't never seen him before. *Preacher Morgan only been imitatin' the likes of this. This here is what preachin' oughta be!*

First the deed of noble darin',
  Born of heavenward aspiration,
Then the fire with mortals sharin'.
Then the vulture,—the despairin'
  Cry of pain on crags Caucasian . . .

The words pulled at me—*fire* and *mortals* (*didn't me and Granny Mandy talk about the very thing gazin' on the foxfire?*) and *despairin'* and *pain* . . . especially *pain*. Why had Andy picked this poem? Was it only to be hurting me? *Oh, God, is You usin' Andy to be rubbin' salt in my open wounds?*

All is but a symbol painted
  Of the Poet, Prophet, Seer;
Only those are crowned and sainted
Who with grief have been acquainted,
  Making nations nobler, freer.

In their feverish exultations,
  In their triumph an' their yearnin',
In their passionate pulsations,
In their words among the nations,
  The Promethean fire is burnin'

Andy's voice rose with the cadence of the poem, drawing me in still—drawing all of us in, holding us there, keeping us captive as he made us feel every word. There wasn't even a young'un stirring as Andy spoke. Those eyes of his burned into ours as he took in everybody in that whole room, making the poem *ours* somehow. It belonged to Jordan's Bend.

Shall it, then, be unavailin',
  All this toil for human culture?
Through the cloud-rack, dark an' trailin'
Must they see above them sailin'
  O'er life's barren crags the vulture?

Such a fate as this was Dante's,
  By defeat an' exile maddened;
Thus were Milton an' Cervantes,
Nature's priests an' Corybantes,
  By affliction touched an' saddened.

But the glories so transcendent
    That around their memories cluster,
And, on all their steps attendant,
Make their darkened lives resplendent
    With such gleams of inward lustre!

All the melodies mysterious,
    Through the dreary darkness chanted;
Thoughts in attitudes imperious,
Voices soft, an' deep, an' serious,
    Words that whispered, songs that haunted!

All the soul in rapt suspension,
    All the quiverin', palpitatin'
Chords of life in utmost tension,
With the fervor of invention,
    With the rapture of creatin'!

Ah, Prometheus! heaven-scalin'!

Andy's chin come up even higher, and he didn't look anybody in the eye no more. Instead, he stared beyond us, seeing much farther than those schoolroom walls.

In such hours of exultation
Even the faintest heart, unquailin',
Might behold the vulture sailin'
    Round the cloudy crags Caucasian!

Though to all there be not given
    Strength for such sublime endeavor,
Thus to scale the walls of heaven,
And to leaven with fiery leaven,
    All the hearts of men forever;

Yet all bards, whose hearts unblighted
    Honor an' believe the presage,
Hold aloft their torches lighted,

Andy held up one arm then, just like he was really holding up a torch. And I swear, a body could fairly see it there in his hand, know the light shining in your eyes, feel its heat reflecting on your face.

And then he finished, shouting out,

Gleamin' through the realms benighted,
As they onward bear the message!

There wasn't a sound then but Andy's breathing, and he was breathing hard as he stood before us, arm raised, chest moving in and out with a force that drew us in and out with it.

"You can't be takin' it from us, Yankees!" Andy hollered suddenly, and I jerked at the strength of command in his words. Andy stared down at Mister Whitaker and Mister Sherman setting towards the back of the room. I glanced towards them, but I didn't give them no notice. It was Andy that I couldn't be taking my eyes off of. "We's proud Southerners, and you'uns may be stealin' our land, takin' what we spilt blood and tears for. And you may be changin' the natural beauty of what God done made, tellin' us what you's fittin' here an' parcelin' over there be better—hidin' yer stealin' behind a pretty picture an' handouts of empty promises. And you may be separatin' kin from kin an' friend from friend, soon by movin' us an' now by the hurt of tryin' to find ways to be livin' with the pain that don't stop . . . don't have no walls to hold it in . . ."

Andy knew. He knew about me and Merry Jo and Verna Mae and Nellie. Knew about Mama and Daddy, Aunt Opal and Uncle Evert, the Arnolds, everybody . . . everybody in Jordan's Bend and beyond. *Andy, how far does them eyes of yers see?*

"But we're carrying this here torch still!" Andy hollered.

"Amen!" come from one hesitant voice somewhere in that room.

"We'uns ain't fergettin' the history of our kin . . ."

Now there were several *amens,* louder than before.

"We ain't stoppin' our way of doin' the everday things. We ain't goin' to be speakin' like no Yankees. We don't aim to be fergettin' the stories that has been passed from kin to kin, generation to generation—the stories that be tellin' who we are an' where we come from an' where we's goin' too. We is Southerners, and you won't be takin' from us what done made us such!"

Shouts arose from all over the room now. Praise echoed. Voices rose as one, truly one.

"They's a fire burnin', flamin' with desire right in this here room. This here torch be us—burnin' with the folk of Jordan's Bend past an' present an' future. An' ye won't be puttin' it out!"

The room like to erupted then as folks stood, shouting and hollering, clapping for Andy and for us—for all of us in Jordan's Bend. Daddy and Mama were standing too, and I saw Daddy blinking tolerable hard.

Surely he was fighting to hold back tears. And Mama wasn't fretting over that atall as tears flowed freely down her flushed cheeks.

Granny Mandy was still setting, but she gazed at Andy with such a look of pride, nodding her head and muttering something over and over, though I couldn't make out what.

When Andy finally lowered his arm and started down the steps from the platform, folks reached out to touch him, patting him on the shoulder and head, applauding still and telling him what a good job he'd done. But before Andy set down, he headed right for Granny Mandy, standing before her, waiting for her to give judgment, it seemed. Only then did Granny stand, and for the first time I saw the mirror image of the two of them before each other.

As they looked at each other eye to eye, I saw the keen sight they both possessed, the way they could "see": Granny, beyond the touchable, and Andy, beyond his years. Stubbornness was carved all about their chins, a sometimes mulelike cussedness that'd like to drive you crazy and at other times a determined persevering that made you know they were *never* going to give up on you, were never going to stop loving you. Both stood square, with shoulders back (even in Granny's bent frame from aging) and feet apart. Like they were ready to take on the world. Sure that they were going to win too.

Did everbody else see it? I wondered. *Did they know that Longfellow's words were Granny's an' Andy's all at the same time? Did everbody here see as I knew from the center of my bein' that Granny Mandy had surely spoken her finest in this here room tonight? That she had passed her burnin' torch to Andy?*

Granny Mandy reached out to him then, placing one palm up against Andy's smooth cheek. He leaned against it for just one moment, closing his eyes and breathing in deeply. When he opened his eyes once again, he looked into Granny's smiling ones. "Ye done said it fine, Andrew," I could hear Granny saying. "Ye done lit the fire again."

There was clapping the rest of the evening for every young'un who sang or acted or read or recited. And when I read my composition on *King Lear*, folks' applause seemed to be right sincere. But there wasn't nothing like the shouting that brought everybody up out of their seats when Andy'd finished his preaching. After the program was over, about everybody come to shake Andy's hand too, pumping it hard and praising him for "speakin' truth," as Mister Harris put it. Even Miz Harris, hard of hearing as she is, shouted at Andy that she hadn't missed "ary a word, but heared it all, an' hollered my *amens*!"

Miz Travis made one last announcement then, thanking folks for coming and inviting them to enjoy the cookies and punch laid out on tables at the back of the room. When most folks moved away to head for the cookies and Andy was finally by himself, I approached him hesitantly.

"Um, Andy, I just be wantin' to say that . . . well, that I was misjudgin' you." I took a deep breath and looked him in the eye. "You done picked a fine poem, Andrew, an' you done a even finer job of recitin' it. I'm right proud to be your sister. An' if James Junior could've been here, well, he would've been mighty proud to be yer brother too." And before I lost my courage—or Andy could run off—I give him a quick kiss on the cheek.

He scowled at me and rubbed at the offended cheek, reddening something awful and looking around to see if anybody else had seen. But seeing that folks weren't paying us no notice just then, he softened a bit, relaxing the scowl, and said under his breath, "Shouldn't be takin' no praise. Granny Mandy helped me."

"I knowed that soon's you started recitin'."

Surprised, he asked, "How? Only Miz Travis knowed that Granny'd helped me pick out this here poem, showin' me its meanin' for Jordan's Bend."

"I just knowed, Andy. Hard to tell anymore where you stop an' Granny Mandy begins. Or where Granny stops an' you begin. One flows into the other and back again, it seems. Wish it were me, but it ain't."

"What?" Andy looked at me in total confusion.

I laughed at him then, appreciating the little boy that still was in him. "Go get you some of them cookies to wolf down before they's all gone. Willie's prob'ly beat you to the best of 'em already. An' try not to be spillin' nothin' on yer Sunday clothes neither!" I teased.

Andy shook his head at me once more before lighting off for the tables of sweets. I was watching more folks come up to praise him when I felt a slight pressure on my shoulder. Turning, I saw Merry Jo, head down, hands hidden in the pockets of her dress.

"Come to say I'm terrible sorry for all I said. Sorry for everthin'." I could hardly hear her, she spoke so softly.

"No, Merry Jo, it's me should be sayin' I'm sorry. You was right. I'm thinkin' I been right proud of my hurtin'. And I weren't wantin' to let go of it any by takin' yer comfortin'." I took a deep breath, struggling to find just the right words. "Folks was wrong to shy away from us when we was needin' them, but I was wrong too to be expectin' more'n what they knowed how to give, just like you said. Seems like neither side was willin' to give." I reached into Merry Jo's pocket, giving her hand a quick squeeze. "'Cept you. At least you tried."

"Tried. And failed. You's right 'bout them times I told you to just trust God. Them words was so easy to say, but there ain't no meanin' behind them, is they?"

"The only meanin' they's givin' to me is more hurt. And guilt." I saw Mister Whitaker and Mister Sherman just then, fairly sneaking out the door. "We all let them Yankees do just what Andy said. Let them pull us apart."

Merry Jo turned towards the door just as they closed it behind them. "Seems a body can breathe easier now that they's gone. I'm wantin' to call them cursed Yankees all kinds of foul names, but ain't we just as bad? We let them do it, Rachael! Why?"

"Don't rightly know. But I'm thinkin' it ain't the Yankees' fault. It's somethin' in us, Merry Jo. And beginnin' in me."

She hugged me then, pulling me to her and whispering in my ear, "Begins in me too. But let's us fight it. Together."

We held onto each other for a moment longer, finding forgiveness and a deepening of our friendship like we'd never known before. When Tommy Lee approached us, we were smiling through tear-filled eyes. "You two be feelin' all right? Ain't catchin' what Nellie an' Verna Mae has, is you?"

"Yer the second one tonight what's asked me that. No, I'm just fine." I glanced over at Merry Jo. "And so's Merry Jo. We's been talkin' some, that's all."

"Gals is always jawin'!"

"An' boys is always eatin'!" Merry Jo teased, poking Tommy Lee in the arm. "Just lookit Willie stuffin' his mouth full. I best go muzzle him before he gulps down ever cookie on them tables. See you all later."

We watched Merry Jo smack Willie's hand and start in to lecturing him, holding back laughter with our hands over our mouths. "You an' Merry Jo workin' out yer diff'rences?"

I nodded. "Got a right good start at them."

"I'm glad for you both. Would you like to tell me 'bout it on the way to home? I asked yer daddy if I could be takin' you an' he give permission."

"I'd surely like that, Tommy Lee. There's so much I'm needin' to talk to you about."

"They's plenty I'm anxious to tell you too." He took my arm and headed towards the cookies. "Come on. Let's us get a couple of Miz

Morgan's ginger snaps before they's done disappeared. Into Willie's mouth, that is!"

We stood near Andy while we ate our ginger snaps (we got to them just in time, seeing how there was only three left—and Willie was ready to grab them up before Tommy Lee beat him to them), listening to compliment after compliment after Andy's reciting. Most of the women folk—and many of the men too—spoke to Andy with tears in their eyes, saying that Andy'd spoke just what their hearts were feeling but couldn't put words to. Andy shook their hands, thanking them all like a gentleman; but he constantly nodded towards Granny Mandy, telling folks that she'd give him help with the "speechin'" (as Andy called it) and the courage to be saying it.

After most everybody had gone on home, me, Merry Jo, Clyde, and Tommy Lee helped Miz Travis put the room back to rights again. We were mostly quiet, not saying much more than "Help lift this, will you?" and "These benches needs be setting back over there" and such as that. Seemed as though the sadness of knowing this was the last time we'd all be here together like this for a school activity hung over us, weighing on us, pushing us all to our inner thoughts and memories of times together.

Just before we went out the door, Miz Travis give us each a hug and a blessing. "Clyde, you've got a good bit of growin' up to be doin' yet, but they's good potential there. Keep that head for figurin'; you can print the neatest column of sums an' add 'em up quicker than anybody I ever knew."

Clyde stared down at his feet as she quickly clasped him to her. "Thankee, Miz Travis," he mumbled shyly, glancing up at her before he again stared down at the floor.

"Merry Jo, you keep practicin' that piano playin'. Not many what play that instrument feel the music like you an' your mama do. Won't be no time at all before you's playin' sounds even the angels will be a stoppin' their singin' to listen to!" Merry Jo was trying so hard not to cry that she couldn't even be saying anything, but she reached out to Miz Travis and they held onto each other for a moment.

Tommy Lee stood a good head taller than Miz Travis now, and she looked up at him, standing on tiptoe to make us all smile in spite of our sadness. "You been a born leader ever since you walked in this here door, Tommy Lee. And that was because you led by example, not askin' any other young'un to do what you wouldn't be doin' first. Them kind of leaders is hard to find—and as valuable as pure gold." She grabbed him to her fiercely, and I saw Tommy Lee hug her back. "Use your gifts wisely, Tommy Lee."

And then Miz Travis moved to me. Wasn't no use to even try to hold back the tears; they'd been flowing ever since I watched Clyde go all mushy and soft over Miz Travis' caring. She put one finger under my chin, pulling it up so I had to look into her eyes. "Mark my words: you'll be the finest teacher this state has ever seen. Because you'll teach your students well. And you'll love 'em even better." Her arms went about me, holding me tight for just one moment before she pushed me away from her too.

Tommy Lee and me walked out the door and down the steps, saying our good-byes to Merry Jo and Clyde, leaving our schoolyard days behind. Tommy Lee helped me into the wagon and we lumbered on down the road a ways, not saying anything for awhile, mourning good days that were over, gone. The only sounds I made were those from sniffling and dabbing at my nose with a tear-soaked hanky until finally I put words to my thinking. "Don't know if you be feelin' this way or not, but it seems like I'm leavin' a part of me behind. Does that make any sense atall?"

"Don't know if it makes any sense, but I'm knowin' what yer sayin'. Guess that be a part of growin' up—leavin' some things behind." He glanced over to me then, his eyes full of caring. "And gatherin' up the new what's up ahead." He cleared his throat. "You ain't cold or nothin' are you?" Tommy Lee asked, suddenly sounding shy.

I grinned to myself. The evening was still tolerable warm, but I supposed the air could be considered just a bit cool. "Um, the air does seem just a mite chilly." I hugged my arms to me, acting chilled.

"Reckon you could move a little closer then. Wouldn't want you to catch no cold on account of bein' out in the night air. Yer mama wouldn't be likin' that atall."

"Nor my daddy neither," I added soberly, moving so I was right next to him.

"Or Granny Mandy."

"And certainly not Ezra nor Nehemiah," I stated, starting to giggle.

"And then they's Eenie, Meanie, Miney, and Moe!" Tommy Lee put in, barely getting all them names out.

"Meanie's gone!"

"Well, she would've cared if she could!" And then we both burst out laughing—laughing in fits so hard we were crying and hugging our stomachs from the hurting of laughing that way.

"Oh, Tommy Lee. It feels good to laugh so. Seems like you just be needin' that now an' then, don't it?" I leaned up against him, enjoying the feel of his arm brushing against mine. It felt natural. Like it was belonging there.

"Takes away some of the heaviness from yer load, I'm thinkin'. My daddy says you can't be no Southerner—an' live among these here poor hills 'specially—if you can't find laughter in the livin'."

"Speakin' on laughin', I seen Daisy go runnin' for you after I done up her hair. An' you was havin' a kindly hard time not to be laughin' at her 'bout somethin'." Tommy Lee grinned. "What was she tellin' you?"

"Wasn't what she were tellin'. Was what she were askin'."

"How's that?"

He shook his head at the remembering. "Said she ain't got no lookin' glass an' was needin' to know if she was pretty." Tommy Lee paused a moment. "No, she were wantin' to know if she were *beautiful*. That were it."

"That Daisy! I swear! What was you sayin' to her then?"

"Said she were indeed right beautiful. Most as beautiful as you was."

I gasped. "You didn't truly, did you?"

Tommy Lee nodded, giving the reins a slap against the mule. "Did too! Got to keep my gals in line—all of them. Daisy best be knowin' you come first, then my mama . . . an' then Daisy!"

I give his arm a good pinch, causing him to holler "Ouch!" and hit the poor mule once again.

"How is your mama, Tommy Lee?"

He smiled. "She's my mama again. Reckon that's the best news I can be sayin', ain't it?" He looked at me, the same peaceful grin easing about his whole face. "Gets up of a mornin' like they was somethin' special to be doin' that day, ever mornin' I'm sayin'. It's like," he paused a moment, glancing towards the woods in his thinking, "like ever day holds a surprise for her. An' she's anxious to be seein' what it might be." Tommy Lee shook his head. "Can't rightly describe it. But it's like she done seen the worst this world can offer. An' now she knows they ain't no more out there—no more to be afraid of. An' so she done decided to *live* her life. Ain't makin' no sense neither, am I?"

"I think I'm understandin'. Remember what Granny Mandy were sayin'?"

"'Bout the fire?"

"Uh-huh. An' that your mama be havin' to choose between the cold fire an' the hot fire. The other world an' this one?"

"Yer granny be understandin' more'n I can even begin to imagine, Rachael."

I sighed. "I try to understand. But I can't be seein' what she sees neither. But I do recollect that Granny Mandy said yer mama must be *choosin'*. An' once she chose—"

"She wouldn't be tempted no more. Yer granny told me the same thing. Ain't been afraid to leave Mama ever since neither. Not since I spoke with your granny, I ain't."

"Tommy Lee, ain't it amazin' that yer mama stared into the fire, an' that Granny told us about the cold fire an' the hot fire. An' then it was the hot coffee what burned her, causin' her to look at your daddy ...."—I grabbed Tommy Lee's arm in my excitement—"an' then Andy spoke on fire tonight. Tommy Lee, he held up his arm like they really was a torch in his hand. I swear I could nigh to see the thing!"

"Didn't rightly know Andy tonight. When I shook his hand, I called him Andrew."

I was quiet a moment, thinking. And then said, softly, "Didn't realize it 'til just now, but I called him Andrew too. Growed up a good bit lately, ain't he?"

Tommy Lee took a deep breath. "Reckon we all has."

"What does the fire mean, Tommy Lee?"

"Bible speaks of its purifyin' ways."

"Purifyin'?"

"Takin' away sin. Cleansin'. They's somethin' 'bout wood, hay, an' stubble burnin', but gold goin' through the fire. Comes out pure."

"Them others burns up, but the gold lasts? Forever?"

"Yup. After it be purified. I reckon that be the point."

I thought on the foxfire then, and the unnatural burning lights that glowed and danced before me. Closing my eyes, I could see it again in all its beauty and glory, drawing me towards it in a most powerful, pulling way. And that pulling was something different than any other wanting I'd known, being of another world, lasting, eternal, *forever*. *But it ain't like that!* I argued back at myself. *You seen that it be dead, just like everthin' else in this world eventually be. Just like Granny Mandy will be someday ...*

"Rachael? Is you all right?" Tommy Lee'd stopped the wagon, pulling it over to the side of the road. He had ahold of my arms and was shaking me.

"What? Why on earth you be jerkin' me about until my teeth be rattlin', Tommy Lee? An' why'd you stop the wagon?"

"Rachael, I been speakin' yer name an' you wasn't hearin' me!" he insisted, panic filling his voice. "You wasn't answerin'. An' you was mumblin' somethin' 'bout fire an' I was afraid that you was . . . that you was doin' what Mama'd done . . . Oh, Rachael. My mama done left once. I couldn't bear it if you was to leave me!"

Tommy Lee pulled me against his chest, wrapping his strong arms about me, hugging me to him protectively. "Oh, Rachael, I'm lovin' you so!" He looked into my eyes for a moment before his lips touched mine. But this time his kiss wasn't no whisper, no soft touch like a dogwood petal or a butterfly's wings. With his arms so tight about me that I could feel his muscles straining, his chest pushing against mine, his breath coming so hard that we were forced to breathe as one, this kiss was a demanding, claiming thing. If there was any doubt in my mind before, there wasn't now. I knew Tommy Lee owned me—heart and body. And there wasn't no other way on earth that I was wanting it to be either.

He released me just as suddenly as he'd hugged me to him, demanding urgent like, "Rachael, why wasn't you answerin' me? You like to scared me to death! What was you thinkin' on so hard?"

I looked away from him, knowing I couldn't lie and yet not wanting to tell him about the foxfire. Not yet. "It's somethin' between me an' Granny Mandy. I can't be tellin' you just now. Can you trust me an' wait—knowin' I'll tell you everthin' when the timin' is right?"

"Is it something what can hurt you?"

I looked into his eyes once again, loving him so for wanting to protect me. Putting my hand to his cheek, I said, "Not physically, it don't."

"You mean it be the heart hurtin' kind?"

I nodded yes.

"Is they some way I can help?"

"I reckon me an' Granny Mandy needs be settin' it to rights. But you are helpin', Tommy Lee. Now. And always."

Tommy Lee turned to pick up the reins once again while I stayed close to him, hugging his arm tight to me. "Best be gettin' on down the road, or I won't be helpin' you none. Yer daddy be trustin' me to get you to home at a decent hour." Since we were just next to the path that led up to the Arnolds' place, he hollered out, "Get on there, mule! No, you ain't goin' to yer stall just yet." We rode in silence for a few minutes before Tommy Lee said, "Must be a terrible hurtful thing if you can't even be speakin' on it."

"'Tis." I stared at the road ahead of us.

"I'll be waitin' whenever yer needin' to talk."

I give his arm a firm squeeze. "I know. Tommy Lee, could you believe how folks talked to us McKenneys tonight—me an' Daddy an' Mama—all on account of Andy's recitin'? They hasn't spoke with us as easy like that since . . . well, since them Yankees first come."

"About time somebody talked some sense into 'em. Took yer Granny Mandy an' Andy to do it." He shook his head in disgust. "Seems to me that were the best preachin' this town done heared in some time. Merry Jo done laid off preachin' too?"

"We both has."

"Both of you?"

"Guess I'm seein' things more clear like now, Tommy Lee. Folks was ill to be avoidin' us, treatin' us like we has the leprosy. An' Merry Jo's advisin' wasn't no help atall. Even hurt." I looked over at Tommy Lee's profile, taking in and enjoying the strength of it and the softness of them eyes at the same time. "But I understand that folks done what they knowed. Give what they was able to. Don't excuse it, but I'm thinkin' I can start to forgive them now."

"Even Verna Mae an' Nellie?"

I sighed. "I'm hopin' to someday. Know I'm still feelin'—what's that word Miz Travis taught us? Skeptical? Feels like I'm crossin' Clear Springs Creek after the spring tide come, like when you can't see the bottom 'cause it's so muddy. An' you's knowin' they's moss on the rocks an' they's terrible slick. Since you can't see 'em atall, you start to step gingerly, terrible careful like."

"And you's expectin' to fall too!"

"Ain't crossed that fool creek yet when she's like that without gettin' drenched. Surely gives O.A. cause to burst into fits. Like to aggravate me to no end when he's crossin' so easy like, not splashin' a drop on him. An' then he goes an' plops through ever mud puddle he can be findin'!"

Tommy Lee chuckled. "Reckon I done the very same."

"I know I'm still terrible put out with Verna Mae an' Nellie, but somehow," I wondered out loud, struggling to put words to my feelings, "it seems I'm feelin' more pity for 'em than anger."

"You's feelin' sorry for 'em when they skipped out on you?" Tommy Lee glanced over at me, amazement written all over his face.

"They missed out on Children's Day, Tommy Lee. The most special one I can ever remember."

"You gals say that ever year."

"But this year I really mean it." I could feel tears threatening as I thought on Andy, standing up there like a man, he was. "I wouldn't of missed seein' an' hearin' Andy for nothin'. Not for havin' Verna Mae an' Nellie there an' givin' our play. Not for all the gold in the whole world."

Tommy Lee made a "hmph" sound. "If you had all the gold in the whole world, you wouldn't be needin' to move. An' Andy wouldn't be needin' to do no speechin' tonight."

An understanding peace settled over me then. Or did it come from inside me, slowly spreading out, fanning out its warmth to pull me in, enclose me with it? "Andy's speechin' were more powerful—more important—than us needin' to move."

Tommy Lee hollered *Whoa*, pulling up the mule yet again. "Is you sayin' that if you could choose between leavin' yer home an' hearin' Andy's recitin', that you'd be choosin' to hear Andy?"

I thought on that a moment and then nodded at him, wondering at myself for saying so. For knowing so.

"Rachael, remember how I told you that I couldn't be findin' God for you? That you needs be findin' yer faith on yer own?"

I nodded again, remembering the pain of that day too well.

"Do you know you's findin' it again? Findin' *Him* again?"

I shook my head, not understanding Tommy Lee's reasoning at all. "They's different. Just because I'm knowin' how much I love Andy don't have nothin' to do with God. Does it?"

Tommy Lee urged the mule on again. "Ain't for me to sort it out for you, Rachael. You needs be thinkin' on all this. Seein' it for what's happenin' in yer heart. What's changin'. An' what's still needin' to be changed."

I leaned heavily against Tommy Lee, wishing I could somehow press the worries out of me, into him, so he could be doing the sorting for me. All the troubling uncertainties were still there: the dark was still hovering just over my shoulder, and the fearing of God was as real as Tommy Lee's shoulder pressing up against mine. But I knew Tommy Lee couldn't sort it out for me. *You must be findin' yer God on yer own, Rachael*, he'd said. Much as I dreaded it, I understood that this was one journey I needs be walking by myself.

"Has your daddy settled on a new farm yet?" Tommy Lee's sudden change of subject caused me to flinch.

"Still lookin'. Me an' Andy keep pesterin' him for answers, but he don't say much. Don't rightly think he's even tellin' Mama everthing about them trips he takes with Mister Whitaker. Mama appears to look at him with the same kind of hungerin' for news as me an' Andy does."

"My daddy's found us one."

"What?" Instinctively I clutched at his arm, holding it even tighter against me.

"It's up north a good bit. Ain't even in Franklin County."

My fear made it hard to talk, and my words come out all short and chopped off like. "But, how can . . . how can you be movin' so far? And when?"

"Daddy says we ain't goin' no place 'til we get all the harvestin' in—corn, fodder, an' the toppin's. Be needin' ever bit we can gather to be startin' up a new farm. An' then too, Daddy's feelin' anxious to be plantin' hay at the new place. A man can't be two places at the same time."

We were rounding the bend just before home now, and I saw the light of our fire shining through the windows. Tommy Lee's news had set me to shivering. *How much longer would this be our place? How much longer would that fire be welcomin' me back to home?* I could feel a tension in Tommy Lee's arm, in all of him. There was more he was needing to be telling me. "What are you sayin' Tommy Lee?"

He turned the wagon into the rutted road by our truck patch and pulled up to a stop. Turning to me and taking my still-clutching, cold hands into his strong, warm ones, Tommy Lee said, "I'm sayin' that Daddy's movin' to our new place right soon." He gripped my hands even tighter, seeing my fear. "Me an' Mama's stayin' put here for now, an' Daddy'll be travelin' back now an' then, hitchin' rides with Mister Whitaker or Mister Sherman whenever he can. I ain't leavin' you, Rachael. Daddy's wantin' me to be workin' the farm here, helpin' Mama, makin' sure she's took care of good. Are you hearin' me Rachael? I ain't leavin' you."

"But you will be!" I could feel panic threatening to rob me of all the peace I'd just been knowing.

Tommy Lee glanced towards the fire-lit windows only a moment before pulling me against him once again. With one arm he held me firmly to him while using the other to gently stroke my hair. Resting his head against the top of mine, he whispered, "Never will forget the first time I took note of yer hair. We was playin' Anty Over at recess an' you was laughin', runnin' to catch the ball. Sun must've been behind a cloud or somethin', because all of a sudden it come bustin' out, shinin' on this hair of yers—makin' it flame like the fire."

I snuggled against him, wondering at my recollection of Mama saying about the same thing. "Ain't never liked my hair. Always wanted hair the color of Mama's."

He pulled it gently through his fingers, feeling of it, caressing it. "Oh no, Rachael. This be part of the special way God be makin' you. Just like addin' them freckles."

I pinched him then, muttering, "Ugh!"

Tommy Lee chuckled, wrapping both arms around me then. "And God made you with yer way of doin' things too. Like the funny way you always sneeze. Seems you's about to explode, an' then you don't make no sound atall!"

"Ain't true."

"Is so. An' the way you hold a book. Like it be pure gold."

I only smiled then, knowing there wasn't no sense to argue with that. "You always be pushin' the hair back from yer forehead."

"Nah. Only do that now an' then."

"You already done it pro'bly a half dozen times since we started out tonight." I grinned up at him. "But who's countin'?"

Tommy Lee smiled back, shaking his head at me. "God made you strong too, Rachael. Though you ain't knowin' that just now. Some folks might say yer strugglin' with the Lord be a sign of weakness, judgin' that you ought to be more weak-willed, merely repeatin', 'It's God's will. It's God's will.' Like some parrot."

"But ain't that so?"

"Rachael, them what do are only play-actin', movin' their lips to say what folks wants to hear, do what folks wants 'em to do. Their heart ain't in it. Their soul ain't in it. They ain't even in the battle what this old sinful world forces a body into. They ain't carin' 'nough 'bout God to be in the fight!"

I pushed away from him so I could look Tommy Lee in the eye. "Are you sayin' that my strugglin', my arguin'—my nigh to fightin' with God be provin' that I *love* Him? Ain't that all mixed up an' backwards?"

"What be folks fightin' over, Rachael?"

I thought a moment, sorting out my understanding. And what Tommy Lee was asking. "Reckon it's what they's believin' in."

"Yes! And what they know is worth fightin' for!"

"Rachael? Tommy Lee? That be you?" Daddy called from the porch. I could see his familiar outline against the light of the window.

"Yes, Daddy, I'm comin'," I answered back, as Tommy Lee hurried to jump down and then come round to help me down from the wagon.

"Hey, Mister McKenney," Tommy Lee called as we walked the short distance to the porch. "I'm much appreciatin' yer lettin' me bring Rachael to home on such a fine evenin'."

Daddy reached out to him, and they shook hands. "Recollect bringin' Miz McKenney home of a night 'bout like this one. Evenin's like this one hadn't oughta be wasted." I just knew Daddy's eyes were sparkling with teasing, even though I couldn't see it in the darkness. "Mighty clear too. Be a right fine day tomorra for layin' by the corn. Talked with yer daddy today 'bout yer new place. Reckon he'll be helpin' you with the corn before he heads up thata way."

"Yes, sir, 'spect so."

"You seen the place yet?" Daddy asked.

"No, sir. But me an' Mama's headin' up this week sometime. See how much work needs doin'. Feels a mite overwhelmin' to be attemptin' to work two farms when one's more'n a body could handle in the first place. Well, reckon I best be headin' to home. Tomorra be comin' quick."

"Holler if we can help ye any," Daddy offered. "Good night, Tommy Lee."

"Good night, Mister McKenney. Good night, Rachael."

"'Night, Tommy Lee." I watched him walk back down to the wagon, knowing his familiar gait even if it was too dark to make out more than his outline against the path. Me and Daddy stood there until the wagon was back out onto the road, calling out our good nights once again as we waved to him. Mama held the door open for us then, and the light from the fire welcomed us.

The dream came again that night—the dream of James Junior slashing at the cornstalks. But this time James Junior not only looked at the flash of the blade reflecting the sun, he stared at it, reveling in it, laughing and enjoying the light dancing in his eyes. Then suddenly James Junior changed into Tommy Lee, and Tommy Lee was urging me, pleading with me to "look into the light, Rachael. You needs be lookin' into the light." But I couldn't look, couldn't bear the searing pain I knew staring into that light would bring. Not until I heard Granny Mandy calling for me, whispering in a soothing voice, "Rachael! The joy's here!" did I dare to glance into the flaming light. And then—oh, the pain to see it!—there was Granny Mandy, being burned, being purified in the flame!

I sat bolt upright in bed, my heart pounding against my nightgown and my breathing coming in terrible gasps for air that I couldn't get enough of, couldn't fill my burning lungs with. Grasping the quilt to my chest, I forced myself to breath more slowly, concentrating on breathing in through my nose, blowing out through my opened mouth. Finally the pounding calmed. My breathing slowed. Opening my eyes, I leaned forward to look out the window towards Granny's cabin, fearing to see—what? Flames surrounding it?

Only the calm of the night greeted me, bathing Granny Mandy's cabin in soothing evening sounds too. The tree frogs were chirping their nightly chorus, and somewhere in the distance the old hoot owl was singing his gentle *who-whoo, who-whooo*. I breathed deeply once more and then snuggled back down underneath the familiar, comforting quilt.

The next morning we all set to work even earlier than usual. Hoeing the corn for the last time of the season was a hard chore, and a long one. We always called it "layin' it by" on account of our work with the corn was now finished for some time—until it was time to strip the fodder from the stalks, cut the toppings (the stalk above where the ear of corn grew) and finally, gather up the ears themselves.

Just like when we first worked our swaths and put in the corn, we each worked a row, moving back and forth across the fields until they were clean of most the weeds, at least. But this year wasn't like the others. Not atall. Seeing how usually we had us a fine, big celebration on this day, challenging our neighbors—Uncle Les and Aunt Samantha, the Pursers (Earl and Daisy's folks), the Owenses, and Tommy Lee's family—to a friendly competition.

Last year had been an especially fine day. I remembered the weather had even smiled on us as a gentle, unusually cooling breeze had blown the whole morning and afternoon, causing puffy, white clouds to block out the sun, and then bring it back in a kindly burst of sunshine. Daddy'd teased all the neighboring men folks, calling them to a challenge. 'Course we didn't really bet nothing; it was all in fun. But at the end of the day, the family who'd finished layin' by first was declared the winner—and set to letting every other family know they were done by ringing the dinner bell, banging on a old bucket, clanging hoes together, and hollering to beat the band.

The McKenneys'd claimed the prize last year, and I reckon we made enough noise for three families, at least. James Junior took to whooping and hollering so that me and Granny Mandy couldn't do much more than set and laugh at him. The women folk had cooked up a feast to celebrate, and once we were all finished (us McKenneys had gone around to the neighbor's fields once we were done, helping them to finish up), we ate chicken and taters and gravy and pie to our hearts' content.

I recollect giving Tommy Lee several shy glances that evening. And teasing him about us beating his family fair and square. He'd promised that the Arnolds would "whup you McKenneys terrible" this year. And now this year had come. Only there wasn't no competition, no laughing, no ringing of bells, or beating on no buckets. Because there wasn't anything to be celebrating this year.

We were making good progress down the Y-shaped field that afternoon when Granny Mandy suddenly stopped her hoeing, staring off towards the direction of her cabin. "They's Yankees comin'. Aimin' to set foot on my place when they comes too. I can feel it in my bones!" And she set off at a quick pace down the hill, supporting her weight with the hoe again.

Daddy glanced over to Mama for just a moment before taking off after her. "Mama?" I asked, questioning what we should do too.

"Best be seein' to her. And see what them Yankees is up to now too. Just leave your hoes here."

We hurried over the rotten footbridge that crossed Dogwood Creek, and then as we come down to the road, we saw Mister Whitaker's car and a big truck setting by Granny Mandy's cabin. "I didn't even hear the car comin'," Mama muttered. "Yer granny's hearin' is better'n all of ours."

"Ain't her hearin', Mama," I said. "It's her seein'."

Andy immediately went to look over the truck, walking around it slowly and marveling at its size, asking, "Ain't nothin' like the Hickmans', is it? Lookit the size of them tires! What they needin' such big ones for?"

Me and Mama just stood there a moment, though, wondering at what had become of Granny Mandy and Daddy. Until we heard something that made Mama and me both look at each other with dread. And caused Andy to come running to us in alarm too.

"No you ain't!" Granny'd hollered, with the sound of absolute fury in her voice.

Now we knew where to find them, and me, Mama, and Andy all took off running frantic like, our panic and fear making us trip over rocks and stumps, abandoned tools, and trash littered here and there. When we came to the family graveyard, Mama put her arms out against me and Andy, blocking us from going any farther. The three of us stood there together, breathing so hard that we all probably couldn't go much farther anyway, we were so out of breath.

Mister Sherman and Mister Whitaker were there, along with two other men—both wearing them government clothes—who were toting shovels. Daddy had ahold of Granny Mandy, had actually wrapped his long, strong arms about her and was keeping her back and away from Mister Whitaker. Pure rage was pouring from her face, streaming from her eyes. She had each hand clenched into a fist and she was straining against Daddy's bonds, leaning towards Mister Whitaker like she would've tore him limb from limb if Daddy'd only let her go.

"Ye won't be touchin' 'im! I'm tellin' ye I won't let ye touch 'im—nor my babies neither!" Granny Mandy hissed between clenched teeth. "Let me go, James Otis! I'm aimin' to fetch my gun! I'll either kill 'em here or they'll be a-killin' me. Ain't goin' to touch my Mister McKenney!"

My confusion at what was happening suddenly cleared to a sickening understanding. Them foul Yankees had come to move the graveyard. They were moving the family plot to higher ground on account of the coming flooding lake. I glanced over to Mama and saw the sick look on her face too. But then something caused me and Mama both to look over at Andy, sensing that Andy didn't appear to be feeling sick or nauseous nor nothing like that. Instead, Andy was just like Granny Mandy. He was mad. No, he was *furious*.

"Andrew," Mama whispered urgently, putting strength and authority in her voice. "Andrew, you stay put. You hear?"

Andy didn't look up at Mama. His face grew even redder, and he also strained at the arm that held him back from Mister Whitaker.

"Andrew?" Mama grabbed at him now.

His eyes narrowed and he took a deep breath before answering, "Yes, Mama." Andy also spoke through clenched teeth, and I saw the familiar muscle twitching in his cheek, a sure sign that Andy's anger was checked—but only temporarily and there still, sure as anything.

"Mr. McKenney, I thought you surely would have explained to your mother by now that we intended to do this." He stood there with a clipboard and papers in his hand, pointing to them. "After we were here surveying the entire graveyard, writing concise notes and taking detailed pictures so that we had a very accurate record of just who was buried here and how we needed to proceed, well, I would have thought you'd have realized this step—the actual moving—was coming. And needed to be addressed for those who are . . . more sensitive, shall we say?"

Mister Whitaker's voice sounded slippery. Cool as Spring Tide Creek. *And kindly insinuatin'*, I fumed to myself. *He's managin' to make all this sound like Daddy's fault—like Daddy's to blame for Granny's anger. And callin' Granny Mandy sensitive that way. Makin' it sound like some bad word. Mister Whitaker'd be feelin' right sensitive over his whole body if Daddy'd only let Granny at him—let her go to tusslin' with him!*

"And it's the right thing to do, too, the civil thing to do," Mister Whitaker continued. "Mrs. McKenney, you couldn't visit your husband's grave if it were at the bottom of the lake, now could you?"

Granny Mandy glared at him, making her eyes nigh to slits. "Any fool'd know ye wouldn't be needin' to desecrate this here ground in the first place iffin ye weren't plannin' on floodin' the best land in the whole blessed county!" I saw Daddy whisper something to her, but I couldn't hear what he said. She seemed to push against him a mite less, but the look of fury still set about her features.

Mister Whitaker turned to Mister Sherman, nodding at him and the other two men. They unlatched the rickety gate and passed through the fence, trampling over the profusion of flowers mixed with weeds that grew everywhere among the stones of the graves. They headed straight for Grandaddy's gravehouse. And proceeded to pull it apart.

I remembered Granny Mandy caressing those words—"James Henry McKenney, God Bless Him That Lies Here"—as she traced them with her finger. And now rough, uncaring hands of strangers—dreaded Yankees!—pulled them down.

Once more I looked over at Granny, expecting to see her fairly storm out of Daddy's restraining arms and light after those men. But instead I saw her close her eyes, leaning heavily against Daddy. I drew in my breath, closing my eyes too, not wanting to see the old boards torn down. Not Grandaddy's gravehouse. Even more, desperately not wanting to see Granny Mandy lose a battle. Not see her weak and helpless. Not *my* granny.

The tearing sound of the boards coming lose was awful, wrenching. Seemed like them old weathered boards hung onto each other, fighting the removing just as we were fighting it—inside, at least. Finally the terrible tearing sounds were over, only to be replaced with the even rhythm of the shovels digging in the dirt, hitting our dark, rich southern clay and then tossing it aside, so careless like.

"Mama?" Daddy asked, gentle caring and deep concern sounding in his voice. Granny Mandy sagged against Daddy now, weariness covering the whole of her. "Andrew, come help me get your granny back to her cabin. We's seen enough here."

Andy come rushing to them, grabbing at one of Granny Mandy's arms while Daddy held onto the other. But Granny only took two or three steps before she nearly stumbled to the ground, causing me and Mama to rush towards her in our fear and concern. Daddy grabbed her up into his arms then, carrying her like she wasn't no more than a tiny babe.

I remembered then how Granny had described our kins' funeral processions to me, how the men carried the casket to the newly dug grave, the women and children following behind, singing hymns, softly. We made a procession now too, the five of us. Daddy carried Granny Mandy (and I noticed how easily he did so, partly because Daddy was so strong and partly because Granny'd grown even thinner lately, I suddenly realized), and Mama, Andy, and me tagged along behind.

The sound of every shovelful of dirt echoed in my ears, and I watched one hand of Granny Mandy's dangling down, helpless like from Daddy's arms, bouncing listlessly as he carried her over the littered and overgrown path to Granny's cabin.

The clouds had gathered this afternoon, hiding the sun and giving us relief from its sweltering rays. Now it suddenly burst forth again, lighting on Daddy's head. And Granny's listless, dangling hand. I grimaced, shielding my eyes from its brightness.

9

The lamb has turned to lion, wild,
With nothing tender, gentle, mild,
Yet once again I am a child,
*   A babe newborn, a fresh creation,*
*   Flooded with joy, swept by elation.*

Daddy tenderly placed Granny Mandy on her straw mattress, and once again I noted how small Granny was, seeing how that old bed didn't give none atall with her slight frame pressed upon it. I tucked her most favorite friendship quilt with the faded blues, yellows, and reds up around her shoulders, worrying after her, touching her constantly, gently, here and there. Mama'd gone to the stove right off to fix tea, and Andy was busy stoking the fire in the fireplace, adding wood and going outside to tote in more. Each of us busied ourselves about the room somehow, hovering over Granny Mandy or fetching this or that, trying to find something that would help, something that would bring back the lively, ornery Granny that we desperately loved. Desperately needed.

Daddy set in the rocker he'd pulled over by her bed, steadily rocking back and forth, making it creak much more'n Granny did when she'd be setting on it. I saw Daddy suddenly lean forward towards Granny and then he reached out to take one of her hands.

"Land sakes, what am I a-doin' abed at this hour o' the day?" Granny asked. She sounded a bit bossy. Sassy. Normal and wonderful. I smiled at her.

"You done took sick, Ma," Daddy answered. He was talking tolerable slow, and I could tell he was choosing his words carefully.

Granny Mandy sat up, looking at all of us, shaking her head. "Don't recollect more'n bein' so durn mad at them Yankees I were ready to skin 'em alive iffin I could catch 'em." She looked over at Daddy. "They still on my property?"

"Now Granny Mandy, you can't be traipsin' after them no more today. I done told you, you took sick. Need be restin' a spell. Miz McKenney, that tea done brewed yet?"

Mama come carrying a steaming tin mug to Granny. "Done just now an' good an' hot." She glanced over to Daddy. "You cravin' some too?"

"Best not. Andy, me, an' Rachael got hoein' to be doin' an' then chorin' after that. Ain't goin' to do itself, that be for sure." Daddy took a deep breath as he got up out of the old rocker. He looked down once more towards Granny. "Sure you not feelin' poorly no more? I ain't leavin' you 'til I know you's all right."

Granny Mandy waved him away, shaking her head at him. "Take more'n fool Yankees to keep me down. Now let me set in my rocker fer a spell. Move it over there by the fireplace. Andy, you been tendin' to my fire so kindly like?" She nodded at Andy, smiling. "Done tole ye before, they ain't nothin' my rocker, a good cup o' tea, this here fireplace, an' a good talkin' with my Lord won't cure. See if they ain't."

Daddy reached out to help her walk towards the warm, now blazing fire, but again Granny Mandy waved him off, giving him a stern look to boot. She plopped down heavily into the favorite rocker that Andy'd moved next to the fireplace and then took a generous sip from the steaming mug. "Tastes right fine, Mae," Granny said, taking a moment to close her eyes and breathe in the sweet-smelling steam. "Reckon you put a secret ingredient in it, didn't ye?"

Mama looked confused. "A secret ingredient?"

Granny's eyes suddenly popped open and she looked over at me, grinning. "Plumb fergot. That's me an' Rachael's secret." She rolled her eyes and then winked at me. "James Otis, now you be gettin' on back to them fields. Andy, you too. A settin' goose ain't got no feathers on its belly. Us McKenneys needs be showin' folks that we aim to beat 'em layin' by our corn again this year. I'll be a-waitin' to hear ye clangin' them buckets an' ringin' the bell."

"But Granny Mandy, we ain't—" Andy began, before Daddy cut him off.

"Hush, Andrew! We's headin' out right now, Granny, an' we'll be winnin', you can count on that." Daddy gave Granny a big smile, but once he'd turned towards Mama, there was worry and concern written right plain on his face. He whispered something to her and then motioned to me and Andy. "Ye both best be comin'. Got a good bit more hoein' to finish off."

I wasn't wanting to leave Granny, but Mama nodded at me and then gestured towards Granny Mandy, reassuring me that she'd be staying to watch over her. Still, I hesitated, giving Granny one more long look before reaching out to squeeze her arm.

"You go 'head, Rachael. After I finish this here tea, I'll just be restin' my eyes a spell." She closed her eyes again. "Fer just a spell."

She sighed, and I watched her breathe evenly for a few moments before I saw her head start to nodding. Just in time I reached out to grab the mug, or it would have clattered across the hearth like it'd done once before. Granny Mandy slept peacefully now, with her gnarled hands setting easy like on her lap and her chin resting on her chest. Her mouth was open just a bit and she snored softly. Mama fetched the quilt and gently wrapped it about her once more.

"Don't be frettin', Rachael," Mama whispered to me as she tucked the old quilt under Granny's bare feet. "I'll be stayin' here with her. Yer daddy needs you to the fields."

"Yes, Mama." I put the dented tin mug in the sink and then, after opening the screen door, turned once more to check on Granny Mandy. The glow of the fire outlined her tilted head, and I saw her shoulders gently rising and falling beneath the frayed quilt. "Keep breathin' easy like, Granny," I whispered. "Please keep on a-breathin'."

We worked the fields hard that day, not finishing layin' by until the sun was well behind the hills and it was nearly dark. But once we were done, we clanged our hoes, banged our buckets, and even rung the bell. Last year we'd done those things with such joy in our celebrating and fun. This time we only done it for Granny Mandy, and I felt sick going through those motions. Even Andy—who generally loved ringing that bell for any reason—pulled the rope with a blank, empty look about his face.

The next day, me, Mama, and Andy went to see what the government men had done to the family burial plot. Nearly took my breath away to be seeing the fence and gate same as always. But the only thing that fence protected now was a couple dozen mounds that were filled-in holes. There wasn't any more gravehouses nor rotted wood crosses nor smoothed, carved rocks saying who was buried there. They'd toted off all of those things. The flowers that we'd planted here and there were either uprooted in the digging or else covered up when them filthy Yankees had trampled over them, filling in the now empty graves.

Mama'd groaned out loud when she saw it, and shaking her head at the terrible pillaging before us, said, "I knowed they moved 'em on account o' it were needful, an' they be restin' now next to the church an' all. But I can understand yer granny's wantin' to fight 'em off. Somehow it just ain't seemin' right to be movin' the dead. This here land be where they was laborin' an' birthin' an' dyin'. I'm thinkin' they'd be wantin' to stay here. Even if that was meanin' they was a flood o' water on top of their graves."

"But Daddy was always remindin' Granny Mandy that they ain't here no more," Andy pointed out. "That's right, ain't it? They is in heaven, Mama."

"You's right, Andy. Yer kin was all God-fearin' people. They was taught to love God an' they taught their young'uns to love Him too. They's in heaven, I'm knowin' that."

"Then why was you sayin' they wouldn't be wantin' to be moved? I wanted to tussle with them foul Yankees. Wanted to help Granny Mandy stop 'em! Why wouldn't you an' Daddy let us?"

Mama stooped down then, reaching out to tenderly caress one remaining daisy that was poking through the fence. "Yer daddy's been readin' to us from the book o' Samuel of a evenin'. Just heared where Samuel"—she glanced over to Andy and then me—"he were a judge, yer knowin'—where this here Samuel went before the Israelites after Saul had done been annointed their king. Well, Samuel was wantin' to point out to 'em that he'd been a honest judge. So he asked 'em if he'd stole anythin' from 'em."

"Samuel was a honest judge, weren't he?" I asked.

"That he was. Israelites done answered him no, sayin' that Samuel'd not took anythin' atall from 'em. Ain't stole no oxen or donkeys or cheated 'em nor took no bribes. An' then Samuel said somethin' what I ain't been able to forget ever since I first heared yer daddy read it. Keep on a-hearin' it repeatin' over an' over in my head."

I leaned down next to Mama then so I could be watching her face close like. Seemed to me that Mama'd always taken God's Word just as it come. As truth, saying just what we were to be living by and because of that, part and parcel of her everyday living. Mama'd never ever told us she was doubting it none or even worrying over some part, trying to work out in her mind how the words were fitting into what had happened to her, was happening to us now. Like I was doing. So I was most anxious to be hearing what she was saying.

"Samuel said that he wasn't holdin' nothin' in his hand. *Nothin' in his hand.*" Mama looked at me then, but she wasn't just staring into my eyes. I swear she was peering deep inside. Into my soul. "Means he hadn't stole nothin', wasn't covetin' nothin', wasn't holdin' onto nothin' in this world. Had his eyes set on doin' right." She looked back up at the destroyed graveyard again then. "Had his eyes set on his God." Mama reached down then, picking up a clump of dirt that the Yankees had thrown, and I recollected so clearly the time I'd clutched this clay in my hand when we were planting Granny's truck patch, the time Granny'd grabbed up a handful too on corn planting day. "Reckon I been wantin' to hold this here land so tight in my fist—" She squeezed the dirt between whitened knuckles until it come fairly squishing out around her slender, work-roughened fingers. "So tight that them Yankees couldn't be takin' it from me ever, couldn't be sendin' us packin' an' away from this here land like no tenant farmers. My land!" Mama suddenly cried out with an anguished longing that once again reached nigh to my soul. She raised that fist now, and me and Andy stared at her in bewilderment, waiting.

Is this my mama—the same mama that I seen drink in the reassurin' comfortin' of the Psalms mornin' after mornin'? I asked myself. *Can she be strugglin' with God too? How can she be knowin' Him them times—and doubtin' Him now?*

But after only a moment she opened that clenched fist, letting whatever bits of dirt that were left slip from her fingers and sprinkle onto the white petals of the daisy before they fell back to the ground. "Had to be learnin' I done stole it," Mama said softly. "My hands wasn't empty like Samuel's be."

"Mama, you an' Daddy never took nothin' what wasn't yers yer whole life!" Andy angrily argued. "You ain't sayin' that Daddy's kin stole this here land, is you? 'Cause this here property been belongin' to our kin for generations! Anyone been thievin', it's been them filthy Yankees, takin' from us just like they always done!"

Mama stood up then, wiping the remaining rich soil clinging to her hand onto her starched white apron. "Andy, Rachael," she looked us both over good, saying, "this here soil only be belongin'—truly belongin'—to One. Be God's land, to use as He sees fit. Reckon we ain't got no choice but to follow what them government people says. I knowed changes was comin'—I feared 'em long ago—an' I can't be sayin' I'm likin' 'em any now. But them Yankees ain't doin' no more than what the Almighty's allowin'. Time we be lookin' at ourselves, askin', 'What do I be holdin' in my hand?'"

Seemed like anger and hurt come fairly bursting out of me then, and I threw my rage at Mama. "Then yer sayin' all them folks—Miz Hickman an' Preacher Morgan an' even Willie Snodderly—was right. That God be doin' this to us to be teachin' us a lesson! That God be punishin' us!"

Mama whipped around to face me, and she took my face between her hands, holding me so tight I couldn't look anywhere but into the piercing blue of her eyes. "Now you listen here to me, Rachael McKenney." She glanced over to Andy for only a moment before looking intently at me again, adding, "And you best be rememberin' my words too, Andrew. I ain't never sayin' God be a punishin' God, lookin' round to find ways to be ill to His children, teachin' 'em lessons by makin' 'em hurt. Or leavin' 'em to be guessin' what it is that He's wantin' 'em to change, guessin' what sins they's doin' to be repentin' of. Bible's right clear 'bout what's sin. And when we's sinnin', then we's knowin' the consequences for the doin'. We's responsible for them sins—like folks not trustin' us on account o' our lyin' or our young'uns goin' hungry if we's too lazy to be workin' our land. Them things be the sinnin', an' we be responsible for the consequences.

"But they's evil in this here world too, Rachael, an' sometimes troubles come just because they is. Just because! Amazin' thing is this," and then Mama's sharp eyes went all glassy and soft, filling suddenly with tears. "Amazin', lovin' thing about our God is that . . . that He be doin' just what them verses say about 'all things workin' together for good.' Our God can be takin' them hurtin' things, them things what tears into yer very bein', makin' you feel pain that wraps round you an' in you an' through you. Pain that Satan was meanin' to be doin' just that too! Why, then God can use them hurtful things to be showin' you where you has weaknesses, showin' you where you needs be growin'.'"

Mama reached out to Andy with one hand, and as she gently rubbed each of us on one cheek, she stared towards the river where the Yankees had cut dozens of trees, leaving bare stumps everywhere. "What them government people is doin' has tore my heart. I seen 'em slowly kill this here land, hurt yer Daddy an' you two. Seen 'em fairly kill yer granny." She stopped a moment and I held my breath, taking a shivering fit after she'd said *kill*. "I ain't never wantin' to know no hurt like this again, but yet . . . yet I know He's teachin' me an' showin' me an' lovin' me through the days an' days of endless hurtin'. An' I'm knowin', truly knowin' what Joseph were meanin'."

Mama's voice had got so soft that I could barely hear her. "What's that, Mama?" Andy asked, with the same softness in his words. He gazed up at her with a look of complete trust and awe on his face.

"Joseph was speakin' to his brothers, forgivin' 'em. Even lovin' 'em." Once more Mama looked into Andy's eyes and then mine. "Said that they was meanin' it for evil, but God were intendin' it for good." She breathed deeply and then turned once more to look over what was left of our family plot. "God ain't doin' this to us for the punishin'. I even reckon He's feelin' the hurt when we does. But God's also usin' this here terrible wrenchin' an' tearin' apart"—Mama gestured towards the empty mounds, waving her arm out over the fence—"He be usin' all this for good." She looked at me with a puzzled expression on her face. Like she was amazed, yet pleased somehow. "*For good.*" Once again her voice was full of emotion. "That be amazin' love."

That night I prayed—or tried to—for the first time in so long. "Dear God," I began, as I held up my hands before me, examining them in the light of the moon that showed through the window across my bed. "Seems I been holdin' onto a tolerable amount of things. And I'm thinkin' I'm not givin' them up as much as You's just plain takin' them away from me!" I paused a moment, my hurt and anger making thinking itself hard work. My attempts to pray were like sharp thrusts of words that fairly exploded from me.

"Even what I was believin' about You—You took that away, and I'm tryin' to ... tryin' to find You again. Know You again. I'm wantin' to believe what Mama said. Like Joseph. But they's somethin' there still. Somethin' what I can't—just can't wade through to find You." Once more I stopped, and then asked, out loud, "Are You really there ... lovin' me?"

There wasn't no answer. Only the gentle breeze blowing at my gingham curtains and the moonlight come pushing through my opened window. And when I slept, the all-too-familiar dream came again. James Junior slashed at them same stalks, and the light of the sun flashed with his jerking this way and that. Once again James Junior suddenly become Tommy Lee, and all the while I was yearning for him to put away the blade so he could pull me into his comforting, reassuring arms and kiss me tenderly. But Tommy Lee kept cutting still, telling me I had to look into the light, needed to be looking into the light. But this time I knew. I knew what was there. It was Granny Mandy in the flame. And I wasn't going to look, wasn't about to see her being burned, even if it was her purifying!

Then the voice came again, a voice calling me so softly, so tender, so gentle. "Come look into the reflection of my eyes. The joy's here!" the soothing voice whispered. I wasn't knowing who it was. But I couldn't resist the tender urging, and once more I looked into the blinding light, the searing pain, and this time I saw—not Granny Mandy, but a mirror, a reflection of me. I was staring into my own eyes!

"Rachael! Rachael, wake up!" Andy whispered hoarsely, shaking me roughly about the shoulders.

"What? Was I callin' out?" I asked him, setting up and remembering too vividly the dream that had become as real to me as being awake. "I was dreamin'."

"Was you ever! An' callin' out? Like to made me jump outta bed, you scared me so." Andy's hair was plastered to his scalp in some places and sticking up all funny like in others. In spite of the terrible dream, I still grinned at him as I watched him rub grubby fists against sleep-filled eyes. "What on earth was you dreamin' 'bout, anyway?"

"Um. Can't remember."

"That's a lie."

"Why are you sayin' that? How would you know?"

"On account o' this ain't the onliest time you done woke me up. Hate to think how many times I heared you. I'm thinkin' you'd recollect right well what you done been seein' that many times."

"You've heard me before?"

He rolled his eyes. "That's what I said, ain't it? Now what are you dreamin'?" I hesitated, and Andy went on, "One time I was dreamin' 'bout haints night after night, an' Granny Mandy done tole me that sometimes it helps to be tellin' somebody else what you's dreamin'. Somehow the tellin' makes you know it ain't real. Makes 'em stop." He frowned at me. "And I'm figurin' I ain't gettin' a good night's sleep 'til yer doin' the same. Now what is the blamed thing about?"

I took a deep breath, quickly asking myself, *Why not tell Andy? He won't understand it no more than me, and maybe it will help me to stop—show me that it ain't real, like Andy said.* I stared out the window so I wouldn't have to see Andy giving me a wondering look if he was to think I was going all queer like or something. "Well, all right. But it ain't about haints or nothin' atall like that. It don't make no sense. And yet it scares me somethin' awful," I whispered. Pausing just a moment more, I gathered my courage to begin putting it to words. "James Junior is cuttin' away at cornstalks, and it's such a bright day and his blade is so shiny that it keeps reflectin' the light of the sun. Flashin' so that it hurts yer eyes, you know?"

I glanced at Andy, and he nodded.

The moonlight streamed through my window and the breeze had gathered strength too, making the curtains slap even louder against the sill. I stared at the curtains flapping. "Well, then right sudden like it ain't James Junior no more. It's Tommy Lee. And for some reason he's wantin' me to look at the flashin' light what would be so painful. Keeps pleadin' with me to do it, sayin', 'Look into the light, Rachael!'"

"Did you do it?" Andy asked. When I turned to answer him, I didn't see any doubting or teasing even written about his eyes. Instead, I saw the same look of trust and awe that I'd noticed when Mama was telling us about Joseph.

"Didn't want to, but then I heared Granny Mandy callin' me, tellin' me—what was it?—'the joy's here'? Yes, that's what she said. But wait a minute. This time it was different. It weren't Granny Mandy callin', it were another voice, one soothin' an' soft an' . . ."

"Lovin'?"

"Yes! How was you knowin' that?" I looked at Andy in amazement.

He shrugged his shoulders. "What happened when you looked? What was you seein'?"

I thought a moment, trying to put together what was different this time from all the dreams before. "When Granny called to me, I seen her burnin', Andy. Oh, it were awful!" Tears come to my eyes, and my throat and chest felt tight.

"Were she cryin' out to you then? Was you tryin' to help her? Is that why you was callin' out in yer sleep?"

"No . . . no. It wasn't like that atall. She were in the flame—but she weren't painin'. She weren't wantin' out. She was wantin' to be there!" The tears started again then, trickling from my eyes and down my cheeks. When I heard muffled sobs, I suddenly realized Andy was crying too. Looking over at him, I saw his tousled head buried on his arms, shoulders shaking. I put my arms around him. "Oh, Andy, I'm so sorry! It don't mean nothin'. They's no reason for us to be cryin'."

Andy looked up at me through tear-filled eyes. "Oh yes, they is. You know good's I does that Granny's dyin'. An' she's wantin' to! None of us can be admittin' it of a day, so we's dreamin' it at night. Knowin' it be goin' to happen."

"No, it ain't! Don't you be sayin' that! And listen, Andy, this time I didn't dream that Granny was in the flame. It was diff'rent tonight because of the other voice that called. It weren't Granny Mandy. And when I looked I seen . . . I seen a mirror."

Andy wiped at his eyes and nose, giving me a skeptical look. "A mirror?"

"A mirror. And in it I seen me, an' I ain't dyin', Andy!" I put my nose right up to his. "I ain't dyin'!"

"Don't make no difference. Granny is, an' they ain't nothin' you or me or Daddy or Mama can be doin' 'bout it! Nothin'!" And then he took off running to his bed, where I could hear him crying softly from beneath his quilt.

I just set there for a moment, debating if I should be going to him, comforting him. But finally I decided that'd most likely only make him angry, thinking he needed time alone for his grieving. Time alone to be crying out his hurt like I'd done lately so many times.

Eventually the creaking of his bed stopped, there wasn't no more sniffing nor hiccuping, and the loft was quiet once again. The only sounds were the flapping of my gingham curtains in the breeze and Andy's steady breathing. I closed my eyes, but like Mama, questions kept on repeating over and over in my head. *What are you holdin' in yer hands?* the voice asked. And then when I'd try to understand like

Mama'd done, try to learn from these hurtful times so that I could be feeling close to my God again, I only heard one thing, one despairing cry that wasn't an answer atall. *Granny's dyin'*! it said, filling me with dread and fear. *Granny's dyin'*!

For the next several days, me and Andy looked in on Granny Mandy often, dreading to see our fears come true, relieved to be seeing they weren't. We were nearly tripping over each other running in and out her door until Granny'd had enough and put a stop to it, telling us both to be giving her some peace.

And then as the days wore into weeks, we were also distracted by Daddy's constant trips with Mister Whitaker to be finding a farm for us. Eventually Daddy did settle on one that he was wanting Mama to see, and then me and Andy took a drive in the dreaded black car to see it too. Granny Mandy still wouldn't have none of it; either she just plain wouldn't be speaking of moving atall or else she'd give us the same stubborn answer: "Done warned them Yankees. They'll have to be floatin' me outta here."

The farm was a mite smaller'n ours, but it was good soil, seeing how it also was on the river. The family that'd owned the place was about all killed in a terrible fire (except for one young'un, who was taken in by her aunt and uncle), and they didn't have other kin to take over the farming. So they'd just put it up for sale when the TVA heard about it through the county offices. Daddy and Mama hated profiting off of others' loss, but as Mister Whitaker put it, "Somebody will purchase the farm, Mr. McKenney. And it might as well be a good farmer—one who'll appreciate this good soil—like you."

Since the cabin'd plumb burned to the ground, leaving only the charred and lonely looking chimney standing, Mister Whitaker promised us the government would help us to build one of those new cinder block houses. The barn wasn't much better off, being so old and tolerable run down. But Daddy said that wasn't as important as good soil, and this farm did have that—dark, rich ground like we were use to for growing good, healthy crops. Of course, there was the usual assortment of sheds, a smokehouse, a chicken coop, and the like scattered everywhere. And we knew the springhouse would have to be rebuilt too, seeing how it also was about to tumble down—although the water coming from the spring itself was clear and sweet tasting.

Everything about the new farm was either pleasing to Mama and Daddy or what wasn't could be fixed by Daddy's hard-working, skilled hands. It had gentle hills and a good view of the river going by. The pasture was still growing thick grass what Eenie, Miney, and Mo could eat from to their hearts' content. And it was a right pretty farm, being pleasing to the eye. I had no right to be complaining nor finding fault with the place. But every mile we traveled to the farm for that first trip—and every trip that was to come—was terrible painful. Because we were driving way south. And Tommy Lee's new farm was north.

It was rare that I got to see Tommy Lee over these past weeks too. He was busy nearly every minute, it seemed, working the fields, helping his mama about the house, and packing up and moving what was needed at the new place. Sometimes he hitched a ride up north to help his daddy there, leaving Miz Arnold for only a day or two at the most, seeing how neither him nor Mister Arnold was wanting her to be alone for long.

And though I dreaded the thought of moving so much that I wasn't calling the farm *ours* yet (stubbornly referring to it always as merely "the new place"), I was wanting to leave Jordan's Bend behind for at least one reason: our once beautiful home was slowly being killed, destroyed, pillaged by them Yankees. Granny Mandy said it was blasphemous, what they were doing. I couldn't be disagreeing with her none.

Trees were being cut everywhere, leaving lonely looking, ugly stumps standing for miles and miles up and down that once beautiful riverbank. Looked plain eerie to see them stumps where there was once woods and birds, coons, rabbits, squirrels, deer—every type of wildlife. Now those critters'd mostly moved on somewhere, on account of there wasn't any protecting cover from mere shaved-off stumps, no food for the gathering where there wasn't any leaves or nuts or fruit, no homes for the building where there wasn't any limbs or shade even when there wasn't . . . wasn't *nothing*.

The Harrises' property was especially awful to be looking at, and passing it every time we went to town was terrible hurtful. Mister and Miz Harris'd moved in with one of their daughters, leaving behind a farm that didn't have much that was worth toting along with them. Oh, they'd carted off furniture (both Mister and Miz Harris had a favorite rocker and they insisted upon taking their rusted and bent old bed frame), some tools, a cow, and one stubborn old mule. But they'd sold most everything else—what little there was worth selling. Or worth buying, from other folks' view.

And then the Yankees had come. First they'd tore down the ramshackle cabin, giving the wood to anybody who was needing it for burning, which was all it was good for. The crooked chimney they left standing, and even the stones the Harrises had used to line a pathway to the door were still there. Marking a path to nothing but a gaping hole that was once a foundation. Looked terrible pitiful to see just a path to an empty place with a crooked chimney.

The Harrises left behind old lard buckets, kerosene pails, pieces of frayed rope, useless harnesses beyond repair, broken tools, torn screens, and scraps of all sorts of things scattered here and there across the bare, trampled red clay. Some of those things people came and took, thinking there'd be a use for them sometime, somewhere. Southerners are like that, thinking there's bound to be a need, eventually, for just about anything, I'm thinking. But even Southerners couldn't be finding possible uses for some of them old things, and they were left laying about, making the place look like it'd been suddenly deserted. Like the Harrises had just been snatched away, right quick like.

Neighbors who didn't have to move were helping with the cornfield. What there was of it, that is. The feeble rows of stalks were so sparse, and the corn so small, there wasn't going to be much needing to be harvested. Miz Harris' truck patch was right pitiful too, but neighbors were picking and eating whatever ripened. Miz Harris had welcomed them to it since they couldn't be traveling back for any, seeing how they were living all the way over to the other side of the county now.

The Owenses had already moved out also (they'd gone to live with kin, too, since they were both eighty-some years old), and so had Earl and Daisy's family, the Pursers. Only those folk had took with them absolutely *everything*. There wasn't anything but stumps and a few rocks left scattered about their places.

Since the Pursers were tenant farmers, working our land, they weren't rightly supposed to be taking the cabin and sheds and the like. But Daddy'd told them to, knowing how hard they had it, seeing how they didn't have land to sell to be buying another farm. So they picked up and took whatever they could carry along, still hoping someday to be owning a place of their own.

Mostly I avoided the north side of our cornfield where the Pursers used to live, but if I did have to be walking up there for some reason, I hated seeing the empty, abandoned place. It looked as though some mighty hand had come along, wiping the earth clean of any signs that anybody had ever lived there, worked there, played, laughed, and cried there. And whenever I thought of Daisy, tears come to my eyes. Recollecting the times she plumb flustered me to death, teasing me about Tommy Lee or flirting with him. The times she made me terrible impatient with her, not listening to me when I was trying to learn her something at school. And then the times she made me love her so, like when she was wanting her hair bow to be just like mine. Only now that she was gone was I appreciating how much I was caring for her.

I suppose there wasn't one inch of the county that wasn't touched by the Yankees' destroying, since there were fires burning somewhere constantly, leaving smoke hanging in the air most always. Sometimes it was so thick and heavy that it made your eyes smart and your breathing come hard like. That smell of burning brush was the first thing we smelled of a morning and the last thing at night. The Yankees told us it all had to be burned, that any left—along with limbs, leaves, and any other plants what couldn't be used somehow and hauled off—were to be burned so that they wouldn't be snagging boats that would someday be floating here. *Boats*, they said. Yankee boats that would be floating on water several feet deep covering our land. I couldn't even begin to imagine it. Nor was I wanting to.

Of course, they'd started in to cutting trees on our property too, and every time I heard another one fall or saw another sawed-off stump, I mourned the loss of a thing of beauty. I hadn't heard any hoot owls for a good while, and even hearing other birds singing was becoming rare now. *Have the Yankees scared away the robins, redbirds, an' bluebirds too?* I wondered. If so, then they'd somehow purposefully bargained to leave behind the loud cawing crows and egg-stealing starlings, since they were still here, pestering at and snitching from Mama and Granny Mandy's truck patches.

Even Tommy Lee's shagbark hickory was gone, sawed up, and sent off to the Roddys' mill. Knowing they were cutting on Tommy Lee's place, I'd got there as soon as I could—but was too late to see Tommy Lee's special "thinkin' place" come down. Tommy Lee wasn't home just then; he was up to the farm that day with his daddy. But after the government men'd gone off, I sat on the lonely-looking stump, thinking thoughts for him, for the two of us.

The places that were to be the shoreline for the reservoir were cleared of even the ugly stumps. After they'd sawed down the trees and burned up the brush, they brought in them big machines—bulldozers, they called them—to be pushing anything remaining from the burned brush towards where the deeper water would be, leaving the shoreline completely bare. Soon there was nigh to a mile or more of that odd-looking, almost fearful, stripped and downright bare land. Those stretches had nothing on them atall but bare, packed red clay and telltale marks from the awful machines. That was the first and only time I ever saw bare land in the hills of Tennessee.

One stretch of that stripped land run right across the Snodderlys' property, and old man Snodderly was bragging once again about how he was going to live right there on the lake, catching the biggest fish you ever saw and eating "high on the hog." Granny'd had her a good laugh over that one, saying it was "Just like Snodderly not to be knowin' the diff'rence 'tween a hog an' a fish!" And then she'd teased, "Reckon he'll go after his hogs with a pole an' hook when it's hog killin' time? Wonder what bait he'll be a-tryin'? Reckon slop'll stay on his hook?!"

I couldn't picture any lake or fish in my mind's eye, no matter how much Snodderly went on about it or Granny poked fun either. He could jaw forever about what was coming, but it didn't make no difference to me. All I ever saw when I looked over his property was ugly, dead land.

One after another of our familiar and beloved places were destroyed—torn down and hauled off. You couldn't barely even recognize places any more, they were so changed. And everything you loved about the river, the riverbank, and this here part of Franklin County was slowly being changed forever. Stripped. Exposed. Slowly choked off and robbed of any dignity and worth. And somehow it felt like they were doing the same to *us*.

We'd already moved a few things to the new place, and Daddy was doing the same as Mister Arnold: trying to work two farms at the same time. Once James Junior heard, he would have none of that and insisted on coming home soon's he could. The very day we got the letter saying that he'd be home in a month or so was such a happy one, the first happy one in so many days—until even that day was ruined.

The four of us—Daddy, Mama, me, and Andy—were traipsing around the new place, exploring the fields, pasture, and woods next to the river. We were even laughing as we tramped along, teasing each other and talking about James Junior and how much we'd missed him and were looking forward to him coming home when suddenly Mama stopped, putting a hand to her heart. There was a stricken look on her face, and she went white, so chalky white that Daddy reached out to her, grabbing at her arm to support her.

"It's a cedar tree," Mama'd whispered, so soft that I could barely hear her. "Look at its shadow. Oh, James, look at its shadow!"

I glanced over to Andy, wondering if he understood what Mama was so afraid of. But he only shrugged his shoulders, shaking his head at me.

"Hush, Mae!" Daddy scolded her, most like a child. "That ain't nothin' but superstition, an ol' wives' tale an' nothin' to be believed.

Rachael, Andy, let's us be headin' back now. We'uns needin' to head on to home."

"But what's Mama talkin' 'bout?" I asked.

"Ain't nothin'," Daddy answered, and in a tone I was knowing right off there wasn't no sense pestering with more questions.

But unfortunately I hadn't been wise enough to let it alone. I'd asked Granny Mandy about it that night, a stuffy, humid night it was, but still Granny insisted on having her a fire in the fireplace. We were setting tolerable close to that hot fire, with me wiping at the sweat that kept trickling down my face, drinking tea together (Granny was always insisting I drink her "secret ingredient" tea these days) when I'd told her what Mama'd done when she'd seen the cedar tree. Granny Mandy didn't go all white like Mama, but she stared at the fire for so long without answering me, without even blinking or nothing, that I had to call out her name before she spoke again. And then when she did start explaining, I reckon I was the one that went all white this time.

"Were the sun high or low in the sky?" Granny'd asked.

"Um, I reckon it was gettin' tolerable low. Why?"

"Cast a good shadow then?" She spoke in a flat-sounding voice. Wasn't any emotion in it atall.

"Yes, Granny, I reckon so."

She was quiet for a moment, gazing into the fire. I was about to call out to her again when she said, "Most folks round these parts won't have no cedar trees. Don't plant 'em. Cuts 'em down iffin they's any on new property."

"Why's that Granny Mandy? Seems a cedar tree's good as any other. Maybe better."

She sighed and took another sip of her tea. "They's a sayin' that iffin a cedar tree casts a shadow the length o' a coffin, means somebody in yer family be 'bout to die."

I sucked in my breath, putting belief to the old superstition quicker than my thinking could deny it. Then I immediately started in to argue with myself, saying, *Ain't true! It's just like Daddy said. Old wives' tale what ain't true!*

But Granny Mandy didn't say no more. Just kept staring into the fire. *She* believed it. And I remembered the coffin she'd had made, setting in her barn. Waiting.

Granny's spells were coming more often these last few weeks, causing me and Andy more concern. She'd talk with Grandaddy McKenney or get all confused about what the Yankees were doing. Sometimes she'd suddenly take sick, needing to lay down or set in her rocker by the fire—her ever-present fire, no matter how hot and sticky and humid it'd be that day. Her cabin was most like a oven, so terrible hot that Andy'd start in to taking off whatever clothes he could soon's he stepped in the door.

The government men were pressing Daddy to have Granny to move in with us, so they could be tearing down her cabin and barn and all, but Daddy put his foot down at that suggestion. He said Granny Mandy needed her cabin, for her health. And he told them they weren't taking down Granny's home before ours. Not until we were all ready to be moving out.

Still, I wondered often if it wouldn't be better for Granny Mandy to be with us, seeing how we all worried about her so. I suppose we were fretting that she'd be burning the place down or forgetting to eat or hurting herself somehow. But she still did fine cooking meals, getting about, looking after her garden, and all the other chores she was insisting on tending to.

Granny Mandy didn't put back on any more weight, but she didn't appear to be losing more neither. If anything, except for her frequent spells, she seemed to be even more wiry and forceful, tiny and bent over as she was. Besides, when Mama tried to tempt her to be eating more, pointing out that she'd got thinner than a split-rail fence lately, Granny only laughed. Said that suited her "dis-po-si-tion" (that was another word Granny Mandy loved drawing out) just fine, and then teased, "Fences be keepin' out meddlesome, thievin' critters, an' I aim to keep out them northern scavengers!"

Her spells didn't seem to hurt nothing really. At least, not Granny Mandy. And except for us wanting to watch her close, they didn't really change anything. They were just terrible frightening to us. Especially me.

Seemed like I'd just put the dark of my fear a ways behind me (it was a race I was constantly running) when Granny'd have another of them spells—and then there it'd be again, pushing down on me, making me know once again I was lugging that familiar terrible weight pressing on my head and shoulders. By the time I went to bed I was so dog tired that falling asleep itself became a chore. The weight made my limbs weak and limp with exhaustion, but my mind would be racing with fighting the Yankees or longing for Tommy Lee or worrying over Granny. Then when I did finally fall asleep, I'd be knowing that same dream, over and over again. I didn't rest of a night no more. I *wrestled*.

Sometimes I thought on what Tommy Lee'd said about arguing with God, and how it was good that I was fighting for something, instead of just giving up, giving in. Not caring atall. And then I'd start in to praying some again, sounding like when I wasn't but a little young'un. The prayers I'd stumble through were simple and honest ones, like I was just talking with a God who was right here and we were pondering over our ties to each other. Same as me and Merry Jo would do. Felt kind of like I was testing praying for the first time really, stepping my way so careful like through a room without no light, no windows, and nothing familiar about to help me feel my way.

There were times I'd get terrible angry with God, and I'd tell Him so, spewing out my hurtful feelings in short, childlike tantrums. But then amazingly, when I'd be waiting for Him to strike me down, show that He was angry with me for being angry at Him, I wouldn't sense none of them things. And once my anger and hurt were spent, I only knew a calm to come. Seemed I could nearly be touching peace. I'd just be reaching for it, longing for it like I'd never wanted anything in my whole life when suddenly another of Granny's spells would come. And the hint of peace would disappear—no, it was swallowed up—in the dark that would come pressing once again.

When Granny's spell had passed and I saw she was going to be all right, then I'd begin all over again. Praying in fits and starts once more. Seemed like I wasn't doing nothing but forever spinning in circles, going round and round with God until I was sure the whirring was making my head ache. *God, I ain't gettin' nowhere!* I'd cry out to Him, complaining in terrible frustration. *I'm ploddin' through this hurt to only end up right back where I was startin'. I can't see no end! Please tell me there's a end.*

My heart ached for Tommy Lee something terrible, since I only saw him a couple times those next several weeks. And when I first told him about the new place—after days and days of wanting to be with him so I could tell him everything that was bothering me—I was so anxious I could hardly talk. He set right in to reassuring me, telling me there wasn't any cause to be fretting atall. "Miles ain't goin' to make no diff'rence, Rachael," he'd said, holding my hands and squeezing them tight between his calloused ones. "I can hitch a ride to see you, an' besides . . ." He'd suddenly reddened, turning away from me and pushing back the hair from his forehead once again. "Since I spoke with yer daddy, well, me an' you is promised, you know. An' it won't be terrible much longer to be waitin'." I remember how he'd cleared his throat real nervous like. "You won't mind the waitin', will you?"

I'd smiled up at him then, possessively reaching to push back the same stubborn lock of hair. "I'd wait forever for you if it was needful,

Tommy Lee. But I'm sure hopin' it won't be too long." And then he'd kissed me again, pulling me to him protectively.

We'd talked about our future then, planning how I'd go on to high school while Tommy Lee continued to help his daddy get fields cleared, planted, and harvested, new outbuildings put up (the sheds on their new property were poorly too), and everything settled in good. Only then could Tommy Lee turn to working other fields that would be ours, ones that still had trees on them but were promised to us by Mister Arnold. They were sure to be tolerable hard work, but as Tommy Lee'd pointed out, it made good sense for me to be getting my schooling while he was working our land. So there wasn't nothing else to do but settle on me going with Daddy, Mama, Andy, and Granny Mandy to the new place while Tommy Lee worked what was to be our land, getting it ready so we could be married in a year or two.

The third week in July began with one of those summer days that sent the dogs to hiding in the shade under the dog trot. There wasn't even a hint of a breeze, and the hot, humid air was so thick that you felt like you were pushing against it to breathe, let alone move here or there. Since the destroying Yankees had cleared most of the trees, there wasn't hardly a lick of shade to be found, but even the biggest old wind-blowed oak wouldn't be a bit of help on this day. You could set and sweat under a tree about as easy as you could in the hazy sunlight. Finding the energy to swat at the bugs that were bothering at you or wave a fan back and forth was the most you were wanting to move about. Unless you were aiming to cool your feet in the creek or Granny Mandy's springhouse. Then a body could be moving along right quick, knowing what cooling relief was waiting for you.

Mama'd promised me and Andy we could head for either of them places this afternoon, but this morning we were working her truck patch, hoeing the weeds, shelling a few late peas, and picking bunches of green beans. Daddy was at the new place, repairing the springhouse there, and Granny had come to help us with the beans, which appeared to be growing and multiplying right before our eyes. Every time we reached in the bushes to pick some, swatting bugs and wiping the sweat from our eyes while we were peering in at them, we'd find a whole passel more that were hiding, needing to be picked.

"Ain't no end to these beans!" Andy complained, rubbing his already sweat-soaked sleeve across his forehead.

Mama'd just turned to answer him when we heard a dinner bell ringing, coming from a good ways off. We all stood still, listening, counting the rings, wondering what it was meaning. I felt sick to my stomach when I remembered the ringing bell of some time ago—the bell warning when them TVA men first come. And then as suddenly as the ringing had begun clanging through the hazy air, it stopped.

"Land sakes, Mae," Granny Mandy said, her voice barely above a whisper. "It be Sadie Youther. Her young'un ain't due yet fer a good while, but that's what it be, sure as anythin'."

Mama looked at Granny Mandy with alarm. "You's right! That be the Youthers' bell. Can't mean anythin' else. Andy, run an' hitch up Old Dean. Hurry!"

Andy dropped his handful of beans into the bucket and took off running towards Old Dean's stall.

"Granny Mandy, you'll need to fetch yer things," Mama added.

Granny'd already turned and was quickly heading towards her cabin. She called back over her shoulder, "I'll be ready soon's I get my black bag packed. Wasn't reckonin' on needin' it this soon."

Mama turned towards me then, dropping her hoe where she'd just left off. "Rachael, me an' you needs to wash up a bit. At least get the dirt off'n our faces an' hands. Can't take time for more'n that; them rings sounded urgent like." I followed her as she hurried towards the cabin. "Then I want you to comb yer hair, pullin' it all back an' knottin' it into a bun. I'll put some food in a basket while you fetch us two clean aprons an' several clean towels."

I grabbed at her arm, stopping her a minute. "Do you mean I'm to be comin' with you? To the birthin'?" I looked up at her in wonder, knowing that my mouth hung open like some fool. And not rightly caring.

Mama took a deep breath. "Ain't usual, I know. But with so many gals moved away—Miz Harris an' Miz Owens, Miz Purser, and Tommy Lee's mama ain't likely to be comin'—well, they just ain't no choice but for you to be comin' an' helpin'. Time was when a unmarried gal would never be . . . never be at no Granny Frolic." Mama gave me a stern look over. "But times ain't what they was an' you's had to grow up faster'n some." She sighed. "Too much faster. Hurry now! Get washed up—an' don't be forgettin' to fetch them things!"

In my excitement, I probably managed to splash more water on the sink and floor than I got on my face and hands, but eventually Daddy's chipped shaving mirror showed that my face was passably clean once again. And after grabbing up one of Mama's best baskets (I knew Mama always took a good one, seeing how the birthing of a baby was such a special event), I carefully folded and placed several towels and two starched white aprons in it, tucking a tablecloth overtop so the towels and aprons wouldn't get dirty. I'd just finished combing and pulling back my hair—why was it being so particularly stubborn just now, sweat-drenched curls escaping every which way no matter what I did?—when I heard Granny Mandy hollering from outside.

"Mae? Rachael? You ready? That young'un ain't likely to be a-waitin' on us!"

Exasperated, I shook my head at the curls that were sticking out here and there, and then running down the steps, I grabbed up the packed basket I'd set by the door. Andy'd fetched the mule and wagon and was holding onto Dean's bit while Mama climbed up onto the seat. I noted with amusement that Granny Mandy was planning on driving, seeing that she had the reins clutched tightly in her aged yet strong and capable hands. "You best be settin' behind us, Rachael, holdin' onto the food an' supplies," Granny warned. "I aim to make this here stubborn ol' mule go faster'n a tidy drunk runnin' to the privy!"

And with that threat barely no more'n said, Granny Mandy whacked Old Dean a good one, sending him to baying and lunging forward, causing me and Mama to grab at our straw hats before they fell off. It also sent Andy into fits of laughter as he watched us rumble down the pathway towards the road.

The Youthers lived just east of the Owenses—what use to be the Owenses' property, that is. Charlie and Sadie Youther were supposed to be moving too, but with a whole passel of young'uns to clothe and feed—they had twelve boys and girls already—and another on the way, they were having a harder time finding a place. Fact was, even though Mister Youther'd plumb wore out his soil, stripping it bare and never rotating crops, he was set on finding a replacement that was the best in the county, some folks were saying. "I 'spect he's just wantin' to ride in that fancy car," I remembered Granny Mandy musing. "Shoot! You wouldn't catch me puttin' my littlest toe in no Yankee automobile!"

"You bring plenty o' towels, Mae?" Granny asked, bringing my thoughts back to today. And what I was about to have the privilege to see.

Mama turned to glance back at me. "Rachael, how many was you packin'?"

I thought a moment, mentally counting up the towels before answering, "Five in all. Grabbed up 'bout ever one what was clean."

Granny nodded. "Good. Goin' to need 'em. That ol' man o' Sadie's so tight fisted, he prob'ly won't allow us to be usin' more'n one o' his blessed towels." She shook her head in disgust. "Iffin he lets us be usin' that."

"Oh, Granny Mandy," I grinned at her, "surely he wouldn't be so stingy. Not for the birthin' of a baby."

Granny chuckled. "Rachael, this be Charlie Youther's thirteenth. Got 'im a baker's dozen with this young'un. Ain't like a baby's arrival be anythin' new fer 'im. Just another mouth to be feedin'. Besides, Charlie is cussed stingy. I knowed him to crawl on his belly under the gate so's to keep the hinges from wearin' out any."

We chuckled at Granny's teasing and Old Dean took advantage of the temporary distraction, slowing down for a minute until Granny Mandy noticed. "Get on there, you ol' mule!" she hollered. "When a gal's fixin' to work on her second dozen, them babies start to pop out faster'n parched popcorn over a hot fire!"

When we pulled up into the Youthers' yard, there was only one other wagon—Aunt Opal's—but Tommy Lee's mama was waving to us from the porch.

"Haddy must've come 'long with Opal," Granny Mandy observed. "Good fer Haddy to be out an' good fer us too. We can surely use the extry help."

Mama nodded. "I've missed seein' her. Reckon we'll get time today to do some catchin' up."

"Hey! Mighty glad to see you all!" Miz Arnold called out to us as we hurriedly grabbed up our baskets and headed towards the cabin. "Pains started 'bout a hour ago. Me an' Opal'd come to visit a spell when Sadie started in to feelin' poorly. Didn't even think on it bein' the baby comin' 'til the pains started in to comin' so regular like."

"That young'un is aimin' to be a good bit early. Might need to call 'im Rooster, I'm thinkin'! How far apart is the pains now?" Granny Mandy asked.

"Oh, I reckon they's comin' right steady ever five minutes or so." She held open the rusted and torn screen door for us, and I followed Granny and Mama into the dark room.

Instantly the odors of rank grease, sweat, and a sour-smelling stench wrapped in waves of sweltering heat reached my nose, causing me to wince and frown. The room was so dark that I just stood there a moment, letting my eyes adjust to the shadowy movements about the room. One was Miz Arnold, as she moved quickly to the fireplace and poked at the embers. They flamed just a bit when she added another log, causing the room to light up a bit and get even hotter.

A tattered quilt hung from the ceiling moved now and then too, and from behind it come low moans that seemed to be echoing about the feverish, shadowy room. Aunt Opal beckoned to Granny Mandy from there, and Granny immediately moved to go behind the quilt while Mama and Miz Arnold spoke quietly by the fire. I saw Mama nod towards me just before she said softly, "Rachael, Mister Youther and the young'uns is waitin' out back. Why don't you go see if they's wantin' for anythin'?"

"Yes, Mama." I glanced at the quilt once more before heading towards the back door, but before I reached it a much louder groan reached my ears. I turned to Mama, expecting to find worry written on her face.

But Mama only smiled at me, a reassuring smile. "Part o' birthin' in this here sin-filled world, Rachael," she said. "Pain before the joy. Go on now."

I was glad to escape the smothering heat and tension of the cabin, but my curiosity pulled at me, making me want to go back inside at the same time. I'd seen countless births on our farm: calves that needed help from Daddy; puppies of every shape, size, and color; kittens by the dozens; beautiful, long-legged foals and squealing pigs too. I knew there was pain in the birthing. I'd seen the mamas struggle in the sometimes terrible long hours it took for the babies to be coming.

But folks is different from animals, I argued to myself. And for some silly, naive reason I wasn't expecting this, this hurting, this wrenching, pain-filled process that made a strong gal like Miz Youther—who'd already birthed twelve young'uns—to be admitting that pain, to be groaning so. I'd seen so many southern women enduring horrible pain—including my mama—by not saying nothing. *Nothing.* And now here was Miz Youther carrying on while Mama merely said, "Pain comes before the joy." Mama admitting to pain? *It must be nigh to killin' a gal*, I worried, shaking my head.

One of the Youthers' young'uns suddenly grabbed me about the leg, looking up at me with pleading eyes. Her dress was unhemmed (it had obviously been handed down from an older sister) and hadn't looked to be washed in some time. And she was tolerable dirty too, from her tousled, uncombed head all the way down to her filthy bare feet. "Cain't I go see my mama now?" she asked, softly. "I'll be gooder'n a angel even. Promise."

I picked her up, smoothing back sweat-drenched curls from her smudged face. "No, you ain't allowed just now. Yer mama's busy." Trying to distract her, I asked, "What's yer name? I forget." The Youther young'uns come to school sometimes, but they certainly didn't attend regular like. And they were one of the few families that didn't go to church atall. Daddy'd said it was Mister Youther's doing, and he obviously didn't care for him much more'n Granny did.

"Martha. But everbody calls me Sissy."

"Well, Sissy, where's your daddy and brothers an' sisters?"

She pointed towards the barn. "They's a-sleepin' in the barn. I's s'posed to be, but I cain't sleep without my dolly. Got to have the dolly what my Grandaddy Youther made fer me."

Sissy started in to sniffling, and then big, silent tears rolled from brown eyes down her cheeks, making ugly streaks in the dirt on her face. "Let's us go find yer daddy first, okay? Don't be cryin' now. We'll see 'bout that dolly if you be clearin' up." She blinked her big brown eyes, trying hard to stop the tears, and I wiped at her face with the hem of my dress.

Carrying her to the barn, I slowly, carefully pushed open the big door, still causing it to make a terrible loud creaking sound. Peeking inside, once more I waited for my eyes to adjust to a darkened room until I could make out sleeping young'uns scattered everywhere—cuddled up next to each other on the floor on an old rag rug, stretched out on piles of hay, on top of a dirty wagon, and two who were snuggled on Mister Youther's ample lap—one in the crook of each arm.

Mister Youther was a tolerable big man, with a rounded belly that bounced when he walked anywhere, legs and arms like tree limbs and several chins underneath his thin, scraggly beard. Granny'd often teased that the Youther's farming was too sorry for him to get that fat off of his own harvest. She said it must've been his mooching off neighbors and kin that kept him "fatter'n a sow totin' a dozen piglets." I smiled when I recollected Granny's description, seeing that Mister Youther himself was sound asleep too; his mouth hung open and he was snoring like a big old sow. I giggled and then so did Sissy.

"I reckon we hadn't ought to be wakin' them up," I whispered, trying to close the door again without making a creaking sound this time. But that door wasn't cooperating any, and before I had it even part way shut, Mister Youther stirred.

He shook his head (which made all those chins bounce), trying to shake off the sleep I suppose, and then glanced at the two young'uns still sleeping in his arms. After easing them onto the hay next to him, he stood up and motioned for me to follow him out the door—and flinched when it made that loud creaking sound once more.

"Been meanin' to oil that cursed door," he muttered, rubbing his eyes in the hazy sunlight. "Serve me right iffin that whole brood wakes up on account o' I been puttin' it off. But oil don't come cheap—nothin' do—when you got twelve, no—best be countin' 'em thirteen now, yes'm, thirteen mouths to be feedin'. Nothin' comes cheap with a baker's dozen."

I remembered Granny Mandy's story about Mister Youther's stinginess and grinned. "Me an' my mama an' granny just come. Mama sent me out here to see if you all is wantin' for anythin'. Young'uns okay?"

"Still sleepin', unless the blamed door waked 'em up." He wiped at his brow. "Weather ain't fit fer nothin' but sleepin', I'm thinkin'. How's my missus? Number thirteen a-squallin' fer food yet?"

"No, she ain't . . . well, her time hasn't . . . the baby's not borned just yet, Mister Youther." I sighed. And then suddenly remembered Sissy still in my arms. I put her down. "Sissy says she's needin' her dolly. I could be fetchin' it for her. Where is it, do you know?"

Mister Youther frowned down at her. "You's s'posed to be sleepin' like yer brothers an' sisters is. Now git on in there."

Sissy's face proceeded to crumple and them big tears started in to falling again, making an even bigger mess on her filthy face.

"I'd be right pleased to find it for her, Mister Youther. It wouldn't be no trouble atall." I looked down at Sissy, reaching out to touch one tear-smudged cheek. "Where is it, Sissy, do you remember?"

"Yes'm. Hit's under Mama's bed. After Daddy put the axe there, I put dolly under her bed too. I's wantin' to hep Mama."

I looked back up at Mister Youther, not understanding atall what Sissy was talking about. "A axe? Under Miz Youther's bed?"

"Land sakes, gal!" Mister Youther exclaimed. "Ain't you learned nothin'? This must be yer first Granny Frolic, eh?" I nodded, feeling my face turn red. "A axe under the bed cuts the pain in two, ain't ye knowin' that?" He chuckled.

I thought about Miz Youther groaning behind that quilt and merely nodded at the superstitious man standing before me.

"An' I know who done brings the baby too!" Sissy claimed excitedly, tugging on my dress and giggling too. "We done heared the ol' hoot owl last year callin', 'Who who! Who wants a baby?' An' me an' my brothers an' sisters run out in the holler to answer him back, callin', 'We does! We does!'"

I looked down at her, smiling at her innocent believing but wondering still at Mister Youther's remedy. *Had he really put an axe there and was he truly believin' such things?* I asked myself. I supposed I'd find out when I went searching for that doll.

"Well, I best be goin' back inside. Mama may be needin' me for somethin'. And I'll be lookin' for Sissy's dolly first thing too."

Mister Youther glanced down at Sissy. "Well, iffin it won't be no trouble, an' you, young'un, be promisin' you be goin' right to sleep once ye get that blamed doll . . ."

"Yes, sir, Daddy, I will," Sissy promised, eyes round and head bobbing up and down.

I turned and walked back to the cabin, a cabin that was, unfortunately, much like Mister and Miz Harris' home had been. Rotting. Leaning terrible on its foundation. Spaces between chipped and weathered boards that wouldn't keep out no winter winds atall. Not a inch of it worth saving, but it would be—since the Youthers were so poor they'd be needing to tote with them everything they could carry to their new farm, even if the Yankees were to help them build a new cinder block home.

Once again I opened the door and stepped into the oppressing darkness, a smothering dark that reminded me suddenly of my own haunting fears. I stopped, trying to collect my racing thoughts and calm my senseless fearing.

"Rachael? Is you all right?" It was Miz Arnold. She reached out to take one of my hands and quickly guided me towards the sink, pouring me a glass of water from a pitcher. "Drink this. You looked right peaked for a moment there, honey. Heat be terrible fierce today."

I drank slowly, finding the water warm instead of cooling—warm like everything else in this room—but still helpful. It at least distracted me from the dark.

Slowly, shadows moved to form recognizable shapes once again, and I saw Aunt Opal helping Mama at the fireplace. They appeared to be boiling a big pot of water there, using it to sterilize whatever it was they were needing, I assumed. Miz Arnold suddenly jumped, reaching for the oven door. "Nearly forgot! If I'd left these here dressin's in there much longer, they'd be burned to a crisp, I reckon! Couldn't be wrappin' no babe in ashes, could we?" She shook her head, chuckling at her own fooling. "Hold out these clean towels for me, will you, Rachael? Need to be keepin' these here dressin's brand-spankin' clean." I held the towels for her and watched as she carefully wrapped up the dressings for the new baby. "Now you can be takin' these to yer granny. She's with Miz Youther."

I stared at Miz Arnold for a moment, fear and indecision keeping me from doing anything. "Um, are you sure I should . . . uh, bother Miz Youther?"

"Yer granny said to be sendin' you to her once you come in, Rachael." She smiled at me then, a tender, loving smile, and I saw

Tommy Lee smiling at me through her features as sure as anything. And then she pushed a stray lock of hair back from her forehead. "Go 'head. Birthin' be a natural thing." Miz Arnold put a hand on my shoulder. "I'm thinkin' yer granny wants ye to see that for yerself."

"Yes, ma'am," I said, suddenly remembering the doll I was to be fetching too. I passed by Mama and Aunt Opal, silently seeking Mama's approval by motioning towards the quilt; Mama nodded her head in response. And then I walked towards that part of the room where the low moans were still coming from. And sometimes, muffled sobs.

Coming around the quilt, I saw Miz Youther was bathed in sweat, and as she writhed with the pain, she clung to Granny Mandy's hand. I watched her, feeling the pain with her it seemed, as I grimaced when she did, moved with her rolling about, and nigh to moaned with her too. Finally the hurting seemed to come to a end and she lay spent, breathing terrible heavy like she'd just run up a mountainside. Panting out between deep breaths Miz Youther whispered, "That was a good 'un, Miz McKenney. They's comin' kindly hard now. Won't be much longer."

Granny Mandy wiped her forehead, saying in a soothing and calming voice, "You's doin' right fine, Sadie. That babe's goin' to be a special 'un, big as he be." Granny grinned. "At first I was thinkin' ye needs be namin' 'im 'Rooster—on account o' bein' so early. Now I'm wonderin' iffin ye might be callin' him Samson!"

Miz Youther smiled but was suddenly gripped with another pain, this one causing her to cry out. Once more she clutched at Granny Mandy's hand, and I saw her squeeze so hard that the muscles and veins in her arms stood out, pulsing like, they were. Mama, Aunt Opal, and Miz Arnold come peeking round the quilt, this time their eyes reflecting surprised concern. And fear.

"Opal, when this pain be endin', I'm needin' you to be holdin' Sadie's hand fer a spell," Granny said softly. We all stood there watching Miz Youther, her body tense and jerking with the terrible pain, moaning and whipping her head back and forth. I don't know what everybody else was thinking, but I was feeling awful. It felt terrible helpless to just watch Miz Youther this way, not being able to do anything to stop it.

When the pain finally stopped and she was gasping for air again, Granny leaned down towards Miz Youther, again talking with a reassuring tone. "It be all right to cry out, Sadie. 'Tis hard work you's doin', an' you's doin' fine. I aim to step outside fer just a moment now. I'll be right back, you hear?"

Miz Youther merely nodded, still spent from the last contraction and trying to catch her breath.

"Haddy, Mae, and Rachael, you be comin' with me."

Remembering my forgotten errand, I said quickly, "Granny, Mister Youther sent me to fetch a doll. Martha's doll. Said she done put it under the bed." I motioned towards Miz Youther, fretting about bothering her with my searching.

"Ain't that like a child," Granny Mandy mused, shaking her head. "I reckon she stuck it there when her Daddy put the axe underneath."

I looked at Granny Mandy in amazement.

"Youthers be b'lievin' the axe cuts the pains, Rachael," she whispered. "Cain't hurt none. Might even help iffin Sadie's b'lievin' it. Go 'head an' fetch the young'un's toy."

I dropped down to my knees, and looking under the old straw mattress (which was sadly in need of a cleaning and new stuffing), I saw dirty rags, a empty kerosene pail, several pairs of old shoes, one filthy doll—and an axe. Quickly I pulled out the doll, brushing off the dust that was clinging to it, and then, nodding to Granny Mandy, followed her, Miz Arnold, and Mama out the back door.

Sissy immediately come running to me, grabbing not at me this time but for her beloved ragged doll. She clutched it to her, cradling the thing in her arms like it was the finest porcelain china in satin clothes. I smiled down at her. "Now, yer to be headin' for the barn. And a good nap, like you done promised." I glanced around for her daddy, but he wasn't anywhere to be found. *Reckon he's gone back to snorin' already*, I thought to myself. I remembered Miz Youther's paining, shaking my head that her old man could be sleeping so easily when she was suffering that way.

"Me an' Miss Emmy is right tired, ain't we, Miss Emmy?" Sissy grinned up at me again. "An' we both says thankee kindly fer the fetchin'." She turned and run for the barn then, making those still rusty and unoiled hinges squeak yet another time.

Why on God's green earth that noise don't be wakin' up that brood is beyond me, I thought to myself. *But it's certainly a blessin' to us all if they stay asleep for a good while yet.*

"Rachael," Granny called, and immediately I hurried over to her, noting the serious tone of her voice. "I done tole yer mama an' Haddy what I been suspectin' ever since I first seen Sadie strainin' so. That baby ain't comin' out right. Goin' to be a breech birth, sure as anythin'."

I frowned and shook my head, knowing something was wrong but not understanding.

"Babies is s'posed to come head first," Granny explained. "But this'n is turned a good bit. Comin' out backside first." She put her hands on her hips, and after taking a deep breath, said to Mama and Miz Arnold, "Goin' to be a hard one, baby's so big—even early as it be an' with Sadie havin' her twelve young'uns before 'im." Granny looked up at the sky then, shading her eyes with one hand. "Clouds'll be gatherin' up soon. She'll be rainin' buckets before sundown. Iffin this here baby's goin' to live, it'll be squallin' before sundown too."

If this baby's goin' to live! I repeated to myself, the phrase echoing over and over, beating like a drum inside my head. And each time it echoed I knew the dark was creeping closer, stealing and hovering over me as we stood there in the hazy sunlight wrapping round us like a smothering blanket. *No God!* I demanded angrily. *You can't be lettin' this here baby die! You can't!*

"What 'bout Sadie?" Mama asked, interrupting my thoughts. "Shouldn't Charlie be fetchin' the doctor over to Crawleysville?"

"I reckon that baby'll be born—one way or t'other—long before no doctor could be fetched, but iffin Charlie's thinkin' it might help, he's welcome to go after 'im."

"And Sadie?" Mama asked again.

Granny Mandy took a deep breath. "Sadie's good'n strong. Ain't thinkin' she be in any danger. Unless . . ."

"Unless what?" Haddy grabbed ahold of Mama.

"Nothin'. Ain't nothin' to be frettin' over," Granny fairly announced, putting authority to her words. "Now let's us be sayin' a prayer for that babe an' his mama."

Granny reached out to Haddy and me, Mama grabbed ahold of Haddy and my other hand, and we formed up a circle right there in the yard. A yard of packed down, bare clay littered with jagged scraps of forgotten tin and iron here and there; a yard with piles of old slop buckets and pieces of glass that had been pitched out the rotted, barely setting on its hinges back door; a yard with stinking piles the dogs left that you had to watch for and step around careful like. And amidst them smells and trash and the sweltering heat that drained you, made your head ache it beat down on you so, we stopped a moment, closing our eyes, shutting out everything around us as we listened to Granny Mandy talk with her God.

"Dear Lord," she began, and I could immediately hear the believing in her voice. The accepting that He was there. Listening.

She ain't just sayin' words, thinkin' they's floatin' up into no empty sky, goin' nowheres. Granny Mandy's talkin' to Someone. Someone who's as real to her as we is standin' here holdin' her hands, I thought to myself. *Maybe if I pretended He was right here—in the middle of this circle—I could be believin' like that too? Believin' that He's here—and carin' too? Lovin' Miz Youther? Lovin' this here baby? Lovin' me?* I squeezed my eyes shut even tighter, shutting out the heat, the smells, the filth all around me, the terrible sounds coming from the cabin. And thought on my God.

"Ye has showed us what love is. Ye sent Yer only Son outta a safe, lovin' heaven into this hurtin', foul, sin-littered world—as a baby, just a wee, needin' baby!—for *us*. Ye done that to Yer onliest Son outta love we can't even begin to be understandin'." Granny paused, taking a deep breath. "Even now, they's another young'un strainin' to be borned, another mama workin' terrible hard to be knowin' her new young'un. Lord Almighty, I ain't no right to be demandin' Ye be doin' what I'm thinkin's best. But we's simple folk here. Watchin' the skies for rain, tendin' the fields what needs that rain, harvestin' the food to be feedin' our families, our young'uns. Yer young'uns, God. How we's lovin' them what Ye has gived us!"

Granny Mandy's voice faltered, and I felt Mama's hand grasp mine even tighter. And I thought about the babies that had died. Granny's and Mama's and Miz Arnold's too. *Sweet Jesus, how are these women survivin' that? How are they still believin' You's a lovin' God when them young'uns has died? Isn't they a-fearin' You like I am?*

"Help me, Lord!" Granny went on. "They's a dozen reasons why we's askin' Ye to be preservin' Sadie. Them young'uns o' hers needs their mama! And Lord, they ain't no sense even tryin' to hide my thinkin' from Ye. I'm needin' to hear that new baby cry. I'm wantin' to feel them tiny fingers a-grabbin' at mine. I'm beggin' Ye to let me see 'im nestled against his mama! Please be showin' us Yer love in the form of a babe once again. Lord, we's lovin' Ye. But still, we's needin' Ye to be teachin' us what it is to be trustin' Ye, b'lievin' in Ye, lovin' Ye! Amen."

I looked up to see Granny Mandy, face raised to the sky, tears streaming down the deep, familiar lines and creases of her weathered face. "Yes'm," she said softly. "Rain's a-comin'."

Mama and Miz Arnold were both dabbing at their eyes and then blowing noses with hankies. Ashamedly, I realized that I didn't need a handkerchief, hadn't even thought on crying. I was too angry. Or afraid.

A sudden piercing scream made us all jump, and we heard Aunt Opal holler, "Miz McKenney! Come quick!" Granny Mandy run to the cabin, throwing open the rickety back door so hard that it banged against the cabin. Miz Arnold run after Granny, but Mama hung back a minute, stopping to put a hand on my shoulder.

"I wouldn't o' brung you today if I'd knowed, Rachael. But maybe God's wantin' you here today for a reason I ain't even seen. Whatever happens, you needs be brave for Miz Youther—an' Mister Youther an' all them young'uns. Do you think you can be doin' that?"

I nodded at her. "I think so."

"Go see to Mister Youther. Tell him what yer granny said an' ask him if he's wantin' to fetch the doctor." She turned to go back into the door but paused once more, her back to me. "Yer granny be a fine midwife, Rachael. Be trustin' in that. But be trustin' more in yer God." She went in then and closed the door.

I hurried back to the barn, but Mister Youther had already come out and was standing in the sunlight, trying once again to rub the sleep out of his eyes. He glanced up at the nearly cloudless sky. "Hotter'n hades today, I'm thinkin'. An' no sign o' rain to cool it off neither."

"My granny says it's goin' to rain this afternoon."

Mister Youther chuckled. "Wishful women-folk thinkin', that be! How's my missus doin'?" He took off his stained, fraying straw hat and run his fingers through the greasy hair that ringed his bald head. "Still no squallin'? What be takin' that there young'un so long?"

I cleared my throat. "Um, Mister Youther, Granny Mandy says the baby ain't comin' right. An' it's goin' to be hard for him to be comin' thata way. Backwards like. So if you's wantin' to fetch the doctor, Granny Mandy says yer needin' to be doin' that right quick."

He put his tattered hat back on and once more stared up at the sky. "Yer granny thinkin' the doctor be hepin' my missus? That there doctor be costin' me good money. I ain't rightly got nothin' to be givin' 'im. Even my hog done wandered off somewheres."

Inwardly I fumed at his stinginess, but respect for my elders kept me from saying anything or even showing it on my face. "Granny Mandy wasn't thinkin' he could be gettin' here in time anyways."

"'Spect she's right. An' the young'un? Ere it goin' to die?" he asked, matter-of-fact like.

The blunt question startled me, and I hesitated a moment. "We prayed it wouldn't."

"Hah! Prayed, did ye? Best be talkin' with them Yankees instead. They's the ones what's makin' decisions round heres these days. Prayed, did ye? Wishful women folk again! Hah!"

I backed away from him then, not knowing how to answer him, what to say. "I'll go see to fixin' dinner for you an' yer young'uns." And then glancing towards the barn door, I noticed a tousled head poking out. "Looks like they's wakin' up. You think they'd be wantin' some beans an' cornbread?"

"Gal, these young'uns'll et anythin'. Anytime. An' anywheres. We'll be a-waitin' fer ye."

Quickly I walked away from him, anxious to be leaving this frustrating man behind. But when I stepped into the cabin, I realized I wasn't escaping from anything since Miz Youther's agonizing moaning greeted me here. I looked over to Mama, questioning her about Miz Youther with my eyes. She shook her head. "Nothin' yet. Mister Youther goin' for the doctor?"

"No, ma'am. Said he prob'ly couldn't be gettin' the doctor here in time. I'm to fetch him an' the young'uns some beans an' cornbread."

I helped Mama gather up bowls and spoons, all the time mopping at my forehead because of the heat, finding it hard to move or even think in the oppressive cabin. And each time I heard a moan coming from behind the quilt, I'd wince. Granny Mandy come out once, asking for her black bag. She took out her cloverine salve, scissors, and thread, and then asked Miz Arnold to sterilize the scissors. "Ain't needin' 'em yet, but I'm wantin' to have everthin' ready," she said before retreating once more behind the quilt.

When we'd toted everything outside, the young'uns come running. And then immediately started into shoveling down those beans like they hadn't had nothing in days. Of course, Mister Youther didn't slight himself none neither. I watched in amazement as he refilled his bowl five times—and then licked it clean, not leaving a spit for the dogs that set begging at his feet.

As the afternoon wore on, clouds started in to meandering their way across the western sky. You could just barely see the sun winking through the haze at noon, but now it was completely hidden, blocked by the gathering clouds. Amazingly, there still wasn't a breath of relief from the intense heat. Instead, it felt like the clouds were holding it in like oven doors, pushing the miserable feverishness up against us until we were so soaked with sweat that our clothes were clinging to us everywhere.

All afternoon I tried to keep the young'uns playing and distracted from the screams that often come from the cabin, but the littlest ones was whiny and kept clutching at my legs, the boys Andy's age were cranky and picking fights, and the oldest ones were—well, they were just terrible frightened. You could see it plain in their wide, staring eyes.

There wasn't anything I could be doing to make them forget, to take that look from their eyes.

Mister Youther went off to work the fields for awhile, but he came back before too long, offering to take the young'uns to the creek for swimming. He asked after Miz Youther, shrugged his shoulders in frustration when I told him the baby still hadn't come (*Was he carin' about them atall? Or was he only put out that this birthin' were takin' so long?*), and then proceeded to traipse off with all twelve of them to the creek. I watched them go, wondering if he'd be the only close kin them boys and girls would be having soon. And then I fretted for them too.

Glancing up at the darkening, cloud-filled sky, I remembered Granny predicting it would rain this afternoon. Certainly was appearing that her seein' had held true again. And then I recollected her warning about the baby too. *Please God*, I pleaded silently, *please be hearin' Granny's prayer*. I stopped a moment, feeling sick to my head and stomach— partly from the sweltering heat and partly from my constant companion, fear. *Please push away the dark*! I cried, clutching at my aching head. *Please be hearin' my prayer*! *Not just Granny's—but mine too*!

"Rachael! Come quick!" Miz Arnold called from the cabin.

I ran as fast as I could, tripping up the steps in my panic. "Is she . . . ? Is the baby . . . ?"

Miz Arnold grabbed at my hand, pulling me towards the quilt. Once more a scream filled the air, echoing through that sweltering, oppressive room and exploding against my pounding head. "Ere the scissors an' thread handy?" Granny Mandy asked, a sense of urgency filling her words.

"Yes'm, Granny Mandy," Aunt Opal answered, as she showed her the clean towel on which the scissors and thread were lying ready.

And then I noticed Miz Youther, and my stomach tensed with fear. She wasn't moving about any more atall now—not flailing her legs or writhing from side to side or moving her head. Not even blinking her eyes. Instead, she stared straight ahead, her eyes wide with terror and fear. The only signs she was still alive were the way she clutched tightly at Mama's hands and the gentle rise and fall of her chest under her soaked shift.

Granny Mandy was at the bottom of the bed, her once soothing voice now demanding, bossing Miz Youther as she barked out, "Push Sadie! Come on now, gal, push harder! Don't you stop workin' on me—fight for it! Sadie, are you hearin' me? I said *push*!"

Suddenly, Miz Youther seemed to come all alive again, and arching her neck and back, she pushed herself nearly up off that old bed in one great effort, letting out a piercing scream that filled the air, surely coming straight from her soul. I covered my ears at the terrible sound, closing my eyes too so I could be shutting out everything around me—the heat, the pain, the dark.

And then, I heard Granny Mandy laughing. *Laughing*. And slowly opening my eyes I saw Granny Mandy grasping a wiggling, slippery, squalling baby gal. And then Miz Youther started in to laughing with Granny, causing Aunt Opal, Miz Arnold, Mama—and finally, me—to laugh too. And then our laughter filled the air where there was once screams, joy rippling through that tiny cabin. Laughter!

While Granny Mandy tended to Miz Youther, Mama and Aunt Opal cared for the crying baby, wiping her gently with warm towels, cleaning ten fingers, ten tiny toes. Her downy head had just a bit of Miz Youther's light brown hair, and she was gazing around her, looking round the room just like she was wondering where she was, where she'd arrived to from so dark a world. Miz Arnold come bringing powder from dry clay that she'd taken from between rocks in the chimney. And then so gently she tended to the babe, patting the little'un's arms, chest, tummy, bottom, and legs and feet. And I watched this amazing sight, everything they were doing, every move this baby gal made—this miracle!—like I hadn't never seen a baby before. Life! Sudden life from pain and darkness and oppressing heat. Life!—when there wasn't none!

And then Mama come bringing the dressings, wrapping the baby up snug, cooing over her and rocking her in her arms for just a moment before handing her over to her mama. A mama who just minutes before had been in agony, screaming out her pain. Now she reached eagerly for the babe, cradling the tiny one next to her—the one who had been causing the pain—soothing her now. The pain forgotten. For the joy had come!

"Best be ringin' the bell, Rachael. Mister Youther an' all them young'uns'll be wantin' to know they has a baby sister," Granny said, smiling at me.

I grinned back at her. "Yes'm, Granny. I'd surely be likin' to do that." Once more I hurried to the back door, banging it open again in my excitement. And then, just as I reached for the rope to be ringing the bell, I felt the first drops of rain on my face. Cooling drops, cleansing drops that splashed on my eyes and nose and cheeks and lips. Turning my face to the sky, laughing at the clouds now, I let the sudden shower cleanse me, let it drench my hair and mingle with my tears, tears that

flowed not from pain this time, but from joy! And I rung that bell—
oh, I rung that bell!

Each time I pulled that rope, sending loud joyful clangs ringing
through the valley, I laughed again, exulting in the knowing that the
darkness had been defeated—by life. *God, I'm knowin' now why they's
pain*, I prayed to Him, knowing Him completely, being flooded with
Him in the rain. *Only through the pain—through the burnin' fire of
pain—can we be touchin' the joy. But we can be escapin' the hurtin',
runnin' from it, leavin' the dark behind. Like I done today, God. It's
gone! The dark is gone and the joy's come!* I cried. *They's no more
strugglin', no more doubtin', no more pain to be meetin' tomorra or
the day after that. They's only joy!*

Soon young'uns come tearing from the creek, shouting and laughing
as they raced to me through sudden gullies and puddles of water
scattered everywhere. "I winned!" the biggest hollered, throwing his
arms over his head in the pouring rain. "What ere it? I git to hear first!
Ere it a boy? I'm guessin' it be 'nother boy!"

Once again Sissy clutched at my leg, and amongst all the begging,
pleading, and shouting of a dozen excited young'uns, I could still hear
Sissy's wail—"Lost Miss Emmy again! Will you find her fer me?"

"Ain't you wantin' to know 'bout your new baby sister?" I asked,
reaching down to stroke her drenched curls.

"Baby sister!" she shouted, pushing away from me and jumping up
and down. "Hit's a baby sister what the owl done bringed us!"

And then the oldest started in to bawling, complaining, "I were
s'posed to be hearin' first! I winned the race!"

Mister Youther rounded the barn then, and to his questioning look
I called out, "It's a baby gal, Mister Youther. Miz Youther be doin' fine
too. She's plumb wore out, I'm thinkin', but she's goin' to be fine."

"What's her name?" Sissy asked, pulling at my skirt to get my
attention again.

I shrugged my shoulders. "Don't know. I was so anxious to come
ring the bell and let you all know that your mama an' baby sister were
fine that I plumb forgot to ask."

"Miz Youther's wantin' to call her Mandy," Mama said, poking her
head out the door and holding out one hand to catch some of the falling,
cooling rain. As she wiped the bit of water she'd collected across her
face, Mama continued, "If that be all right with you, Mister Youther,
she was sayin'."

"Ain't makin' no never mind to me," Mister Youther drawled,

shrugging his shoulders. "Ere she wantin' me to come see the baby gal yet?"

"Reckon so." Mama held the door open for him, and Mister Youther plodded through with all twelve young'uns tagging along behind.

Mama smiled at them, and I giggled. "They's certainly most excited about this one," I said, following them in and watching them crowd around their mama's bed. The quilt hanging from the ceiling had been pushed back, and Miz Youther sat propped up, her arms cradling the now sleeping baby. The poor little thing must've been plumb wore out too. I marveled at all those young'uns being quiet as they stood transfixed, staring at the sleeping baby. "Wouldn't you think they'd be use to new young'uns by now—not gettin' so excited?"

Mama shook her head, smiling still as we both watched over the pleasing scene before us. Miz Youther held out the baby for each one to be seeing, and they cooed over her, reaching out to touch the soft blanket that she was wrapped in. "I reckon it don't matter how many they'd be addin' to the family. Each new one is still special, a new life, a reason to be thankin' and praisin' God."

Once each young'un had touched her, causing the baby to wake up with all the commotion, Miz Youther handed this new little Mandy to Mister Youther. She looked so small in his huge, clumsy hands, and Mister Youther held her up against his broad chest awkwardly. He poked one fat finger at her cheek and Mandy turned to it, rooting for her mama's nipple. The young'uns laughed.

"She's hungry as that new litter o' kittens is, Daddy," one boy giggled. "They's always rootin' for they mama!"

"Then I 'spect she's needin' to go back to her mama," Granny Mandy announced, taking the baby from Mister Youther and handing her back to Miz Youther. "After she's done eat, yer mama's goin' to be needin' her a good rest. An' that means," Granny lectured, putting her hands on her hips and turning so she could meet every young'un's eyes in turn, "that means that you all is to be eatin' yer supper on the dog trot right quiet like, mindin' yer manners an' obeyin' yer daddy, an' then you's goin' to bed early. No tusslin' an' no whisperin' neither!"

They started in to whining and complaining about that, but Aunt Opal and Miz Arnold herded them outside to the porch, where they'd already set out another pot of beans. And then it wasn't no time atall before it was quiet again except for the sound of the steady rain and several spoons scooping pinto beans into hungry, waiting mouths.

Once the young'uns were settled onto their various beds, cots, and blankets scattered across the floor—and Miz Youther was sound asleep—Granny gathered up her scissors, thread, and cloverine salve into her old black bag. We were almost out the door when Granny Mandy stopped, and turning towards the baby, she went over to give her one last look.

Baby Mandy was all snuggled up against her mama, but she wasn't sleeping like Miz Youther was. Instead, her eyes were wide open, and she gazed about her surroundings once again like she was interested in everything she was seeing. Like she couldn't hardly wait to be exploring this here new, exciting world.

Granny Mandy reached out, putting a finger against the little one's smooth, unblemished fist, and the baby immediately curled all five tiny fingers around Granny's one, clutching at her. Granny smiled. "I'm right proud ye be named after me," she whispered softly. "'Tis fittin'." Stopping suddenly, Granny Mandy swayed just a bit and I moved towards her, worried that the tiring day had brought on another of her spells. But Mama grabbed at my arm.

"Leave her be a moment," Mama said, and there were tears choking at Mama's words. I looked up at her, wondering at her stopping me, but Mama only shook her head and left the cabin.

"'Tis fittin'," Granny whispered once again. "Pain before joy. Life amidst death." She sighed, closing her eyes. "Oh, thank Ye, dear Lord. How I'm a-thankin' Ye. An' now, baby gal, ye needs be lettin' go. Cain't be clutchin' at me no more." And then Granny Mandy turned to look at me, staring deep into my eyes.

I was awake this time, but suddenly the dream was there with me, and I was living that dream just as sure as I stood in the Youther's filthy, tumbledown cabin, hearing the even breathing of a dozen young'uns all around me. A flash of pain blinded my seeing, and reflected in Granny's eyes I saw only a mirror. And in that mirror I saw myself.

Completely alone.

10

Those powerful jaws have snapped the tether,
Have freed me to the wind and weather.
O Lion, let us run together,
Free, willing now to be untame,
Lion, you are light: joy is in flame.
—*Madeleine L'Engle*

The next morning I set on my bed staring at my feet, attempting to clear my muddled memories, sort out what was real and what was the dreaming. Instinctively, I squinted, recollecting too well the piercing light that shined in my eyes when Granny'd looked up at me. *Was it real? Or was I only rememberin' the dream—imaginin' it all after the close, tense an' tirin' long day?* I shook my head and rubbed at my sleepy eyes, but there wasn't any understanding about what was the dream and what wasn't.

"Rachael!" Mama called, hollering up at me from the bottom of the steps.

Startled, I jumped up to answer her, stubbing one toe into the leg of the table by my bed. "Ouch! Yes, Mama?" After hobbling to the top of the steps, I plopped down there and hugged the throbbing toe against me.

"Are you all right? What happened?"

"Just stubbed my fool toe. Is you needin' me to help with breakfast?" I asked, still wincing at the pounding. How could one little toe hurt so much?

"No, but I am wantin' you to do a extry chore for me. Need you an' Andy to go to mill this mornin'. Might be the last time before we's movin', so's I'm wantin' you both to tote two sackfuls." Mama nodded at my toe. "Granny Mandy always says a stubbed toe'll feel better once it stops the hurtin'." She grinned up at me. "You reckon that's a true sayin'?"

I smiled then too, recollecting the seriousness in her voice every time Granny'd said the very thing to me. "Reckon so." Glancing towards Andy's side of the loft, I asked, "Andy up yet?"

Mama's voice trailed off as she headed towards the kitchen. "Been up a good while. You best be hurryin' along. He's most anxious to be leavin'."

I set for a moment longer, frowning and shaking my head, thinking over what a miserable morning it was sure to be—and especially so coming after the joy of yesterday's birthing. First I'd felt so terrible groggy, not being able to sort out the dreaming from waking. Then I'd gone and plowed into the table with my toe. And now this.

Going to mill was a point of manhood for young'uns around here, and Daddy'd sent Andy by himself for the very first time only a few months ago. Every time Andy'd gone since then, he'd been all puffed up the whole morning, teasing and pestering at me, acting like he was all growed up or something. I swear I could tell he was going to mill the very day just by the way he smiled at me when he set down to breakfast. More of a smirk than a smile, it'd be. Plain irritated me to death.

And now today Mama was sending me with Andy—since she was needing more meal to be moving with us to the new place—and that was surely going to make Andy madder'n the widow Campbell was when Miz Hickman told her her coffee was thick enough to plow. Granny Mandy'd said widow Campbell set so many sparks flying, you could've lit fireplaces round this here whole county. Again I frowned and shook my head. Didn't make no never mind why Mama was sending me with Andy; I was just knowing he wouldn't be wanting me tagging along. The sparks'd be flying from Andy all morning too. And they'd be aimed at *me*.

My toe was done paining, and so I went to get dressed, eat breakfast, and do my choring, managing to avoid Andy completely (except for breakfast, when he'd glared across the table at me the whole time) until it was time to be heading to mill. Mama met us at the door with two sacks of corn setting on the breezeway. She pointed to them, saying, "Andy, there's two for you, and Rachael, two for you also. You already got the eggs, Rachael? Good." Andy glanced over at me just long enough to give me another of his scowls. I noticed he had his favorite straw hat on again—the one that looked like Old Dean had chewed on it for a spell.

"Still don't see why I can't go to mill by myself," Andy complained, sending me yet another scowl. "I can tote them sacks just fine."

"Andrew, that ain't so an' you know it," Mama said. "You'd be spillin' out more'n you'd be totin' home. Can't spare the mule an' wagon. Yer daddy be needin' 'em. Now be sure to say *hey* to Mister Buchanan," she added, using a corner of her apron to wipe at a smudge on Andy's cheek. "We'uns'll be missin' him. He always done us fair, an' millers ain't often like that." She sighed and then said, "Now off with you, an' come on to home when them sacks is full. Daddy's needin' you both for chorin' in the barn once yer back."

Andy set off at a good pace and I trudged along behind him. *Ain't no sense tryin' to talk to him,* I muttered to myself. *He'd only grumble back at me—and pull that old hat farther down over his eyes. Don't know how he's seein' to where he's goin', he's got the blamed thing pulled down so far.* I smiled to myself. *Sure wouldn't mind seein' him trip over somethin'. Serve him right for bein' so ill!*

We were just passing Tommy Lee's farm—and I was busy studying on trying to catch a glimpse of him somewheres about the place, not watching where I was walking—when I tripped over a branch, causing me to drop one of my sacks and spill out some of the precious corn. After picking up what'd been lost, I then carefully checked over the meal sack for any signs of dirt. Mama'd took great care when she'd stitched up these sacks out of a heavy, cream-colored material. There was a straight blue stripe running along the edge of each side, and up in the corner of each one she'd also sewed in *McKenney Way* in her perfectly neat little stitches. I rubbed my fingers across our name now, a deep feeling of sadness suddenly coming over me. *Would we still be known as havin' McKenney Way corn at the new place? Could we?*

"Rachael! Have you gone plain deaf?" Andy hollered. He stood staring at me, the frown still on his face.

"What? I were thinkin' on somethin' else."

"Thinkin' on somethin' else? A body would think you *was* someplace else!"

"Well, maybe in my mind I was. What was it you was wantin' anyway?" I took up the two sacks in my hands once again and walked on, motioning for Andy to follow. "We can't be stoppin' for no jawin'. You know what Mama was sayin' 'bout Daddy needin' us to home."

"I didn't stop—you did!" Andy growled at me. "You was standin' there starin' at the meal sack like you ain't never seen one before. Come to think of it, you had 'bout the same look on yer face first thing this mornin' when I walked right past you."

I glanced over at him warily. "When was that?"

"I said, first thing this mornin'. You was settin' on yer bed. Starin' at yer feet like you'd done just discovered them too."

I could feel my face redden. *How many times a week does he make me do that anyway?* I fussed silently, blaming myself for letting Andy make me blush time and time again. "I was thinkin' on somethin' then too. Is they a law against that?"

Andy chuckled and pushed his hat back farther on his head. "Only if you go simple in the head, I reckon, an' keep a-starin' at yer feet for days an' weeks on end!"

I ignored him. "You never said. What was it you was wantin', anyway? When I dropped the meal sack?"

Andy kicked at a stone. They were all over the road now, since towards town just a ways the government men had poured even more truckloads of rock on all the roads leading to the dam site. But if we were pleased that they'd improved the roads, we surely couldn't be saying that about the scenery all around us. It made me sick to see the acres and acres of stripped land, chopped-off stumps. I kept my head down and my eyes on the stone Andy kept on kicking. Looking ahead or to the left or right was too hurtful.

"Was just wonderin' if you'd had that there dream anymore. You was actin' so strange like this mornin' that I thought maybe . . . maybe you'd been bothered with it again."

I jerked my head up to look at him, wondering at the note of kindness—and concern maybe?—in his voice. "Andy, have you ever had a time when you wasn't knowin' for sure if you was awake or if you was still asleep, and dreamin'? And I don't mean like when you wake up of a night in bed. This was . . . well, it happened at the Youther's."

"What happened?"

"The dream come to me. At the Youthers'. When I was just standin' there, waitin' for Granny Mandy. The baby'd been a-holdin' onto her finger and then Granny looked up at me. Andy, I swear I seen the flash of light and it hurt so, painin' me terrible!"

"Did Granny Mandy say somethin' to you?"

I thought a moment, vaguely recollecting something, but not able to remember just what it was. "I think so. But I can't recall what. Why? Are you thinkin' that be important to remember?"

Andy shrugged his shoulders. "Was just askin'."

"You ain't still frettin' over Granny Mandy, are you? 'Cause Andy, you should've seen her yesterday. Why, she worked the whole day over Miz Youther, and she didn't once have no spell come over her. Many a time I've heard it said that Granny done the best midwifin' round the whole county. Now I know it's true! Mama, Aunt Opal, an' Miz Arnold was all sayin' nobody else could've saved Miz Youther and that baby gal. Not even the doctor could've done what Granny Mandy done!"

Andy'd been kicking that same stone this whole time, but now it suddenly tumbled down a gully and rolled away into the Harrises' abandoned front yard. Andy stared after it a moment and then suddenly turned, heading off down the road at an even faster pace. I saw him shove that hat back down over his eyes before he stuck both hands into the pockets of his overalls.

Nearly running to catch up with him, I called, "Andy! Why're you tearin' off like that? And didn't you hear what I said 'bout Granny Mandy? Means that silly old dream of mine doesn't mean nothin', just like I told you. Ain't you happy?"

He turned to me, slowly shaking his head and giving me a look that took me off guard once again. With softened features and them eyes deepening with caring, Andy's look was one of *pity*. Softly he said, "They's daylight showin' through yer words, Rachael. Can't you see it? Or is it that you just ain't wantin' to see it?"

I stopped a moment, watching Andy's back now as he walked away from me, leaving me standing there with my mouth hanging wide open. I'd took blame, pouting, and plenty of anger from Andy, but I wasn't taking no pity ever—from Andy or from nobody else. Ever! And I recollected too well Andy saying the very thing once before. About the daylight showing. I stood there fuming inside until finally my anger reached the boiling over point, it seemed, and I kicked at another big old rock. Kicked it *at* Andy. "Don't you dare say that about me!" I hollered at him. "You said that 'bout them Yankees! I ain't no stinkin' Yankee. An' I ain't no liar!"

Andy spun around then, the pity gone and throwing as much fury back at me as I'd aimed at him. "Yes you is! Only you ain't lyin' to nobody but yerself! The only time you's got the courage to be admittin' the truth is when you's dreamin'. Well, it's time you be wakin' up, Rachael. I never knowed such a coward! Even when you's seein' it with yer eyes open you's still believin' the lies. You best stop it . . . stop it before—before it be too late!" He stared into my eyes a moment, like to pleading with me he was, before turning around and trudging off down the road again.

Once more I knew the pain from staring into someone else's eyes, but this wasn't no blazing light. And it wasn't a dream coming to haunt me in the daylight neither. I put my hands over my eyes, shielding them from—from what? *Oh God*, I prayed. *I wish I was dreamin'*!

I ran to catch up with Andy then, but I didn't ask him anything more, and he wasn't offering to talk any more with me neither. We walked on, quietly, begrudgingly, each one avoiding even glancing the way of the other. Only my thoughts weren't quiet, and they come attacking at me like a swarm of yellow jackets: *Am I lyin' to myself? 'Bout what? Could it have somethin' to do with what Granny Mandy said to me yesterday at the Youther's? What was it? Why can't I remember?* I knew now that it was something important, something I should be thinking on. My head started to ache I concentrated so hard, and I rubbed at my sweat-soaked forehead. But it was as if I'd plain blocked it out of my memory. Wiped it away like Miz Travis cleans the blackboard. *Why, oh why couldn't I remember?*

I struggled over it all the way to town, finally putting the puzzle aside when it was time to call our *heys* to folks as we were passing through. When we come to the Hickmans' store, I went in to drop off the eggs and Miz Hickman started in to questioning me all about the Youthers' newest young'un. Knowing there wasn't no use trying to escape without jawing with her at least for awhile, I listed off what most women folks were anxious to hear: yes, Miz Youther was in terrible pain for hours and hours (at this point I was interrupted by Miz Hickman, assuring me that her labor pains were even more awful, she was sure of it); the baby come out backwards—but healthy just the same; Granny was thinking she weighed close to six and a half pounds; she measured twenty-one and one-quarter inches long; and they'd called her Mandy, after Granny Mandy.

When Miz Hickman started in to asking me to tell her exactly how long Miz Youther'd been in labor and to even describe how loud she'd hollered, I told her she was needing to ask Aunt Opal or Miz Arnold those things since I'd been outside with the other young'uns most the day anyways. And then I scooted out the door right quick. Before she could be asking me anymore of those kind of questions.

When we passed by Old Man Snodderly's bench I noticed it was empty, but I didn't think too much of it until we come to the mill. Then me and Andy both groaned aloud. "Now don't this just beat all! George Snodderly an' Ol' Man Snodderly is both here at the mill!" Andy complained. "I ain't goin' to get one moment's peace with the two o' them pullin' my ear this mornin'." He turned to glare at me. Like I was the cause of it or something. "This be enough to make a cat spit. I'm to be standin' here all mornin' with Ol' Man Snodderly, George Snodderly, and you. Did you ask Miz Hickman to come join us too? If she was to come an' start to jawin' in my ear too, I'd be deaf as Miz Harris quicker'n I could find my own bottom in the privy."

I glared at him. But seeing there wasn't any use to waste no words arguing—or trying to make him feel any better either—I turned and headed towards the door of the mill house where the Snodderlys and Mister Buchanan stood talking about what everybody was these days: the dam. Mister Buchanan turned and smiled at me, pulling at his hat.

"Hey there, Rachael. Needin' some meal a'ready? Fool dam's to blame, I reckon."

Mister Buchanan always talked in short sentences, taking his good sweet time too. Fact was, you'd plainly try to help him finish his speaking sometimes, he was so slow to talk. And seeing how no Southerner was ever in a hurry to be spitting out words, that meant Mister Buchanan was tolerable slow all right. Granny'd told me she once watched a spider spin him a web that stretched from Mister Buchanan's ear to his elbow while he was telling her a story. I wasn't believing her, but it certainly did seem possible sometimes when you were waiting on him.

"Yes, sir. Mama's wantin' extra, seein' this is to be our last trip. Me an' Andy's both totin' two sacks." I nodded towards the Snodderlys. "Hey. Good mornin' to you."

They both nodded back, saying *hey* and smiling at me and Andy. *Only a Snodderly smile is more of a sneer than a smile*, I thought.

"Grindin' two sackfuls afore you," Mister Buchanan drawled. "Shouldn't take too long. Nice day fer it."

George Snodderly glanced up towards the sky. "Iffin she should rain, hit be a fine day fer fishin'." He hitched up his frayed, dirty overalls, sliding even filthier fingers round the suspenders. "Ain't many knowed we was to git us'uns a lake on Snodderly property. Was you knowin' hit? Well, come next year, I figure me an' my daddy'll be yankin' them fish outta that there lake faster'n Daddy can chew an' spit. Ain't that right, Daddy?"

Ol' Man Snodderly grinned and then proceeded to pucker up and spit a stream of ugly brown tobacco juice from between toothless gums. Right next to Andy's feet. Andy's eyes narrowed dangerously and he took a step towards the both of them, but I quickly stuck out my arm in front of Andy, handing Mister Buchanan one of my sacks. "Have you opened the gate yet, Mister Buchanan?" I asked. "Me an' Andy's needin' to get home to help Daddy with chorin' soon's we can."

"Not yet. Best get to her." Mister Buchanan turned then and slowly walked towards the gate that, once opened, would allow the power of the water from the combined Mills and Poplar Creeks to turn the large millstone which ground the corn into meal. It was a simple method, one that folks'd been using for centuries, according to Daddy. But it still worked fine—as long as there was enough force to the water and there was a need. Once the dam was finished, though, the government people were promising that Jordan's Bend would have electric power, and that we wouldn't have a need of places like this here mill anymore. I watched

Mister Buchanan going about the chores that he'd done for so many years now, wondering how he felt about this new dam. And George Snodderly bragging on the very thing.

Mister Buchanan lumbered back towards us, taking off his battered hat and scratching his head with one hand. "Current's unusual slow today. Even after yesterday's rain." He put his hat back on and nodded towards the river. "Fool dam's to blame, I reckon. They's workin' upriver too. Goin' to take a good while fer the grindin'. You all be wantin' to stay?"

I glanced at Andy, instantly noting the often present scowl coming over his features again. Or had it never left his face from when he'd first seen the Snodderlys? "I reckon we'd best just wait, Mister Buchanan," I said, ignoring Andy's disgust. "Mama's needin' that meal, and I'm thinkin' she'd be wantin' us to stay. Won't do us no good to go home empty-handed." I sighed. It was going to be a long day all right.

"Hey, Andy!" a voice called out, and I turned to see Clyde Travis coming up the road. He was toting two sacks of corn too.

Fortunately, I saw Andy's face ease just a bit as he leaned against the old hickory tree that grew next to the mill, giving everybody that waited here a much appreciated cooling shade. *Thank You, Lord*! I muttered under my breath, knowing that Clyde's coming was surely no less than a blessing. He'd distract Andy, keep him busy talking and therefore hopefully not picking no fights with the Snodderlys.

"Hey, Clyde!" I greeted him warmly, causing Clyde to glance over at me in amazement. We hadn't spoke much since Children's Day, when I'd been right put out with him for acting just like one of the littlest young'uns.

"Hey, Rachael." Clyde give me a wary glance, stepping round me and then turning towards the Snodderlys. You'd've thought I was a poisonous snake—or smelled worse'n them Snodderlys—the way he was acting. "Hey, Mister Snodderly, an' you too, Mister Snodderly." Clyde shook hands with them and then nodded towards the mill. "Mister Buchanan workin' the mill today?"

"Just startin' her up," Andy answered him. "Snodderlys is ahead of us. Me an' Rachael brung four sacks since Mama's needin' meal to be lastin' her a while. Mister Buchanan says the mill's turnin' slow like though, on account o' the current ain't fast. You in a hurry?"

"Me? I got me the whole blamed day," Clyde laughed, putting his sacks on the ground and plopping down at the bottom of the hickory tree next to Andy. "Say, did you hear what Lena done?"

I turned away from the two of them, knowing Clyde would keep

Andy busy talking the whole time we were there, and for that I was mostly thankful. Of course, the bad of it was that that left me to listen to the Snodderlys brag on what good fishermen they were, how many fish they'd be catching, and how big they were all going to be, measuring them every time with their arms wide apart. Seemed like I'd heard every fish story that was ever told before Mister Buchanan finished grinding our corn, since the Snodderlys had even stayed after theirs was ground, knowing they had them a captive audience, I was figuring.

Finally, it was going on to late afternoon when our meal was finished being ground. Mister Buchanan took out the "toll dish," a wooden dipper which he used to measure out a portion of the meal as payment. I was just thanking him like Mama had told me to do when we all looked up at the same time, for coming down the road towards the mill was a mule and wagon, at a tolerable good speed for a mule.

"It's Ol' Dean!" Andy exclaimed. "An' Tommy Lee Arnold's a-drivin' our wagon!"

I nearly dropped the sacks I was holding, knowing that something had to be terrible wrong. Tommy Lee drove Old Dean right up to us, and soon as he'd pulled him up to a stop, he called out, "Rachael, Andy, climb in quick. You's needed to home."

"You's wantin' me to finish up, Rachael? Measurin's mostly done," Mister Buchanan pointed out. Now his slow, drawled-out words nearly drove me to distraction.

"Um, yes, sir. Can you be doin' it quick like?"

He nodded. "Reckon so. Anybody hurt, Tommy Lee? Want Clyde here to fetch the doctor?" Mister Buchanan measured out his meal, but we weren't watching him. I reckon every eye—including them nosy Snodderlys and Clyde too—was on Tommy Lee.

"It's Granny Mandy. Took bad sick 'bout a hour ago. She don't want no doctor, but she's askin' for Andy an' Rachael." Tommy Lee looked over at me then, and I saw the caring in his eyes again.

For a moment, it seemed like everything else in the whole world just fell away. There wasn't no mill nor miller nor meal sacks in my hands. The Snodderlys plumb disappeared and Clyde and Andy along with them. There wasn't no ground beneath my feet nor sun beating down on my head. All I saw or knew was Tommy Lee's eyes. And then the horrible fear come, starting with a terrible knotting in my stomach which turned quickly to nausea, sickening nausea. *Oh God, no!* I pleaded. *Not my granny. I can't be bearin' it if somethin' should happen to Granny!*

Somehow the meal sacks got lifted into the back of the wagon, and then me and Andy climbed up on the seat next to Tommy Lee, but I really didn't remember doing any of those things. Once again I was struck by the fact that I wasn't knowing for sure if this was real—or if I was only dreaming. *Let it be a dream,* I prayed. *Let it only be a bad dream.*

"How bad off is she?" Andy asked, bringing me back suddenly, rudely, to the bright sunshine, the wagon being pulled along by Old Dean and Tommy Lee's urgent message. I felt my stomach turn again.

"Can't say. Only know yer daddy said to fetch you quick." Tommy Lee glanced over at me, his eyes asking if I was okay. "Rachael?" he asked.

I shook my head at him, closing my eyes to the pain I saw in his. Tommy Lee loved Granny Mandy too, and surely he was worried sick over her. I was knowing that. But mostly Tommy Lee was hurting because of me, since he knew how much I loved my granny. And how much I needed her.

Tommy Lee drove Old Dean hard. We fairly flew through town, barely waving at folks as we passed by, calling out that Granny Mandy'd took sick and we were hurrying to home. But once we were on the other side of town, we all fell silent. Every now and then Tommy Lee'd need to call out to Old Dean, urging him on, but otherwise not a word was said. Can't say how many times I'd rode that path from town to home, but this was the longest trip I'd ever took.

When we pulled up next to Granny Mandy's cabin, I saw Mama open the screen door. She looked terrible white, though Mama had tanned a good bit these past weeks from working her truck patch. Her mouth was set in a straight line, and about her face I saw worry—worry evidently for us as she first searched Andy's face and then mine. And then, amazingly, Andy did something that I hadn't seen him do in years. After jerking off his dirty hat, he went straight into Mama's arms, where she held him, resting her head against his as she swayed slowly back and forth. I stood there stiffly, resentment building in me as I watched them. *Why is they just standin' there? Why is Mama wastin' precious time?*

"How's Granny Mandy?" I asked curtly. "And why didn't you have us to fetch the doctor?"

Mama didn't look at me, but kept her cheek nestled against Andy's tousled hair. "Yer Granny wouldn't have it. We's just respectin' her wishes, Rachael. They ain't nothin' we can be doin' anyways," she said softly. "Granny insists it's so, an' me an' yer daddy's believin' 'tis true. Been comin' for some time. Surely you knowed that?"

"Ain't so!" I hissed at her, and this time Mama jerked her head up, staring up at me with a bewildered look. "Can't rightly believe her own kin's puttin' her in the grave before she's ... before she's ..." I stopped, giving Mama, Andy, and Tommy Lee one more glare before jerking open the rusted screen door and making sure it slammed hard behind me.

"Andy here?" a weak voice asked, and I heard a slight lilt of amusement in the question.

Granny Mandy was in bed, and the favored quilt was tucked up around her chin. One hand stuck out at the top, a tanned hand, one with fingers worn, wrinkled, and bent with pain from years of choring. Such a familiar, beloved hand. Her fingers nervously worried back and forth across the frayed edges of the once colorful quilt. Daddy set on the rocker next to her, and he give me a confused look when I come to her bedside. I kneeled down beside her, taking the dear hand between my own. Instead of finding the ever warm one which I had always known, it was terrible cold. I flinched at the feel of it.

"No, 'tis Rachael," Daddy said, soothingly. "Andy's here too though. Is you wantin' to speak with 'em both—or one at a time?"

Granny's head jerked back and forth against her pillow, just like I'd seen Miz Youther do just yesterday. *Yesterday? Were it only yesterday that this same woman was workin' feverishly like a strappin' young gal, savin' a baby and its mama? It can't be! Surely everbody's mistaken. Granny's goin' to be just fine!*

The door creaked open again and Mama, Andy, and Tommy Lee come in. Tommy Lee hung back, not wanting to intrude on us, I assumed. But Andy come right up to Granny's bedside, kneeling down beside her on the other side of the bed. Suddenly Granny stopped her jerking, and she opened them sparkling eyes, favoring Andy with a sweet smile. "Andrew McKenney," she said, barely above a whisper. "I'm always a-seein' yer daddy in ye. An' yer grandaddy too. Come from good stock!" She giggled just a bit, and then coughed from the effort the laughter took. In a raspy voice she asked Andy, "Ere ye knowin' yer heritage, Andrew McKenney?"

Tears started to glisten in Andy's green eyes, and I saw him blinking terrible hard, trying to hold them back. "I think so, Granny Mandy." He cleared his throat, nearly choking on the words. "I'm thinkin' I know what yer sayin'."

"Musn't just think. Ye must *know*," Granny persisted.

One tear escaped, running down Andy's cheek, but he took no never mind of it now. I watched it slowly work its way down his face until it fell onto Granny's quilt, dropping on a red square where it left a dark spot on the faded color. I stared at the wet spot. "Is you meanin' that I'm to be like my grandaddy an' my daddy?" Andy asked.

"I'm meanin' that ye already is so like 'em," Granny said, her voice sounding suddenly stronger. "They's a knowin' in ye, way beyond yer young years," Granny said. "Only comes from the Holy Spirit a-leadin' ye an' teachin' ye. But to be growin' even more—so that ye truly be like yer grandaddy an' daddy in ever way—ye needs be listenin' to Him even more, Andrew. Must be fightin' the stubbornness that comes over ye, takin' over yer will an' heart an' mind. When you's doin' that, you's shuttin' Him out same's closin' the door on a neighbor what needs feedin'."

Granny paused a moment, evidently gathering strength to finish what she was wanting to say. "Ye must be strong 'nough to be makin' the decision to be seekin' Him, Andrew. Let Him show ye His innermost thoughts, an' then He'll let ye see the deepest thoughts an' feelin's inside o' ye. An' then Andy—an' only then in the wellspring of our Lord's everlastin' love—can ye see yerself as ye truly is, seekin' humble repentance for the ugly sin ye'll be findin' there. Then ye can grow in Him, becomin' most like Jesus. Our sweet Jesus." She took a deep breath, continuing in a much weaker voice, "Some folks is never knowin' the how of it, Andy. But ye will. Such a gift! Yer so like yer daddy. An' yer grandaddy."

Granny Mandy closed her eyes once again, and then Andy's silent tears give way to muffled sobs as he buried his face on the bed. His shoulders heaved and the crying that come from deep down inside seemed to echo throughout the otherwise quiet cabin. I watched him, feeling a lump form in my throat, but no tears came from my eyes. I felt like I was watching everybody from a distance. Like spying through one of those looking glasses at people I was hardly even knowing. Maybe it was that I wasn't wanting to know them just now.

Granny slept peacefully, and time seemed to just set still in that old cabin. Andy eventually got up, wiping away the remains of his crying but showing the telltale signs from the bright blotches on his cheeks and a glistening in his eyes still. Mama cooked some supper and Daddy got up from the rocker to eat, along with Andy and Tommy Lee. Mama coaxed me to come, but I stayed by Granny, setting on the floor next to her bed, still holding her hand, stroking the fingers between mine. *They's all wrong*, I said to myself, over and over. *She's sleepin' so peaceful like. Granny's goin' to be just fine.*

Darkening shadows moved into the cabin as the day slipped into evening, and the fire's light shone in Tommy Lee's eyes. I only glanced at him now and then. But I knew he was watching over me most every minute, rarely taking his eyes off me.

"James Henry? Ere that you?"

I started at the sudden sound of Granny's voice. Her eyes popped open, but now there was a glazed look about them, the same odd staring I'd seen every time she'd had one of them spells. Though I'd been holding her hand all this time, I now let go, pulling back from her in dread.

"Won't be long now." Granny glanced towards the window. "Before the night's touched the mornin', I'm thinkin'." She reached out the hand that I had held just a moment ago, acting like she was reaching for something in the air. "Funny, but I ain't never seen that before. Now I can most touch it—feel them things in yer world, James Henry, the unnatural world just beyond. The world where the foxfire grows."

I winced at the remembering. But Granny smiled.

"Veil must've hid 'em from me. 'Bout gone now though. Soon I'll be a-touchin' ye again too, James. An' also my . . ." her voice broke, and now Granny Mandy began sobbing, only weak like, as if she had no strength left for the crying even. "My Jesus . . . I'll be touchin' my Jesus . . ." Daddy anxiously moved next to her side, but Granny ignored him, crying out, "Oh, Rachael, where is ye?"

Her eyes searched over the whole room for me, frantically looking right past me, not seeing me. I grabbed up her hand again, holding it up to my cheek, and then Daddy started in to soothing her, caressing and stroking a few curls of snow-white hair that clung to her dampened forehead. "Rachael's here, Granny. She's right here at yer side," Daddy said softly.

Finally Granny calmed again as she found me. Some of the sparkle come back to her eyes as she smiled at me and I smiled back. I clung to her hand, willing her to hold onto me as tightly as I clutched at her. "Rachael?"

"I'm here. What is it, Granny?"

"Oh, Rachael." She blinked them eyes, and once again I felt just a hint of that uncanny, frightening pain flash in my eyes. "I'm in the garden," she whispered.

A wave of terrible disappointment swept over me. *Not now*! I pleaded silently. *Don't be havin' no spell now, Granny, please*! I took a deep breath and patiently explained, "Granny Mandy, you ain't outside in the garden. You's safe in yer cabin. In bed. Inside."

"No," Granny said insistently, disappointment filling her voice too.

She jerked her head back and forth. "Be listenin' to my heart, not my words, Rachael. Not my truck patch. I'm in the garden. His garden. Gethsemane, child. *Gethsemane!*"

I shook my head at her. "I'm not understandin' you, Granny. Why're you in Gethsemane?"

"It be the place o' struggle, Rachael. Wantin' to go. But knowin' the cost, oh, the cost. 'Tis agony!"

I saw the torment pull at her features, noticed the pain in her eyes. The sorrow of the struggling set plain over my granny as a heavy mountain fog.

But even seeing that—so clear and so close that her struggle was reaching out to me, touching me with grasping fingers—still I looked away from her, shrugging my shoulders, shaking away the feelings that were trying to pull me in. Stiff like, resolving to take all feeling out of my words, I said, "You can go if you's needin' to."

Granny's head jerked up off the pillow, and with surprising strength she reached out with her other hand to pull my face full toward her again. Them piercing eyes bored into mine, and the torment she was knowing poured into her words. "Go? Child, ain't ye knowin' you's the onliest one what ain't let go o' me? You's the reason I'm strugglin' so—the reason I'm feelin' a longin' to be leavin' this painful world, yet feelin' guilty fer the goin'. Fer leavin' ye alone, when ye ain't ready yet. Ye needs be lettin' me go, Rachael, let me put the garden behind. Ye can't be clutchin' me no more!"

And then suddenly the room before me changed as the edges that divided everything melted and disappeared, making windows and floor and chairs become one in a mighty roaring sound that flowed in me, through me. My mind had time to grasp just this: it was the dream come true for real, and there wasn't no denying it, no doubting it this time. With blazing swiftness, I was sucked into the center of a swirling darkness, a vast empty hole that pushed me to the place where all those edges now suddenly come together once again, defining my whole world with one understanding, one final knowing that become everything. It was *pain*, a piercing pain that stabbed at my eyes and cut down all the way to my soul.

"No!" I cried out, reaching and grasping at the tattered quilt, searching for something to break and stop the reality of the horrible dream and the unending pain that it brought. "I can't bear it—I won't!" I shouted now, raising my face to the dark cloud that hovered over me. "You done took everthin' away from me, God—my home, my land, even Tommy Lee's goin' to be miles away. Granny's my only way to be touchin' You, to be knowin' You has any love atall for me. I won't let you take Granny Mandy too! I won't! *I can't!*"

I jumped up and run from her then, slamming open the door once again and running from the pain of the dream, the accusation from Granny Mandy, the threat I'd thrown at God. Blindly I ran, not knowing where to go in my despairing and intense pain, but instinctively following the worn, familiar path that led to the river.

Sobbing, with tears flooding my eyes and soaking my face, I run past barely visible sawed-off stumps in the growing darkness, hated reminders of the Yankees and all that they'd brought into our lives, *my* life. Everywhere I looked there was the evidence of destruction, hurting, agony. And I knew that really it all began with me, flowed from me, from my heart.

Then, without even realizing I'd headed just this way, I come to the place where—wasn't it years and years ago?—the place where Granny'd guided me off this old path by the light of her old lantern, the place where the foxfire lay hidden under a rotted stump. "Yes!" I spit out. "This is just where I should be a-comin', even though I wasn't plannin' to. Somethin' led me right here—right to this lyin' place. I'll destroy it, just like everthin' else's been destroyed—my home, my Granny, everthin'!"

Furiously I started pushing at every stump in my way, not recollecting just where the hated foxfire was, but knowing it was here, somewhere, hiding from me. I stumbled, falling over a branch and scraping up my shin, causing me to cry out in my hurt and frustration. And then, when I looked up to see just what I'd tripped over, I recognized the familiar rotted stump setting just next to me.

The foxfire stump. The place where natural and unnatural come together, forming truth. Forcing me to see the real—who I was and all I was wanting to be. Who I was and all I wasn't. I couldn't run no more, couldn't clutch at Granny to be saving me, couldn't deny no more what I knew. I was like Mama's fragile china cup. Broke. And there wasn't no fixing it. No fixing me.

I lifted my face to the sky once again, but suddenly there wasn't any fight left, no accusing. I whimpered, "I feel throwed away, God. You done made it plain You ain't wantin' me no more. Hurtin' me like You done, time after time. Why is You so cruel? Was You ever lovin' me? Was You?" I dropped to my knees, feeling a weakness flow through me. "You ain't never loved me. Never."

With the last measure of strength I could gather up, I give the stump a great push, sending it splintering against the ground, it was so rotten.

And then through tear-filled eyes I looked down ... and stared into the most beautiful blue-green glow winking back at me. The foxfire. Gleaming, shimmering, mesmerizing me even now with its captivating beauty.

I blinked several times, trying to clear the tears from my eyes, trying to know for sure if the sight before me was real. But the foxfire didn't go away. If anything, it glowed brighter, dancing once again to the delicate fairy music, celebrating with joy and inviting me to join them in that other world—the unnatural one.

Something in me broke then, feeling like a thread that's stretched too far and suddenly snaps. "Oh God, it's *real*," I whispered. Reaching out with shaking hands, clutching at the edges of the stump to steady me, I sought to find some reassurance in the feeling of the splintery wood in my hands. "The foxfire's still here and it's real. Then Granny weren't lyin' after all. But I'm still not knowin' for sure if ... if You was ever lovin' me, if You's wantin' me even now. I feel so alone, so terrible alone an' lost." I closed my eyes, concentrating on my need. "If You really is a-lovin' me, then You must be showin' me. I'm needin' to feel Yer arms round me, now!"

And then suddenly strong arms were around me, enfolding me into a firm embrace that pulled me against a warm chest, a beating heart, and the sounds of a soothing voice cooing, "I's here, Rachael. Let my arms be God's for you. Let me be His touchable love."

After months and months of being lost, I was found.

Tommy Lee held me for some time as I cried softly. There wasn't any more furious anger. No paralyzing fear. Not even the deep pain that I'd known every time I'd cried before in his arms. This time there was only release. A cleansing. A new beginning between me and my God. Though Tommy Lee'd done the touching, I knew it was His love washing over me in waves, filling my heart, my soul with a deep sense of belonging. I felt like a young'un that woke up in the night, feeling so utterly alone as it searched, hands reaching in desperate need for its mama—until the babe was tenderly held, soothed, loved. And with that come security and a sure *knowing* of ... what?

And even as I cried and was comforted in the protection of Tommy Lee's arms, I knew this for sure: that I didn't have all the answers, and the future still stretched before me with so much uncertainty and a measure of fear too. But somehow this new beginning had given me a calmness to face it. Because I'd faced my greatest fear already, I could now turn and move into that uncertain future.

My tears stopped their flowing and the two of us stared into the foxfire, entranced by the shimmering lights before us.

"Tommy Lee?"

"Yes, Rachael."

"What is faith? I've found mine again, but I'm still not knowin' for sure all that it is. All that it should be. Does it mean I can't be afraid at all of the future? Or angry at the Yankees? Or worried 'bout Granny Mandy? And just, well, askin' all them questions I been askin' for so long?"

"Can't be givin' you all the answers, Rachael. You's knowin' that. But I do know one thing. Faith and doubtin' ain't opposites."

"They ain't?" I snuggled up closer against him.

"If they is, then David an' Peter an' Paul surely wasn't knowin' much 'bout faith. Is that right?"

"No, can't be. But they wasn't strugglin' like I been, was they?"

"Ever man struggles in the pathway God's give 'im to walk, Rachael. God never promised us this life would be a easy one to hoe. Only said it'd be worthwhile."

"Do you think God loved me, and then stopped . . . and now He loves me again?"

He chuckled and then tightened his arms about me. "You answer yer own question."

I sighed. "Well, I'd surely like to think He always loved me. But I were thinkin' God's love were like this here foxfire, and it changed. Oh, it changed terrible, Tommy Lee. You should've seen it in the daylight!"

"Foxfire's one o' His creations, Rachael. Can't be explainin' it no more'n I can be understandin' why God loves us in the first place. But I know He does—even though we ain't deservin' it. An' He 'specially loves us when we think He ain't."

"Even when I can't be feelin' it?"

"'Specially then."

"When . . . when Granny dies . . ." I stopped a moment, trying to keep talking when the words were still feeling like they shouldn't be spoke, shouldn't be thought even. "When Granny Mandy dies, I ain't goin' to feel like He loves me."

"Maybe not. But He will be, Rachael. You was right—His love ain't never stoppin', an' I think you's beginnin' to understand that, knowin' that deep down in yer heart."

I stared at the foxfire a moment longer, drinking in its glorious beauty, gathering courage. "I need to go back to Granny Mandy." A sudden need to see her made me push away from the comforting arms about me. "It ain't too late, do you think?"

"No. Yer Granny ain't said good-bye to you yet. I'm thinkin' yer granny never done went anywheres but when she was good 'n ready to be goin'. But we best be hurryin' anyways." Tommy Lee stooped over the foxfire, waving his hand back and forth like Granny'd done so long ago, making it shimmer once more. "Wait an' let me right the stump best I can. Poor thing's 'bout rotted away."

I watched him pick up what was left of the stump and place it over the blue-green glow. Once again I hated to see the light blocked out, cut off from my sight. And then turning towards me, Tommy Lee took my hand firmly in his and we headed back along the worn path towards Granny's cabin.

The firelight shining through Granny's windows welcomed me as it had done so many times before, but suddenly I hesitated, feeling my heart start in to pounding.

"What is it?" Tommy Lee asked.

"This could be . . . could be the last time."

He nodded. "In this ol' world. They's another one, Rachael. An' there yer granny'll be whole, an' happy, an' with all her kin. A homecomin'!" I could just glimpse his reassuring smile in the firelight.

Slowly I walked the last few steps to the cabin and pushed open the door, where I saw Daddy, Mama, and Andy gathered round Granny Mandy's bed. All three looked up at me, but Granny's eyes were closed. "She ain't . . . ?" I asked, fearing Daddy's answer.

He shook his head. "Come now."

Once more I knelt by her bed, but when I took her hand this time, I wasn't clutching, wasn't holding her back. Instead, I remembered Granny talking so long ago about Grandaddy, and how she'd memorized the feel of him before he died—his roughened flannel shirt, his worn-smooth overalls, his calloused, strong hands. I gently rubbed the wrinkled one between mine, imprinting the feel of this dear hand on my heart's mind. The slender, bent fingers, the deep lines and calluses, the cool feel of her slim gold wedding band and how it moved up against the enlarged knuckle.

When I looked up at Granny's face, she was smiling at me once again. My eyes moved over the familiar face then too, as I sought to memorize the forehead and the way her snowy hair framed it, the tiny nose, the high cheekbones like Mama's, a tender yet somehow firm mouth (was that having to do with her stubbornness?), and of course, them sparkling, twinkling eyes. *Why, they was most like the foxfire!* I hesitated only a moment before letting my hand follow where my eyes had just been, lightly moving over the dear face, imprinting the feeling of each line and hollow, working hard to always remember. Always.

When I'd finished, Granny smiled and sighed. "Ye done seen it again, haven't ye?" she asked, excitement ringing in her words, even though they were weak like. "I can fairly see the reflectin' glow still about yer face."

I nodded. "Yes, Granny. Headed right there, even though I wasn't meanin' to."

Granny looked puzzled. "Ye mean ye wasn't goin' right to it for the comfortin'?"

Shaking my head 'no,' I answered, "I were afraid to be goin' back there. Ever since . . . ever since I seen it in the daylight."

She raised her eyebrows, looking puzzled. No, it was more questioning, like a teacher asking for the truth. Knowing the answer, knowing the outcome. "I seen you'd been there before. Found the stump uncovered an' had to right it. What was ye seein' then?"

I looked away from her eyes, squirming in my remembered hurt and anger over the foxfire—and the blame I was putting on Granny Mandy for it, the separation I'd put between us because of it. Softly, barely above a whisper, I said, "It were terrible ugly, Granny. Terrible."

Now Granny put a hand to my face, and as she tenderly pulled my face towards hers, there were waves of love coming from her. "It were the same foxfire, Rachael. The very same. One's of this world—one's of the unnatural one. You's understandin' that, ain't ye?"

I closed my eyes a moment, still remembering the pain of the foxfire, still feeling the flashing pain of my dream. "I ain't understandin' Granny. I thought God's love were like the foxfire—beautiful an' glowin' an' lovin', always. But it ain't. It ain't! Sometimes it hurts. An' sometimes it's awful . . ."

"Oh, Rachael, my dear Rachael. Open yer eyes, child! Look into mine an' be listenin' to the Truth what God has tole us. Starin' into the fire be painful, since we's seein' ourselves as we truly is—sinful, terrible sinful! But we can be bearin' it because of His love. A love what ain't shocked by what we sees in ourselves. 'Tis a love what accepts us, just as we is. A love what ain't never changin', never. Ain't portioned out. Cain't earn no more. Cain't be punished an' be gettin' less. We's receivin' ever bit He has to be givin'. Lookin' into the blindin' light of the Light o' the world be terrifyin'! But in the seein', Rachael, we's knowin' His deep love reflected back to us. An' that love ain't never changin' none."

Still firmly holding onto me and keeping them blazing eyes riveted to mine, Granny now raised her other hand, motioning and waving it around the cabin. "But now everthin' round us—the happenin's, the seasons o' life, the bad what comes to ever creature—them things shift an' change. But they ain't the real. They ain't the things what be tellin' Who He is an' how much He's a-lovin' us."

She paused a moment, taking a deep breath. "These old worldly eyes looks on the terrible things o' this world, an' we sees the ugly foxfire, the awful, the foxfire o' this here natural world. An' we's thinkin' them's the truth. But ye must believe God, not what them things is sayin'. An' ye must not believe what them things seem to be sayin' God is—hurtful an' cruel an' unlovin'. True faith, Rachael, be a decision. A decision to be believin' God and that He's lovin' no matter what's happenin' all round us."

"But the foxfire did change," I whispered.

"Did it? Or was it the way ye was a-lookin' at it? God's love itself be a burnin' fire, Rachael. Seems like it done like to burned me to death sometimes, but He wasn't lovin' me no less them times. It were the purifyin'. Ain't no cruel thing. Was gived outta love. In the hurtin' of the day. Durin' the beauty of the night."

I searched her face for more understanding. "But how can I be believin' them times when I feel so, so awful inside. So hurt an' angry an' lost an' . . . without no joy, like Preacher Morgan's always a-sayin' we oughta be havin'. I haven't been knowin' no joy! All I been knowin' is pain an' hurtin' an' anger! Granny, they been followin' me like a mist what's right behind me ever moment."

She gently caressed my cheek, wiping the tears away. "Rachael, them things is feelin's, an' they's comin' an' goin' with the things of this here world. 'Course you's feelin' them things. I be knowin' 'em too—seein' what them Yankees is doin' to my land, my dreams for the future, my loved ones! But feelin's change, Rachael. Change with the happenin's from this year t'next. Now joy, though. Joy be different."

Granny Mandy struggled to set up then, and a shining glow come to her features, a glow that seemed to pulse from her in touchable waves. "Joy is a *knowin'* down deep in yer soul. A knowin' that it don't make no difference what be happenin' to me—whether it be pain or sorrow or terrible anger or anythin' an' everthin'—nothin', *nothin'* can be changin' God's love for me. Nothin' can be takin' Him from me. Whether the foxfire be glowin' in all its glory or lookin' terrible awful in the light o' day, *it don't make no difference.* God's love ain't no changin' thing, Rachael. It's real an' alive an' livin' in me. An' joy is a-knowin' that!"

Granny's words washed over me, completing the cleansing, bringing understanding, allowing a soft and gentle healing to reach my soul at last. I gazed deeply into her eyes, letting all that Granny'd said pour into me and through me, letting the words penetrate my heart—and live there. So I could be owning them. So I could say, *I know*.

Granny Mandy wearily leaned back onto the pillow, her energy spent, the glow quickly fading into memory. I determined to remember every word she'd said, every expression on her face. Mama and Daddy helped Granny settle the dear head onto the pillow once again. But I had one more question for her, one more concern that I needed Granny's reassurance of. "So the foxfire'll always be there, waitin' for me, just like God's love?"

"Always."

"Just like yer love for me too?" I was knowing just how she would be answering me. But I needed to hear her say it. Just once more.

"Yes, Rachael. An' ever time you be gazin' at its glowin' colors, peekin' in on the unnatural world, ye will be knowin' that yer God an' yer granny is always lovin' ye. Always."

Suddenly another worry struck me, but even as I blurted it out, I knew it was too late. "What about when we move? Granny?"

But there wasn't anyone to answer it. Only the crackling of the fire invaded the stillness of the dying. Granny Mandy had already closed her eyes, took one last deep breath, and then breathed no more. I watched her weary face slowly ease and relax, and somehow the aged, burdened look that I had always known her to carry was gone, replaced with a gentle peace. A slight smile pulled at the corners of her mouth, and I saw a young woman again, a young woman with her Lord, her beloved husband, and the children she had said good-bye to so many years ago. Mandy McKenney was home. Truly home.

Funny how I remember the sounds and smells of those next hours more than the seeing. We spent some time there gathered round Granny's bed, crying softly, talking of what she'd meant to us, reminiscing about favorite times. After awhile—I have no idea how long we were there, whether it was five minutes or an hour or more—Andy went to sound the dinner bell, ringing it sixty-two times, Granny's age. Seemed like the haunting sound would go on forever, echoing through the gathering mist of the evening, creeping into Granny's cabin, seeming to become a living, breathing thing ringing inside my head. When it finally ended, all of us stopped what we were doing, suddenly looking up at each other, knowing the finality of it. Like an amen.

Daddy and Andy went to fetch the casket from the barn, the very casket that had brought so much fear to my heart. I looked at it now without really seeing it, but the still-new smell of the oak forced me to know it was real, to know its purpose. When I reached out to feel of it, a splinter immediately pushed into my hand. "You best not be touchin' it no more 'til I get her smoother," Daddy warned. "Reckon help'll be comin' soon."

After me and Mama'd gently prepared Granny Mandy, bathing her, dressing her in the favored and Sunday-best dress with the yellow flowers on it, carefully combing the snow-white hair, and placing a nickel on each eye to keep it shut, the help did come—Aunt Samantha and Uncle Les and Aunt Opal and Uncle Evert. I can hear their voices still, soft and low in their respect for the dead, but I can't recollect how they looked atall, what they wore.

Both Les and Evert stayed outside, bedding all the young'uns on the porch and taking turns helping Daddy and Andy sand down the oak box until it was kindly smooth to the touch and they could stain it with a light brown varnish. Even from inside with the fire still burning I could smell that varnish carrying through the air. When it was dry, Daddy would add the brass handles that Granny'd purchased some time ago too. Handles that were cool to the touch even on a hot day.

Mama's kin had come prepared to care for body and soul: Aunt Opal and Aunt Samantha, each toting baskets packed full with food, hugged us to them soon as they'd come through the door. They immediately set to work making the lining for Granny's casket—cotton batting and quilted white satin. Mama'd suggested we could use Granny's favorite worn quilt instead, since Aunt Opal'd brought the satin and we all were knowing how hard off they were by the needing to move too. Satin was a rare treasure for anyone in these parts and terrible expensive too, but Aunt Opal wouldn't have none of it.

"Somehow I just knowed Jamie's mama weren't goin' to be makin' this here move," Aunt Opal'd said, reaching out and lightly touching Mama's hand. "Miz McKenney were right good to everbody round these parts. Me an' Evert knowed her help with the birthin' o' ever one o' our baby boys. I traded for this here satin soon's I heared 'bout the dam. Wanted to have it. Wanted to be ready." She rubbed her hand over the soft material once more before placing it in Mama's arms. "Miz McKenney be deservin' white satin. It's for her."

Mama smiled then, giving her another quick hug before we all set to work stitching up the quilt that would soon soften Granny Mandy's resting place, caressing her roughened skin like no worn quilt had ever done before. Often while we were working I would touch my cheek to it, pleasuring in its softness, breathing in the fresh new smell. I would never see a bolt of satin again without closing my eyes, remembering how it felt that day, recollecting how it smelled.

Outside I could hear the soft sleeping sounds of the young'uns, the tree frogs giving their nightly concert, and the men working at the casket, murmuring now and then as they went about their chore. When they come inside, saying they were waiting for the varnish to dry, other folks come—Preacher and Miz Morgan, along with Merry Jo (who immediately pulled me into her arms, telling me she was knowing how much Granny Mandy meant to me, to us all); Miz Travis; the Hickmans (amazingly, even Miz Hickman was quiet in her respect); the Travises (Clyde walked around me once again, but this time I knew he did it out of shyness and caring); and Mister and Miz Arnold, along with Tommy Lee.

When Granny Mandy died, Tommy Lee'd hugged me once before quietly leaving, knowing that we needed some time as a family—just the four of us, together, alone. But now that he'd come back with his mama and daddy, I suddenly realized how my thinking on family had changed. Though we'd just spent time as only the four of us, I knew that from this moment on I'd always think of Tommy Lee being just as much a part of me as Daddy, Mama, James Junior, and Andy were. Maybe I was needing to fill the empty place that Granny'd left. Or could it be that I'd already begun to think of him as my husband? Whatever the reason, I knew a need for him like never before. Glancing into them doe's eyes moving over me with looks of concern and caring, I also knew a comforting, a sense of being complete, now that he was there, that only Tommy Lee could be providing.

As we set up of a night together there in Granny Mandy's cabin, we did what folks round these parts always do for the wake: we sang together, seeking comfort, mostly finding it. The sounds of those voices mingling like I'd never heard them before softly lulled me, soothed me with the familiar refrains of "Amazin' Grace," "Savior Like a Shepherd Lead Us," and Granny's most favorite of all, "The Old Rugged Cross."

Suddenly I remembered how so long ago I thought we were singing as one when Mister Hickman led us through "Rock of Ages," waving his arms like he does. And then I recollected too well the pain of feeling pushed away, abandoned by these same folks. That oneness I'd sensed mocked me then, bringing even more pain. Now, as I looked about the room at caring faces, eyes raised to the ceiling in adoration of Him, voices wanting to give us comfort from the deep meaning of these hymns, I knew oneness again.

Only this time, it wasn't a gushing feeling that I responded to, no naive wanting from folks that couldn't give what my childish needing was demanding of them. I understood now that Miz Hickman would always be the town gossip, hurting those that felt the sting of her tongue (like I had). And Nellie and Verna Mae most likely wouldn't say what was on their hearts, or maybe it was that they just couldn't. Even Preacher Morgan had his faults. As Granny'd said, he was needing to care for his sheep instead of hollering at them. Giving love in understanding, seeing the world through another's pain—not giving out simple phrases and answers that didn't help anybody when they were really hurting.

But now, I looked into each one of those faces, knowing them, accepting them for what they were and what they were able to give back to me, understanding that it was a decision that I was making to love them. Be one with them in unity as we were singing a hymn or listening to Preacher Morgan or caring for a birthing mama or whatever it was we were doing to worship our God together. And I knew too that each one'd have to make a decision to love me too—Rachael, the one who pushed them away in her pain, the one who blamed anybody and everybody for the hurting, the one who couldn't even accept Merry Jo's love when it was offered, the one who could only see and know and care about what she was feeling. That selfish Rachael was needing to be accepted for what she was too. And loved in spite of it all.

Just after midnight we sung one last hymn, in such hushed voices that it seemed but a whispered prayer. I didn't look into other faces now, but instead closed my eyes, needing to peer into my heart, search out if I could truly sing this hymn with believing and trust.

When peace like a river, attendeth my way,
When sorrows like sea billows roll;
Whatever my lot, Thou hast taught me to say,
It is well, it is well with my soul.

Though Satan should buffet, though trials should come,
Let this blest assurance control,
That Christ hath regarded my helpless estate,
And hath shed His own blood for my soul.

My sin—oh, the bliss of this glorious thought,

My sin—not in part, but the whole,
Is nailed to the cross and I bear it no more,
Praise the Lord, praise the Lord, O my soul!

And, Lord, haste the day when the faith shall be sight,
The clouds be rolled back as a scroll,
The trump shall resound and the Lord shall descend,
"Even so"—it is well with my soul.

It is well . . . with my soul . . . ,
It is well, it is well with my soul.

I found that I could sing with believing that night, could know in my heart that those words were true. But it wasn't the kind that I used to think was believing—an untried faith, really a kindly lazy one that was most like setting in a rocker on a breezeway, watching the world go by. Pointing out what was good and what was bad, dismissing the bad easy enough since it wasn't no part of me. The bad belonged with the likes of the Snodderlys, folks like that. Good come to them like us McKenneys, and things from the past like Granny's young'uns dying I could pass off easily as "God's will." Those things hadn't touched *me*. Until the government men come.

I'd learned me some hard lessons all right. Not that I was thinking I knew everything there was to be knowing. No, I understood better'n that. But I wouldn't never forget what Granny'd said about it not mattering what was going on all around me—and whether I was afraid of a pursuing darkness or angry at God or mourning the passing of one so dear. Because I'd found there was a knowing deep down inside of me. Granny was right. Joy is a knowing.

Folks left soon after that, except for Aunt Opal and Aunt Samantha, who stayed all night to set up with the dead. I tried terrible hard to be staying awake with them, but soon's I saw Andy drift off, my eyes just got heavier and heavier too. Before I knew it, it was morning and I was waking up to the sounds of Mama putting wood in Granny's old wood stove.

I remember the smell of frying ham and baking biscuits, and then the feel of Granny's battered tin mugs holding hot, steaming coffee that we all sipped gratefully after the long night. *Wonder if this'll be the last time we use Granny Mandy's stove and the fireplace?* I asked myself, letting my eyes roam over the blackened old stove and then the ancient fireplace, the heart of Granny's cabin, I was thinking. *How I'll miss her fried pies, specially brewed teas—even the ones with "secret ingredi-*

ents"— *and her old-timey oven cornbread.* My eyes filled with tears again as I remembered the many times we'd baked and talked, somehow finding the answers I was searching for as we worked together with our hands covered with flour, making dough of some kind.

All too soon Daddy and Andy lifted the now-filled oak box into the back of our wagon, and Old Dean started in to taking Granny on one last ride to town. I saw Mama give Daddy a hurtful look, and I knew she was aching for James Junior to be here, to help Daddy and Andy with bearing the coffin in his rightful place. Daddy'd said he'd wire James Junior once we got to town, but there wasn't no helping him to be getting here in time. The burying couldn't be waiting, no matter how hurting it was for Mama—and all of us. With a sudden stab of pain, I realized how much I was wanting James Junior too, needing him for his strength. Somehow needing him here to complete saying good-bye to Granny Mandy.

We rode slowly, passing by that stripped, ugly land much too slowly. You couldn't help but stare at it, much as you hated to. There just wasn't anything else to be looking at no more. *Death's not only all round us,* I thought to myself, *it's right here in this wagon, makin' us know its touch, its smells, its sounds.* They would all be remembered.

When we went through town, folks nodded, men tipping their hats in respect. Most everyone was heading towards the church for Granny's funeral and burying. And from the looks of the number of wagons already setting outside the church and folks standing around talking, that room'd be right packed.

"Whoa there, Dean," Daddy called out, and then I remembered the Sunday me and Granny left the all-day singing together, stopping Dean along the way home to eat under a tree. *Funny how everthin' brings back a memory of Granny Mandy,* I thought. A rush of feelings and happenings and pictures were constantly running across my mind, causing me to look out at the world in the present through all those memories of the past. *Will I always be this way? Or will the gnawin' ache in me for Granny slowly slip away, leavin' only memories what rarely come? Or never come? I don't want to lose her!*

"Can I be helpin' you down?" a familiar voice asked, breaking into my thoughts. Looking up, I saw James Junior standing next to Mama, reaching out them long, strong arms for her.

"James Junior!" Mama cried then, nearly falling off the wagon seat into his waiting arms, being lifted up once more as he held her fiercely to him. "You's here! You's here!" Mama cried over and over, joy and pain telling in her voice.

Daddy and Andy both come running, waiting until Mama'd stepped aside and then they were snatched up into James Junior's arms. First was Andy, who'd grown a good bit, I suddenly noticed, and then Daddy, who first give James Junior a look of disbelief, saying, "Can't hardly b'lieve 'tis truly you. Best get me a hug to be knowin' it for sure!"

Finally it was my turn, but I hesitated a moment, feeling suddenly shy. And then James Junior winked at me—that familiar warm, loving wink that never ceased to make me smile or forgive him or feel just a bit more at ease or whatever was needed at that moment. That wink pulled me into his arms faster'n I could even begin to wonder why I was feeling shy or what it was I needed. I only knew that once I was hugged tight up against him, the grieving for Granny Mandy could come full circle.

Now I wouldn't feel the need to be storing away the memories of today for James Junior; he could be doing that for himself. Instead, each of us could grieve in the way that we were needing, still caring for each other, finding strength in who and what we were as a family. So the needing for drawing in and then the giving out would bring us round the circle, back to our starting point: Granny Mandy, and Granddaddy McKenney and their mamas and daddies and so on. It was family I was needing. A sense of heritage that would then give me hope for the future. Me and Tommy Lee's.

James Junior held me at arm's length then, looking me over, smiling and nodding his head. "You's changed," he said softly. "Granny told me you would be." Before I could ask him what he meant he turned to Daddy, saying, "Mister an' Miz Hickman wired me last night, Daddy. Sorry I wasn't here before she passed on, but me an' Granny had us our talk before I left. I'm thinkin' she were knowin' somehow, like she always was knowin'."

Daddy nodded. "Reckon that's so. Yer mama an' me's just happy you's here now. An' right beholdin' to the Hickmans. What they done has . . . has made me . . ." Daddy stopped then, reaching for the handkerchief that he'd stuffed into the pocket of his starched white shirt, wiping at his eyes. He pushed it back into the pocket and then cleared his throat, visibly straightening his shoulders. "Ere we ready now, Miz McKenney?" Daddy asked, his voice strong and sure once again.

"Yes, Mister McKenney, we is," Mama answered.

And then Daddy, James Junior, Uncle Les, and Andy reached up for the simple oak box, sanded and varnished with great care, handled now gently, tenderly. As they silently carried the precious burden into the church, even the whispering hushed, and folks filed into a solemn line behind us.

Once we were all setting down, someone started into ringing the church bell. We all just set there, staring straight ahead, listening to the rhythmic *ding! ding! ding!*, seeing nothing but a simple oak box.

Miz Morgan played the piano for a while and Preacher Morgan read some and prayed, but I don't remember what was played, what was said. Those things didn't pull at my attention. I felt Tommy Lee's eyes on me, and once I turned to glance back at him. For reassurance, I suppose. Once I heard a baby fussing. And for a few moments I stared out the window, watching a squirrel setting on a tree branch. But mostly it was like there wasn't nothing else in that whole room, nothing in the whole world—nothing except that oak box.

Finally the service was over and Preacher Morgan opened the lid of Granny's casket for one last viewing. Folks filed silently forward, passing her, some reaching out to touch a hand, most women folk grabbing for handkerchiefs to be wiping eyes and noses. All too soon, the room was empty except for Preacher Morgan, Daddy, Mama, James Junior, Andy, and me. And Granny Mandy.

"Is there anythin' you'd like me to be sayin'? A prayer or somethin'?" Preacher asked.

Mama looked up at Daddy, but he shook his head. "Just give us a few minutes please, Preacher. An' then at the gravesite, if you'd be readin' them verses like I asked you to, we'd be most thankful."

Preacher Morgan nodded and then turned to leave. "Yer mama was stronger than most folks round here," he said softly. And then turning towards Daddy, he added, "She was stronger than I am. To my shame. To her praise." And then he left us alone.

Mama reached out, gently placing one of her hands on top of Granny's. I noticed Granny's wedding band and remembered the feel of it between my fingers. "I'm rememberin' how many times she were like a mama to me, lovin' me just like I were her child too," Mama said. She glanced up at Daddy. "They was many a time she helped me carry my burden, when I knowed she had her own to tote. Kindly never knowed how much I depended on her 'til that day in the field, when we was layin' by the corn. Thought of bein' without her filled me with fear. 'Cause I'd always followed her, followed her example, followed her wisdom."

The feelings of that day come rushing back to me. Sickening fear over Granny's spell, deep confusion for Mama's reaction to it. *Why wasn't I understandin' then that Mama was just as scared as I was?*

"Knowed right then how much I'd always looked up to her. Death ain't makin' no difference. 'Cause I always will."

Mama reached for Daddy then, tucking her hand through his arm and pulling him against her. She looked up at him once more, searching his face while he stared at his mama, waiting for Daddy to find the words he was needing to say. He took a deep breath. "I'm recollectin' how many times I were lecturin' her when Daddy died, remindin' her how that body were only his shell an' that grievin' for him so weren't admittin' the truth we was knowin'." He stopped a moment, shaking his head and looking into Mama's face like he was gathering strength from her. "Truth is, what I'm rememberin' now—an' grievin' for—is able hands what soothed my wounds, strong arms what give needed comfortin', knowin' eyes what peered into mine—makin' me look at myself somehow.

"Reckon it's time I done somethin' I been puttin' off. Need to nail up Daddy's gravehouse, seein' that them words Mama was always wantin' there is back where they's s'posed to be. I'm understandin' the need for 'em now. Then I can run my fingers 'long 'em like she use to. An' once I finish them gravehouses . . ." I glanced up at Daddy in surprise, knowing nobody put up gravehouses anymore. He'd only tolerated Grandaddy's for Granny's sake. ". . . I'll touch her final restin' words too, findin' comfort there like she always done at Daddy's. I reckon God'll give me the words what is fittin' to put there." Daddy leaned down then, softly touching his lips to Granny's forehead. "I love you, Mama."

I'd never seen my Daddy cry like that before, never seen tears allowed to flow so freely, so unashamedly. We just stood there for several minutes, waiting, listening to the sounds of Daddy's tears. Sounds we hadn't never heard before. I noticed we were all crying with him, but we cried silently, as if there was a whispered *hush!* over us. Somehow it wouldn't have been fitting for us to be making no sounds atall. Would've been like intruding, I was thinking. This was Daddy's time and his alone. When his crying had quieted he turned to James Junior, nodding to him to come pay his respects.

I noticed the changes in James Junior then too, the confidence of his every move, the way he handled himself that was somehow like he was before—and yet so different. He also reached out for Granny Mandy's hands, but instead of just touching them, he grabbed them up into his own, tucking them completely under his browned, strong fingers. "I always was, an' always will be, most proud that she were my granny," was all James Junior said, and then he also bent down, giving Granny Mandy a tender kiss.

My mind raced furious like, sorting through the many questions I wished I'd asked Granny, the tender and funny stories I wished I could hear again, the countless lessons there was still to be learned from her. But I knew those times were past. What was needing to be said, Granny Mandy had give me. Now it was for me to sort through all them lessons, applying them to the questions that I'd be facing tomorrow, and the next day, and in the years to come. I leaned close to her, one last time working to memorize the tiniest details that I was so fearing I'd forget—the cowlick that always made a stubborn curl on the upper left side of her forehead, the small mole under her right eye that give her a mischievous look, the hint of a dimple on her chin. I whispered, "I love you, too, Granny, and I won't never forget. Never. I know now. I know!" And then I too brushed her forehead with one last kiss.

Andy stood before Granny Mandy now, staring, his hands pushed way down into his pockets, his hair messed up as usual, his feet restlessly shifting weight from one to the other. He glanced nervously up at Mama and Daddy. "Ain't rightly knowin' what to say," he mumbled, his words coming out in a rush.

Daddy smiled down at him. "Maybe you a'ready done said everthin' they was needin' for."

Andy merely nodded and backed away, shuffling his feet slow and awkward like. Mama started towards Andy then, but Daddy held her back, shaking his head. "Leave 'im be."

"But he didn't even kiss her," she whispered to him. "Shouldn't he be . . . ?"

Daddy shook his head again, putting his arm around her and giving her a hug. "Ain't fittin' to force him. If Andrew were wantin' to, then . . ."

Suddenly we all stopped, watching Andy, feeling humbled by the simple tribute, touched by a young'un's way of loving. And knowing just what was fitting to show that love. Andy'd put one hand to his mouth and blown Granny Mandy a kiss. *They's a knowin' in ye, way beyond yer years,* I could hear her saying. *Yes, Granny Mandy, you's right.*

We waited until Uncle Les and Uncle Evert had nailed down the lid, and then Daddy, James Junior, Uncle Les, and Andy carried the coffin one last time. We followed them in simple procession—a plain oak box with a line of silent mourners trailing along behind—up the winding, worn pathway to the graveyard. Seemed funny to have this many folk gathered together without hearing any jawing, laughter, bragging, or swapping of stories. Yet though the quiet was kindly strange, I knew it was fitting and proper and the way folks had always done the burying.

Still, I couldn't help wondering if this'd be what Granny Mandy really wanted. Seemed to me she might ask a whippoorwill or two to come light on her coffin and sing a cheerful song. Wouldn't even mind if that made folks laugh right out loud, I was thinking. And then if that reminded the widow Campbell of a story Granny'd once told her, and she was wanting to share it with us, well I just knew Granny'd be wanting her to go ahead and make us all laugh in the telling too.

A soft breeze pushed wispy clouds along a bright blue sky. I squinted up at the sun as it moved from behind one of them clouds, lifting my face to it, enjoying the warmth of it on my skin. It was a glorious day for Granny Mandy, one that she would've called "one o' God's smilin' days." I smiled now, remembering how her eyes sparkled when she said it, recollecting how she lifted her face to the warmth the same way. *Oh, Granny*, I thought to myself, *of course you would be buried on a smilin' day, teachin' me still, you are. Showin' me that though I'm cryin' and grievin' for you—and always will in some measure—that laughter will come. And should come again. You of all folks would want me to laugh*. No more would I close my eyes to the bright glare! Instead, I lifted my face with joy, letting its beauty and warmth and brightness shine into my soul. *Yes'm, Granny, it be a glorious day*!

And that was why some folks would criticize me later, saying I wasn't respectful of the dead—didn't even love my granny—because I'd stood with my face raised to the sky. Smiling. The whole time Preacher Morgan was reciting the twenty-third Psalm.

> The LORD is my shepherd; I shall not want.
> He maketh me to lie down in green pastures: he leadeth me beside the still waters.
> He restoreth my soul: he leadeth me in the paths of righteousness for his name's sake.
> Yea, though I walk through the valley of the shadow of death, I will fear no evil: for thou art with me; thy rod and thy staff they comfort me.
> Thou preparest a table before me in the presence of mine enemies: thou anointest my head with oil; my cup runneth over.
> Surely goodness and mercy shall follow me all the days of my life: and I will dwell in the house of the LORD for ever. Amen.

Truth tell, it didn't bother me none what they said.

Seemed like the days after that fairly rushed by as we filled them with harvesting, packing, moving. The summer and autumn had brought good weather, and we brought in the last crop of McKenney Way Corn. A crop to be proud of, it was, and we toted it in wagons to the new place along with Eenie, Miney, Moe, and one sow tagging along behind, a sow that would hopefully produce a good number of piglets in the seasons to come.

We took nearly every outbuilding we had along with everything inside them. The day we toted the chicken coop certainly was one to remember. Daddy'd put chicken wire over the door so they couldn't be getting out, but them chickens sure raised a fuss—squawking and carrying on so, flailing themselves up against that wire. Me and Andy rode in the wagon with them, trying to keep them from hurting themselves. But they just plain didn't take to no moving. I remember smiling to myself, thinking that Granny most likely would've acted about the same way.

By the time we'd moved the barn and all the smaller buildings, the place was surely starting to look strange, almost fearful to me. I'd never got used to how the Harrises' property looked when they'd left, and now ours was beginning to look the same way. When I'd wake up of a morning, the first thing I'd do was to look out over our land, noting what had disappeared from the day before. And even though I was helping in the work, slowly carrying away every bit of whatever it was that had belonged on McKenney land, still it looked to me as if somehow everything was just disappearing, all by themselves in the night. Almost like a mighty hand was snatching them. Gave me shivers nearly every morning.

The day we moved everything out of Granny's cabin was such a mixing of the past and future. The old rocker looked so lonely without Granny giving it a good working, the wooden spoon she favored still had some flour stuck to it from the last time she made biscuits, and the tin mug brought back sweet memories of healing teas—with secret ingredients. Sometimes the memories brought tears, but mostly they were tears of joy since me and Tommy Lee were taking most all Granny's things to be ours, to help us start our home in a few years. We were even taking that old wood stove, filthy as it was. We'd work on it some day, cleaning it up best we could, hoping I'd be able to make fried pies, biscuits, and gingerbread good as Granny's were. Well, maybe almost as good.

Once Tommy Lee'd hauled off all our things to his new place, Granny's cabin looked terrible empty and lonely. But then it wasn't no time atall before Uncle Evert come to tear down the cabin itself, toting it off with them since they were needing a bigger home for all the young'uns they had.

I stood and watched the men for awhile, saw them pull down shutters and doors, ripping away board after board until I couldn't even recognize it as Granny's anymore. But I didn't stay very long. It was too much like losing my granny again to watch the touchable reminders of her tore apart and hauled away. I run off soon as the tears started pushing at my eyes again.

Finally all that was left on McKenney soil was our cabin and the last of our furniture—beds, the stove, a table, a bit of food, and some pots and pans. Once we got those things loaded onto the wagon, Daddy, James Junior, and the other men that come to help started in to tearing down the walls that had sheltered us for so many years, the place where I'd known so much love, laughter. And hurting. This time I couldn't run off, couldn't keep from watching a beloved home become nothing but a pile of boards, pieces, bits of something here and there. Looking at the mess, I wondered, *Was this once really a home? Was it our home?*

Me and Tommy Lee stole away for a few minutes while Mama and Daddy were thanking folks and saying their good-byes. There weren't any trees to be hiding behind no more, no cornfields to give us privacy, not even no rock at Lookin' Point to be setting on. The rotten Yankees had moved even that, saying it would be a danger to boats. But we ran to the river anyways, finding a place that, though it wasn't pretty anymore, at least had moss that was soft and made a spot where we could set and stretch out our feet, dangling our toes in the water like we'd done so long ago, so many times before.

"Ain't goin' to be easy bein' apart," Tommy Lee said, reaching for my hand.

I took a deep breath, trying to keep any more tears from coming. I'd cried too much these last months. "I know."

"I'm thinkin', though, the waitin' will go faster if we can keep busy. An' be happy."

I glanced over at him, frowning, searching his eyes to see if he was fooling. "How can I be tellin' myself to be happy? And especially when I'll be missin' you kindly terrible?"

Tommy Lee shrugged. "Guess you can't. But I still think we can live like Granny Mandy done."

"How's that?"

He stared out across the river, squinting at the sun reflecting off the water. Suddenly he picked up a stick and threw it in. We watched it bob along, carried by the current. "'Member when we was on the chicken boat drinkin' them Nehi's?"

I smiled at the memory. "It were a wonderful day. I'm never goin' to forget it, Tommy Lee."

"I throwed one o' them bottles in the river, 'member?"

"Sure do. Was a wasteful thing to be doin'."

"Do you recollect why? An' what I said?"

We watched the stick slowly disappear from sight as it headed towards the dam. "Somethin' 'bout the bottle only changin' the river for a moment. An' how she'd keep flowin', keep goin' on forever."

"With nothin' really changin' her. Not no bottle, no stick, not even no Yankees."

"Well, it surely weren't true! Look how them Yankees has changed everthin'. This here river, our land, our very lives!"

"Has they, Rachael? Look at the river. She's still flowin' south, still pulsin' with beauty an' power. Them Yankees didn't invent her power for no electricity. They's only usin' it! Ain't goin' to stop her from never floodin' again, neither, though they's thinkin' they is. An' yes, they may've changed her round, sent her flowin' different like for a bit, blocked up a lake with a dam. But she's still the Tennessee, a God-made body of water a-flowin' over this here soil. An' they ain't a-changin' that!"

I stared at the river's beauty with new eyes, seeing the current moving along, lapping at the banks, hearing her familiar sounds. Beloved sounds. "But what about us, Tommy Lee? Look what they's changed. Look what they's forced us to do."

He took both my hands in his once again, and I turned to look into them eyes. "Nothin'! Nothin' what matters has changed, Rachael McKenney. Our God is still lovin' us. Me an' you is still lovin' each other." He grinned shyly when he said that, letting go my hand for a moment to push back a lock of hair. "An' one more thing. You've learned to let yerself be loved by God."

"Let God love me? Seems all backwards to be puttin' it thata way. Why was you thinkin' I wasn't lettin' Him love me?"

"'Cause you wasn't knowin' how big God's love is. And you wasn't likin' yerself."

I thought on that a moment, recognizing the truth in what Tommy Lee was saying, holding dear the memory of the foxfire now. "How is it showin' that I've changed?" I sighed. "Seems I've come a good ways, but they's still so far to go."

"Oh, sure they is, for all of us they is, Rachael. But yer learnin' to love others, lovin' them cause yer able to be likin' yerself. An' you can't like yerself 'til yer knowin' God's love. Really knowin'."

"Granny talked 'bout knowin'. Said joy come from the knowin' that He loves you."

"An' that's how she lived, Rachael. Knowin'. Decidin' ever day to trust Him. That's what faith be. Ain't nothin' on this here earth can change them things, take 'em away from us, destroy 'em. That's how yer granny lived. An' that was her gift to you."

I could hear Granny's voice then, singing and mingling with Tommy Lee's, hear those words ringing like the sound of a dinner bell through my heart, and savor the repeating of them in Tommy Lee's explaining about the river. I smiled at him, feeling so thankful. Knowing I'd received a precious gift. From Granny and now from Tommy Lee. "What was Granny Mandy's gift to you then?" I asked him, gazing into eyes that mirrored my love.

"That's easy," he grinned back at me, pulling me to him and brushing his lips against mine. "She give me Rachael McKenney."

The mighty Tennessee River hurried on past, not paying us no mind. She flowed on by the McKenney land, the adjoining Dickerson property, and then on into Jordan's Bend. Finally she rounded the bend that edged the new dam, peeking at where she would soon send sprays dancing for joy, sprouting rainbows in the air. And then the swelling tide of the Tennessee hurried on to the next town, and the one following that, wherever that may be. Endless coursing. Never-changing river. Flowing through the heart of the land, washing and cleansing the soul.

Epilogue

I've been back many a time to see the lake that stretches across what use to be McKenney land. And yet every time I go there, I can still see the valley where Spring Tide and Dogwood Creeks come together, still picture the rich corn growing there and the homey cabins where smells of wood stoves and fresh baked cornbread come floating from the chimneys. Closing my eyes and letting my musing take me back, I can 'most hear Granny's rocker creaking against the loose boards on her porch, hear Ezra and Nehemiah barking as they chase after Andy, hear laughter—Daddy's, James Junior's, mostly Granny Mandy's.

I recollect too just how the land looked when we left it that day so long ago. Granny's and our chimney stood alone, standing there like silent sentries to those who'd gone before. Rocks formed paths that led nowhere. Empty spaces. Bare patches marking where small outbuildings had set. A people moved on. And only such a few reminders left behind to tell us that they'd ever even been there. Soon them things would be erased too, covered by tons of water.

Now I'm a granny myself, and I can't even begin to tell how many times I've taken a solitary walk to the woods that grew just next to our pasture, seeking out a special place, a secret spot that never failed to give me courage, understanding, and the strength to go on when the weariness would threaten to set about me like a black fog again.

You see, just before we moved from the McKenney homestead, I made one last visit to that foxfire and I dug it all up, putting it in an old bucket. It was daylight when I'd done it, and that foxfire was just as ugly and terrible looking as the first time I saw it that way. Took me a good while to find the courage to touch it, to go ahead and do just what I'd set out to do. My feelings were ones of fear and revulsion and horror—just like they were before—but it was the knowing in my heart that finally made me put the shovel into the ground, helped me to place all that ugliness so gently into the bucket and then later bury it on our property, me and Tommy Lee's. Every step of the way I could hear Granny's voice, hear her whispering in my ear, *Whether the foxfire be a glowin' in all its glory or lookin' terrible awful in the light o' day, it don't make no difference. God's love ain't no changin' thing, Rachael. It's real an' alive an' livin' in me. An' joy is a-knowin' that.*

Funny thing was, over the years it got so that I made that trip to gaze at the foxfire just as many times during the day as I did at night. Whenever I was a fighting with God, feeling the pain of living so much that I couldn't be feeling His love, the sight of that foxfire in the sunlight give me nearly as much strength and reassuring as it did during the night. Knowing that whether it looked terrible—or wondrous beautiful—it was the same, the very same. The foxfire. And God's love. *Oh, Granny, I know*!

I've been back to visit Granny Mandy's gravesite many a time too, always finding comfort there, and peace. It's just a brisk walk from there to the dam, and that dam is such a wondrous thing, channeling the force of the Tennessee to do all those things that the Yankees had promised. I've stood at the top of that amazing structure, drinking in the beauty of the lake, feeling awe at the power they're making there, watching with fascination as men control the water and other folks do indeed ride them fancy boats across its gentle waves. But for all the strength and depth of those feelings, they aren't nothing compared to what I'm knowing when I stand next to Granny's gravehouse and run my fingers over the lettering Daddy put up there so many years ago.

Has complete healing come in the telling? I'm thinking there's always going to be a measure of hurt there, like a scar that's tender from the burn and always will be. But it's enough for the healing, enough of an end to the pain that I can be seeing through it now, know what be worth keeping and what be the chaff. Know what to cling to and what to send down the current with the water, letting the gentle flow carry it away, knowing what's left behind, what really matters, won't really change none.

The precious words, lovingly carved in wood by Daddy, call me to touch them just as sure as Granny's dinner bell drew me to her side. And like the foxfire, they never fail to remind me, to help me to know, to give me renewed hope. Daddy told us the verse come from the book of John, and that it was meant to describe John the Baptist. But when he saw it, he knew God was showing him those words were surely intended for our granny too—and Who it was that she loved so dearly.

I gently trace my fingers across them, caressing them not just with mere touch, but with feelings that flow from and then back into my fingers, as I follow the gentle curves of the simple words.

Here lies our beloved Granny Mandy McKenney.
She was a burning and a shining light.

Acknowledgments

While living in Tennessee, I was intrigued by the history of the Tennessee Valley Authority, but mostly I was fascinated by the beautiful lakes formed by the Watts Bar and Chickamauga dams. I don't think I ever passed one of them without wondering, *What would it have been like to leave my homestead? How would it feel to know that I could never return? That it would never be the same because my land was at the bottom of that vast body of water?* Those questions were the seeds from which my novel grew.

My story is based on fact; however, I created a fictional town by combining the factual areas of Chickamauga (in Chattanooga, Tennessee) and Chatuge in Clay County, North Carolina. The history of Chatuge is particularly amazing: in just seven months from July 1941, to February 1942, literally everything was removed from the area to be flooded. When the gates were finally closed and locked, only a few chimneys and rocks lining pathways to nowhere remained. How did those people survive such an overwhelming crisis? And most importantly, I wondered, how did this affect them spiritually?

The research for this project was, at times, nearly overwhelming as I attempted to locate a variety of books about the South—some written during the Depression years. I am in debt to so many of those valuable resources: *God's Valley: People and Power Along the Tennessee River* (Willson Whitman); *The Tennessee Valley Authority* (Marguerite Owen); *The Valley and Its People: A Portrait of TVA* (R.L. Duffus); *What My Heart Wants to Tell* (Verna Mae Slone); and lastly, the *Foxfire* series, an incredible source for insight into southern culture.

Madeleine L'Engle's poem from *The Irrational Season* fit the flow and theme of my novel so perfectly, and I judge that I am forever in her debt for the gift of her books. I have read every one.

My heartfelt thanks go to my wonderful family for encouraging me to chase a dream and to my believing husband, Craig, who never doubted my abilities. Or me. Lastly, I praise and worship the Lord who is the reason for this novel, the One who made joy a knowing because of His gift, Jesus Christ. I love You, Lord; help me to really love You.

About the Author

Carolyn Williford, a wife, mom, author, and seminar leader, is a graduate of Cedarville College with a degree in English. She loves working alongside her husband Craig in his pastoral work, taking care of him and their two sons, reading, and writing. Her desire is to know God more and more each day and to help others on the same journey. Carolyn hopes that as readers visit the imaginary town of Jordan's Bend, it will help them to know God better.